D0459462

THE
VIRTUE
OF
SIN

THE

VIRTUE

OF

SIN

Shannon Schuren

PHILOMEL BOOKS

PHILOMEL BOOKS
An imprint of Penguin Random House LLC
New York

Copyright © 2019 by Shannon Schuren.

Penguin supports copyright. Copyright fuels creativity, encourages diverse voices, promotes free speech, and creates a vibrant culture. Thank you for buying an authorized edition of this book and for complying with copyright laws by not reproducing, scanning, or distributing any part of it in any form without permission. You are supporting writers and allowing Penguin to continue to publish books for every reader.

Philomel Books is a registered trademark of Penguin Random House LLC.

Visit us online at penguinrandomhouse.com

LIBRARY OF CONGRESS CATALOGING-IN-PUBLICATION DATA
Names: Schuren, Shannon.
Title: The virtue of sin / Shannon Schuren.
Description: New York, NY : Philomel Books, 2019. | Summary: Miriam, sixteen, is chosen for marriage by someone other than the boy she loves and begins to question her entire life in New Jerusalem, a desert compound safe from the world's evils. Identifiers: LCCN 2018042988 | ISBN 9780525516545 (hardback) | ISBN 9780525516552 (e-book) Subjects: | CYAC: Cults—Fiction. | Love—Fiction. | Arranged marriage—Fiction. | Deserts—Fiction. Classification: LCC PZ7.1.S336555 Vir 2019 | DDC [Fic]—dc23 LC record available at https://lccn.loc.gov/2018042988

Printed in the United States of America.
ISBN 9780525516545
10 9 8 7 6 5 4 3 2 1

Edited by Liza Kaplan.
Design by Ellice M. Lee.
Text set in Granjon LT.

For every woman
who has ever felt
like she doesn't
have a voice.

1

MIRIAM

But because of the temptation
to sexual immorality, each man
should have his own wife and
each woman her own husband.
—*1 Corinthians 7:2*

The girls never get a choice.

Recite your Prayers, report for Lessons, respect your Elders. Do unto others and as you are told. Keep your hair tidy and your thoughts to yourself. There is no choosing—not of intentions, not of words, not of spouses. This has always been our way in New Jerusalem.

Sixteen years ago, my father chose my mother at the first Matrimony, on a spring night just like this where the Elders were paired as husband and wife. I know this because it's part of our community's historical record, not because they told me. My parents would never speak of anything so personal. That's between them and God. Well, and Daniel.

Even now, as my mother and I swelter in the Communal Kitchen to finish last-minute preparations for tonight's feast, I know that whatever questions I have about tonight will go unanswered. I know only this: At some point during the night, one of the boys will call my name, announcing our union. That will be my cue to leave the bonfire and head toward the opening of the lava caves at the foot of the mountain. As a woman, it will be the one and only time I'll be allowed in the Marriage Cave. Afterward, I will be forbidden to talk about anything that happens inside. I can't imagine why. I can only suppose the proceedings are too sacred to speak of, or too profane. My own father is the only man I know well enough to ask the reason behind all the secrecy, but I doubt he'd tell me. If I even see him between now and tonight's ceremony; he only steps foot inside a kitchen if he needs something. Though our Leader says there are no menial tasks, it often seems like the women get stuck with the less noble jobs.

Like the chores I've been assigned today. Soak the beans. Seed the peppers. Wash and peel the potatoes. Tend the fire in the wide oven wall, where the goat has been slowly roasting for the past twelve hours. Bite my tongue and don't complain about the temperature, which has been steadily climbing throughout the day in this long, airless room.

Our eyes meet, and my mother reads something in my expression, because she looks away first, scraping the juicy jalapeño pulp across the surface of the carving table with the dull edge of her knife. "Not now, Miriam." She turns to pull a tray from the bank of ovens that span the width of the room. A tendril of steam escapes a crack in the top of the perfectly browned corn bread.

I've spent the past ten days eating nothing but vegetables and drinking nothing but water, as is our custom before a celebration of this magnitude. Yesterday, I would have clawed someone's eyes out for a piece of that bread, but now the stifling heat and the smell of the charred goat turns my stomach, and all I can think about is the row of windows that tops the tiled walls and how I'd begged to tilt them open, even a fraction. But Mother says the dust will spoil the food.

"Are Rachel and Delilah as nervous as you?" She dumps the bread onto a cooling rack beside the stove, then uses the back of her wrist to wipe sweat from her forehead.

"I'm not nervous."

My mother raises an eyebrow.

Even if she doesn't believe me, it's not a lie. I'm curious and excited, but I'm not nervous. Delilah and Rachel, though, are terrified. They know just as little as I do about tonight, but perhaps they have more to lose. I have no reason to share their fear. I know which boy is going to call my name tonight, which boy is about to become my husband.

My husband. In just a few hours, I'll be allowed to speak those words aloud. My skin prickles into gooseflesh at the thought.

"My husband." I can't resist. I say it low, under the wet slice of the potato peeler, but my mother still hears.

"I don't know who it will be. And even if I did, I couldn't say," she whispers, though the room is empty aside from us. The others have already left to set up Outside. Only my mother has volunteered us to stay behind to finish up, to avoid leaving the safety of the city for as long as possible. She grew up Outside, without our Leader's guidance, in a faraway place called San Diego. Whatever happened to her there left her tight-lipped and afraid, and more than willing to sacrifice a few moments of freedom for the stifling confines of the Kitchen. Just the few steps she will take through the gates tonight, to witness my marriage, have had her worried and fearful for weeks.

Unlike me, she and the other Elders have been on the other side of the fence, many times. They used to hold all kinds of celebrations in the sacred tunnels as well as out in the middle of the desert. But that was before one of Daniel's Children betrayed their faith and broke their trust.

She once told me that being on the other side made her feel exposed. Actually, the word she used was *naked*. What I didn't tell her was that I've yearned for that same feeling. That secretly, I think I might like it. *That* I would never say aloud. Like many of my thoughts, it's unsuitable and liable to earn me a punishment. The Elders say I'm incapable of keeping anything to myself, but sometimes I manage. Still, it's impossible for me to keep entirely quiet, especially on a day this special.

"Why does everything about tonight have to be a secret? It's in the Bible. 'He who finds a wife finds what is good and receives favor from the Lord.' Proverbs 18:22." I'm allowed to quote Scripture; sometimes it feels as if that's all I'm allowed. For mainly this reason I've retained a great many of the passages we've studied in the classroom, a skill that both delights and frustrates my mother. "And anyway, I don't need you to tell me who he is. I already know."

"What?" She holds her knife aloft, the newly skinned potatoes lying forgotten in front of her. "There's no way you could possibly know that. Unless—" She narrows her eyes. "Has one of the boys tried to speak to you?"

My mother has always possessed the ability to look past my babble and straight into my heart. "Of course not," I say, the words tumbling out in my haste to explain. "No one's spoken to anyone." This is not a lie, and so hopefully will pass her scrutiny. "I just . . . I dreamt of him. There was music, and a bonfire. And we were in the cave—"

Her eyes widen, and she drops the knife to grip my hands. "Who told you this?"

"No one." I shake loose. "I told you, I dreamt it."

Her face relaxes into a smile, and she presses her forehead to mine. "I knew it," she whispers. "I knew you had a gift. He'll be so proud."

Her declaration sends a thrill through me that's almost as good as a gust of cool air. As the reincarnation of the Prophet, our Leader has always been the one to interpret the messages we receive from the Lord in our dreams. But I'd always secretly hoped that one day, God might choose to communicate with me directly. "Who will be proud? Father? Or Daniel?"

"Yes. Both. They both will." My mother wipes her hands on her apron, moves the clasp on her crucifix to the back of her neck, and adjusts her head scarf, checking for loose hairs with a practiced finger. There aren't any, of course.

"Did you love him?" I ask.

Her hands still. Her face changes. "Who are you talking about?"

I've spent years studying her every expression. She's taught me to interpret the faintest sign of displeasure, but I don't need any lessons to read the annoyance in her face.

"Father must have loved you," I say. "Because he chose you. But on that night, did you know—"

She presses her lips together. "Stop. Do you want to risk a Shaming?"

"Surely you can tell me *something*. In a few hours, I'll be a woman, too. What will a few details matter now?"

She turns away to tend the meat, so I can no longer see her face. I watch her hands instead, their choppy quick movements as she uses the poker to stir the coals. "The less you expect, the better," she says. "Marriage should feel like a gift, not an obligation."

"After sixteen years, what's one more obligation?" I toss the potatoes into a bowl, angry at myself as much as her. What did I expect? She lives to obey; in this regard she's exactly like Rachel. Or Rachel is like her. This may be the one thing the Bible has gotten wrong. Familiarity doesn't always breed contempt. Sometimes it breeds likeness. After Rachel's mother left New Jerusalem, my family took Rachel in and raised her. And though they have no blood ties, my best friend is more my mother's daughter than I am.

Rachel comes in just then, as if I've summoned her with my disloyal thoughts. And behind her, my father, trailed by a passel of small children. None of them are his; younger kids just always seem drawn to Father, despite his complete indifference to their adoration. I think it's his bald head they find unusual.

"What's taking so long?" He wrinkles his nose as he surveys the necessary chaos that comes from preparing a meal for over one hundred people. "The men are getting hungry."

"The music has started!" Rachel says, darting over to me. "Can you believe it? It's finally happening." She fans herself, sweat already beading on her upper lip. In a few more minutes, her dark hair will be as frizzy as mine. "Whew. It's hot in here," she says. "What can I do to help? The faster we finish, the sooner we can go Outside."

My mother turns pale.

"Ruth. You look tired," says Father.

Why is it men never curb their tongues? Of course she's tired. We've been cooking in this furnace for the past six hours. Personally, I think Father looks stiff and uncomfortable, the lines on his face more pronounced today. It could be the heat, or the unfamiliarity of the kitchen. Either way, I keep this to myself.

"Miriam. Haven't you been helping your mother?" He takes a step toward me and trips over Delilah's youngest brother. "Damnation, Ezekiel! Why are you always underfoot?"

"I'm Zacharias. And I'm small." He bursts into tears and dives under the table, upending the bowl of potatoes.

Mother holds the platter of meat high, stepping carefully around the errant vegetables rolling across the floor. "Everything's fine, Boaz. Miriam's been a big help. In fact, I'm pleased to see how much she's improving. She's going to make someone a wonderful wife."

He makes a noncommittal noise in the back of his throat and crosses his arms. Mother glances at his gleaming white linen shirt and pants and then looks for somewhere else to set her tray, while I kneel to gather the spilled food, the back of my neck prickling under the weight of Father's stare.

Rachel goes around to the other side of the table to coax Zacharias out. She crosses her pale eyes and wiggles her thick eyebrows, and he giggles through his tears. "I want my mommy," he says, as he crawls into Rachel's outstretched arms.

We all have our talents. Rachel's is mothering. Mother's is cooking. Mine isn't either one. I'm also not going to make just *someone* a wonderful wife. He has a name. But like any woman here, my mother never really says what she means.

"I'll get this," she says. Mother pulls a potato from my grasp and waves me off. "We're nearly done here anyway. Go and help Rachel with the children. It's too hot in here for them, and there's no one in the Medical Shed to treat heatstroke today." Like my mother, the other nurse has been temporarily relieved of her Vocational Duties to help prepare for tonight's festivities.

I hesitate, but freedom tugs at me like the devil's hand. Besides, she's used to cleaning up our messes. It's how she shows her love.

I stand and brush off my skirt, then Rachel hoists Zacharias onto her hip, and I grab the tray of vegetables and corn bread my mother has carefully arranged. Father holds the back door, and as we step out I'm rewarded with a rush of fresh air that cools my heated skin so quickly it makes me shiver.

"Straight to the feasting tables. No dawdling," Father says to me, then turns to the other children. "I need to move the benches from Chapel out to the bonfires. Who wants to help me?"

Some of the older children raise their hands and follow him toward the city center, while the rest scatter, leaving Rachel and me to deliver Zacharias and the rest of the food.

The sun is slipping low in the sky, hovering above the mountain ahead and blinding us, so that we have to make our way to the front gate almost by memory. We cut through the welcome shade of the Pavilion, the open-air shelter where most of our communal Gatherings take place, including our yearly Last Supper and the Epiphany Festival. This used to be as near to the sacred tunnels as we ever got. But tonight, because it is the most important of all our celebrations, Daniel has decreed that the Matrimony will actually take place inside them.

It won't be the first Matrimony—that was the marriage of my parents and the other Elders of the First Generation—but it will be the biggest. This is the first time God has spoken to any of the Second Generation, and the first time He's spoken to so many at once. And most important, at least to me, it's the first time He's spoken my name.

My heart sings with excitement as our feet lead us down the path and through the gates stretched wide to allow the men through as they carry out the tables and benches and other equipment needed for tonight's celebration. Once we cross Zzyzx Road, we are officially Outside for the first time in our lives. I am overcome by a feeling

I struggle to name. This road that stretches on forever, the endless expanse of desert and sky, unblemished by gate or guard—these are the things the Elders have warned against, and yet, here I am. Untethered. Free. At least for one night.

Rachel grabs my arm and points to the flags waving in the distance, stark white against the dark rock of the mountain to mark the entrance. "There it is! The Marriage Cave!" She raises her voice to be heard above the rhythmic blend of harp, reed, and bells streaming from big speakers into the open air—the same sound system that in just a few hours will be used to announce our futures.

We hurry past the girls' bonfire, skirting a cluster of younger girls playing hopscotch in the sand, and over to the feasting tables. The lavish buffet I helped my mother prepare will soon be set out; until then, the rest of the women straighten tablecloths and arrange bread and sweets into piles. Delilah is here, too, moving a plate from one side of the table to the other and then back again as her mother, Chloe, supervises.

Zacharias bursts into tears at the sight of his mother and squirms to be put down. When Rachel releases him, he runs to Chloe and buries his face in her skirt.

"There you are! Your sister and I have been looking everywhere for you!"

Delilah rolls her eyes heavenward. "I told you he was with Rachel, Mother."

"And I told you to keep an eye on him," Chloe says, but she sounds only mildly exasperated.

Normally, Delilah is tasked with wrangling her many brothers and sisters. But today is a special occasion. With no Lessons, and the Elders preoccupied with Celebration preparations, it's expected that the children should also get a chance to enjoy this tiny taste of freedom. Plus, it's her wedding day.

As Rachel and I hand over the trays of vegetables and bread, another mother, Judith, slips the crying boy a cookie, and his tears immediately evaporate.

"Delilah, move those cookies to make room," Chloe orders.

Delilah wrinkles her nose as she sticks her tongue out at us, her freckles blurring into one sandy cluster, but she does as she's told. Until we serve our husbands, we must serve our parents.

Judith hands us each a cookie and wipes her calloused hands on the apron tied over her dress. The women are all in nicer clothes tonight, the dresses they normally save for Chapel. Rachel and I and the other girls will wear white for the wedding, while Judith and the other Elders are dressed in traditional cream linen. "How are you girls feeling? Nervous? Excited?" she asks.

I'm tongue-tied all of a sudden, and to cover, I shove the cookie in my mouth. Judith is almost as good a cook as my mother, and she's definitely a better baker. Not that she looks it. She's thin and wiry, like she never eats. And maybe she doesn't. With a husband and six sons, maybe the food never makes it to her plate.

"We're excited *and* nervous," Rachel answers for both of us.

Judith smiles. "The boys are the same," she says, waving a hand toward the glow in the distance. "I finally sent Caleb and Marcus away. They were more hindrance than anything."

"Oh, I can't imagine *Caleb* being a hindrance. Can you, Miriam?" Delilah asks.

I choke on my cookie, and Rachel gives me a raised eyebrow and a tiny shake of her head. "What can we do to help?" she asks the women, too loudly.

"There's still the meat—" Delilah's mother says, but Judith interrupts.

"Let them go, Chloe. This is their special night." Judith winks, and this time I'm sure it's at me.

Delilah doesn't give her mother time to reconsider. "Let's go." She crams the cookie in her mouth and links her arms through both Rachel's and mine, pulling us away from the food and the fire and into the darkness of the night desert.

We walk, mostly because we can and everyone else is too busy to stop us, but we're careful to keep Zzyzx Road and the city fence to our left, while the voices of the women and children fade at our backs. We weave our way slowly between scattered rocks and the spindly Joshua trees with their branches raised toward heaven in prayer, like their namesake at the Battle of Jericho. But what do these trees pray for?

Sometimes I imagine they were once people, like us, stuck out here so long they grew roots. A blasphemous thought, I know. I pluck one of the waxy blossoms sprouting from their outstretched arms like pale fingertips and tuck it behind my ear. Unlike other wildflowers, these don't bloom every spring. Their appearance is the very reason we're all out here tonight. It's a sign God has finally called for another Matrimony.

Rachel finishes her cookie and dusts the crumbs from her face. Then she squints into the darkness. "It's time to go back."

I don't ask how she knows. Rachel's sense of duty is as inborn as the dent in the bridge of her nose, the one she rubs when she's nervous.

"You two go on," I say. "I'll follow in a minute."

"Or you could just come with us now. We still have to change out of our work dresses."

I sigh. "I have to pee, Rachel."

She wrinkles her nose, then massages the dent. "There's no toilet out here. You can go at the house."

"I can't hold it that long. I'll go behind this tree."

Delilah's eyes widen with glee; Rachel's with shock. "You can't," Rachel says.

"Of course I can. The men do it all the time. I've seen them."

At her gasp, I amend my words. "I don't mean I've actually seen them. I mean, I've seen my father go off by himself, behind the Pavilion. So why can't I?"

"Because you're a girl?" Rachel counters.

"But it's still pee," Delilah says. "There's no difference between male and female pee."

Delilah has done enough diaper changing to know, and Rachel gives up the fight. "Even so, I'm not going to stand around while you pollute the desert. Come on, Delilah."

"That's why I told you to go ahead," I call after their retreating backs. "And it's not pollution if the animals all do it." I don't actually have to pee, but my argument is still valid.

I walk a bit more until I'm far enough away from the bonfire so that if I squint, the flames are hands holding up a column of climbing smoke as an offering. The sun has slipped all the way behind the mountain now, and above me, stars decorate the sky like thousands of candles lit in honor of tonight's marriages. The magnitude of all this beauty, all this freedom, leaves me breathless. I know this is the same desert I see every day, but Out here, it's wild and untended. Here, the ground is unswept, the sand coarse and rocky, the bunches of yucca and desert paintbrush scattered by God instead of gardener. The farther I go from New Jerusalem, the less evidence I see of any human hand.

I walk until I see the guards. I knew I'd run into them eventually, and that I'd have to stop before they caught me. We were told they would be patrolling during the celebration. Even Outside, there are still boundaries we can't breach. But it doesn't matter, because I've come far enough. I turn and duck behind one of the taller trees, my heart pounding in the stillness. For the first time tonight, I am afraid. Not of being chosen, but of being caught—here, at the boys' fire. Tonight, of all nights, I shouldn't risk this.

But I need to see him one more time.

2

MIRIAM

Scarcely had I passed them when
I found the one whom my soul loves.

—*Song of Solomon 3:4*

Their fire is built close to the mountainside, and they gather round it, dark shapes that move and ripple in the light of the flames. My skin tingles at the sound of their laughter. Girls aren't allowed to speak in the presence of boys, and because we're always separated, they rarely speak in ours. The only time I see any boys for any length of time is at Chapel. And at Chapel there is no speaking unless Daniel invites us to respond. That's a rule even I have never broken, though going a whole day without talking is the worst form of torture.

But these boys—they're so loud! As they jostle and play, they seem more alive than the girls I talk to every day. I taste jealousy, sour and hot in the back of my throat, at their easiness with themselves and one another. At their right to speak their thoughts aloud. I'll never know that.

And then I see Caleb.

He is illuminated, his skin bronze against the white of his shirt, his blond hair shining as the others fade until they are but a gray fuzz and only he remains. We were friends, up until the age of Separation, which was when Daniel decreed the oldest of the Second Generation must begin Lessons. Before that, we all used to play together, though I don't remember Caleb making me feel like this. Mostly, I remember him as quiet. And determined. Once, when the chain kept coming off an old bike Rachel and I shared, he'd fixed it. Even after my father told me it was my own fault, and that seven was too old for riding bikes. Caleb had waited until my father went to a meeting at the Council House, and then he'd squatted in the dirt at the foot of the driveway and worked on it until it was done. I still remember him like that, holding my handlebars with muddy hands, a big smile on his face. "I cleaned out the links. It should work fine now."

That was the last time we spoke. It was also the last time I saw the bike. Father said it was time for me to put away childish things and gave it to one of Delilah's brothers.

Caleb turns to say something to the others, and his deep voice carries through the darkness, wrapping me in its warmth. I should feel guilty for listening, but it's only fair. He has heard me speak since the Separation. A few months ago, Rachel and Delilah and I were lingering outside the girls' schoolhouse after Lessons, in an effort to avoid going home to our chores. I was last to leave, and as I turned to go, I saw him around the corner of the building. I don't know where he was supposed to be, but I'm sure it wasn't standing there, spying on us.

When he knew I'd caught him, he didn't blush or bolt. Instead, he smiled. Then he bent down, traced something in the sand with his finger, and pointed at me before he slipped around the other side of the building. By the time I rounded the corner, he was gone. But he'd left me a message, written with the same coded language we use for

Bible Study. A heart, an ear, and a mouth with sound waves coming from it. *I love to listen to you speak.*

Even now, months later, the memory makes me shiver with some thrilling emotion I can't name. I should have felt obligated to report his infraction, but I didn't. Instead, I stared at those precious symbols until they were burned into my memory. Then I erased the evidence and kept his secret.

Will he keep mine?

He stares into the darkness where I'm hiding for a long moment, his body still as the others move around him. His gaze is drawn to mine like a magnet, though he can't see me here. Can he?

Then the corner of his mouth curves upward, like the crook of a finger. It isn't just a smile, it's an invitation. The tether between us grows ever stronger, the heat that infuses my body far greater than the desert sun. Surely this must be love. Has God sent him dreams of me? Will I finally know what it's like to speak to him? Hear his secret thoughts? Touch him? Be touched—

"Aha! Caleb. I knew it!" a voice calls from behind me.

"What are you doing out here?" I whisper, though I want to shriek.

"Running away." There's no whispering for Delilah.

"What? Why?" I peer behind her into the blackness. "Running away from who? Where's Rachel?" If we get caught out here, especially on this night, our punishment will be severe. And Delilah's pale skin glows in the moonlight, a beacon for anyone who looks in our direction.

But she's oblivious to my concern as she flops down beside the tree. "I'm teasing. I followed you. I didn't believe your pee story for a minute. You're trying to get a better look at the boys, aren't you?

Why didn't you invite me?" She picks up a stick and traces a pattern in the dirt. She's always doodling—in her notepad, in the sand. Even on her clothing. About the only place I've never seen her draw is in her Bible.

As I crouch beside her, I see this isn't just any doodle. It's a circle with an arrow pointing out the top. *Husband.*

Caleb left me this symbol, too, just last week. Right after the Matrimony was announced. Along with another circle with the curlicue tail—*choose*—and the circle above a cross—*wife.*

"Don't worry," she says, still drawing. "Caleb will pick you. I've seen him watching you at Chapel. He likes you." She moves her hand, and I see she's made the jagged scribble for *fear.* Does she know about our secret communications? Has she noticed me scouring the sand for evidence of his interest?

She brushes her hand across the sand, smoothing it out. "I just wish there were another option."

There are nine girls taking part in the Matrimony tonight, and of all of us, Delilah is the least interested in marriage. She's also the youngest, fourteen to most of our sixteen, so she's had two fewer years of her mother extolling the virtues of the institution. Rachel and I are the eldest of the Second Generation. Some of our Brothers and Sisters are too young for the responsibilities of marriage. Privately, I think Delilah is one of them. But she has bled, so the Lord has determined her worthy of a husband; she must go forward tonight.

"What other option would there be?" I ask. "The Lord wants us to be wives and mothers."

"I don't know. A vessel for knowledge, maybe? We could be teachers. Like Phoebe."

It's only because I love her so well that I don't remind Delilah of the shame Phoebe endured before becoming a teacher. She says we are all her children, but none of us really believes that. "I think even Phoebe would rather be a mother."

"That's not true," Delilah argues. "Phoebe says knowledge is the most important gift."

"She has to say that. She's a teacher. Obviously, the gift of life is the most important."

Delilah rolls her eyes. "There are plenty of smart women in the Bible who didn't marry or have babies. And don't tell me you've never wondered what it's like Outside."

I can hear Rachel's voice in my head, a firm *never*, leaving no room for doubt.

But I have.

Oh, I know all about the dangers. The rest of the world does not live as we do. Only when we're locked inside the gates are we safe. Outside, people do unspeakable things to one another. My secret shame is that I've tried to imagine these things. But all I can ever picture is this vast desert, stretching on and on. Sometimes I dream of others, faceless people out beyond the mountains, their bodies contorted in something other than prayer. But the images are hazy and jumbled, and they fade when I wake, because I have nothing concrete to compare them to. Though I've been taught all about the dangers of sin, no one wants to tell me what it looks like.

"I'd rather go Out there than be chosen by a Faithless man like Azariah," Delilah says.

Azariah was Phoebe's husband. He betrayed her with another woman and then ran away, leaving her behind, childless and alone, to live with the shame.

"But . . . that would never happen to us." Would it?

"How can you be so sure? What if I get picked by a husband I can't love? Or what if he decides he doesn't love me?" She tosses her stick aside. "This is it. We can't be chosen twice. If they betray us, we'll be forever Stained. Just like Phoebe."

Before I can think of a response, the world goes dark. Someone's doused the boys' fire. I look for Caleb one last time, but he's hidden behind the cloud of hissing smoke. Then the music cuts out on the speakers above, and a sharp squeal reverberates off the mountain walls.

Delilah bounces to her feet, her hands pressed against her ears.

"We have to get back," I say. "If we're late . . ." I don't finish. Like everything else about this night, I don't actually know what will happen if we're late. Will we be Shamed? Held in Contempt, our names forever excluded from the Book of Truth? All I know is there's no time for keeping to the shadows. I take Delilah's hand in mine and break into a flat-out run, the rocky sand dragging our stride and chafing inside my yucca-leaf sandals.

I slow to skirt an outcropping of dark boulders. I think we're safe from punishment now that we're within view of the gathering; the clumps of Joshua trees have thinned enough that we can see the dark silhouettes of the women and girls as they move in and out of the torchlight near the mouth of the cave. But I don't see the boy until it's too late.

I trip over his body and go down hard on my knees, the coarse sand scraping my bare legs with granules sharp as glass.

"For heaven's sake—" The rest of the words die in my throat at the distinct and deadly sound. I know the night amplifies everything, but the snake's rattle is still impossibly loud. It comes from every-where at once, and fear puckers my skin like a thread pulled tight at my neck. Hours pass in a matter of seconds as I bite my tongue and try to gauge how likely a target I am to the unseen reptile. I've lost a sandal, and my skirt is twisted about my knees, leaving a good expanse of ankle and calf exposed. My muscles twitch, urging me to run, but movement will only tempt it.

"It's moving away." Delilah's voice is low, for once. "Give it a minute." She must be standing behind me, though I don't dare turn my head to look. Instead, I watch the boy who lies beside me, eerily still. He may be dead. The thought hits me sudden and hard, like the rock that struck Goliath.

"Are you all right?" The words slip off my tongue before I can catch them back. The sand is cold, which must be why my hands tremble as I reach toward the shock of blue-black hair. I turn toward Delilah. "It's Aaron."

"The Outsider?"

"He's not an Outsider anymore." The words are more my father's than my own. As a member of the Church Council, he is constantly reminding me of our obligation to welcome new members into our fold. And it's been many months since Aaron's family renounced sin and joined our community. They are family now, or so I'm told.

"Are you alive? Can you talk?" I press my fingers against his neck, and relief warms them as I feel the fluttering of his pulse. "Do you need help?" I move my hands along his arms and then down his legs, searching for the wound. "Where did it bite you?"

"My . . . foot."

His hand clutches mine. Thankfully, the night conceals my blushing as I lean toward his foot. There. In his heel. Two tiny pin-pricks, each oozing a dot of blood.

"Poison?" His voice is muffled. "Will I . . . die?"

"Lie still," I say, though he hasn't moved anything except his hand since I fell over him. I pull my scarf from around my neck and wrap it around his ankle—snug, but not so much it cuts off his circulation. I hesitate only a second before I press my mouth to the bite.

Delilah inhales sharply, and Aaron's foot jerks, but I hold it firmly and suck a mouthful of blood from his heel, careful not to swallow before I spit it onto the ground beside us. My heart pounds with fear, and my tongue tingles from the venom, but I keep going, sucking and spitting, as I mentally count my sins. I shouldn't have spied on the boys. I shouldn't have spoken to *this* boy, much less touched him.

"Miriam?"

The sharp, imperious voice isn't Delilah's. Delilah would need more than three syllables to convey that kind of superiority. No— someone else has seen us. Of all the people to witness this, did it have to be Susanna? Her willowy beauty, though the envy of us all, masks the heart of a viper. Though that probably won't keep her from being chosen first tonight.

"Did you just *touch* him? With your *mouth*?" Susanna steps around the rocks, her words coming out in a hiss, as if by whispering in his presence she will manage to avoid the punishment I am certain to receive. But she's right; I definitely shouldn't have put my lips on any part of his body. "What is the quote from James? 'The tongue is restless evil, full of poison'?"

I spit one last time into the sand and wipe my mouth. "His foot is full of poison," I counter. "And you're forgetting Proverbs. 'Death and life are in the power of the tongue.'" I don't even have to search for the quote; it comes as if by magic. There is a buzzing inside my head, a hum with no rhythm. My hands shake and my heart pounds and I am aware of everything at once: the cooling sand beneath my knees, the moon rising behind us like a spirit, the blood flowing through the foot that still lies in my lap. I hastily push it aside and spit again. Maybe I've been poisoned.

"I wonder what Daniel will have to say about your tongue?" asks Susanna.

Delilah wrinkles her nose. "Aaron was bit by a rattler. Why are we still talking about tongues?"

" 'Confess your sins to one another, and pray for one another so you may be healed.' " Susanna's voice is mocking now. "How can you heal, Miriam, if we don't confess this incident?"

I shake the sand from my missing sandal and pull it back onto my foot. "What was I supposed to do, let him die?" But we all know there's no denying I've sinned. If Susanna shares what she knows, I'll be punished for sure.

"Brothers and Sisters!" Daniel's voice cuts through my threat. He does see all, even in the dark.

"People of New Jerusalem!"

My heart stutters. Our Leader is speaking through the sound system to everyone. Not just us. I haven't been caught. Yet.

Muted cheers waft toward us, and then the crowd quiets to hear his message.

"Tonight, we join in celebration, as the first members of our Second Generation—" Louder cheers this time, and he waits for them to quiet before continuing, "take the next step on their journey to Righteousness!"

Aaron scrambles to his feet, though I'm not sure if it's our bickering or Daniel's words that shock him into mobility.

"Slow down," I say. "You're going to spread the poison otherwise. You need to lie back and elevate your foot."

"Stop talking to him," Delilah pleads. "We need to hear Daniel's Word."

"As you know, the world Outside has become a dark place," Daniel continues. "The dreams I had in my first lifetime, they are all coming true. People worship at the feet of false idols instead of their One True God. Nations fight wars, driven by great beasts of leaders who've been corrupted by the horns of power and greed." He pauses, and I can feel the crowd hold its breath.

"The world is doomed. And I dreamt it all. And then I wrote it down. I shared it with the world, in the Bible, as the Book of Daniel, all those years ago, so that many could be saved. It became Gospel. But what happened? They looked, but did not see. They heard, but did not listen. They read, but did not believe. And so the Lord asked me to return. He granted me visions once more and ordered me to gather my flock of dreamers, my True Believers. To build a new city, a new beginning, a New Jerusalem. A sanctuary in the desert. A second chance at Salvation. Seventy years until the Tribulation! Seventy years to save our souls!"

Another pause. More cheers. It's a story we've all heard many times, the history of how our community came to be. Tonight, with Daniel's voice echoing hollowly off the mountain, it makes me feel small. Scared. Like everything else, his words are easily swallowed by the vast Outside. But maybe that's the point.

"In New Jerusalem, do we fear the Tribulation?"

We all join the chorus of "no"s, Susanna most fervently.

"Of course not!" Daniel agrees. "Why would we? For though we know that the world is destined to come to a terrible end, the

Children of Daniel shall be spared! Through our dreams, God has called us to Salvation!"

The crowd grows louder, more excited at this news that isn't new.

"You share with me your dreams, and I alone interpret His word. All dreamers worthy shall have their names written in the Book of Truth. And all in the Book shall be delivered! Tonight, let us add the names of these couples to the Book!"

The crowd erupts into screams and cheers.

"Is that true?" Delilah asks. "Once we're married, we're in the Book? Phoebe never said that."

"There's a lot they don't tell us," I say.

Aaron meets my gaze and bobs his head in silent thanks. Then he bolts, sand churning in his wake as the darkness swallows him whole.

"He's stalling," Susanna says, finger-combing through her lustrous hair.

"Looked like he was moving pretty quickly to me," Delilah says.

"Too quickly," I add. He's probably worried about being late for the Matrimony, but he should be looking for one of the nurses. There's no way to know now if I got all the poison. If I didn't, running will only spread it faster.

Susanna smirks and shakes her head. "I wasn't talking about Aaron."

But before we can ask what she means, the microphone squeals a second time, and another voice booms out across the desert. "I choose Susanna."

Exclamations drift from the darkness, though I don't know why anyone is surprised. Delilah rolls her eyes, but Susanna's face is curiously blank as she says, "He will pay for that."

"Who will? You recognize the voice?" I ask. "How? And why will he pay?"

"Keep faithful, *girls*." She leans hard on the last word, an unnecessary reminder she is the first of us to become a woman, before leaving us to head toward the cave in the distance.

"She makes me so angry, I just want to—"

"Don't say it." Delilah curls slender fingers around my fist. "Don't let her goad you into sin. Trust me, it's not worth it. Besides, what are the odds she'll remember to report your breach, on a night like tonight?"

I wish I could believe her. Delilah may be willing to burden herself with my secrets, but Susanna will be under no such obligation. Still, that isn't why I'm mad. Clearly, Susanna knows something about tonight she hasn't shared with the rest of us.

We trudge back toward the warmth of the fire. From this distance, I can see the gathered crowd of our friends and family, though I can't make out any one individual. I halfheartedly scan the sand, looking for evidence of Aaron's passage. "Do you think he found help?"

But Delilah isn't interested in his well-being. "What was it like? Touching him?"

"I only did it to save him. I didn't *enjoy* it," I say, scrubbing at my lips again, trying to remove any last traces of sand or memories of his skin against mine. I'm glad the darkness hides my face. Because truthfully, a part of me did like it. Not just because he was a boy, or because I saved his life. But because it was my decision to do it. I chose to sin, and I enjoyed it. What does that say about me? About the state of my soul?

Another strange voice bounces off the mountain, distorted by the echo and the amplification, this time calling Rachel's name.

I grab Delilah's hand and squeeze. "Who do you think he is?"

Delilah's shoulders hunch further. "How would we know? Maybe if we knew what order they were choosing in," she says.

"Do you think it's random?" But we both know that's unlikely. Nothing about our lives is ever left to chance.

As we come up to the back of the crowd, Phoebe squeezes between us and unclasps our hands, taking them in both of hers. "Girls. Where have you been? And why haven't you changed?" Even her look of worry as she scans our dusty work clothes can't mar our teacher's perfect features. I've always thought Phoebe must resemble the Virgin Mary. Only with shorter hair. And minus the virgin part.

"There was a rattler," I whisper back, trying to brush the sand and dirt from my apron.

"We've been here in the back the whole time." Delilah speaks over me, silencing my thoughtless confession.

"Never mind." Phoebe pulls us close. "I've been trying to find you. I wanted to pray with you. One more time."

"Did you pray with Rachel?" That was rude, but I'm honestly curious. Phoebe has never liked Rachel, more because of Rachel's mother and father than anything Rachel has done.

Red spots appear on Phoebe's high cheekbones and she ducks her head. "There wasn't time," she says, her voice clipped. "I didn't expect her to be chosen so early."

Delilah chokes back a laugh.

"That's not what I meant." Phoebe squeezes my hand. "Do you have any questions? Before—"

"Phoebe." My mother pushes her way through the crowd. She's shorter than Phoebe, and her covered head next to our teacher's bare one makes her look a decade older, but she carries herself with a grace that makes up for the rest. "Surely you weren't about to . . ." She stops without naming Phoebe's sin, which somehow makes it worse. "You know better."

Phoebe bites her lip. "I'm not sure about any of this."

Before my mother can respond, before I can ask Phoebe what she means, another voice ripples over our heads in a wave and crashes into the mountain, shattering the calm of the night. "I choose Miriam."

Caleb is big, but his voice is smaller than I expected. Soft. Hesitant. My mother's words echo back at me: *The less you expect, the better.* Serves me right. My heart pounds furiously as I squeeze Delilah's hand in goodbye and prepare myself for my future.

The crowd surges, pushing me forward. My mother grabs my hand, briefly, to help me up over the black jumble of rock, but then she slips away from me and I'm alone, the dark hole of the Marriage Cave yawning at my feet like a mouth that will swallow me whole. I've never been this close to the edge of anything.

A ladder rests at the lip of the pit. I grab the top rung and swing my leg around, but my skirt twists at my ankles and I miss. The crowd buzzes above me as I dangle, the damp clawing at my feet. A sickening sense of familiarity comes over me as my hands slip and I fall into the abyss.

I've had dreams like this.

Strong arms catch me before I hit the ground.

Caleb holds me, the two of us bathed in a pool of moonglow from the opening above. This isn't a dream. It's real. This is his body pressed against mine, his arms strong around me, his hands hot on my back. But there's no smile on his face. And suddenly I realize— positioned here, at the bottom of the ladder, he can't have spoken my name. My head spins. My mouth goes dry.

What has happened?

"I wanted . . ." These are the first words I've spoken to him in years, but my throat is too tight to finish.

The desperation in his eyes mirrors my own. "Me too," he whispers, and an electric jolt surges through me at the sound of his voice.

Then I'm pulled from his grasp, from the protective alcove where we stand and into a dim, low-ceilinged cave filled with men. My father escorts me, disappointment flickering across his face, or perhaps it's a trick of the light? The rest of them swim past on waves of heat and confusion, or maybe it's me who is moving, shoved away from the rock walls scorched by the tongues of a thousand flames and into the center of the cave, where the latest fire still burns low in a pit.

Our Leader stands on a flat rock at the far end of the cavernous space, casting a long shadow across the wall and completely obscuring the boy beside him. Daniel is like the sun, the source of all light. He holds out his arms to me, and though I don't intend to move, I'm drawn like a thirsty traveler to water. His voice washes over me like warm rain, though the thunderous beating in my chest drowns out the words. When I step up to meet him, he pries my hand from my neck and joins it with the boy's, pressing them tightly together within his own. Fingernails gouge my palms; they could be mine.

"God has sent you a vision of your wife?" Daniel asks.

"He has."

"And which woman does he wish for you to take?"

"Miriam."

And just like that, Aaron and I are married.

Another man steps forward and holds out a basket. I take it automatically, staring in confusion at the tufts of angora wool and the glittering instruments stabbed between them.

There are so many things I didn't know about this night, so many questions my mother wouldn't answer, and perhaps this is the biggest surprise of all. Not only have I been given to the wrong husband, but I've been assigned the wrong livelihood as well.

Fat tears spatter the wool.

I am a terrible weaver.

3

CALEB

I am supposed to marry Miriam.

This knowledge is a certainty, as much a part of me as my blood and bones. So when Aaron—the *Outsider*—speaks her name, I think I must have misheard. The cave is crowded; his voice is muffled. But then she is in my arms; we speak, and just as quickly, she is gone. Taking vows.

With Aaron.

This is a nightmare. Why can't I wake up?

I've done everything right. I've obeyed all of Daniel's laws. And God's. I studied. I dreamt. I prayed. It should be me standing next to her. Me shielding her. Me touching her, instead of all the rest. Their fingers on her shoulders, her hair, her face. She's a married woman now, and I know this is part of the ritual—wives do not have authority over their own bodies—but it bothers me. Aaron is supposed to assert his power as her husband and stop them. So why isn't he trying? Miriam twists away, and my heart does the same. I clench my fists and try to push through the crowd. But just as my fingers graze her thick curls, Daniel takes a single step forward and everyone else falls back.

Finally! He prayed with me. He knows God intended me to call her name tonight. I'm not sure why he let this go on so long, but I know better than to ask stupid questions. Daniel will stop this.

But he doesn't. Instead, he cups Miriam's chin. "May this union be blessed."

I both wish and fear she'll say something. Deny Aaron as her husband. Daniel doesn't like women to speak. Even when spoken to. But surely this is an exception? Someone needs to do it. But she only shakes her head, back and forth. I know the feeling. This is all wrong.

"Miriam."

The whispered voice is Boaz, her father. I don't know what he wants to say, because he doesn't speak again. And even though every cell in my body is screaming at me to do something, I can't. No one interrupts Daniel.

Shadow flames dance across Daniel's face as he studies Miriam's . . . Aaron. But Aaron's face gives nothing away.

"Marriage is a journey," Daniel says. "There is no mercy for those who stray from the Path of Righteousness. I suppose only time will tell."

"What?" Miriam asks, her voice shaky. "What will time tell?"

Daniel presses three fingers against her mouth, silencing her, until she winces.

I don't know if I should laugh or cry. It isn't Miriam who's strayed. Can't he see that?

He removes his hand, and she must agree, because she whispers, "Where is my mercy?"

But Daniel isn't feeling merciful. He turns his back as Boaz squeezes her hand and pushes her and Aaron into the shadowy doorway of the tunnel that leads back to the city.

"Caleb." I don't know how long Father has been standing beside me, or if he understands the disaster of what's just happened.

He snaps his fingers in my face. "Daniel is waiting. Step up to the podium and choose."

So, no. Father has no idea that Aaron has just married my wife. He spent many nights questioning my older brother on his choice, but never asked about mine. I wanted to believe it was because he trusted me to make the right decision. But most likely he only asked Marcus because he only cares about Marcus. "I can't," I say, trying to sort out what I should do. "Aaron—"

He puts a hand to my shoulder, as if to shove me, but stops, maybe remembering I'm bigger than him. Ever since Daniel offered me a place on his Security Council and advised me to begin strength training, Father hasn't raised a hand to me. Tonight would be a bad time to start again.

"You're embarrassing me," he hisses, his jaw clenched. "Go to the podium."

He is still my father, and I am still an obedient son. I move as if in a dream, though not a good one. Not like the one where Miriam and I . . .

"Caleb." Daniel holds the microphone out to me, and his words are both an invitation and an order. "Be a man. Choose your wife."

He's asking me to join their ranks, and I've never wanted anything more. To make decisions. To be taken seriously. To stand beside him and Father as equals. But that's exactly why I can't choose. Can't Daniel see that? A man does the moral thing. Miriam is already someone else's wife. If I were to say her name now, would that make me an adulterer? Adultery is punishable by Banishment.

What does Daniel expect me to do? It feels like one of our Lessons, where we must decide who is righteous. I almost never get those right. Even now, I feel like the other brother in the story of the prodigal son. Where was his reward? *I* am the faithful. *I* am the righteous. *I* am the son of a Council Member. Aaron is none of these.

I'm not saying I'm perfect. I shouldn't have spoken to her, not even those two small words. It's against all the rules. But when Aaron said her name, I was in shock. And when I heard her voice—*I wanted*—so soft, yet so earnest, it was like someone else took over. I wasn't a Seeker of Wisdom, or strength trainer, or devoted pupil of our Leader. I was just Caleb. And I wanted her.

So maybe this is my punishment. Maybe Daniel knows, somehow. Maybe I'm supposed to choose another wife to show my contrition. Except I'm not sorry. Instead, I regret not saying more. Why didn't I talk to her, instead of leaving those stupid messages in the sand? Surely that punishment couldn't be any worse than the pain I feel right now.

I could have told her how I've loved her since before the time of Separation. Back when we were still allowed to play together, and Marcus liked to give us biblical riddles and then show off how smart he was when we couldn't solve them. I was usually the slowest, and I took the brunt of his teasing. But Miriam never laughed, even when the others did. In fact, once she stumped Marcus with a riddle of her own. He'd just given me one: Who came close enough to Heaven to kiss the gate, but ended up in Hell? The answer was Judas, though I hadn't guessed. In the midst of everyone's laughter, Miriam had spoken up. "Who broke every commandment?"

Marcus had snorted a laugh, so sure he was right. "That's easy. If you're going to play, Miriam, at least try to come up with a riddle that doesn't have the same answer as mine."

But he was wrong. "It's Moses," she'd said, making sure he got it before she'd looked at me. "He dropped the tablets. Broke the commandments. Every single one." Then she'd hopped on her bike and ridden off, her hair blowing behind her.

I love her hair. I should have told her that. It's like a spring of coiled energy that can't be contained—just like her. I love her voice, too. My family sits near hers at Chapel, and I can hear her voice above everyone else's. It's like a kind of prayer. Or I could have told her about the way her laugh makes everything inside me tingle. Or that I've dreamt of her. That I meant to choose her.

I should have tried harder. I don't know how many of my messages she got, or if she even understood them. It took me a long time to figure out how to say *I love the way you sing* with just a stick in the sand. I settled on a heart and a music note. *I dreamt you were my wife* was just a cloud and a circle-cross. I'm not good with words. Even less when I'm limited by symbols meant for godly worship instead of forbidden love. Though it wasn't really forbidden. I was supposed to choose her. I just wasn't supposed to let her know.

Now I'll never get the chance. Especially not if I marry someone else.

"Caleb," Daniel says again, his voice even more commanding than his magnetic stare. "Choose."

"I can't." I drop to my knees. "I will do anything, any sort of penance, if you will just—"

"God has a message for us," Daniel says, stretching out an arm as his voice carries across the cave. "Brothers, close your eyes, so that He might better communicate."

The men obey.

Daniel presses his thumbs over my eyelids. "You too, Caleb. Listen for His instructions."

I kneel in the dirt, my eyes pressed tightly shut. So faint is the voice of God as He whispers in my ear, "Delilah."

Delilah? The redhead? She's the same age as one of my younger brothers, a child. I shake my head, once, then more firmly. "No," I say, opening my eyes and struggling to my feet. And then, "I won't choose." I say it louder, into the microphone this time, my denial echoing off the cave walls. It worked for Aaron, when he spoke Miriam's name aloud.

And so it must for me, because though Daniel's gaze burns with a dangerous light, he merely tilts his head. Then he says, "So be it."

I barely feel Father's hand as he pushes me into the tunnel. Alone. I don't know where I'm supposed to go now or what will become of me.

The reality of what I've done presses on me like these suffocating walls. I've defied Daniel. And God. I've refused to take a wife. No man in New Jerusalem, other than our Leader, has ever gone unmarried. I've never felt so scared, or so lost.

I've also never been this angry. With a roar that comes from deep inside, I beat my fist against the rock wall. Pain winds from my blood-slick knuckles up my arm, and I'm glad. It pushes out all the other feelings, at least for a second.

Daniel says my temper is my weakness. Tonight, it feels more like Aaron's problem.

4

MIRIAM

My skin still burns from the feel of their hands on me—my arms, my shoulders, my head. Every man I know took a turn. Once I was married, they were allowed to touch me, so they did. It's actually one of the few things I knew would happen tonight. Phoebe told us in Lessons, after swearing us to secrecy. She said she wanted us to be prepared, but I didn't realize how belittling it would be.

What else have I neglected to consider?

Aaron stumbles, and I reach out to steady him automatically, before I remember what he's done. His skin is sallow, and beads of sweat line his forehead. I don't know him well enough to tell if his discomfort is pain or something else, and though Church law states that since we're married we can speak, for the first time in my life I can't find the words. Instead, I study the tunnel we've been shunted into.

Every Child of Daniel has been taught the importance of these tunnels. Many years ago, after Genesis but before the birth of Christ, lava flowed beneath the earth in certain sacred spaces. When the lava cooled and drained, it left behind tunnels. Their existence was foretold to Daniel in a dream, and they are the reason New Jerusalem was settled here, at the base of the Soda Mountains, away from the rest of the corrupt world. The tunnels and the Marriage Cave are sacred spaces, and before tonight, I'd never been in either. Now that I'm finally here, the damp, craggy space lit by flickering candles is yet another disappointment in this nightmare I thought would be a celebration. Maybe the reason none of the Elders talk about this night isn't that they want to keep the memory private, but that they'd rather forget.

Aaron sags against the tunnel wall, eyelids fluttering. "How bad is it?"

I kneel to examine his heel. It's red and puffy near the wound, but the redness hasn't spread past my scarf, which is still tied around his ankle. My fingers itch to snatch it off, to turn and run. But then I remember the handwriting. As in the Bible, the hand of God wrote a coded message on the wall of the tunnel for Daniel, giving him directions for forming our community. This is my first and only chance to see it.

"Look, I know you're pissed." Aaron pushes off the wall. "And you've got every right to be. But just tell me, am I going to be okay? Shouldn't I go to a doctor or something?"

"Pissed?" I don't know this word that sounds like steam escaping a kettle.

"Okay, super pissed." He throws his hands in the air and bumps the candleholder, and only then, in the sputtering light, do I see it. The handwriting of God. Aaron has been leaning against it.

I shove him aside, both so he won't deface it any further and so I can read it.

But I can't. And it feels like yet another mistake in a night of many. Though I've been taught the message is a code only Daniel can comprehend, deep down I always imagined when I saw it, I'd understand it. But this is just a bunch of drawings and scribbles. Caleb's messages are easier to decipher than this, and they are mere scratches, easily erased by a footstep or a soft breeze.

Aaron watches me run tentative fingers over the stick figures and shapes.

"You act like you've never seen them before. They're petroglyphs."

I glare at him, and he holds up his hands in supplication, more careful of the flame this time. "Or maybe not. What do I know?"

"Nothing." I pinch my lips together and manage to hold back my tears. How foolish of me to assume that once I was married, my husband could teach me. Now I'm married to an Outsider who knows even less than me.

"Let's go," I say. "My mother is a nurse. She can take care of your foot. Although you should have done that earlier." If only he'd gone for medical attention, maybe Daniel would have halted the Matrimony and we wouldn't be here now.

"A real nurse?" he asks.

"What other kind is there?"

When he doesn't answer, I keep walking and he limps behind. The silence is broken only by the occasional crunch of rock beneath our feet, until the path grows steep and the walls narrow, and we emerge into the city from a rocky outcropping wedged behind the guard shack. The old wooden door that normally blocks this tunnel has been rolled away, and as I step into the cool night air, I choke.

New Jerusalem is bigger than the cave or the tunnel, but the fence is impossibly high and the floodlights perched atop it blindingly bright and I'm suffocating. I turn back—to run, though where would I go? But my mother steps forward and holds out her hands, and I force myself to breathe. One breath. Then another.

"Mother. What are you doing here?"

"I'm here to welcome you home," she says. "You left here tonight separately, as children. But you return as husband and wife."

The words sound flat, rehearsed. She's adopted a mask of serenity, but I have had years of practice, and I know her tells. The thinning of her lips as she surveys my dingy work dress means disappointment. The wrinkles in the corners of her eyes convey worry. Does she know this marriage is a terrible mistake? Does everyone? Or is this how every wedding night begins? Maybe she isn't concerned about the Matrimony. Perhaps it's the night to come that worries her.

It certainly worries me.

"Miriam?" she asks.

"Aaron's been bit." I point to his foot.

"In the tunnel?" Her mouth puckers, and the wrinkles spread to her forehead.

"No. Before . . ." He doesn't finish.

She kneels beside him, and he lifts his foot and pulls off his sandal, her fingers lingering on the fabric knotted at his ankle. She must recognize the scarf; it's my favorite, the same shade of light purple as the Mojave asters that grow wild along the fence. Aaron winces but doesn't protest as she moves it aside and probes the heel with expert fingers.

I think of the men, back in the cavern, with their grasping hands. How does he like it? Has he ever been touched by a woman he barely knows? But if he feels anything other than pain, it doesn't show.

"I think you got lucky," Mother says, standing and brushing dust off her long skirt. "It must not have been poisonous."

"Really?" Aaron grimaces as he shifts weight back onto his injured foot. "I was sure it was a rattlesnake . . ." He trails off.

She gives me a sharp look and waits a beat. When I don't speak, the creases in her forehead deepen. "About one in four rattlesnake bites are dry—they don't inject venom. We should keep an eye on it, of course. Miriam can help. She knows all about first aid. Apparently."

Can Aaron hear the suspicion in her voice, or is it only me? Surely she knows I couldn't leave him to die. No matter what his gender.

"Why don't we get you two settled in your apartment? Get you off your feet."

As we walk past the front of the guard shack, Aaron glances back at the tunnel. "I didn't realize . . . is that the only way in?"

My mother pauses, turning her back on the gates, which still stand ajar. "No. There's also the cave."

He ducks his head. "Oh. Right. I'm just . . . a little turned around."

Maybe Mother is wrong about the bite, and the poison has spread to his brain.

Mother begins walking again, toward the newly renovated Cooperative Dormitory. It used to be a motel, many years ago, when New Jerusalem was a health facility for the spiritually unwell, but that was before our time here. For most of my life it was an empty shell, waiting for a purpose.

"Every new couple has been allotted a dwelling space," she tells us, as if we don't already know. The boys helped fix and furnish the dilapidated stucco building. As for the girls, my friends and I snuck over many times to wander the open-air corridors that ring both stories of the building. We tried to peer in the darkened windows and ran our fingers over the corroded brass numbers on the doors and argued over who would be lucky enough to get the apartments overlooking the lake. But mostly, we talked about what we thought marriage would be like.

I never imagined it would be like this.

"It's been furnished with everything you need to start your lives together." My mother trips over the last word. "That way, you can spend time getting to know each other, without the worries of daily life intruding."

That strangling feeling comes over me again, and I cling to the iron railing as she leads us up the stairwell. Daily life? I don't want to think about one day with this man, let alone a life with him. Everything is happening so quickly, and I don't know how to stop it. I can barely remember how to breathe.

Once we've entered the building, we pass Susanna's mother, just leaving, on our way up the stairs. Are Susanna and her husband, whoever he is, already settled in to their new home? I open my mouth to ask, but Lydia nods at my mother, glances at Aaron, and then scowls at me, so I snap it closed. The woman shares her daughter's warm personality.

"Someone will be bringing by your meals for the time being," my mother says as we walk down the outside corridor until we've reached the door to our apartment. Her smile falters for only a moment, and she almost catches her lower lip between her teeth. "Myself or one of the other Council Members' wives. These first few days you'll be free from Lessons and Vocational Duties. There will still be Prayer, of course. Thrice daily. More, if you wish. It helps with the . . . adjustment. That and talking. I imagine you have much to say."

This is directed at me, but for once it sounds more like a plea than an admonishment.

She opens the door and leads us inside. It's smaller than I pictured. There will be no room for me to avoid my new husband here. Our "house" is essentially one room, broken only by a half wall. My mother switches on a table lamp, but the light does nothing to improve my view. The window beside the door looks out over the corridor we just left. On the wall to my right, there is a couch and an end table with the single lamp. Centered above the couch hangs a large portrait of Daniel. To our left, a small table and two chairs, and behind it, a door I hope leads to the bathroom. In the far corner, a short countertop juts from the wall, partially obscuring a small refrigerator and cooktop.

The double bed lies just beyond the half wall in front of us.

"Daniel will come by soon. To . . . visit," my mother continues, stepping around me to pat at the couch cushion.

Aaron sinks down on the couch with a grimace. "How soon? Tonight?"

Her teeth try to grab her lip again. "Probably not. Maybe tomorrow. He will talk with you about your new Lessons. And your duties."

"What kind of duties?" he asks.

I struggle to keep the desperation off my face as I wait for her answer. Please, let her mean the weaving. I don't want to think about my other duties. Not with him.

She pauses to prop Aaron's foot on a pillow, then says, "I'm told you will both be apprenticing in the Woolen Mill. Daniel will also answer your questions about . . . other things."

Aaron collapses back into the cushions and closes his eyes.

I'd scream, but panic has taken my ability to both breathe and speak.

In a moment, my mother will leave, and we will be alone. And then what? I'm not naïve. We do our own work in this community. I've seen the barn animals. I know the basic premise. I have also studied scripture. *But if they cannot exercise self-control, they should marry. For it is better to marry than to burn with passion.* 1 Corinthians 7:9.

Why have I never noticed the passage is exclusionary? Can the two not exist together, passion and marriage? I have allowed myself to imagine what both might be like. Cooking dinner in my own kitchen while I hum softly to myself, no one there to quiet me. Walking to Chapel in the middle of the city, hand in hand in hand with our children. Waking up next to Caleb, the sunlight stretching warm fingers across his chest.

But only Caleb. Never have I pictured another man, and certainly not this near-stranger.

My mother kisses my forehead, then hesitates before she kisses Aaron's. "I have to go help Rachel settle in to her new home."

The pang of longing is so sharp I almost cry. How I wish I were with Rachel, back in the bedroom we've shared since we were babies, instead of here in this unwelcoming apartment.

"Where is Rachel? Who did she marry?"

"Phoebe escorted her, so that I could come with you," she says, not really answering either of my questions. So that much hasn't changed.

"Phoebe?" I pray Rachel's been chosen by a more suitable husband than I have. If not, if she has doubts like me, Phoebe is the last person she'd want to share them with.

Mother knows this, too. "I should go to her and leave you to get acquainted." But she doesn't. Instead, she hovers near the door. What is she thinking? Is it difficult to leave her daughter with a man she doesn't know? This is our custom, and I've never questioned it. Not until this moment. But she also once sat in a strange room with a man she had never exchanged so much as a single word with. That man became my father. She must know this panic welling inside me. So why doesn't she console me?

To calm myself, I think about what Daniel would say.

He would tell me to keep faithful. That we are the chosen, the Children of Daniel. That Aaron isn't a stranger, he is my Brother, in the way we are all Brothers and Sisters of God. And now, he is also my husband.

Aaron is silent, maybe from the pain. Or maybe he's asking God for forgiveness. It's a little late for that. I turn my back on him. My mother's eyes are shut, too, but her lips are moving. She is praying. I take her hands, and her eyelids flutter open.

"You need to watch over him tonight. If you see signs of—"

"This is a mistake," I interrupt, the words finally free. I grip her hands as tight as I can. "I can't stay here. Help me fix this before . . ." I don't finish. We both know what "before" is.

"There are no mistakes." She starts to hum a song she used to sing when I was a child, about love giving us strength to try "once more," whatever that means. I don't plan to try at all.

Maybe she understands, because she squeezes my hand quickly and releases it. Takes a deep breath. Straightens her back. "This is a sign, Miriam. God must have wanted this union."

"Why?" I ask.

"Only He can answer that. You must get down on your knees and ask Him."

"Mother, wait. I have to know. Did you . . . you and Father. Did you know he was going to choose you?"

She pinches her lips together and looks down at the floor. Her face is a mixture of warring emotions—love and anger; fear and resolve. Without meeting my gaze, she nods, once, and then she is gone, the door clicking shut behind her.

I don't know when I'll see her again, or if I'll be able to forgive her when I do.

She knew. Just like I did. The difference is that she was right, and I was wrong. She married the man she knew she belonged with. I have married . . . someone else. I stand for a long time with my hand pressed against the door. When I turn, Aaron is still lying on the couch, dark eyelashes fluttering against his pale cheeks.

"Why did you choose me?" It's a reasonable question. I've earned the right to ask. I'm his wife, after all. But my words come out pointed and sharp, and his eyes fly open.

He shrinks back into the couch so I have to lean forward to hear him. Even so, I can hardly believe what he says.

"I was late. And I panicked." He looks away toward the window, which holds no view at night, only our distorted reflections. "It's been a long time since anyone's been nice to me."

His stupid answer only fuels my anger. "Nice? You picked me because I was *nice*? What about God? Your dreams? Isn't that how this is supposed to work?" I don't actually know how it's supposed to work. But Caleb's messages . . . he dreamt of me. And I of him. That must mean something.

Aaron plucks at the textured fabric of the armrest. "I never thought . . ." He leans forward and digs his knuckles into the corners of his eyes. "I screwed up. It wasn't supposed to happen this way."

"What 'way' was it supposed to happen?"

"You saved me back in the desert. With the snake. I had to choose, and your name just popped out. I'm sorry I messed up your plans."

"My *plans*?" I ask. "As if my marriage, my . . . my future were just an outing I'd been looking forward to and had to cancel?" I pound my hands against my thighs until they ache, though it's nothing compared to the pain in my heart. "You need to undo this. In the morning, you must go to Daniel and tell him you've made a mistake."

Aaron drops his head into his hands, and his shoulders shake. At first I think he's crying, but when he looks up he is laughing. "God, Miriam. Do you really think it's that easy?"

"It has to be. There has to be a way."

"Tell Daniel I messed up." He swallows convulsively. "Does he strike you as a forgiving kind of guy?"

"*God* forgives. Daniel leads us to repentance. We need a firm hand to guide us, not a soft one."

"Well, *soft* is definitely not a word I'd use to describe him. Harsh, maybe? Punitive?"

"He is the Prophet, reborn. Who are you to insult him?"

Aaron tilts his head to the side, as if he can't grasp what I'm saying. As if I'm the strange one. "The prophet Daniel. Like in the Bible." He makes a choking sound deep in his throat. "How do you know that? Because he told you? Where's his proof?"

"He doesn't need proof!" I don't think I've ever been this angry before. I clench my fists and back away until I bump up against the bathroom door. There's nowhere else to go. I'm trapped, married to a man I don't know, a man who blasphemes our Leader as easily as he might talk about the weather.

"Keep your foot elevated," I finally say. "If it looks like the redness is spreading, you may need to have it amputated."

Then I leave him alone in our living room with his swollen foot and his empty apologies. I won't speak to him again tonight, and I surely won't share a bed with him. But since married women are allowed to speak, I refuse to waste the privilege any longer. I take my Bible into the bathroom and turn to Song of Songs.

"'On my bed by night I sought him whom my soul loves; I sought him, but found him not.'" I read aloud until my voice goes hoarse and the night sky turns a dusky gray, the stars fading into oblivion.

5

CALEB

Two guards are waiting as I exit the tunnel. Abraham, Aaron's father, steps in front of me when I turn toward the dormitory.

"The apartments are for married couples," he says.

He's shorter than me, but solid. The faint scar across his cheek is evidence of at least a passing knowledge of violence. He's one of the few men here I don't think I could beat in a fight, though tonight I'm itching to try.

Maybe he can tell, because he grabs a gun from the wall and holsters it. The other man, Thomas, points his flashlight at me. "Daniel says you're to go to the Council House."

It makes sense. It's where Daniel lives, along with Phoebe, the only other unmarried person in the community.

"Caleb." My mother's soft voice is the last I expected to hear. She's standing in the shadow of the guard shack, near the road. My youngest brother, Matthew, is perched on her hip, his sleeping face buried in the curve of her neck. The others must still be at the celebration.

"Mother." I don't want her here to witness my act of defiance. While she would never punish me—that is Father's duty—her disappointment will almost be worse.

"Let's go." Thomas waves the flashlight toward the road. "I'll take you."

"Of course." Mother bows her head and turns to follow, but falters when I don't move.

"I know the way." I'm keeping my temper in check, but just barely. "And I don't need an escort. I'm a member of the Security Council. Just like you."

"Are you, though?" Thomas asks.

Matthew squirms in Mother's arms, and she shushes him as she shoots a nervous glance between Thomas and me.

I stand taller, careful not to let them see my fear. The boys were all assigned their Vocational Duties last week. Tonight was to be the official announcement, but that's just a formality. My marital status has nothing to do with my job on the Security Council. Does it?

Abraham claps Thomas on the shoulder. "I think they'll be all right."

Thomas glares at me as he flicks the flashlight off and on and then off again. Finally, he shrugs off Abraham's hand. "Fine. Go on, then."

I should be grateful to Abraham, but I'm not. Most of this is his fault. He brought his family here, after all. He's also the one responsible for the new apartments, along with all the added work and the renovations that followed. Sure, Daniel had already been concerned about where the newly married couples were going to live. Abraham wasn't even the first to suggest that we renovate the old motel. But he was willing to do more than talk, and that lit a fire under the Council. Soon after the vote to accept his family, we received deliveries of paint and lumber, along with a new van to haul it all.

Miriam is probably in one of those apartments, right now. With a man who isn't me. I scan the terrace, and the lighted windows beyond, aching for a glimpse of her. Until Abraham clears his throat. When

I look back, Thomas has gone inside the shack, but Aaron's father is standing in the doorway. Watching me.

"Caleb," Mother calls softly.

She starts down the road and I follow, feeling Abraham's gaze on my back long after we're out of sight.

We pass the now-darkened Medical Shed and the Gymnasium and the Kitchen before Mother speaks. "Why did you do it?" she asks. "You can't live on your own. Without a wife. Who will take care of you?"

Her voice seems unnaturally loud in the empty streets, but it can't be, because Matthew doesn't stir. Still, I hear the admonishment. In what she says, and in what she doesn't. *How could you be so foolish? Why would you make a decision like this without thinking it through? What did you think would happen?*

"I don't know," I mumble, kicking a chunk of rock, and then another. She wouldn't understand, even if I were allowed to tell her about the dreams, about the hours spent in prayer with Daniel, waiting for a sign from God. The farther into the city we go, the more alone I feel, which makes no sense. Mother and Matthew walk beside me. We're inside the gates, safe. Headed to Daniel's house, the holiest of places. Usually, the thought of Daniel is enough to calm me.

Not tonight.

It's like there is an invisible rope pulling at me, tugging me back toward the apartments. To Miriam. It's so strong, I know that if I follow it, I will be able to find her. I want, no, I *need* to see her.

It would be so easy to go back. To find Aaron. Punch him. There's a physical pain inside me that won't be appeased until I do. But Daniel ordered me to the Council House. He must want to talk to me. I should do the right thing and keep walking there, all the way up the path. It's the wrong thing that got me here.

Mother stops at the walkway leading to the Farmhouse and turns to me. "Come inside. Let me make you something to eat. Daniel will understand, won't he?"

Part of me wants nothing more than to run up to the Farmhouse, just like normal. Follow Mother inside. Let her make me tea and brown-sugar toast.

But I don't belong here anymore.

"Thank you," I say, kissing her cheek. "But Daniel is expecting me. I shouldn't keep him waiting."

"I know," she says. "It's just . . ." She blinks back tears. "This path you're on . . . can you really make it on your own?"

Past the barns and grazing pasture, the path to Daniel's house winds steep and potentially hazardous in the dark. But this isn't the path she's talking about.

"I'll be fine." I turn away so the darkness hides my lying face. "You go on home. Put Matthew to bed." And because I'm a man now, she does what I say.

The Council House is Daniel's home, a three-story, gleaming white building topped with a domed roof. It sits on a hill in the far corner of the city, opposite the front gates, so that he can keep watch over the whole community.

I stop to catch my breath at the bottom of the steps. The pillars stretching above me always make me feel small. They represent the angels from Daniel's visions, the ones who urged him to lead his followers away from sin and depravity. The dome on top is an almost perfect sphere. It's left over from the first settlers, who used it for something called radio, which Daniel says is an ancient technology no longer in use. Marcus says it reminds him of a soap bubble, but Daniel likened it to the firmament in Genesis and so built his house around it.

I push open the tall doors and step into the dark foyer. I've never been here at night. Only during the day, when sunlight streams through the tall windows and shines on the marbled floor. Now, everything is black. Even when I flip the light switch, shadows still blanket the staircase that climbs the wall to the second- and third-floor balconies.

Abraham told me to come here, but he didn't tell me what to do next. What would make Daniel angrier? Waiting for instruction? Or taking initiative and choosing my own room? Be a man, they said. So I will.

The first floor is taken up by Council business in the left wing and Daniel's personal rooms on the right. There is a small kitchen in the back. I climb the staircase. The second floor is where Phoebe lives, alongside several other unoccupied rooms. I'm not sure it's appropriate to share a floor with her, but taking a room on the third floor, so far from Daniel, feels cowardly, and I can't give in to fear. I've already given up too much. I choose an empty bedroom to the left of the staircase, separated from Phoebe by the balcony that runs the full width of the foyer. That should be acceptable.

It's furnished with only a bed and a desk, which don't offer much distraction. I circle the plain room, muscles tense. What I need is to move, to push myself, to feel the burn as I struggle against the weight machine. That struggle I know I can win. I've worked hard to hone my body, though as Daniel reminds me, my strength is a necessity and a gift from God and should never be viewed with prideful eyes. It doesn't matter tonight; my weights are back at the Farmhouse.

I drop to my knees on a threadbare rug and begin a set of push-ups. I try to lose myself in the rhythm, but the blankness won't come. Every time I close my eyes, I'm back in the cave. The flickering light, the bodies pressed tightly together.

Newcomer. Must. Choose. First.

Each word a thought. Each thought a hard, upward thrust.

Why?

Don't. Question. Daniel's. Word.

But. Aaron. Is. Late.

Then. Marcus.

He pushes his way to the front. Climbs the podium. Takes the microphone.

Even from far in the back, hidden in the shadowy pit near the ladder, I can tell by the set of my brother's shoulders that something isn't right. When he says Susanna's name, Daniel moves forward. As if to stop him.

My arms cramp. I've lost count. Forty? Forty-five? I keep going, keep pushing on. Marcus has loved Susanna forever. Surely God knows that. So why did Daniel seem surprised? Speaking your wife's name is the first step. Pronouncement. Marriage. Consummation. It's the only Path to Righteousness.

My arms go slack.

I should be starting down my own Path tonight. With Miriam. Instead, Aaron has somehow laid claim to her. So I'm here, alone. Unmarried. What will happen to me? Will my name be stricken from the Book? Somewhere on the other end of the city, Miriam is lying in a strange apartment. In a bed just like mine. With Aaron.

That thought pushes me to my feet. I want to break something, to hurt something. Feel something other than this twist in my gut that's like a tight muscle I can't loosen.

"Caleb. The disciple whom I love."

Daniel's voice interrupts my thoughts. He stands at the door, and my heart swells, edging out a little of the anger. No admonition for the room choice. For once, I've made the right decision. And now he will make this better. The way he does everything. I may be imperfect, but he still loves me. He just said so.

"What happened tonight?"

He knows what happened. But he wants to hear it from me. "He must have misinterpreted . . . somehow." I catch myself. *Daniel* interprets. It will do me no good at all if he thinks I'm laying blame at his feet. "Why would God send us dreams of the same woman?"

"Misinterpreted? Are you suggesting for even a moment that he didn't know exactly what he was doing? This was no accident. This was deliberate."

Deliberate? Why would he . . . ? "Are you saying he *ignored* God's word? And chose Miriam instead . . . instead of . . . ?"

Daniel cocks his head. He does this in class sometimes, when one of us has said something very intelligent. Or very stupid. I have no idea which I've done.

"You're referring to Aaron."

"He chose Miriam. *I* was supposed to choose Miriam. You told me that was what my dreams meant." The anger boils again, my skin going hot. I think I'm even madder than Daniel . . . Wait. "Who are you talking about?"

"Are you suggesting," he says, pressing his fingers together as he paces the room, "that somehow I am at fault here? When the rest of your Brothers and Sisters are happily married? While you and Delilah remain stubbornly unwed?" His peppered hair skims the collar of his purple ceremonial robes. He came here directly from the cave without stopping to change. I'm not sure if I'm flattered or terrified. "You claim that Aaron stumbled. But what about you? God spoke to you, did He not? Called on you to choose a wife? You yourself told me you were ready. Worthy. Yet when the moment came, you refused. Why do you see the speck in your Brother's eye but not the log in your own?" His eyes blaze with something other than the fervor he usually carries. This looks a lot like rage, an emotion I know well. Maybe we're not so dissimilar, Daniel and I.

It shouldn't surprise me, the swift shift of blame. I've seen him do it to others. I've watched my Brothers talk themselves into corners—and worse—too many times to defend myself now. I refused to name a wife only because I thought it was the right thing to do. Because the dream God sent me was of Miriam. And I couldn't choose a woman who was someone else's wife. Or a wife I couldn't love.

But none of that is what Daniel wants to hear now. This is always my problem: I usually know what *not* to say; rarely do I know the right thing.

"I just want to fix this. I'm supposed to be with Miriam."

His voice sharpens to a flinty edge. "Have you spoken to her about this?"

"No." I squeeze the answer out the way I push out another rep on the bench press. It isn't a lie. He's asking about after. "I haven't spoken to anyone since the Matrimony, other than the guards. And my mother."

My answer seems to calm him. "Supposed to be." He chuckles. "There is no 'supposed to be.' There is only what exists."

"What exists are my feelings for Miriam," I say. I'm not great with words, but these come easy. They're the truth.

Daniel manages to look sad, even as he smiles. "What you need to remember, Caleb, is that each of our actions causes a ripple. And enough ripples cause a flood. Like the one that brought about the end of nearly everyone in Ur."

I have no idea what he's trying to tell me. He's referring to the story of Noah and the ark, but after that I'm lost. Does he want me to build a boat?

"What would you have me do?" Daniel says. "Tell our brethren you're unhappy with your choice? And then what? Perhaps you think it better if I say the entire evening was in error." He spreads his arms. "But who will believe that? That I allowed Matrimony between all the wrong people?" Tiny lines feather out from his eyes like arrows. "Does that seem like the kind of mistake I would make?"

"Of course not," I say, the words automatic. Daniel doesn't make mistakes. But neither does God, so . . . what is tonight, then? If all that is real is what exists, that means Miriam and I were never meant to be together at all. And that can't be true. My head begins to pound, and my body shakes.

Daniel puts a firm hand on my neck as he guides me to sit on the bed. "Since you cannot live with the married couples, I'll allow you to stay here. For now. What choice do I have? But you will be responsible for your own meals and your own housekeeping. After all, this is not your mother's burden to carry. Nor is it mine." His voice is warm in my ear, strong, when he says, "Your refusal to marry is the mistake, Brother. A sin. And one I'm not sure you can recover from."

Once again, I've managed to do the wrong thing. I bow my head. "I'm sorry."

"Oh, it's not me you need to beg for forgiveness. This is between you and God. I hope for your sake He's feeling merciful. Because there's no room for the Faithless here. Not in my community."

I'm not Faithless! I want to scream it, but he is already gone. And maybe he's right. I have sinned. Willfully. I ignored God's voice. I refused Daniel's orders. How can I expect forgiveness? I'm lucky to still have a roof over my head.

6

MIRIAM

WHEN THERE IS A PROPHET AMONG YOU,
I, THE LORD, REVEAL MYSELF TO THEM IN
VISIONS. I SPEAK TO THEM IN DREAMS.

—*Numbers 12:6*

Caleb and I walk across the sand, hands intertwined. But this isn't the sand of our desert; this sand is white and fine and sifts through our bare toes like sugar. Ahead is water, as far as I can see. It undulates like a living creature, fierce and blue, roaring louder than any animal I've ever heard. Caleb tugs me forward and I resist, laughing, ecstatic at the chance we've been given to be together, to be free. He tugs again, and this time the water sweeps forward to meet me, licking me with its icy tongue. Then Caleb pulls me into his arms and leans in, his lips inches from mine.

I wake, heart pounding, my mother's song in my head and Daniel's voice in my ear.

I hope you still feel small when you stand beside the ocean.

"'Let the morning tell of your unfailing love, for I have put my trust in you!'"

For a moment, I think he's there with me. That he has read my forbidden thoughts. But it's just the morning Call to Prayer. These messages always sound timely and personal, but by now I know they're prerecorded. Daniel can't be everywhere at once. Our house—my parents' house—had several speakers for delivering his Word, but this tiny apartment has only one, and it's mounted above the couch where I finally fell asleep.

Never have I missed a Call to Prayer. But then, never have I been given the opportunity. I'm just so tired. Between the Bible passages and my fevered dreams, I barely got any sleep at all. Instead of getting down on my knees immediately, I close my eyes, trying to hang on to the carefree happiness of my dream a little longer.

Dreams are prophetic. Daniel founded New Jerusalem based on his own dream of a peaceful society, with no war or suffering. It's a requirement of all members of the community to record our dreams in our journals, and to share them with Daniel, so he can interpret the messages God sends us. But my dreams of Caleb seem self-explanatory. And more than that, personal. Just not prophetic, given that I am married to someone else. But my mother said she thought I had a gift. Is she right? Does this dream mean that there is still a chance for Caleb and me to be together? Perhaps I need to pray, as she suggested.

But before I can slide onto my knees, an insistent voice stops me. "I screwed up." This time, it isn't Daniel. "What the hell . . . now?" Aaron asks.

My Bible is open on my lap. I shift carefully, cracking an eyelid. The front door is ajar, and through the tiny gap I see Aaron standing in the outside corridor. But whom is he talking to? The drawn curtains obscure any view I might have.

"It's not great, but what's done . . ." A woman's voice, though I only catch part of what she's said. "Abe and I . . . make this work. Keep your eye on the . . ."

Abe is Aaron's father, so this must be Sarah, Aaron's mother. Neither of them have heeded the Call, which is more like the behavior of Outsiders than True Believers. Are they talking about me? Am I the screwup? If so, then I'm also apparently "not great" as a bride, at least according to her. I clench my fists. Who is she to judge me? Besides, I don't plan on staying married to her son any longer than I have to.

"They're friends . . . she can help," Sarah says.

What does she mean, "they're friends"?

"She doesn't want . . . made that abundantly clear . . ." Aaron laughs bitterly, while Sarah's laugh is light, almost musical.

"So make her want . . ." But I can't hear the rest of the sentence.

What is he supposed to make me want?

"You can be charming when it . . ." she continues. Then her voice hardens, and I have no trouble hearing her next words. "You need her. Remember that."

The apartment door bangs open, followed by quick footsteps across the carpet. I squeeze my eyes tightly shut, trying to figure out what this all means. Why does Aaron need me? Because he still feels like an Outsider?

The slam of the front door hits me like a slap, and only after muffled footsteps move past me do I open my eyes.

Aaron stands in the kitchen area with his back to me, and in daylight he might as well be a different boy from the one I tripped over last night. I stare, mostly because I can and no one will rebuke me. I've never seen a man move about the kitchen in this way. He opens drawers, takes out silverware, tense and controlled, like a wire about to snap. His blue-black hair stands nearly straight, adding another inch to his lean frame. He reminds me of a push broom.

I stretch my cramped legs and stand, trying to brush the wrinkles from my skirt. My hair has escaped its binding, and I pat uselessly at the tangled mess, pulling a crusty tendril off my cheek. I start to gather it with tired fingers, but then I remember I'm married to a man I've no wish to impress, so I leave it and walk barefoot into the kitchen.

"Should we have some breakfast?" Aaron asks, his back to me.

My mouth waters at the mere mention of food. When was the last time I ate? The day before yesterday? It doesn't matter. Only one night of marriage, and already he wants me to serve him. I won't do it.

He turns, and I stumble. His unbuttoned shirt hangs open, revealing the biggest expanse of naked male skin I've ever seen. I slap my eyes shut and promptly run into the counter.

When I open them, he takes in my embarrassing entrance, rumpled clothing, and crazy hair without comment.

"I'm not hungry," I say, and my stomach groans at the obvious lie. My cheeks flush hotter as the ghost of a smile flits across his face.

I debate fleeing to the bathroom, but a knock at the front door stops me.

"Can you get that?" Aaron asks, turning away so that he misses the glare I give him.

I go to the door not because he asked, but because it will be my mother, bringing us breakfast.

Only it's not.

"You aren't—" I open the door to Sarah, looking happy and relaxed and not at all like my mother, or for that matter, like any mother who just had a disagreement with her son. Has she been out here the whole time? Waiting? For what?

"You don't . . ." I trail off. She isn't the wife of a Council Member, so she doesn't have access to the kitchens.

But that all would sound rude, so instead I say, "Welcome. Thank you for coming."

She smiles and pushes the basket she's carrying farther up her arm as she takes my hands in hers. Her grip is surprisingly strong considering she's so thin I can count the bones of her wrist. Is it hard to find food Outside?

"Good morning, Miriam. Or should I say 'daughter'?"

I pull my hands free. "Miriam is fine." I move aside to let her into the apartment, but she remains in the doorway. She's shorter than me, and probably easily a foot shorter than her son, so that her long brown skirt brushes the tops of her sandals. Her head scarf, by contrast, is a riot of color, bright greens and reds. I imagine she must be my mother's age, but she doesn't have the waxy look of the older women here. Her skin is smooth, lighter than Aaron's, and standing this close I can see a dusting of freckles across her nose. The only thing she really has in common with her son is the pointed chin.

"And you may call me Sarah." She studies me with the same scrutiny. "I just wanted to come by and drop off some goodies from the Commodities Exchange." She pulls back the cloth to reveal a pile of brown eggs, some ground meat, and a loaf of bread.

"You didn't have to do that," I start to say. My mother was very clear on where our food would come from.

"It gives me an excuse to check on Aaron," Sarah says, dimpling her cheek with a smile. "He's my only son. I worry."

"About what?"

She moves to put the food on the counter and waves her hand, a tiny, fluttery movement that makes me think of moths. "What do all mothers worry about? The usual."

I don't know what all mothers worry about. My own mother

worries about damnation, and possibly me embarrassing her, but I don't think that's what Sarah is alluding to. "Do you mean the snakebite?"

Her dark eyes snap to her son. "What is she talking about?"

"It's nothing. Just a tiny snake. Not even poisonous." He looks at me from across the counter, as if daring me to contradict him.

I don't, but only because I think this small lie will make Sarah leave faster, not because I have any desire to share secrets with him. Besides, he's sort of right. I sucked the poison out. And his foot doesn't look swollen, nor does he look like he's suffering any other ill effects.

He pulls two eggs from the basket and cracks them into the pan, one after another, where they sizzle and snap. "We live in the desert now. There are many dangers here."

Something in his voice makes her face go blank. "Watch out for him, Miriam," she says, her eyes on his back. "He doesn't always say the right things. But he has a good heart."

I don't care about his heart.

"Isn't it time for you to go? Mom?" Aaron grips the spatula so tight I'm afraid it might snap in half.

A spatula. I've never seen my father so much as slice a piece of bread. "You know how to cook?"

He scrambles the eggs in the pan, then dumps them onto a plate. When I don't move, he walks it over to me. "See for yourself."

I take it, as much from shock as from hunger.

Sarah takes his chin in her hand. "Such a good boy." She lays her other hand on my elbow. "Eat up, Miriam. You need strength." For a second, her clawlike grip turns painful. She's stronger than she looks. Then she releases me, and the moment passes.

"Strength for what?" I ask, raising my voice as she opens the front door.

"Your journey on the Path to Righteousness," she says, after only a tiny hesitation.

She's learned well. It's exactly what my mother would have said. So is the "keep faithful" she leaves us with.

When she's gone, I drop my gaze to the plate in my hands. I'm tempted to refuse it out of sheer spite, even though I'm so hungry I feel faint. What kind of husband cooks? But my stomach groans in protest, and I weaken and take the plate to the table. The eggs are cooked perfectly, golden and so fluffy they melt on my tongue. When Aaron brings over sausage, browned and sweet, I can't get the fork to my mouth fast enough.

He watches me and shakes his head. "Slow down. I don't want to have to Heimlich you."

I scowl as I see the smile bumping at the corners of his mouth. How can he be so casual about all of this? Or maybe this is just him trying to be charming.

"What?" he asks.

I duck my head and continue cutting my meat.

He puts a hand on my wrist. "Tell me what you're thinking."

It sounds like a command, and I tense. This is the moment, then, when all I have been taught must be put into action. *Obey your husband. Submit to him.* It was only a matter of time.

He pulls his hand back. "Sorry. That sounded pushy. I just . . . We're allowed to speak, you know. So tell me. What do you think of my cooking?"

I swallow. "It's good."

"That's it? 'Good'?" He leans back in his chair and laughs.

"What happened to the girl who broke the rules and spoke to me last night in the desert? The one who read aloud all night just because she could? What's the matter? Do you only speak when it's forbidden?"

His words shock me, and I drop my fork with a clatter. He quirks one eyebrow so it forms a kind of question mark.

As angry as I am, at him and this situation, he's right. I do use my words to shock people. I'm much less adept at normal conversation, especially with a man. And this man, although technically my husband, is still practically a stranger. After all, it wasn't that long ago he was an Outsider.

I've never spoken to an Outsider until now, though Aaron and his parents aren't the first I've seen. Sometimes people will visit our community to meet with Daniel. Most of them leave soon thereafter. On rare occasions, some ask to stay. But Aaron and his family are the first to pass the Council and become True Believers, at least as far back as I can remember. We aren't allowed to ask them anything about their time outside New Jerusalem. That life no longer exists.

But now I'm married to one. And as he reminds me, we're allowed to speak.

I push my plate away. "You'd like me to talk? Fine. Tell me about the Outside."

His gaze flicks to the speaker on the wall before dropping to the table. He shakes his head, once, and for a moment I think he's refusing. But then he says, "You say 'Outside' like it's its own place. Like this compound is its own world, and outside is another. You've never been out, then. Not even to Barstow? Disneyland? Vegas, maybe, so Daniel can prove he's right about the fall of society?"

I've never heard of any of these places, and I suspect he's making them up. "I've been to the desert," I say, crossing my arms.

"The desert. Jeez, what must you think . . . ?" He shakes his head. "The world is way bigger than that. This place, this"—his eyes bounce toward the wall once more—"this . . . city? It's just a dot on the map."

"What map?"

"God, you can't be that sheltered."

I wince at the casual way Aaron uses the Lord's name.

He leans forward and drops his voice. "I'm willing to tell you about the outside." He lays a hand over mine. "But it comes at a cost."

I yank free and push my chair back.

"What? Did you think I meant . . . God, I would never . . . Not a physical price. I'm talking about punishment. If Daniel finds out I've told you anything, he's going to be piss—angry."

"Because it's so bad out there?"

He groans and covers his face. "Damn it. I can't answer that. I wish I could. You have no idea." Then he shoves back his chair and goes to the window.

We stay like that for a long time, Aaron staring out over the lake and me staring down at the table. I'm scared by this stranger, by his presence and his words.

Though of course the Elders all grew up Outside, as far as I know, only Daniel and a few members of his Security Council have ventured back Out since the city was founded. None of them ever talks about what they see. But Aaron must know as well as they do of the pain and the filth and the sin. Maybe not talking about it is really a way to protect himself from the memories.

Aaron takes our plates from the table to the sink and turns on the faucet, and my curiosity about the Outside is replaced by an even deeper, unsettled feeling about this man I married. This man who cooks and cleans up after himself. In all the days of my life, I've never seen such a thing. My mother told me marriage would be a revelation, and she wasn't lying.

"She's wrong, you know," I say, "your mother. You don't need me. And the only thing I need from you is help undoing this marriage."

The soft clatter of dishes ceases, his shirt tightening across his shoulders. But he doesn't say anything about my eavesdropping. Instead, he asks, "And how do you suggest I do that?"

"If I knew, I would have already done it." I dig my fingernails into my palms so I don't bang them on the table. "This was your choice." *Your fault*, I think but don't say.

He scrubs furiously at a pan, sloshing water onto the counter. "Don't worry about it, okay? None of this matters. It isn't real. It's just, like, playacting."

"How can you say that? This is my life. My future." I jump up from the chair. "I'm not supposed to be married to *you*." The words are much harsher than I intend, but he deserves them.

"Point taken." He braces himself against the counter, his back to me. "What I meant was, just because Daniel says we're married, that doesn't mean we are. The state of California won't recognize it."

"We aren't governed by the state of California," I say. "We govern ourselves."

He pounds his fist against his forehead and mutters something about brick walls.

"What?"

"Never mind. Let's try this. How old are you?"

"Sixteen. And you?"

"We're both underage, then," he says.

"Sixteen-year-olds can marry with consent from their parents."

I watched my parents sign the form before the Matrimony, but hope blooms, full in my chest. "Did your parents not sign?"

"No, they signed." He tosses a sponge into the sink, and a handful of soap bubbles go flying. "So what are our options?" he asks. "You've lived here longer than me, but even I can tell Daniel is not the kind of guy who takes criticism well. So tell me. How did they undo the marriage the last time someone wanted out?"

I watch the bubbles float gently into the wall and pop, one after another, as the reality of his words hits me. As far as I know, no marriage in New Jerusalem has ever been undone.

7

CALEB

The sun is just rising when I finally give up on sleep. It peeks through my curtains, red and swollen with fury. I don't blame it. Lighting the whole world has got to be one hell of a thankless job. Like how Daniel must feel most of the time, trying to bring us all Salvation.

I shake the wrinkles out of my pants before putting them back on, but I can't shake the questions I have about last night. God did call on me to choose a wife. Daniel isn't wrong. But it was Miriam. It was always Miriam. Once I mentioned her in my dream journal, Daniel came to me. Together, we prayed for guidance. And then the Lord told him I was ready to choose. And I was. I am. Except Aaron took my wife. Why am I the only one who can see that something's not right?

My jaw aches from clenching, and when I get to the bathroom I have to massage it in order to get my toothbrush past my lips. Aaron is the one who misspoke. Aaron is the reason I am unmarried. But Daniel seemed more upset with me. I shudder when I remember his final words last night. *There's no room for the Faithless here.* As if he looked into my head and saw my worst fear: to be sent out to wander the desert like an animal, as King Nebuchadnezzar was sentenced in the Bible. As far back as our community goes, only one person has ever been Banished. It happened before I was old enough to understand or remember, but I can't imagine Daniel having been any more disappointed in her than he is in me.

As Daniel suggested, I spent the night on my knees. I don't feel like I received absolution, but I did get an idea. I'm going to confront Aaron. Make him tell me why he did this. He may think he loves Miriam. But it isn't enough to want to be with a woman. God has to want it, too. Maybe this isn't the way things work Outside. But he lives here now. Someone needs to remind him of that.

Or it could be he doesn't belong here anyway. Yes, we say that we accept Outsiders. People hear about Daniel and his teachings and they come to us, looking for the Path to Righteousness. Usually, it's a single lost soul who's been abandoned by everyone else. They are sometimes fervent in their wish to join, which makes sense. They've lived the horrors we've only heard about. But they are often found to be Unworthy, too tainted by sin for any hope of Salvation, and cannot become True Believers.

Abraham and Sarah and Aaron were the first family to pass the scrutiny of the Church Council. Didn't Daniel find this suspicious? I know my father did, at least until Abraham pledged his loyalty to Daniel and offered to get him everything he needed for the renovations of the old motel. After that, all it took was one vote of the Council, and it was unanimously decided to invite them into our fold.

I spit into the sink and scrub my face with a wet cloth. It feels good to have a plan. I didn't just wake up one morning and decide to be strong. I exercised. I lifted. I increased my stamina. Four reps became eight, eight became twelve. And so it is with this. I'll get Aaron's confession. And I'll take it to Daniel. Then he will see. I'm not Faithless. I'm the one following the word of God. I'm the one fighting for what is right. Not Aaron.

Even Marcus would agree, and he's usually the one cautioning me to keep my mouth shut. He's smaller than me, but he's smart. It used to drive me crazy, the way he'd sit in Bible Study, not speaking. Even when he knew the answers. And there I was, struggling to figure out what exactly Daniel expected me to learn from all of it. Like the story about God asking Abraham to sacrifice his son. Would he really have done it? How come when we talk about that story, we're so focused on Abraham? What about the son? How did he feel? Did he understand? Or did he think his father had gone crazy? When I asked Marcus, he just told me, "A fool who keeps silent is considered wise." And Marcus is wise, I'll give him that.

Because it's so early, I don't see anyone in the hallway or foyer when I leave my room. But from the steps of the Council House, I can see all of the city. Daniel told us that after the Matrimony we would see with new eyes. At the time, I thought he meant something about our duties as husbands. But I'm not married, and he's still right. New Jerusalem looks smaller somehow today, as if the metal fence that surrounds us has been cinched tighter in the dark. Even the goats on the Farm have shrunk, tiny black ants that swirl and swarm toward the barn. It must be milking time.

I take the path down the hill, slowing as I near the Farm. My father's words come back sharp—*You're embarrassing me*—and I wince. It's not the first time he's said it. And it shouldn't bother me anymore. I'm a man now. I don't need his approval.

But my feet move toward the barn door anyway. Maybe if I explain it to him, he'll realize why I couldn't choose. He'll understand that I was only trying to follow God's word. And maybe—finally—he'll respect me.

I nearly run right into my mother as I push the side door open.

Buckets in both hands, she holds her arms wide and takes a few steps back, trying to keep milk from sloshing onto her brown work skirt. "Caleb! What brings you out so early? Have you had breakfast? Isaiah and Matthew have already eaten, but there might be something left."

"Leave him be, Judith. He's not your problem anymore," Father says, slapping the rear end of a goat and sending it scurrying into the holding chute between the milking pen and the pasture.

Though this was my home my whole life, until yesterday, he is quick to remind me I am no longer welcome here. I ignore him and the gnawing emptiness in my belly that my mother has somehow named before I can. "Let me get that for you." I grab for the handle.

"It's her job," Father says. "Unless you think she's incapable?"

Mother smiles wearily and hefts the buckets. "I'll leave you men to talk."

Father turns his back and continues to herd the goats through the chute. Now that he's rebuked me, he sees no need to further acknowledge my presence.

I clear my throat. "I wanted to explain," I say. "About last night. Aaron—"

"Aaron? I don't want to talk about *Aaron*." He curls his lip. "I want to know what the hell you were thinking. Did you give no thought to the shame your choice would bring this family? And you've made Daniel incredibly upset."

I flinch in the face of his scorn. "Why do you assume this is my fault? I'm not the one who messed up!"

Father kicks at the last of the goats, urging them through the holding pen and into the pasture. "All you had to do was say a name. Daniel talked you through the ceremony, what? A dozen times?

Honestly." He slams the gate and snaps the lock into place. "How did I raise a son so weak?"

I rear back, the words as harsh as any physical punishment he could've doled out. "I'm not weak. You know how hard I've worked, the reps, the practice—"

"I meant morally weak." Father wipes his hands on a rag and tosses it at my chest.

When I let it drop, he takes a quick step toward me.

I flinch, an automatic response. But Father doesn't strike me, just shakes his head in disgust and walks away.

My body is throbbing with a rage so deep and so consuming, for a second I can't breathe. Then I snap, howling out my pain and my anger. "I'm the weak one? I'm the disappointment? I'm your son!" I scream and I punch and I kick, gaining no satisfaction from the sound of the fence post splintering or the physical impact.

"Caleb. Caleb!"

I stop, leaning against a wooden beam to catch my breath.

Mother reaches out a tentative hand, brushing a tear from my cheek. Then she looks down at my hands. Behind us, a goat bleats repeatedly.

Mother turns, and with a small exclamation, hurries to the pen, where one straggling goat has been left behind. It quivers in the corner and sinks down into the dirt, as if witnessing my temper has exhausted it. Mother enters the pen, clucking soothing nonsense words until she can get close enough to gather the small animal in her arms.

"Is it okay?" I ask, my voice hoarse.

"He's fine," she whispers, rubbing his belly. Her eyes meet mine. "But son. Your anger . . ." She shakes her head. "You can't let it get the best of you."

I close my eyes. She's been telling me this for as long as I can remember. She could say the same to Father. But she never does.

"You know I'm right. It scares me, the way it takes over."

"I'm fine." I hold out my hands, palms down. "See? Only scratches."

"It's not just you I worry about." She buries her face in the goat's neck, then sets it on wobbly legs and clicks her tongue until it bounds out into the pasture. "If you keep this up, you're going to end up hurting someone you love."

My anger deflates as I watch her walk away, leaving me empty and wobbly. Just like the poor goat. The only difference is he has my mother to comfort him. I have no one.

8

MIRIAM

WHOEVER SPREADS GOSSIP BETRAYS
SECRETS; THE TRUSTWORTHY
KEEP A CONFIDENCE.

—*Proverbs 11:13*

I attempt to tie my head scarf for the third time, then yank it off and stare at it in disgust. The same piece of fabric I used to wear around my neck with no problems now seems ridiculously small for the amount of hair I have. They should come in other sizes. Our shirts and skirts do, but that's so we can wear them loose to keep from revealing too much of our shape. Apparently we don't need the same consideration for our head coverings.

When I hear Daniel's voice, my heart flutters and drops to my stomach. I ball up the scarf and press it to my mouth to hold back the scream. The mirror above the sink reveals white knuckles, tumbleweed hair, and eyes shiny with fear. But what do I have to be afraid of? Aaron and I didn't . . . do anything, last night. But Daniel doesn't know that. And he doesn't know I've dreamt of Caleb. Even if he did, it only proves I'm supposed to be with him. It's a message from God. My reflection nods, mirror-Miriam looking much more confident than I feel. My mother used to sing me a song about the girl in the reflection being different from the one inside, and now I finally understand.

I toss the scarf onto the back of the toilet.

"New wives, the Lord has called you to Lessons. New wives, the Lord has called you. Report to Lessons."

It's only the speaker, calling us to yet another obligation. Strange. My mother told me we wouldn't have to go to Lessons the first few days after the Matrimony. For once, I wish she was right. I'm anxious to see Rachel and Delilah and find out who has chosen them, but I don't know if I'm ready to face the rest of the girls, for them to know I've been given to the wrong husband.

Am I the first woman to ever think this? Am I the only woman who believes this after last night? Perhaps this sort of suffering is commonplace among the Elders. But how could that be? That's why we're here, in New Jerusalem. Because it's the only path to Salvation. To eternal happiness. We pray, and God answers.

And what if Aaron prayed for you? Dreamt of you? a tiny voice whispers in my head. What then?

I shake this thought loose. Only God knows how to make all His children happy. It isn't for me to say. No matter if I think I know better.

When I leave the bathroom, I notice the front door is open. I'm drawn toward the sun as it peeks over the mountains, warm tendrils of color slipping through rocky crevices. The scent of mildew mixed with butane wafts from the fountain in the middle of the lake, where the fire burns eternally in the bowl on top, even as the water flows around it. It's a message, a reminder that evil exists, even in the midst of goodness.

Aaron is standing on the balcony, a mug of something in his

hands. When he sees me, he straightens and holds up the cup. "Can I get you some tea?"

He's naked. From the waist up, at least. "No." I shake my head. "Thank you," I add grudgingly. I wish he'd stop being nice to me, especially now that I know it's just an act, a directive from his mother. But mostly, I want him to put on some clothes. "Where's your shirt?"

"It's going to be a hot one," he says, leaning his arms on the railing.

I don't want to talk about the weather. Daniel says idle chatter breeds sinful thoughts. Usually, he's saying this to me. Is that why God wants me married to this Outsider? To show me where all my talking might lead?

"That's why you need a shirt. The heat's much worse without it. The fabric absorbs your sweat, keeping your skin cooler. And it prevents your skin from burning. You'd know that . . ."

"I do. Thanks, though. I appreciate your concern."

If you were one of us, I was going to say. But he isn't, and if he doesn't care, then I don't either. Certainly not enough to worry about him. "I have to go to Lessons."

"I heard. That seems odd, doesn't it?" He sips his tea, watching me over the rim. "Your mom said we wouldn't have to."

"My mother isn't a *liar.*"

He widens his arms, and I have to look away from his body. "Hey, nobody's calling anyone a liar. I just wondered why the sudden switch. Almost like Daniel's making it up as he goes."

His constant criticism of our Leader is starting to grate. "Maybe he wouldn't have to, if you hadn't chosen so poorly."

Aaron winces and rubs his face. "Point taken. But listen. I don't think it's a good idea for you to be saying that to people. You could get us both in trouble."

"You can't tell me what to do."

We both know this is a lie. He's my husband. He can make me do almost anything. But he shrugs and ducks his head, as if agreeing. All part of his plan to charm me, I suppose.

It isn't going to work. I won't listen to him. I'll tell whomever I want about my mistake of a marriage.

I grab my journal, wincing as I remember I never recorded any dream. Too late now. Maybe in the wake of last night's excitement, Phoebe won't bother to collect them today.

I stomp down the stairs, following the paved path past the Lake of Fire and the courtyard, slowing behind some of my Sisters heading in the same direction. We've done this every day of our lives, except for the Lord's days. Yet somehow, today is different. Is it because we're married now? Or walking from the apartments, instead of the family housing circle?

In front of me, Leah and Eve bump hips, whispering and smiling, and I realize what has changed.

They are happy.

And suddenly a new thought barges in: Is one of them Caleb's wife? I've been thinking this problem involves three of us—myself, Caleb, and Aaron. But there is a fourth. And I don't even know who she is. Does she love him? Did she want him to choose her? Did she want to be married?

And then another, more insidious question. Caleb left me messages that said he would choose me. But when Aaron called my name first and I was no longer a choice, he had to make a decision. How long had it taken him to utter another name? How many seconds before he replaced me?

The questions make me dizzy, and I have to stop to catch my breath.

"Miriam." Rachel runs up behind me and links her arm through mine. Her dark hair is pulled back, a white scarf tied neatly around her curls. Married women must wear head coverings in public.

I clutch at my own bare head.

Rachel smiles. "Miriam, Miriam. How did I know you would forget?" She reaches into the pocket of her apron and pulls out an extra scarf. "It's our first day. I'm sure Daniel will allow you one transgression, but maybe we shouldn't risk it."

Between talking to two different boys before the Matrimony and dreaming of a man who isn't my husband, I've already reached my limit on transgressions, but I don't tell Rachel. Though we are nearly the same age, she has even less patience with my failings than my own mother. Instead, I hug her, quick and fierce. "What would I do without you?"

"You'd probably be thrown to the lions. Now hold my journal and turn around so I can tie this."

"You can try, but it isn't going to fit," I say, pushing at my wayward hair.

"That's what you think." She slaps my hand away and pulls my hair back with practiced strokes, the way she has a thousand times before. "I married Jacob," she whispers, and her happiness is evident in the tremor in her voice. "What about you? Who is it?"

This simple request sends my heart into my throat. I shouldn't have come to Lessons today. I should have pled illness and gone to the Medical Shed. What was I thinking? Aaron was right. Speaking about my marriage in public is wrong; the act of uttering his name will seal my fate.

I pull away, leaving a chunk of hair wound through Rachel's fingers.

She blinks. "I'm not finished."

"I have to go. I forgot . . . something . . ."

"I'm sure Aaron can wait until you get back. After all, it's only been a half hour since breakfast," Susanna says, planting herself behind me so that I run straight into her when I turn around.

"Aaron?" Rachel's hands go still at the back of my neck, then rest on my shoulders with a tiny squeeze.

Susanna tosses her hair. She isn't wearing a head scarf either, though I assume her lack is intentional. "I could see if you were in a hurry to get back to, say, Caleb. But since he didn't bother to choose, I guess none of us get to reap those benefits."

The sound of his name is like an electrical shock.

Caleb didn't take a wife?

Susanna has a talent for knowing exactly what's going on in the city at any given time. I don't know how she does it, but she's usually right. Which is the only reason I give her words any consideration now.

Behind me, Leah and Eve erupt into excited chatter. "Is that allowed?" and "What was he thinking?" and my body continues to hum with a low-level current as I try to take in the implications of what Susanna has just said. When faced with the choice between me and someone else, he chose . . . no one? What does that mean? Is there still a chance for us to be together?

Rachel squeezes tighter.

Susanna watches me, like a coyote eyeing a fresh carcass. But I refuse to give her the satisfaction of letting her know she's stunned me.

"And who is it you married, Susanna?" I ask. "You seemed to know last night before you even saw him. How'd you recognize his voice?"

Her eyes narrow. "Are you accusing me of talking to one of the boys? After what you did? Is it any wonder the Outsider chose you, after you all but threw yourself at him last night?"

My vision blurs as I blink back sudden tears. I can't be with Caleb, even if he isn't married. Because *I* am. It doesn't matter what I want. I'm only a woman. I don't get to choose.

"I know it's hard to keep your hands off him at first," Susanna continues. "But don't worry. Evening will come soon enough, and then you and Aaron can—"

"We shouldn't be talking about this." I can't listen to her go on, and not just because I have only an abstract idea of what she's talking about. Based on her casual reference to marital relationships, her husband wasted no time in introducing her to all aspects of marriage. And judging from the embarrassment on Rachel's face, and the way Leah and Eve look away, this is probably true for the rest as well. But only Susanna is brazen enough to say the words out loud.

She throws back her head and laughs, golden hair cascading down her back. "We're married women now." She shares a glance with the others. "What are we to discuss, if we can't talk about our husbands? Surely this is a benefit of marriage. Not the best one, of course." Her eyes gleam wickedly. "Besides, it's God's will. Wives must submit to their husbands." She cocks her head. "You have submitted, haven't you, Miriam?"

I fear everyone can read the answer on my face.

Susanna spreads her hands wide, encompassing everyone. "It might be said that wives who don't wish to boast about their husbands' . . . assets . . . have something to hide."

My mouth is suddenly dry, but I manage to quote Psalm 94:4: "'They pour out their arrogant words; it is the evildoers who boast.'"

Then I stumble away from the girls, drop my things, and vomit into the dirt.

I wipe my mouth and run blindly down the path toward the housing circle. The concrete-block houses are all the same, but I have no trouble finding mine—left side, just around the curve. I've been running here for as long as I can remember.

But this isn't my house anymore. I won't be allowed to stay, or even go inside. How could I have forgotten? I stumble and fall to my knees on my parents' front terrace, a prayer on my lips that God, in his infinite wisdom, can help me find my way home. Wherever that is now.

9

CALEB

The walk to the apartments passes in a blur of longing and resentment.
Both Daniel and Father think last night was my fault. By not choosing a wife, somehow I've become the sinner. I need to make them see
that they're wrong. Aaron is the Faithless. Not me. He took my wife.
I don't know why, but the easiest way to find it out is to ask him. Right
after I beat him senseless.

The girls have all been called to Lessons, but I don't pass Miriam
on the path. Is she already in the classroom? Or running late? Maybe
I'm too late. *I wanted*, she said, but she didn't say what. What if one
night of marriage has changed her mind? One night of . . .

I have to physically shake the paralyzing thought from my head.
I can't get distracted. I need answers. I slow in front of the building, scanning the doors on the first floor as I pass by. I don't know
which apartment is theirs. The easiest way to find out would be to
stand out front and yell his name. What would he think, that runt,
if he heard me roaring outside his door? He'd probably pee himself
a little.

What the hell. "Aaron!" I yell.

I jump back as droplets spatter the dirt beside me.

When I look up, Aaron stares down at me from over the railing a
few doors down, a coffee mug dangling from his fingers.

"I figured Daniel would come himself, not just send a lackey," he says.

I don't know what a lackey is, but I'm not going to ask. I sprint for the stairs, running up and around the open corridor at the front of the building. He's waiting for me, lounging against a doorframe with his hair wet and his shirt unbuttoned. Like he's perfectly at home here. Just the sight of his smug face makes me want to hurt him. Does he walk around half naked in front of Miriam?

I walk right up to him, fist cocked.

He sees it coming and ducks, and I just graze his jaw. His head snaps back, but he recovers quickly and delivers a sharp jab to my gut.

I double over. Damn. He doesn't look like a fighter, but he knows how to hit.

He backs up, tripping over a metal chair on the terrace. He manages to stay on his feet but keeps his distance from me. He may have caught me off guard with the punch, but I'm stronger and he knows it.

"Let's not do anything we're going to regret." His eyes flick to the apartment doors on either side.

But I don't care who hears us. "I don't think I'll regret this."

After that, I'm not sure what happens. One minute I'm lunging at him, the next I'm up against the side of the building. Aaron shoves my arm back and up, so my fist is pointing at my shoulder blade. Then he leans in, the stucco cutting into my cheek as he whispers in my ear. "Listen, you fucking ape. Beating me up might feel great. For about a second." He leans harder on my arm, and my vision goes blurry. "But it's not going to get us anywhere."

I suck in air through my teeth. "Get. Off. Me."

"Not until you promise to stop acting like a Neanderthal and listen. Can you do that?"

I try to nod, my face scraping against the building. It's enough of a concession for him. He shoves one last time, pushing his weight off me.

I gasp at the sudden relief and turn slowly to face him as I try to rub feeling back into my arm.

He holds his arms wide in a gesture of surrender. "Look, man. I was late. I know. It sucks, and I'm sorry. But none of this was my idea."

I roll my eyes. Does he honestly expect me to believe anything he says?

"Don't believe me? Ask your brother."

"What does Marcus have to do with it?"

He glances down the corridor and lowers his voice. "Like I said, talk to him. The important thing now is Miriam. Neither one of us wants her to get hurt."

"Miriam is mine. Not yours." God, I hope that's still true. Is he in love with her, too? "I don't even want to hear you say her name."

"Jesus," he says, almost under his breath. He runs a hand across the top of his hair, and it springs back up. "Look, I get that you're pissed. And I'm not saying you don't have a right. But she doesn't *belong* to anyone. You get how messed up that sounds, right?"

"She's supposed to be my wife. God whispered her name to *me*."

He crosses his arms over his bare chest. "So what? Maybe He whispered her name to me. You can't prove that He didn't."

This is exactly what I was afraid he'd say. But it isn't possible. How could God make a mistake like that? Aaron has to be lying.

"Anyway, we're married now," he continues. "From what I hear, that's not going to change. So if you love her like you say you do, let it go. You keep up this fight"—he circles a finger between us—"all you're gonna do is piss off Daniel. Just be patient and play it cool, man, and it'll all work out. Trust me."

"Trust you? Why in hell would I trust you?"

He opens the door behind him and steps backward into the apartment. "Who else are you going to trust? Daniel?" He snorts a laugh and slams the door in my face.

I raise a fist to pound the door, catching sight of the blood on my knuckles. The tender flesh of my cheek throbs with every breath as I lower my hand. Daniel says anger accomplishes nothing, that it's an emotion for the weak-minded. I know he's right. I have to control my temper. It's just that turning the other cheek never feels as good as punching someone else's.

10

MIRIAM

I manage to pick myself up off my parents' yard before anyone sees me, leaving the housing circle and turning down the dusty path to the girls' schoolhouse. I've been following this road since I was old enough to walk. Everything else in my life may have changed overnight, but not this. Square and squat, the schoolhouse sits at the bottom of the hill beneath the Council House. Close enough for Daniel to watch over us, but far enough that the mountain shadows at the longest part of the day just brush the eaves of the shiny metal roof.

I slip in quietly, but I'm late. The others are already praying, so I slide onto one of the juniper benches, the swirled surface worn smooth by years of this same motion. Only the newly married women have been called this morning. Our younger Sisters have apparently been given another free day, and because of their absence, there is more room than I anticipated. There aren't that many of us of marriageable age. Instead of thirty-seven whispering and giggling Sisters, now we are only nine. But inexplicably, the benches have been clustered together on one side of the room, where we all must huddle, hot and breathless, the air thick with the secrets we're guarding.

My Sisters are reciting Ephesians, and Phoebe is nowhere in sight. I resist a sigh of relief. At least this much is familiar. We still start the day with our repetitions, and I know the scripture well enough that I can go to another place in my head. I imagine myself floating above the room. We all look alike, at least on the outside, especially now that we must cover our hair. But is this all we'll ever be? One bowed head in a sea of wives? Despite the stifling heat, this unsettling thought leaves me cold.

Leah is on my left, and on her other side, Eve. Susanna is in the front row, along with her close friends Tabitha and Elizabeth. On the bench across the aisle to my right, Rachel holds her head high, her voice clear, while Claudia sits beside her, looking like she'd rather be anywhere else. I can't tell if she's unhappy with her marriage; Claudia always looks like that.

Where is Delilah? I count again, but there are only seven other scarf-covered heads.

From across the aisle, Rachel sees my confusion and gives me a tiny frown as she pulls at her own cotton work skirt in an effort to get me to straighten mine.

Delilah? I mouth, raising an eyebrow.

Rachel pinches her lips into a thin line and gives one small shake of her head.

What does that mean? Where is she?

Rachel begins the next passage, and the others join in. "'For a man must leave his mother and father, and cleave to his wife, and the two shall become one flesh.'"

Usually, I love recitation. It's the most we're ever allowed to speak out loud. Today, instead of washing over me, the words sting like tiny insects. *Leave. Cleave.* How can two words that sound so similar have such different meanings? I flip them around as we recite. "For a man must cleave his mother and father, and leave his wife, and the two shall become one flesh." One tiny change, and the words take on ominous tones of murder and abandonment. Did Paul think about that as he was writing his letter? Or am I the only one who sees marriage as a threat?

Leah wrinkles her nose. Though she's kneeling right beside me, she probably can't hear my actual words, just enough of the discordant sounds to cause her to stumble over her own.

I study her from beneath lowered lashes. Whose wife is Leah? She's tall, like many of the boys. Her height and her strength would be an asset to a husband. I try to ignore the sweat pooling on the back of my neck and press my hands to my cheeks to stop the heat. The rest of the girls all look equally flushed. Equally dazed. Are they all having sinful thoughts of their own? They probably have more experience to base them on. All I have is an embrace, some longing glances, the whisper of two words—*me too.* Does my love count less than theirs?

Phoebe hurries in, her skirt wrinkled and her blouse buttoned wrong, as if she came here right from her bed. As if the call to Lessons this morning surprised even her. She presses a hand to her chest as she reaches the front of the room. "I apologize, girls. Ladies. Women of God." She pauses to catch her breath, smoothing her hair with two quick strokes, then holds out her arms. "Welcome. I see you started without me."

A few titters of laughter. Most of my Sisters look to Rachel, and Phoebe follows their gaze. "Rachel. I trust I have you to thank for that." But she doesn't sound especially thankful.

So Rachel started Prayers. It doesn't surprise me. She's a born leader, and she hates being behind schedule. Rachel ducks her head, but not before I see her pained expression. Marriage may bring blessings, but it will not bring her freedom from Phoebe's judgment.

"Where is Daniel?" asks one of my Sisters. Normally, a query like that would have come from Delilah, whose constant questioning Phoebe calls "natural curiosity," though her irritation is often evident. But today it's Susanna displaying an avid interest markedly different from her normal disdain. Maybe marriage really does change people.

Phoebe takes a moment to put her books on the table and collect herself, then frowns in Susanna's direction. "Daniel has never taught your Lessons. Why should today be different?"

"Because we weren't supposed to have Lessons today. So when he called us, I thought it might be to offer some kind of specific instruction. About marriage."

"Daniel is . . . busy . . . this morning. And besides, he is espoused to the Word," Phoebe says, touching the crucifix around her neck. "Since he has never taken a wife, he has limited insight into these particular Lessons."

"You were hardly a wife yourself," Susanna says. Several of us gasp. Susanna has changed, all right. Marriage has made her even meaner.

Phoebe appraises her coldly. "Be that as it may, I'm the only teacher you've got. So." She clasps her hands together. "How is everyone feeling this morning?"

How am I feeling? Lost. Angry. Terrified. But I don't know how to say these things, even to Phoebe. Especially Phoebe. Aaron's caution holds me back. Do I want everyone to know I've been chosen by the wrong man? That I don't want to be married to him? What will happen then? A Shaming? Or worse? This is exactly what Delilah was worried about.

"Where's Delilah?" I call out.

Phoebe flinches, then smooths back her hair and crosses her arms. "Delilah was not chosen at the Matrimony."

My heart begins to pound. First Caleb, now Delilah. And I'm married to Aaron. What happened last night?

"What does that mean?" Rachel asks. "Does she go back to her parents' house? To Lessons with the younger girls?"

Of course. That makes sense. She's younger than us. Even Phoebe looks relieved at this suggestion. "Perhaps. It is up to Daniel." She turns away from Rachel. "Does anyone have any questions about the Matrimony? Or marriage in general?"

"How did they decide?" Once again, I speak without thinking. "The boys, I mean. How did they . . . know? Whom to pick?"

Fabric rustles against the benches as my Sisters shift in their seats. Have none of them wondered? Or maybe they'd rather not know.

Phoebe clears her throat. "They pray, of course."

"And their dreams? Do those count?" I ask.

"I expect so. I'm afraid there's not much about that side of things that I can tell you. Because I simply don't know."

Phoebe has always been honest with us, more so than our own mothers. If any woman would know how it works, it would be Phoebe. "But they're just boys," I say. "So it's possible they . . . that some of them got something wrong, right? That they misunderstood, somehow?"

Phoebe looks more alarmed the longer I speak. But as I finish, her face clears. "That's what we have Daniel for. He's the Intercessor. Between God and self. He makes sure there are no mistakes." She studies me a beat longer. "Miriam? Is there something else—"

"Do they ever get tired?" Susanna interrupts, and the rest of the room explodes into nervous laughter, dragging Phoebe's attention from me.

"Everyone gets tired. Eventually," she says, to more laughter. Her face flushes and she tilts her head. "But that's okay. That's what's supposed to happen. This initial"—she searches for the word—"attraction, it changes. Into something deeper. Stronger." She makes a fist.

I can't help but wonder if she was married long enough for any of that.

"And what if we get tired before they do?" Eve asks, her brow furrowed. "Or what if we're . . . bleeding?" She whispers the last word. "What do we tell him?"

Susanna snorts. "Like he'd care."

"You're allowed to tell him that, Eve," Phoebe says, shooting a glare at Susanna. "He's your husband. You can talk to him. Remember, scripture urges husbands to love their wives. But that love need not always be expressed physically. He will understand."

"But wives must submit. That passage comes first," Claudia says. She's a stickler for details.

I'm pretty sure that everyone in this room has submitted already. Everyone but me.

"Try not to think of submission as something passive," Phoebe says. "It's active. An act of love. Do as he asks, and love will follow. For your husband, and for God."

Is that all it takes? I want so desperately to believe her, and yet something inside me resists. It's the same voice that insists on speaking whenever I am forced into silence. Sometimes I think that voice might be stronger than even Daniel.

"And remember," Phoebe continues, "he can ask you to submit. Order you, even. But he can't hurt you. And he can't force you."

Susanna snorts again.

"That's not true," Eve says. "Vashti resisted, and the king took a new wife." Her dark eyes are wide, as if she can't imagine a worse fate than Queen Esther's predecessor. And maybe she can't. Eve doesn't have a lot of imagination.

"I don't think that's the lesson—" Phoebe begins, but Leah interrupts.

"Well, he did ask her to dance naked for his friends, so I don't know if it's the same thing." She nudges her best friend. "Don't worry, Evie. I doubt Peter will ask you to do that," and they both dissolve in laughter.

So, Eve married Peter. I never talked to Eve about the marriages, so I don't know if she wanted him to call her name or not. But she doesn't look particularly upset this morning. No one does.

Claudia frowns and holds up her Bible, already open to the correct passage. "Scripture says he asked Vashti to dance wearing her crown. It doesn't say only her crown."

"Well, it doesn't mention any other clothing, either," Leah points out.

"Does it matter?" Susanna asks. "If my husband asked me to dance, naked or not, I'd do it."

No one doubts this.

"And who is your husband, Susanna?" I ask.

Susanna sits up straighter and tosses her hair. "Marcus," she says, as if it should be obvious. And in some ways, it is. She's beautiful; he's handsome. They both know it.

It still doesn't explain how she recognized his voice.

"Okay," Phoebe says, clapping her hands together. "I think we're getting a little off topic. It occurs to me that with the excitement of last night and this early morning call to Lessons, some of you may not have had a chance to record in your journals. Why don't we take a few moments to do that? While your dreams are still fresh."

My journal. I check the bench on either side of me, though I know it won't be there. I dropped it. Outside. After I fought with Susanna . . . I look at Rachel, and she holds it out to me.

Thank you, I mouth, reaching across the aisle. She just shakes her head. She probably thought that once we were married, she'd be looking after her husband instead of me. I'm going to need to pull it together, unless I intend to tell everyone of my concerns. What's worse? Staying married to Aaron? Or the punishment I'll endure for speaking up?

I draw a spiral, an unending line that twists on and on. How can I record my dream of Caleb? Daniel will read it and Shame me for dreaming about another man. Or worse, his interpretation might have nothing to do with Caleb. I can't risk him taking the memory from me. "What if we didn't dream last night?" I ask Phoebe.

"A favorable dream is a sign of a favored marriage," she says, touching her crucifix again. "I'm sure you dreamt. You probably just need a moment to call it to mind." She smiles with her mouth but not her eyes.

Once, I dreamt of the fountain in our lake, so writing about that isn't quite a lie. Only in my dream, I was the fountain, and words flowed from my lips like magic, as clean and slaking as water. And beneath me in the lake, everyone talked, all day long, about everything they saw and everything they felt. Daniel told me then that it was a warning: If everyone is talking, then no one is listening. The fountain was meant to take away my words and my sin, washing me clean.

Perhaps if I repeat that dream now, I will finally believe it.

11

CALEB

Whom do I trust? Daniel. Of course, Daniel. I stare at Aaron's door for a while, but he doesn't come back out, so I head down the stairs.

I'm still angry, but mostly at myself. I should have stood my ground. So what if Aaron says God promised him Miriam? And that he and Miriam are going to stay married? What does he know about any of it? Clearly, he wanted to be with Miriam—who wouldn't?— and somehow he made that happen. I'm the one who failed. Father is right. I am weak.

I glance at the Lake of Fire as I stomp past, through the row of fat palm trees, then do a double take. Marcus is climbing the fountain in the middle of the narrow lake, wearing what looks like overalls made from trash bags, and rubber gloves pulled up to his elbows. He's stretched tall along the column that holds the bowl of fire, his fingers gripping the brass edge dangerously close to the flame.

"Marcus! What are you doing?"

He jerks and almost slips off the cement base at the bottom. Then he sees me and raises a hand halfway in the air. Weak, as far as greetings go.

I wave back.

How did he get out there, along with that bucket and mop? What is he . . . is he cleaning the fountain? My head aches from all this confusion. Miriam is with Aaron. I'm unmarried and without a home. Marcus, the golden boy, is doing manual labor. Nothing is as it should be, and I'm already tired of trying to figure out why. Marcus is smart. Maybe he can tell me. Isn't that what Aaron said? *Ask your brother.*

I wave my arms again, this time in an arc. Gesturing him over.

His shoulders slouch. Then he inches his way down the three cement steps at the bottom of the column, backward, and eases himself into the water before turning toward me and the shore. I find myself holding my breath, as if he's swimming. Or I am. The water gets shallower as he gets closer, and I'm relieved to see him emerge from the water unsinged. I know, deep down, that the water isn't actually flammable. That this isn't the real Lake of Fire from the Bible. Still, it's not like I've ever thought to chance it and take a dip.

Marcus drags his legs through weeds and muck. When he's nearly ashore, I extend an arm and he grabs hold. His grip is tight around my wrist, and the rubber from his glove pulls at the hair on my arm.

"Thanks, Brother." Thick mud splatters on the pavement as he stomps off his boots.

"What were you doing out there?" I ask. "Cleaning?"

He eyes me warily as he pulls off his gloves and runs his fingers through his long, sweat-soaked curls. "What can I tell you? Menial tasks for the unrepentant."

"There are no menial tasks." I repeat the phrase because it seems called for, not because I believe it. We both know there are, and they're usually reserved for those who've strayed from their Path. "Jesus washed—"

"Jesus washed feet. He didn't scrape bird poop into fetid water." He finishes my thought, only better. Typical Marcus.

Then I realize what else he's said. "Unrepentant for what?"

He won't meet my eye as he slaps the gloves against his rubber pants. "Daniel is angry. That I chose Susanna."

My stomach aches, and not just because Aaron has a sharp right hook. This is that Outsider's fault, isn't it? He chose wrong. Not my brother. "What do you mean? Why would Daniel be angry with *you*? You love Susanna. You said you dreamt of her."

He nods. "I do. I did. We had it all worked out. As long as I went first and Aaron went second, nobody else would've been affected."

"But the Newcomer chooses first." That was Daniel's rule. It makes as little sense now as it did when he first said it, but who am I to question his word?

"Yeah, well, I figured Daniel would be less likely to stop me than Aaron. Assuming he even wanted to stop us."

The hair on the back of my neck rises higher each time he mentions Aaron. "What are you saying?" He can't mean . . .

Marcus grimaces and shakes his head. Once. "We switched names."

I shake my head, back and forth, as if trying to shake loose some kind of understanding. It doesn't work. "So *you* were supposed to choose Miriam?"

"No!" He scratches at his cheek with the back of his hand. "I did dream of Susanna. Every night. You know that. But during my Dream Sessions, Daniel said the only dream that mattered was the one I had of Rachel."

"You dreamt of Rachel?"

"One time! Back when she was the first to . . ." He holds his hands in front of his chest, fingers spread. "You remember."

I do remember. We'd all noticed Rachel's changing body, especially once Jacob called it to our attention.

"I'd forgotten all about the stupid dream, until Daniel pointed it out in my journal. He said that since she was the first girl I'd dreamt about, God's directive was clear." He rubs hard at the stubble on his chin. "But I knew it had to be a mistake."

"You thought Daniel made a mistake?"

He doesn't answer my question. "Since the blossoming, the only one I've dreamt of is Susanna. Since Aaron wanted Rachel, the answer seemed simple."

"Simple?" I want to yell, but I lower my voice instead, afraid of letting the anger overtake me. This is so like Marcus. To just assume he's in the right. And usually he is. But not this time.

"There are so many things wrong with your story, I don't even know where to begin," I say, clenching my fists, as if my temper is a physical thing and I am holding it back as tightly as I can. "How did you know Aaron wanted Rachel? Did you talk about it? Because that's Blasphemy. And anyway, he didn't choose Rachel. He chose Miriam."

Marcus talks faster. "I don't know what happened. Aaron was late. I mean, he was supposed to be late. But only a little. Enough for me to choose Susanna, But then he didn't show up, and Jacob went next. He chose Rachel, which didn't surprise me. You know how he's always staring at her."

I can't make sense of anything he's saying. "So you all dreamt of Rachel? You and Aaron and Jacob? But how can that be?" We'd all wondered what would happen if God sent more than one of us dreams of the same girl. But Daniel assured us that God wouldn't make a mistake like that. We might, though. That's why we need Daniel to interpret for us.

"I told you, I only dreamt of Rachel that one time. It didn't mean anything."

"And Aaron told me God whispered Miriam's name to him. Not Rachel. How do you explain that?" Actually, he'd said I couldn't prove He didn't. Either way, he was lying. If not to me, then to Marcus.

"I don't know why Aaron chose Miriam. That wasn't part of the plan." Marcus sighs, but I can't tell if he looks repentant or just exhausted. It doesn't matter. Even if he is sorry, do I owe him my forgiveness? These are the kinds of things I should know. But scripture has always seemed a slippery thing to me, full of contradictions and loopholes. The same book that urges us to turn the other cheek also asks for an eye for an eye. So which is it?

"Aaron wanted Miriam, so he took her. Just like you did with Susanna. What kind of men decide to replace God's will with their own?" I ask, even though I know the answer. The kind of men who think they're above everyone else. Smarter than everyone else. The kind who deserve to lose an eye.

"But isn't God's will for us to be happy?" Marcus asks, in that irritatingly clever way he has of twisting my words. He pulls his gloves back on as he continues, "If we pray hard enough, and Follow the Path to Righteousness, He rewards us with a full heart. That's how it works." The rubber snaps, and I wince. "So what happens if our Path and our hearts diverge? Which way do we go?"

Marcus waits for my answer, but I don't have one. My Path and heart have not diverged, and yet, I'm the one with no wife and no home. Not him. "We're not all happy. I'm not happy!" So much for keeping my anger in check.

He flinches, then stands with his hands spread, as if waiting for a blow. And if I'm being completely honest, there are times I've thought about hitting him. Who hasn't? And now that I know this is his fault? That while I spent the night alone, trying to calm my rage, he got to lie with Susanna? And Aaron got to do the same with Miriam. Just because they thought they could get away with it. So yes, a part of me wants to punch him in his satisfied little face.

But he's my brother. He's my blood.

He senses my weakness and grabs my arm. "You're not with Miriam, and I know that must be killing you. But hurting me won't change that. I'll survive Daniel's disappointment, as well as his punishments. But I can't live without Susanna. It would be no life at all."

This is my chance—to yell, to scream. Tell Marcus he ruined my life. That he traded my happiness for his own. That he's a selfish bastard, and that I am going to make him pay.

But maybe we're more alike than I realized, my brother and I.

When given a choice between his heart and his Path, Marcus chose his heart. Based on the effect it's had on the rest of us, I'd say he chose wrong. But if I'm being completely honest with myself, when God whispered another name to me—a name that wasn't Miriam—I did just the same.

So instead, I say, "I know."

And I leave the tarnished golden boy to his polishing.

12

MIRIAM

If we confess our sins,
He is faithful and just to forgive
us our sins and to cleanse us
from all unrighteousness.

—*1 John 1:9*

When the door swings wide, everyone turns, like sunflowers toward their namesake, drinking in both the cool breeze and the light of his presence.

"Sisters!" Daniel cries, and our greetings surpass his in jubilation as we swarm him like drones to a queen. He bestows greetings, touches, and smiles upon all of us before dropping his arms and zeroing in on our teacher. "Phoebe." He takes in her narrowed eyes and folded arms. "Are you upset with me, Sister? Because of the unexpected call to Lessons this morning?"

I shift my weight nervously from one foot to the other and hold my breath as Phoebe says, "Of course not. I am happy to serve." The rest of my Sisters look as relieved with her answer as I am, except for Susanna, whose smirk gives way to a pout of disappointment.

"I know you are." Daniel tilts his head, just slightly, and Phoebe looks away from him, her cheeks going pink.

"We're happy you could join us. What an unexpected treat." Her gaze flicks to Susanna and then away. "We were just about to read from our journals. Who would like to start?"

I go as still as the statuary in Chapel, willing Phoebe not to look in my direction. It's one thing to write a false dream in my journal, quite a different sin to lie about it in person, especially to Daniel.

Daniel circles our tiny group slowly, stroking his beard. I keep my head down even as he pauses in front of me, until it's uncomfortably clear that he wants my attention. When I finally look up, I am lost in the depths of his deep blue stare. It's as if he sees only me, as if only he and I exist, and we will stand here, forever, wordlessly. There is no need to speak, as he can read my thoughts.

"Miriam?" Phoebe asks, breaking the spell. "Could you share with us from your journal?"

I press my lips together, but my fear is whispered aloud by the fluttering of the pages clutched in my trembling hands. Daniel must already know, but the rest are waiting. What should I tell them? That I dreamt of a man who is not my husband? I scan the pews, imagining their reactions. Eve will be shocked, Susanna delighted, Rachel disappointed. My gaze falls on the empty seat beside her. Only Delilah would understand.

"What's going to happen to Delilah?" I blurt.

There is a collective intake of breath, and then the room goes silent. It is not my place to question our Leader, and thus my sin is twofold—Disobedience and Insubordination.

Only Daniel seems unsurprised by my boldness; his calm is divinely bestowed, and it's nearly impossible to shock him. In fact, he almost looks amused. "Your concern for your Sister is touching," he says, fiddling with one of my escaped curls before leaning down and snatching my journal off the bench. "I believe I can relieve at least some of your concerns. Excuse us," he tells the others. "Please, go back to your gathering of knowledge."

He clasps a hand to my shoulder and propels me toward the door, pushing me past Phoebe and her troubled stare and out into the unforgiving sunlight.

When we are alone, Daniel twists me to face him, and I choke on his unique scent of body odor and woodsmoke. He looms over me, blocking the sun—no, he is the sun, and this is the closest I've ever been to his scorching presence. "Dear Miriam. First Blasphemy, now this? I have grave concerns about the state of your soul."

Blasphemy is the crime of disrespecting the laws of New Jerusalem. How is asking about Delilah an act of Blasphemy? Or is he talking about the journal? "I didn't ... I'm not ... I'm just worried about Delilah. Phoebe said she wasn't chosen at the Matrimony. What will happen to her? Please tell me."

"Delilah will be dealt with in a way that God deems fit."

This should be enough for me. Daniel is the One True Prophet; he is more than capable of taking care of Delilah. But something about the way he says "dealt with" makes my skin go tight around my skull.

"What does that mean? Has she been ... Banished?" I don't wait for him to answer; I can't. "Delilah's young. She can attend the next Matrimony. Until then, she can live at home. And go to Lessons with the younger girls. Right?" I'm talking more than I should, more than I ever have in Daniel's presence, but I have a growing fear of what he might say when I stop.

He shakes his head slowly. Is he *crying*? "None of your Brothers were sent any dreams of Delilah. Clearly the Lord doesn't think she is fit to be a wife. Not now, not later."

So their dreams *do* matter. This is what I suspected. But why was Delilah even called to the Matrimony if no one dreamt of her? "What if the boys made a mistake? About their dreams?" I whisper.

He tips his head back and laughs, as if sharing a joke with God himself, though I don't see the humor. "I see. You think the boys are incapable of understanding God's message. And how about you? Do you think you are any better?"

Yes! I am good at deciphering the meaning of my dreams. It is my talent, what I do best. My throat burns with the need to say it, to shout it, but the impulse is snatched by the desert air and blown away with Daniel's next words.

"You? A woman?" His words are like a slap.

"I dreamt of Caleb." I know at once I've gone too far. I should already be on my knees. There will be no easy forgiveness for this. But I can't stop now. This is my last chance. My only chance. If no one else will tell him, I must. "He should be my husband. Not Aaron. We are meant to be together."

"Not all dreams are prophetic, Miriam. Because not all dreamers are prophets." Though he says it quietly, there is no mistaking his anger; I can read it in the tightened cords of his neck and the curl of his lip.

"I kn-kn-know." I quake in the face of his fury. "Y-you are the only Pr-Prophet."

"And yet my word—God's word—is still not enough for you. What happens to the Faithless, Miriam? Those who question the authority of the Lord?"

This is another one of those traps, I can sense it, but I answer anyway. I can't help myself. "They will be Banished. Thrown out in the desert, where they will wander like animals. For seven years. But I'm not—"

"Have you ever been to the middle of the desert, Miriam? In daylight. Alone. With no food or water?"

He knows I haven't.

I open my mouth, but my answer is choked by a cloudful of dust, as the hot wind kicks up and scratches at my face with sandy fingers.

"It's a lot like Hell."

"What are you saying?"

"It's not what I'm saying. It's what you're saying." He paces in front of me, slow, controlled steps that take him just far enough to blind me with the sunlight, then plunge me back into sightless shadow.

I blink furiously, but all I see is a bright pinprick surrounded by darkness.

"It sounds like you want a divorce," he continues. "And divorce is a sin." He pauses with the sun burning over his shoulder so I have to shield my eyes. "Sinners are cast out. I'm afraid the Lord is clear on this. My hands are tied."

"Fine." I raise my chin. "Send me Out, then. Delilah and I can go together."

"So impulsive." He shakes his head. "Death, rather than marriage? Is that what the Lord would want?"

Death? Is this what will happen to my good friend? My heart stutters in fear, but I push on. "Not everyone out there dies. What about Aaron and his family? And Naomi."

He tilts his head. "You still don't understand. Locked Outside the gates, with no food or water? With only the slim hope of God's mercy? If an Elder like Naomi didn't have the faith to survive, what chance have you?"

Something breaks inside me, the pain as much for Rachel's loss as for my dying dreams. In all the stories we'd made up about Naomi's

Banishment, this was the one ending we'd never spoken of. "Naomi is . . . dead? Does Rachel know?"

He ignores both questions, but finally answers another. "Delilah isn't being Banished. She will be sent away for Counseling and Education. If she is found to be faithful, she will return."

"That's not fair! She doesn't even get a choice? Why do none of us get a choice?"

Daniel leans in, our foreheads touching. "But you do, don't you? Tell the truth. Did you speak to him?"

I jerk back, cracking my head against the wall. The fabric of my head scarf snags on the rough cement and pulls free. My vision goes bright and then dim, and Daniel's face is a fuzzy blur surrounded by a halo of sunlight. "Caleb?" I ask, grasping at his question through the cotton in my head.

"Don't be stupid."

The world snaps back into focus, but both the words and the face are those of a stranger, not our loving leader.

"Aaron," he says. "Did you speak to Aaron?"

"He's my husband. I'm allowed. That's always been the rule." As Susanna pointed out, there are some benefits to marriage within our community. But my speaking has gotten me into trouble once again. "Wait." I hold out my palm, but I don't dare touch him. "If we hadn't spoken on our wedding night, would that have made a difference? Because all we did was talk. And very little at that. We didn't consum—"

"No, no, foolish girl." He slaps my hand away. "Before the Matrimony. Did you speak to him before?"

Suddenly everything I need to know is in those six little words, soft and disappointed, like wilting flower petals. I go cold, as if the sun has slipped from the sky the way my life has slipped off its expected Path.

The speakers crackle to life above us, calling us to Prayer, and we fall to our knees as one. I don't need the recitation of scripture, harsh and blistering in my ear, to know this is all my doing. Daniel's strong voice leads me through Bible passage after Bible passage, as my transgressions and my guilt build until I can no longer breathe beneath them. My knees ache until the ache becomes a constant burn; my tongue dries until the mere act of speaking cracks my lips. He trembles beside me, and his voice grows hoarse, but he does not leave me or slow our prayer, not even when the turkey vultures circle overhead.

13

CALEB

I get caught outside for the Call to Prayer. I manage to duck under the shade of the Pavilion, so I'm not burnt, but churned-up sand dusts my body, and my throat feels like I tried to swallow a fire. I need water and a shower—in that order—but before anything else I have to talk to Daniel.

Cool air washes over me like divine intervention when I open the doors to the Council House. As I wait for my eyes to adjust to the darkness, I try again to sort through what Marcus said. He was counseled to choose Rachel, but he chose Susanna instead. Because he dreamt of her. And now he's married to Susanna. But he's been assigned Janitorial Duty, the lowest of all Vocations. Aaron dreamt of either Susanna or Rachel or Miriam, depending on whom you ask. And he is married to Miriam. With no repercussions, other than the blow I landed on him. Does that mean God is pleased with their union? No. He can't be. And what about Jacob? I have no idea whose name God sent to him, but he called Rachel's. These are the facts. No matter how much I twist them or how hard I beat at them, they don't come together.

And then there is my wrongdoing.

"Did you need something, Caleb?"

I blink and step farther into the room, wiping grit from my eyes. It's Susanna, sitting at the desk outside Daniel's office.

My skin tightens to gooseflesh, and not because of the air-conditioning. "What are you doing here?"

She tosses a wave of golden hair over her shoulder. "I was assigned as Daniel's secretary," she says, picking up a pencil. "Do you have an appointment?"

Something stirs inside me as she sticks the end of the pencil in her mouth and ever so gently bites down on the eraser. She smells like flowers and soap, and I'm gritty and tired and in no mood for her games. I clear my throat. "I don't need an appointment," I tell her. "I'm his Security Officer. He'll . . . he'll want to speak to me."

"Maybe. But he's not here." She stretches, arching her back, so that I have to look away before I start to think about her and Marcus. Together.

"Daniel is praying." She leans forward, as if she's letting me in on a secret. "With a sinner. It may even lead to a public Shaming." Her face has the appropriate concerned expression, but her tone is gleeful. Normally, I'd ask who it is, but I don't want to spend another second in Susanna's presence. Especially now that I know she's partly the reason I'm alone.

"I'll just wait in his office," I say, walking past her before she can protest. What could she possibly do to keep me out, anyway?

Daniel keeps his Inner Sanctum dark, velvet curtains the color of dusk drawn against the sun. Thick carpet muffles my footsteps and cushions the solid wood of the desk and chairs. The office itself is small, almost cramped, and despite the heat a fire burns in the hearth. It reminds me of the Marriage Cave, which may be his intention. Daniel believes strongly in symbolism.

Today, I'm more interested in answers.

"My servant, Caleb. 'He has a different spirit and has followed me fully.'"

I let out a hard bark of surprise. I didn't hear Daniel come in, yet when I turn he looks as if he's been waiting for me, not the other way around. The only signs to the contrary are the redness of his face and the sand clinging to his beard and hair.

I rush to the adjoining bathroom to get him a glass of water. He accepts it with a "Bless you, Brother," and gulps it loudly, water streaming down his beard and wetting his shirt so I can see his chest hair through the fabric.

When he left me last night, he was disappointed, perhaps even angry. But his familiar greeting has given me hope. Maybe there is still a way to make this right.

When he finally stops for breath, wiping his mouth, he says, "I was expecting you earlier. What revelations have you achieved?"

I don't know how to start. He wants the answers I received from God, through prayer. But God was mostly silent last night. And I want, no, I *need* Daniel to tell me something that makes all of this make sense. That he knows what Marcus and Aaron have done, and that he is going to make it right. That he is going to let me be with Miriam. But the fear that he won't holds me back from asking.

Instead I say, "I talked to Aaron. He says that he heard Miriam's name, too. Is that possible?"

"Are you asking me if God makes mistakes?"

"N-no. I know he doesn't," I stammer. In my head, I hear the whisper once more. *Delilah.*

Daniel stares at me for a long time, unblinking. I can't match his intensity, so instead I watch a drop of sweat roll slowly down his cheek and drip onto his collar, my own neck growing hotter and hotter. If God doesn't make mistakes, what does that mean? God sent me dreams of Miriam, night after night. And in my Dream Sessions,

Daniel assured me we were meant for each other. But God also whispered a different name to me at the Matrimony. It can't all be true. But if it comes from God, it also can't be wrong.

"How do we know what is God's will?" I ask, my voice cracking. "And what is . . . someone else's?"

Daniel raises an eyebrow, first at me, then at his reflection in the mirror behind the desk. "Why are you here, Caleb?" he asks. "In New Jerusalem?"

This is my home. I was born here, I almost say. But that isn't what he's asking. I pull up the words I remember from a thousand Lessons. "We're here to follow the Word of Daniel on the Path to Righteousness," I say, and the rest comes automatically. "'Those who are wise will shine like the brightness of Heaven, and those who lead many to righteousness will shine like the stars for ever and ever.'"

"Excellent." He holds up a finger as he takes another drink. "And you, Brother? Do you think you're wise?"

This is an insult, and my neck grows even hotter.

Before I can answer, Daniel continues. "If one is not gifted with wisdom, what other path is available?"

It sounds like a riddle, and I've never been good at riddles.

"Leadership," he continues. "If you can't be wise, you must lead others to righteousness. It's right there in the verse." He slams the glass down on his desk, and I wince at the unexpected show of emotion. "Are you questioning my leadership, Caleb?"

"Of course not," I say. "It's just Marcus told me—

"Marcus," Daniel interrupts, his voice mocking. "Tell me, Caleb, do you *deserve* happiness? More than Marcus?"

It's as if he knows what Marcus and I talked about, and he's using my own words to trap me. None of us deserve happiness *more* than anyone else. But at the same time, no one deserves it less, either. Maybe what he's really asking is: What kind of man resents the happiness of someone he loves?

"The devil takes many shapes. A coyote, a wolf in sheep's clothing. Sometimes even a brother." He pins me in place with his hypnotic gaze, and I struggle not to blink. What is he saying? Does he think I'm the devil?

Daniel moves to the fireplace and picks up a poker to tease a log at the bottom of the pile. It shifts, and an ember catches my wrist. I try not to wince as he turns to look at me. "There is no room here for the Faithless," he says, repeating his words from last night.

Unlike last night, this time I summon the strength to answer him. "I am not Faithless."

"I want to believe you," he says, "but our enemies are looking for a crack. Evidence that I am weak." He inches closer as he speaks, his anger palpable, so strong it edges out my own. "How will it look if someone on my very own Security team is asking questions about the Matrimony? Telling my flock that he is unhappy because I misinterpreted all their dreams? That I sanctioned the wrong marriages?"

He moves closer still, until I am backed up against the desk, pinned by his hot, sour breath. Like the cornered animal I am, I don't see the trap until too late. It was never a choice between sacrificing my happiness or my Brothers'. It's Daniel and Miriam I must choose between.

"Caleb?"

If God doesn't make mistakes, if Daniel, the One True Prophet, is infallible, then the marriages must be upheld. All of them. No matter how they were chosen. Since I've already betrayed Daniel by questioning his leadership, it's only fitting my punishment should be giving up Miriam. It doesn't matter what my Brothers did, or what I want. What matters is Daniel's law.

Something gives way inside me. I can't tell if it's a breaking or a letting go. "I understand," I say.

"Miriam was never right for you anyway. From the lips of an adulteress drips honey."

My blood heats, and my muscles tense. She isn't an adulteress. Still, now I can't get the picture of her lips covered in honey out of my head. And I can't look Daniel in the eye.

He circles me. "Her speech is smoother than oil." The words hit like a slap.

She does quote scripture smoothly. No. I clench my fists. "It isn't like that. We didn't do anything wrong." Even as I say it, I wonder what he knows.

"Not you, my Brother. *Her*." He makes one more, tight circle around me, then stops and lifts my chin. "She was with Aaron. Before the Matrimony. Did she tell you that?"

I shake my head. "No. That's not poss—" But he forces me to look at him, and there I see the truth. His anger. Susanna's glee.

Miriam is the sinner he prayed with.

"Do not blame yourself. This is the way of the adulteress. She deceives you as she deceives us all."

How could I have misjudged her? The connection we had? Why was she with him? What did they do?

"Forget her," Daniel says, with a flick of his hand. As if it's that easy. "We have important work to do, and she is not a part of it."

Even as I mourn, a tiny part of me takes hope in his use of the word *we*.

"There is a coyote in our midst," he continues. "Here, in the city.

I need you to find him and bring him to me." He returns to his desk, pausing before he sits. "But first, there is the matter of Delilah."

"Delilah?" My heart stills. I've given up Miriam. Isn't that enough? *Dear God, please don't make me—*

"Yes, Delilah. She was not chosen, so I'm making arrangements for her to be sent Out. For Education. It will take me a few days to locate a place for her. When I do, I will need you to provide Security for her exit." He looks down at his desk and waves at the door. "That is all."

I stumble from the room, feeling weak from relief. Or maybe it's just freedom from the burden of everything I've given up.

14

MIRIAM

Beware of false prophets who
come to you in sheep's clothing but
inwardly are ravenous wolves.

—*Matthew 7:15*

Aaron jumps to his feet when I enter the apartment. The dark circles under his eyes and his swollen lower lip make me finally understand the expression "suffer the consequences." I've created these consequences, and this punishment is one we all must endure.

"What did he do to you?" he asks, blending both compassion and horror into his question.

There is only so much I can take. My knees still ache from the hours spent praying in the desert sun, begging God—and Daniel— for forgiveness. I won't accept Aaron's pity.

"I deserve it," I say. "It's my fault." Confession is a dam that, once opened, is hard to plug.

"You can't really believe that." He peers at me, then presses me gently to the couch. "Your lips are chapped. Let me get you some water."

"'With much seductive speech she persuades him; with her smooth talk she compels him. All at once he follows her, as an ox goes to the slaughter, or as a stag is caught fast till an arrow pierces its liver; as a

bird rushes into a snare; he does not know it will cost him his life.'"
My lips move of their own accord. "Proverbs 7:21." My voice is but a
whisper, and Aaron is in the kitchen, so I don't think he hears me.

"'If the other person injures you, you may forget the injury,'" he
says, returning and handing me a glass of water, "'but if you injure
him, you will always remember.'"

My hand trembles, and water splashes into my lap. "Is that
scripture?"

"It's not scripture. It's poetry. Kahlil Gibran."

My body has begun to shake uncontrollably, though I can't tell if
it's a delayed reaction to my confrontation with Daniel or a response
to Aaron. "This Kahlil. He is your prophet?"

A smile tugs at the corner of Aaron's mouth, and he winces as he
touches a finger to his fat lip. "That's funny. But he's not a prophet.
He's a poet. Like Frost. Or Wordsworth."

I draw a blank at the strange names. This is not right.

"Shakespeare?"

I try to put my cup down. It spills across the table, but I'm too
weak to pick it up. Instead, I slump into the couch and hold my shaking hands over my ears. I don't know what he's saying, but his words
terrify me.

"How is any of this your fault?" His voice is muffled, but I can
still hear him. "I called your name. You had no choice."

"But I spoke first. I spoke to you." I have to work to get the words
out, as if I've reached the end of my finite allotment.

"So? I was bitten by a rattler. Wouldn't letting me die be a bigger
sin?" He goes to the kitchen and brings back a wet washcloth. "Is
that what this is all about?" As he folds the cloth into thirds, he asks,
frowning, "How would Daniel even know about that? I didn't tell him."

The cool relief as he drapes it across my forehead almost makes me weep. I don't deserve it. "Don't." But I'm too weak to throw it off. Instead, I let the water drip down my cheeks and soothe the salty burn.

"'Do not withhold good from those to whom it is due, when it is in your power to do it,'" Aaron says. "I can quote scripture, too. The real test of goodness isn't in words. It's in actions. You people should have thought about that, before you chose your *prophet*."

He spits the last word at me and stalks away, and I'm too tired to argue anymore. I'm not sure what I'd say anyway. Everyone knows you can't reason with a heretic.

Even if he is your husband.

15

MIRIAM

WHAT CAUSES QUARRELS AND FIGHTS
AMONG YOU? IS IT NOT THAT YOUR
PASSIONS ARE AT WAR WITHIN YOU?
—*James 4:1*

I've been married for exactly one week, though I wouldn't believe it if I hadn't been counting. It feels much longer. The days blend together, hot and dry and monotonous, broken only by the cold nights spent alone in the bed I'm supposed to be sharing, watching the moon creep slowly across the windowsill and listening to the coyotes in the distance. Why do they go on, night after night? Crying doesn't change anything. Or perhaps I'm only imagining the mournful notes on the end of their howls. Maybe they're just trying to be heard above the sound of the spring sandstorms whipping across the desert. There was another last night, the roar of the wind like a scream, and I had to hold my pillow over my mouth to keep from joining in.

A week, or an eternity, during which I've tried my best to avoid both my mother's pleas and Daniel's instructions on obedience and submission. The Council continues to send food, and I refuse to cook it and instead go to bed early each night, alone. Truthfully, though, neither of these seem to bother Aaron. Nothing does, really. Not even the calls to Lessons, which, despite my mother's assurances to the contrary, come every day except the Lord's day.

I don't know what the men are learning, but so far, instead of talking of wifely duties, we women have studied Eve, Deborah, Mary Magdalene, and my namesake. If anyone else finds Phoebe's choice of topics strange, they don't say so, and I certainly don't complain; these women and their stories are a welcome distraction from the nightmare that is my marriage. But even at Lessons, Rachel and I rarely have time to say more than a quick "keep faithful," and we certainly don't have time to talk about Delilah. For once, though, Susanna's ear for gossip has proven useful, in that she tells me Delilah is still here, spending time with her family before she is sent away. I haven't been allowed to see her, but I take comfort in knowing she is nearby.

Saturdays we spend in Chapel, from sunup to sundown, like always, only now we sit with our spouses rather than our parents. The Call to Prayer still comes thrice daily, and so far the only complaint I can make against my new husband is this: When we are alone in our apartment, Aaron ignores the calls. At first, I pray harder, to make up for his refusal. But when no one questions him or comes to punish him, I start to ignore the sunrise call, too. After so many sleepless nights, it's a sinful relief to spend those extra minutes in bed. And I've stopped recording my dreams. After my punishment outside the schoolroom, Daniel kept my journal, so it's only a matter of time before he reads it and I get punished for that, too. In the meantime, I should start another, but what's the point? I'll have to fill it with either more lies or evidence of my wicked heart.

I continue to dream of Caleb, though I haven't seen him. I'm not sure I want to, either. My disobedience began with him, with reading those messages and believing them. If I hadn't, would I still be burdened with this unhappiness, this inability to accept Aaron as my husband? Maybe this is Caleb's fault. Maybe he didn't pray hard enough. Or maybe he never meant to choose me at all. Sometimes when I first wake, I can almost convince myself it was all a dream—the drawings in the sand, Caleb's strong embrace, the ache in my heart that won't go away. Then reality settles on me, like the layer of grit that coats everything in this awful apartment. I feel raw inside, too, like sand has gotten in through my cracks and settled in corners I can't reach, constantly chafing.

Today, the morning call is immediately followed by an order to begin our Vocational Duties. I thought Aaron might ignore this summons as he's ignored the prayer calls, but he finishes his piece of toast and brushes off his hands in the sink. "Ready?"

He waits as I tie on my head scarf: gray, like my mood. "I didn't even know we had a wool mill," he says, as I lead him out of the apartment and past the courtyard, toward the spindly wooden building on the edge of the city. "I never learned to knit. Do you suppose that matters?"

I slow and stare at the back of his head as he moves in front of me. Does he even know what weaving is? Possibly not. It's a woman's duty. He'll be in charge of maintaining the equipment. But he knows how to cook, so it's not a completely ridiculous thought. "Is everything opposite Outside? Men do women's chores and women do men's?"

"What?" He frowns, maybe confused because I've asked my own question instead of answering his, but then he says, "No. There aren't . . . people aren't just one thing. Men and women do a lot of the same things."

"The same things." I snort. If only that were true, I'd be much less worried about Delilah being sent Out. "You're telling me men are willing to scrub toilets? Mend socks? Or how about bleeding? Birthing children?" Even Outsider men can't be that different from us. They're still men.

Aaron rolls his eyes. "You asked about chores. Not biology. And yes, men are capable of household chores. Mopping and sewing are not functions of your uterus."

My cheeks burn with embarrassment. I hope no one has overheard. Aaron has even less desire to hold back his words than I do, if that's possible. And the paths are bustling with all our neighbors this morning, everyone relieved to get back into the pattern of our daily lives. I nod at their hearty greetings, but I don't return them. Don't they know that nothing will ever be as it was? Though even I can't deny the satisfying pull of the familiar. Life is much easier when you know what to expect, and what's expected of you. Maybe my dark thoughts will fade once the routine of my life as a weaver takes hold. The dull, monotonous routine.

Just before my thoughts send me screaming toward the gates, Aaron stops and squints into the sun. "That's the mill? I thought it was an old barn nobody'd bothered to tear down."

"What need would we have for another barn?"

"What need do you have for a mill without a water wheel? Where's the river?"

I thought he was handling this marriage better than I, but maybe not. Maybe he's finally gone crazy. "There is no river here," I say slowly. "We're in the desert."

"Yes, but a mill needs . . . Never mind." He pulls open the door and holds it for me.

I promptly trip over his feet and sprawl across the planked floor. Dear Lord, I'd forgotten how much I hate this place.

Aaron puts out a hand to help me up, but I ignore it. Instead, I get up and yank at my skirt to straighten it while I wait for the thick cloud of dust and humiliation to clear. I haven't been in this wide, high-ceilinged room in some months, but time hasn't wrought any improvements. Sunlight still pierces the gaps in the boards, haphazardly splashing the sinks and counters lining the east wall as well as the long table in the center of the room. It even encircles the heads of the Elders standing at the table, like halos.

But Lydia and Mishael aren't angels. They're Susanna's parents, and more important for Aaron and me, they are the weavers who will be conducting our Vocational Training. I know the basics of weaving. Growing up in New Jerusalem, it was one of the skills I was required to learn. The Second Generation regularly practices all of the chores needed to keep the Community running smoothly. Once our talents emerge, Daniel and our parents begin to talk of Vocations. At my Vocational Sessions, we talked about the Chapel Choir and secretarial duties, but weaving was never mentioned, and there's a reason for that.

Mishael is the first to break the awkward silence. "Welcome, Brother."

No greeting for me. Not that I want one. Mishael has always made me uncomfortable. He is also a Council Member, like my father, and has attended many Gatherings at my house. Gatherings where he talked loudly over my mother, as if she weren't there, though his red, piggish eyes followed her around the room.

The way they follow me now.

"Good morning, Lydia," I say, turning away from him and toward his wife. She is his opposite in nearly every way, brittle and dried out where he is greasy and swollen. Her threadbare tan shirt hangs off her bony shoulders as if it's given up, while her apron is cinched around a waist so tiny I can't believe she doesn't snap in half. I've seen cactus spines wider. Lydia looks like Susanna with all the life drained out of her. Maybe by Susanna herself. I almost feel sorry for her. It can't have been easy, having a daughter like that.

Lydia sniffs, and the crucifix that all the Elders wear bounces against her bony chest. "Your hair is showing." She thumps a fist against a head scarf as washed out as she is, then goes back to plucking her thin, wax-bean fingers through a batch of wool laid out on the table in the center of the room.

Then again, maybe there's a reason Susanna turned out the way she did. I yank off my scarf and tousle my curls.

Aaron shakes his head, a subtle shiver of warning. I'm tempted to ignore it. I can tell by the way he watches me, by the small wrinkles that form at the bridge of his nose when I do or say something inappropriate, that he thinks I'm going to get us in trouble. Already I'm learning to read him, though I don't want to. I should be grateful one of us is trying. Instead it's one more thing I have to resent him for. I'm Second Generation. Shouldn't I be the one teaching him our ways? But I knot the fabric anyway and twist it back into place, tucking stray curls as I go.

"What are we doing today?" Aaron asks, taking my hand.

Without thinking, I slap it away.

Lydia stares, her hands frozen clawlike above the rough-hewn table.

"There's a Gathering for the newly wed this evening." Mishael drops his gaze to my shirt front as he hefts a bucket of fleece and dumps it onto the table, covering the clump Lydia is picking through. "But it's not for the Shameful."

I duck my head and rest my fingers loosely in Aaron's, resentment and guilt bubbling in my chest. It's my fault we can't attend tonight. I had hoped that since Daniel hadn't held my Shaming publicly, it would go unnoticed by the rest of the community.

I should have known better.

Daniel is throwing a dinner in the Pavilion to welcome the newly married couples into the fold. Up to this point, we have attended Chapel together but gone separately to Lessons and otherwise kept to ourselves in our apartment, per Daniel's instructions. But he announced this morning that tonight, for the first time since the Matrimony, the new couples can appear in public as husband and wife. For Aaron and me, this means we must start *acting* like husband and wife.

Only tonight, we'll have to do it at my parents' house instead of at the Gathering.

"Start the water," Mishael barks.

Lydia's hands still, and her face tightens before she turns silently to the sinks behind her.

"We'll pick. The women can clean."

This sounds like a dismissal, so I move to Lydia's side. She stares down into the deep cast iron sink as it fills slowly with water.

"Temperature's the important part," she says finally. It's clear she doesn't want to teach me, any more than I want to be here, but as usual, I, *we*, have no choice. "Too cold and the lanolin congeals. Too hot and you'll shrink the fiber."

I nod, though she can see me only in the reflection of the water.

"First, we soak." She digs through the pile on the table and yanks out a fleece, the one she was working on.

"First, we *pick*." Mishael's voice is louder than it needs to be. He and Aaron have their backs turned, so only I see the angry curl of Lydia's lip when her husband speaks.

"And what if we forget to pick?" I ask. Not just because I don't like the way he corrects her and speaks around her but never to her; I'm also curious. This job seems so insidiously boring, I'm sure someday I'll forget a step.

"What if we just throw it in the water?" I touch the fleece in her hands, rubbing it between my fingers.

"Every step of the process is important. If you skip even one, the wool is useless." Lydia pulls the wool from my hands and shoves it into the water, giving the faucet a hard twist.

"Surely the weaving is more important than the picking or the washing? Without the weaving, you'd just have wool."

Lydia snorts. "Without the washing, you'd have a blanket of goat dung."

I press my lips together as I pull up my sleeves. As usual, my mouth has done nothing to help the situation. Better to keep it shut and try not to mess up. I plunge my hands into the water to turn the sticky wool.

"Get your hands out of there," Lydia snaps, and I snatch them back. "You don't want to agitate it."

Of course not. We don't agitate anything around here, do we? This time I manage not to say my thoughts out loud.

"If you move it too much, the wool will felt," she says.

The back of my throat burns with the unfairness of it all. Surely this must be punishment for some grievous sin, something much worse than speaking out of turn. But what did I do? Covet? I don't know how to stop wanting. Each night I pray for these feelings to go away, but each day I awaken with the memory of Caleb's arms around me, and a dull ache settles in my chest as I realize it's just another dream.

Aaron works on the other side of the table, his dark head bent over a matted cloud of wool. Each strand must be picked free of sand particles and other debris, using a contraption that looks like a narrow rectangular box filled with nails. Once the wool is placed inside the box, a panel is slid back and forth across the wool. It looks every bit as boring as washing, and maybe more tedious. I can't imagine how any of this can possibly turn into something beautiful. Then again, the wet mass in the sink no longer looks like the thick coat of the Angora goats. Already it's become something else. Something other.

I tug at the fringe of my own woolen head scarf and feel the heat radiate off Mishael as he moves behind me.

"You should learn to use the picker as well," he says, sliding the nail box in front of me and wrapping his hands around mine.

Unlike the other Elders, Mishael had letters inked on his knuckles before he came to New Jerusalem. I've seen them before, but today is the first time I'm close enough to read them. Together, they spell out LOVE on the left hand and HATE on the right. Who or what did he feel so strongly about—and so conflicted—that he needed the words on his body as a constant reminder? I know exactly whom I love. And what I hate.

I'm pinned against the table, his engorged belly pressing into the small of my back. Even Aaron has never dared to touch me like this. And Mishael is a married man the same age as my father. I shoot Aaron a pleading glance across the table, and he frowns, but I can't tell what he's thinking. Maybe he feels trapped, just like me. Maybe he doesn't know how to resist without causing a scene. Or maybe he isn't thinking about me at all. Maybe he's wondering how it became our life's purpose to serve at the mercy of these people.

I slam the panel against the side of the box, pinching Mishael's *H* finger.

"Damnation!"

He grabs at the injured digit, and I take advantage of his distraction, slipping out from between him and the table. "I'm sorry," I say. "I guess I need more practice."

He glares. "It's not that difficult."

He's right. It certainly doesn't need two pairs of hands. Aaron seems to be doing fine all on his own.

Mishael stomps away to grab another fleece of wool.

How long will I have to endure this? Tears blur my vision, and my hands shake as I untangle the wool from around my fingers and carry the pile over to the sink.

"My husband seems to feel you need his attention," Lydia says.

It's the first time she's initiated conversation with me, and her words suggest something so disgusting, they shock my tongue loose.

"Well, I don't."

"You'd best find a way to mind your own chores, then." She turns and yanks a fleece out of the water bath, swinging it onto the table with a wet slap. "Completely ruined."

I stare at the soggy mess. "It looks . . ." *Fine*, I start to say, but that would be a lie. It does look pretty bad, but it's wet wool. "What's it supposed to look like?"

"Not this. It's felted." She jabs a spindly finger at the pile in the center of the table.

Does she see the irony? That the other meaning of *felt* is the past tense of *feel*? How we process emotions? Like anger. Agitation. Despair. I stare down at the submerged wool, and it's hard not to imagine it as a lost kid, agitated and trapped. Drowning. A tear splashes the surface of the water, rippling out, as the baby goat is replaced by the image of my own face. My skin is hot, as if Lydia has burned me with her mocking smirk.

"You'll need to start over."

"Start over? But I didn't . . ." I bite my tongue. There's no use arguing with her, even though there's no way this was my fault. "Fine." I reach toward the wool, but she sweeps it to the floor.

"Not just this. All of it. Fresh wool. Fresh water. Everything has to be redone."

I wipe my sweaty forehead with the back of my wrist. "But that will take hours."

"It must be done tonight, or we'll have nothing dry to work with tomorrow. Isn't that right, Mishael?"

Her pleading tone doesn't escape my notice. Though she's enjoying this chance to belittle me, the power really rests with her husband. He will say whether we have to stay or not. It all depends on which of us he dislikes more.

The pause before he speaks is infinite, and this time when Aaron takes my hand, I let him.

"Miriam will stay and clean the wool." Mishael doesn't say she's right, but it's Lydia's victory all the same.

My body sags in defeat. I'm tired of this already—the monotonous work, Lydia's biting comments. The way Mishael speaks, as if his words hold momentous importance and not just punishment and innuendo.

"Daniel teaches that all our jobs are important. Do you disagree?"

Aaron squeezes my hand and answers. "No, sir. We don't. And we'll fix it."

"The practice will do you good. The more you do it, the sooner it will become muscle memory," Lydia says as she returns to the table, tossing a new basket of wool into the middle.

"Muscle memory?" I begin slowly picking through the wool one more time.

"When your body is so used to doing it, your mind doesn't have to think about it." Lydia glances over at her husband. "You can be somewhere else. Anywhere else."

Something about the way she says the word *body* makes me shudder. She isn't just talking about the wool. Where does she go, in her mind, when she doesn't want to be here?

Lydia is one of the original Elders. She and Mishael were joined at the first Matrimony, just like my parents. But where my mother's face is serene and unlined, Lydia's skin is worn thin. From disappointment? I can't fault her for that. Perhaps this is what comes from being given to a man you don't love. This is our way. I'd better get used to it.

"I'd say it's a shame that you'll have to miss dining with your parents now, but I suppose they have come to expect that kind of disappointment, what with only birthing one child."

And just when I was starting to feel sorry for Susanna's mother, now I hate her for pointing out my own mother's weakness. Even though the acid in Lydia's words is mostly for my parents, it still stings.

Daniel encourages procreation in order to grow our flock. There is strength in numbers, he says. But for reasons only God knows, my mother has never been able to produce another child. She holds her head high above the whispers, but I know it bothers her. I have memories of her coming home from the birthing of her Sisters' babies and sitting alone in the kitchen, staring at nothing, her fists pressed tight against her own flat belly.

Lydia awaits my reaction with the hungry look of a vulture ready to pick over a carcass.

I take a deep breath before I speak—the only way I know to control at least part of what comes out. "My mother will be happy to see us, whatever the time. She's used to keeping dinner warm for my father. He believes in the philosophy of Colossians: 'Whatever you do, work heartily. For the Lord and not for men.'" And I brush past her to drain the tubs and start again.

Her irritated sniff is a tiny victory, but it's all I have, and I savor it.

16

CALEB

The sun's rays are no longer directly overhead and the sky is clear, but everyone still clusters under the corrugated roof of the Pavilion, behind the Communal Kitchen. Council wives new and old are carrying out dishes for a feast, the table piled with grilled eggplant, bread slathered with saguaro butter, bowls of black tepary beans and dandelion greens, and pitchers filled with cinnamon-scented horchata.

My stomach growls like an angry mutt. I haven't had a decent meal since I moved out of the Farmhouse. Daniel is letting me stay in the Council House, but he says being unmarried is my own choosing, and it is up to me to figure out how to carry out those wifely duties for myself.

I haven't. When Lydia's back is turned, I snatch a thick slice of bread from the tray and cram it into my mouth, whole.

The scent of charcoal hangs in the air, along with a general buzz of uneasiness. The uneasiness might just be mine. I don't think I'm supposed to be here. Daniel didn't specifically tell me to stay away, but this Gathering is for married couples. I don't fit in anywhere anymore; I don't belong with the husbands, and the younger boys who haven't yet been called to Matrimony don't want anything to do with me. It's almost as if they're afraid of me. Like my bad choice will rub off on them. So I go about my business on my own, wandering the city like a spirit, searching for Daniel's coyote, and tightening weak spots in the fence. Trying not to look for Miriam.

I haven't seen her since the night of the Matrimony. When I held her in my arms and heard her speak to me for the first time. But that was before Daniel told me of her betrayal. Before I promised him I'd forget her.

It isn't like I haven't tried. I've avoided all the places she might go. I moved my seat at Chapel, arriving early and sitting in the front so I don't see her enter or leave. All of these safety measures only prove it's easier to stop seeing her than it is to stop thinking about her. Not an hour passes that I don't wonder why she lied to me and what she and Aaron are doing. I've spent most days half hoping she'll seek me out, only to collapse into bed at night both relieved and disappointed.

But she will be here tonight. Which means until someone tells me to leave, I have every right to look at her. To speak to her, even, if I can find the right words. I can ask her what she was thinking. If this is what she wanted. It will be like the burn in a muscle stretch. Painful, but pain that must be endured because it's the only way to achieve results. It will be better once I know.

I lean on a support beam near the front of the Pavilion, trying to look inconspicuous. Something about the Gathering tonight bothers me, but I'm not sure what. Then I realize that even though they're allowed to mingle now, my Brothers and Sisters have fallen back on our tradition of separation. The new husbands hover around a large picnic table near the food. Most have a plastic cup in one hand and one eye on the group of wives who've clustered around a table near the back. Some of the women have their backs to me, and since they have their scarves on, I can't tell which one is Miriam.

"Brother." Marcus is at my side with a cup of horchata before I can figure it out.

I know the drink is a peace offering—isn't there something in the Bible about offering water to your enemy?—so I take the cup. I haven't seen Marcus this week either, not since our quarrel. But I've heard Daniel is keeping him busy. And the fountain looks brand new, the brass shiny beneath the constant flame.

"How is living in the Council House?" he asks.

I swallow the last bitter crumbs of bread. "Don't."

"I said I was sorry about Miriam—"

"Caleb! I didn't expect to see you here." Susanna swoops in between the two of us and links her arm through Marcus's, leaning her body against his. "What were you two handsome men talking about? Did I hear you mention Miriam?" She blinks wide, innocent eyes in my direction, and I will myself to stay calm.

She doesn't know I was going to choose Miriam. She can't know. Unless . . . I look at Marcus, but he is too busy beaming at his new bride to pay me any attention.

"She and Aaron aren't here." She leans in and lowers her voice. "I heard it's because of her Shaming." She grips my forearm with icy fingers. "Mother says she's a mess. No idea what she's doing, in the Mill or in her marriage. Can you believe it? It's almost as if Aaron chose the wrong wife."

Her wolfish grin gives way to a sunny smile, and she straightens. "Hello, Hananiah. Judith. How wonderful to see you," she says, as Father and Mother walk up behind us.

I stand taller, too. If anyone is going to order me away from this Gathering, it will probably be Father.

But he has other sins on his mind. "Susanna." Father frowns. "Most women find marriage keeps them too busy to gossip."

Marcus pulls his wife closer. "I asked her about Miriam and Aaron, Father."

I'm shocked at how easily my brother takes the blame for her. Susanna is the picture of innocence, her hands clasped and her gaze cast demurely to the floor.

Father scowls and mutters under his breath, "It's no wonder . . ." then stops when Mother lays a hand on his arm. "Can we speak privately, Marcus?" He gestures toward the road, and Marcus has no choice but to obey.

I watch them walk away. "Why didn't you defend him?"

Susanna takes a sip from her cup and peers at me over the rim. "Why? He's my husband. He's supposed to defend *me*. We both know you'd do the same for your wife. If you had one."

She turns away before I can respond.

My hand is wet. Rice milk, cold and sticky, drips from the crushed cup in my hand.

"Here." Mother hands me a napkin, then glances around to make sure we're alone. "I've put together some food for you as well." She holds up a small paper sack.

I hurl the sopping mess into the garbage. "Thanks," I say, "but you don't need to feed me. What would Father say?" I scrub at my hands with the napkin.

"He wishes you had a wife. We both do. But he won't begrudge you a few bites of food."

"Won't he?"

Mother doesn't hear me. "He's preoccupied with Marcus these days."

I snort and ball up the wet napkin. When isn't he preoccupied with Marcus? My whole life has been about Marcus. Marcus is smart, Marcus is clever, Marcus will make a great leader someday. Never Caleb. My work and my loyalty and my faith went completely unnoticed. Maybe that's why Father didn't bother to kick me out of the Gathering. As far as he's concerned, I've always been a ghost.

"Daniel has revoked Marcus's invitation. To serve on the Church Council." When Mother looks at me again, her eyes shine with unshed tears. "You know how much that meant to your father. To have his son serve Daniel."

There is a hollow pit in my stomach that no amount of food will ever fill. "His son *is* serving Daniel," I say. "He has more than one, remember."

She flinches at the venom in my voice and holds out the sack again, but I turn and start walking. Away from the food, which I no longer have any appetite for. Away from my mother and her weak defense of Father. Away from all the husbands and wives.

The streets are deserted this time of night, and for once I am happy to feel invisible. There is no one I want to talk to. The Council House is dark, and I head for the staircase and my room, but the sound of raised voices from Daniel's chambers draws me in.

I quietly circle Susanna's desk and push on the door behind it, then shift my weight as it cracks open, leaning my upper body against the doorjamb.

"Your son disappoints me, Han."

Daniel's voice is so cold, I shiver.

"No apology?" Daniel continues. "No remorse whatsoever? From either of you?"

"I have nothing to apologize for. Susanna was meant for me. So I chose her."

"Shut your mouth, Marcus! Remember whom you're speaking to! You've embarrassed yourself and our family." Father gets this look when he's angry, his face going white and still, like it's carved from stone. That is how I picture him now. For once, it's Marcus experiencing the coldness of that look. Finally, it's he who is the target of Father's rage and disappointment instead of me. I thought I'd enjoy it, but my brother's humiliation chokes me as if it were my own.

"I've already been punished," Marcus says. "You revoked my seat on the Council, humbled and degraded me with work duty. What else do you require? Beat me or berate me. None of that will change the fact that she is my wife. It is God's will."

"It isn't God's will," Daniel says. "God asked you to choose a different wife. Yet you conspired with your Brothers and ignored His voice."

I hold my breath. So Daniel does know that Marcus and Aaron switched names.

"I didn't." Marcus's voice is strong, too. No hint of the lie he's telling. "God spoke to me. He told me to choose Susanna."

Our leader quotes scripture, the words spewing forth as if from an erupting volcano. He speaks fast and low, and I can't follow most of it. I hear the words *marriage* and *obligation* and *undefiled bed*.

"We've met all our marital obligations. Every night."

"Don't be vulgar."

Marcus says, "I chose my wife. We took our vows. You sanctioned the marriage. All is as it should be. Why do you think otherwise?"

Daniel continues as if Marcus hasn't spoken. "You know exactly what you've done. And not just you. Who else was involved?"

"I don't know what you're talking about."

Daniel's laugh is humorless. "Like Judas, you've grown a spine far too late. Get out."

I press myself against the wall, but my brother doesn't even notice me as he hurries out and bangs through the front door.

What is happening? Will this one Matrimony be the end for my family? Clearly Daniel believes that he sanctioned the wrong marriages, despite what he told me. And he's angry.

Yet even in the face of that fury, Marcus held firm. What is it the Bible says about liars? Something about perishing in the Lake of Fire. Maybe Marcus is afraid that if he confesses, he'll be punished even more severely. Not only will he lose his wife, he'll lose his life. By keeping quiet, he's managed to keep both.

Now I'm more confused than ever: Does lying make him weaker than me, or smarter?

17

MIRIAM

"Are you ready to hit the road?" Aaron asks.

I yank the stopper on the sink one last time. "Why would we hit it?"

His smile wavers, and he jams his hands into his pockets. "Never mind. It's just an expression. Are you ready to go?"

He waits as I untie my apron and hang it beside the drying hanks of wool. Muted voices and laughter drift toward us from the Pavilion at the other end of the city as we step out into the dying light, but the street is shadowy and deserted.

"Are you nervous?" I ask as we head in the opposite direction, down toward the housing circle, which lies in the lowest part of the city.

"About dinner with your parents?" He takes my hand. "They're still your parents."

I stare down at our hands, and he snatches his back.

"I'm just saying, you've only been gone a week. Not that much has changed."

He's half right. Almost nothing. Only everything.

We walk toward my old home in silence. I long to chatter to fill the emptiness, but I don't dare. The longer we go on with our sham of a marriage, the harder it is to keep up this appearance of normalcy. I once thought nothing could curb my tongue, but a day with Lydia and Mishael has finally muted me. There are too many ears here, too many Brothers and Sisters close by, and our strained conversation will give us away. What do real couples talk about? There's no one I can ask without admitting to my marital failings. I'll have to become a silent listener, an observer. Watch my classmates closely whenever I encounter them as a couple.

It's what Daniel has been preaching my whole life—women should keep their questions to themselves. Perhaps getting me to shut up was his intention all along.

"Is it that unusual?" he asks.

So it's true what they say of married couples? He can read my mind? "My not talking?"

His forehead wrinkles. "What Lydia said back there. About you being an only child."

"Oh." I sigh, sucking in the first cool, whispered breath of evening. "It's a source of embarrassment, especially to my mother. We're supposed to be fruitful and multiply. Your mother must know what that's like, you being an only child, too."

"I'm not . . . I mean, it's not unusual to be an only child. Outside of here."

"Yes, but you . . ." I stop before calling him an Outsider. "You're not Second Generation." Marriage has already taught me to curb my tongue, and I want no part of it, so I ask the question anyway. "Is that normal for women Outside? Not being able to procreate?"

My caustic tone doesn't seem to bother him. "It's not *ab*normal.

But I'm not sure why you assume it's your mother's fault. Maybe it's your father. Has he ever been tes— Never mind." He jerks his gaze from mine and shakes his head. "Not everyone Outside has kids. Some people don't want them. Others are worried about population growth. They say if we keep reproducing indiscriminately, there won't be enough resources for everyone."

I stare off into the distance, at the wall encircling our city, and try out this new word. "Indiscriminately." It sounds sinful. I like it. "How many people are out there?"

"On Earth? A couple billion. I don't know the actual number."

I shiver, though the day is only beginning to cool. "How is that even possible? Where do they all fit?" I whisper, rubbing my arms.

"Well, it's a big world out there," he says. "Seven continents and five oceans. There's a lot of space, but it's not all usable. Population is increasing, while the land is shrinking and the oceans are dying."

Dying. The word sits heavy in my chest. It's not as if seeing the ocean was a real possibility for me, but I still mourn the loss.

"Don't look so sad. That's the point of all this, isn't it?" He waves an arm. "Cocoon yourselves so you don't have to worry about the rest of the world's problems?"

But never before has the safety felt so confining. Is it worse for Aaron, having known such openness before he came here? Most Outsiders call New Jerusalem a refuge, but I've never heard him use that term.

"Is that why you're here? Your family wanted a cocoon?" I ask.

"Something like that."

He sounds bitter, but I can't ask any more questions. My mother is waiting at the door; I can see her from here. Shiny brown hair tucked away under her scarf, perfect heart-shaped face, cocoa-colored eyes that light up when she smiles. She hugs me first, then Aaron. "I'm so glad you're here," she says. And if not for the circumstance that brought us, I'd believe her.

My father hovers behind her, one hand resting on her shoulder as he cups my cheek. He's older than her, and after being away from them for a week I see it more clearly than ever—in the brown spots that speckle his head, in the lines around his mouth. They had a Matrimony, just like us. But they were First Generation, so their union occurred when New Jerusalem was formed, not when they came of age. My mother was eighteen, not sixteen, and my father was in his thirties when he chose her, but this is all I know for certain. Everything else about their past is a mystery, a box I've never been allowed to open or look inside. Did they love each other? Do they now?

They invite me—us—into the only home I've ever known, and for a moment, none of this feels real. Not their happiness, not my life here. It's all orchestrated, a carefully blurred reality, like the skits Rachel and Delilah and I used to perform on Saturday afternoons after Chapel.

Who are these people?

My father is a member of the Church Council. My mother, as the wife of a church official, organizes most of the community Gatherings. If there is cooking or cleaning to do, my mother handles it or delegates the task to someone nearly as competent. She's also a nurse. She heals people. I've always been proud of her accomplishments and a bit envious of her composure, but today, I add *resentful* to the list. There is so much she could have told me about marriage, had she chosen to put me before the rules, just once.

On the night of my marriage, her composure cracked a little. From her response, I knew something had gone wrong. Yet she did nothing to help me or to correct it. And watching her now, with her serene smile in place as she ushers us to the table, there is no hint anything unusual happened. This frightens me. I had thought support, if I'm to have any, would come from her. Surely as a member of a founding family, she hadn't intended me to be married to an Outsider. So why doesn't she speak up? Why maintain her silence, even in my time of need?

Because this is what women do in New Jerusalem?

"I've kept everything warm," she says. "It will just take a few minutes to set the table."

"Why don't you show me your room while we're waiting?" Aaron asks with a bland smile.

No boy has ever set foot in my bedroom. Actually, I can't remember a boy ever being in our house, though perhaps we spent time together in the yards when we were younger, before the age of Separation. He looks unimpressed by the plain cream-colored walls, the spare furniture, the neatly made twin beds tucked close enough together that Rachel and I used to be able to hold hands until we fell asleep. But what did he expect?

"What was it like? Living here as a child? It's so . . . empty."

There's a kind of longing in his voice, or maybe it's pity, but it riles me. "My life was *not* empty. We had Lessons every day, and chores or Bible Study at night. Chapel on Saturdays."

"I meant the room is empty. Where are your toys? Your decorations?"

"Toys? I'm not a *child*. I gave up my toys at the age of Separation."

Aaron massages his hand over his mouth, as if physically trying to pull the words from it. But he doesn't speak; he just looks at the bare shelves and empty beds.

Suddenly, I think of Mimi. My mother crafted the rag doll to look just like me, with pale blue thread for eyes, black yarn curls, and a red puckered mouth sewn permanently shut. No matter how many secrets I whispered in Mimi's tiny cloth ear, she could never repeat them. I went to sleep every night with Mimi tucked between my cheek and my pillow, and by the time I was seven, she was flat and nearly bald. But I'd still loved her fiercely. When I'd had to give her up to Delilah's baby sister, I'd cried as if I were losing my own child.

Aaron squats beside one of the beds—mine—and slips his hand beneath the mattress.

I clench my hands at my sides to keep from pulling him back. Maybe he won't find it.

But then he grins, and I know he's found the hole in the box spring.

Our eyes meet as he slides the sheets of paper from beneath the mattress. I snatch them away. "How did you know?"

"It's the same place I used to hide things." A veil comes down over his eyes, and I know he means Outside.

I'm not sure what shocks me more—that despite all our differences, we should have this in common? Or that I must think like an Outsider?

He peers over my shoulder.

"Don't." I roll them into a tube. They aren't for anyone else to see. I hid them after Mimi was taken and I realized I needed a better way to protect what was important.

"I knew you weren't that boring. So tell me, what secrets does Miriam keep?"

"None of your business."

"And how about Rachel?"

"Ha! You clearly don't know Rachel." I lift my own mattress as he peeks under Rachel's, intending to put the papers back, but he comes up behind me and shoves it down.

"Take them with you," he says. "You don't live here anymore. And obviously these mean something to you. You should keep them close."

I cradle the roll like a baby. He's right, they do mean something. But other than clothing, we're not supposed to take any physical tokens of our childhood into our married homes. And I have no way of getting them out of the house without my parents seeing.

He pries the tube gently from my hands, unfurls the papers, and folds them into a small square without reading them. Then he puts it into his own pocket. "I'll keep your secrets safe. Promise." He raises his little finger.

His words are an eerie echo of the pacts Delilah and Rachel and I used to make. My Sisters, I trust. But my husband?

I stare at his hooked pinky with a strange sense of trepidation as I ask, "How did you know that was my bed?"

He shrugs. "Lucky guess. I figured you'd want to be close to the window."

How can he know me this well, when he's spent the past week virtually ignoring me?

When we are all seated around the dinner table and my mother is finally satisfied that my father has everything he needs, she speaks.

"How is the weaving coming?"

A week ago, I wouldn't even have noticed, but I've spent the last seven days taking my meals with Aaron. Seven days in which he cooked, served himself, cleared the table, and cleaned up after both of us. Until I saw him do these things, it never occurred to me any man could.

"I'd like some water. Father, could you pour me a glass?" I gesture to the pitcher.

They all stare at me. My father stops eating, a peculiar expression tugging at the corners of his mouth, but he doesn't get up. Instead, as he always does when perplexed by female behavior, he calls on my mother. "Ruth?"

My mother pours the glass and sets it beside my plate.

My father clears his throat. "We need to discuss your sin. Daniel has asked us to make some things clear."

"Not now, Boaz. After dinner," my mother murmurs without looking up.

Heat rises in my cheeks. I can just imagine which "things" are to be made clear. I have spent this past week longing to come home, and now that I'm here, I have no idea what I thought I was missing. My father, lecturing us on Daniel's wishes? My mother's meek reproach, almost worse than Daniel's thunderous anger? I love my parents, but they have betrayed me. Their lack of support has split our family, the injury so jarring nothing will fix it. Eating with them only serves to slap a bandage on the gaping wound, but I do it.

The sweet, soft squash is like paste, gluing my mouth shut and trapping my voice.

"Miriam used to be quite the talker, Aaron," Father finally says. "I'm not sure if it's you that's cured her of the habit. Or perhaps Daniel has finally managed to get his point across." He turns his attention to my husband. "Either way, this is how it should be."

I clench my fists under the table.

"I won't take credit for that," Aaron says. "Miriam has a lot of good thoughts to share. Honestly, I prefer it when she talks."

Both my parents swivel their attention from my husband to me and back, although my mother looks less confused than my father. His gaze rakes across the two of us, scrutinizing. I feel naked. He is no longer looking at me as his daughter, but as another man's wife. I work hard to keep the giggle of hysterical laughter down in my throat. My poor father. If only he knew. He has nothing to worry about on that front.

Soon, I know, I will have to give in. Submit to my husband, as it says in the Bible. I have so far refused, though *refused* is probably too strong a word, since Aaron hasn't asked. As the days march on, my refusal feels less like a point of principle and more like a pointless gesture that accomplishes nothing save isolating me from my faith and my community.

Still, I can't bring myself to lie with him. Should it not be as in the Song of Solomon, with a man I love and not a stranger? All my life I have been taught to expect something magical, and the ordinariness of our married life is both a disappointment and a horror.

"They are newly married, Boaz," my mother says softly. "There is a lot to take in. I expect Miriam's focus has turned . . . inward, for the time being."

My father makes a sound in the back of his throat, though whether he agrees with her or is choking is unclear. He points at Aaron. "It's your job to keep it there."

I open my mouth and look at my mother, who gives me the tiniest of headshakes. "It is for the best," she says, laying her hand across my father's.

Aaron mimics her gesture but then grabs my hand firmly. "If Miriam wants to speak, I won't be the one to silence her. I'm surprised you would."

And just like that, my husband has become my closest ally.

Maybe my only one.

18

CALEB

I don't have time to cross the room before Daniel and Father see me, so I duck under Susanna's desk. It's a tight fit. The corner of a drawer bites into my shoulder, and my head is bent at an almost impossible angle. Luckily for me, it's dark, and the chair glides without so much as a squeak when I pull it into place.

"Are you sure about this?" Father asks, his voice amplified as he pauses beside my hiding place. "Maybe Marcus was telling the truth. Maybe it's all a simple mistake."

"Don't be stupid." Daniel sounds annoyed. "Of course I'm sure. This was no mistake; this was anarchy."

Daniel knows what Marcus and Aaron have done because he's the one who interpreted their dreams. But if he really thought they were defying God's will, why didn't he stop the Matrimony? Why let them commit . . . anarchy in the first place?

"I'm losing control," Daniel continues. "It was a mistake to let them speak at all. I should have called the wives' names."

"Pronouncement is the first step on the Path to Righteousness," Father says. As if Daniel needs reminding.

"Screw the Pronouncement! I give this generation the tiniest bit of power, and look what happens. They think they can do whatever they want, and damn the consequences! They don't think they need me. Why is that? You all understand. Why we're here. What I've done. What I've built."

"Because we witnessed it firsthand," Father says.

"So why don't you teach your children, then? Do you need reminding that because of me, your offspring have never known suffering?" A pause, then, "Perhaps they need to be taught a lesson."

The hair raises up on my arms. What kind of lesson is he talking about?

Father's voice is calm when he says, "If you fear you're losing this younger generation, maybe the answer to keeping them isn't telling them what they want, but asking."

"Asking?" Daniel snorts. "They're children; it doesn't matter what they want. I know what they *need*." The floor creaks as he takes a step closer to the desk. "Careful, Han. My patience for insubordination wears thin this evening."

"Your patience? What about mine? I gave up my best goat in sacrifice. And for what? Marcus still lost the Council seat. And his Vocation at the Farm."

My muscles burn from holding still, but I can't move now. Father made a sacrifice so Marcus would be named to the Council? And aren't our Vocations determined by our specific talents? This is what we've always been told. My pulse pounds in rhythm with my unspoken questions. What about me? Is my spot on the Security team due to my hard work? Or Father's?

"Jacob hates the Farm; what could be a more fitting punishment than to have to toil in the dirt for all his days? And as I told you, Susanna is unqualified to be a Council wife. If Marcus wanted that placement, he should have done what was asked of him."

Asked of him by God? Or by you? The question must come

from somewhere outside me. I would never entertain such disloyal thoughts.

"Your son's rebellion will be an example to the others, and I won't have it!" Things crash down around the chair: pens, a desk calendar, a stapler. I bite my knuckle to keep from crying out.

I wait for their argument to fade before I allow myself to breathe. It doesn't take long; Daniel is the only person Father ever backs down from. As their footsteps recede, I shove back the chair and untangle my legs from the cramped space. They burn as blood flow returns, but the discomfort sharpens my senses.

Which makes it all the more painful when my head scrapes against the bottom of the desk, and again when I whack it on the partially opened drawer as I stand.

"Damn!"

My voice echoes loudly in the empty hall, and I freeze, waiting. My gaze climbs the stairway, and I crane my neck to scan the balcony above. No sign of anyone.

I kneel to pick up the items Daniel's thrown. The desk calendar has come free from its leather binding, and as I try to work the corners back in, something flaps loose. An envelope. The handwriting on the front is thin and precise, but that isn't what catches my attention. It's the names. Not just Daniel, but Daniel Howe. And in the upper left corner, Naomi Walker.

I know only one Naomi. Rachel's mother. When Rachel was a baby, Naomi and another member of the community, Azariah, committed a sin so Contemptible, Azariah ran away and Naomi was Banished. None of us is allowed to speak of the incident. Or of them.

I turn over the envelope and see it's already been opened. I know I shouldn't, but I pull out the lined sheet and unfold it.

Dear Daniel,

Rachel is sixteen today. Do you remember? Maybe not. While I was lying in a bed, barely older than she is now and begging the midwife to let me die, you were elsewhere, doing what you do best— preaching and being revered. I couldn't see at the time how messed up that was, but I guess that's what blind faith will do to a girl.

You dumped me in the desert, alone and afraid. You left me there to die. But I didn't. It took me a long time to find a place where I felt safe. Even longer to shake off your insidious "teachings." To stop seeing the world as the evil place you painted it. Sure, there are bad people out here. But there are bad people in there, too. Which is worse, I wonder? The devil you read about in the morning paper, or the devil who sleeps beside you?

But this is about Rachel. I want her to know ordinary freedoms. Sleeping late on a rainy day. Grabbing a burger at a drive-thru. Texting with a girlfriend. Smiling at a cute boy in the park. Bike riding. Window shopping. Reading the backs of all the novels in the bookstore. Reading ANYTHING. Have you given them books yet? I doubt it. That would be dangerous, letting them know other people have voices. I'm betting yours is still the only narrative you allow in there.

That's why I'm writing. I've contacted a lawyer. and I'm suing you for custody. There's a hearing in

thirty days. Consider this your notification. I was
underage when I signed away my parental rights. And
there isn't a jury in the world who could fail to see your
influence over me as "undue."

I have friends, Daniel. And with their help, I'm
going to take you down. You aren't as powerful as you
think, or as clever. It turns out you were right. The end
IS coming, just not the way you predicted.

The pounding of my heart and the rattling of the paper in my shaky hands must be loud enough to drown out everything else, because I don't realize anyone is watching until I hear a voice.

19

MIRIAM

DO NOT FORSAKE YOUR MOTHER'S TEACHING.

—*Proverbs 1:8*

After dinner, my mother invites me to help her with the clean-up while my father and Aaron step outside for an evening walk. In her cozy kitchen, nothing has changed. Though we've just finished dinner, nothing is messy or out of place. Even the dirty dishes are stacked neatly on the washboard to the right of the sink. The only decoration is still her calendar, hung on the side of the refrigerator, where she carefully crosses off each day that brings us closer to the Tribulation. With the sound of running water and the feel of the threadbare dish towel between my fingers, it's as if I've slipped back in time. Was it only a week ago I stood here, staring out this same window at the tiny strip of sand, stone, and desert holly as I tried to pry whatever information I could from my mother about married life?

Now that I know firsthand, I'm angry at that naïve girl.

"This is the last time we can feed you," my mother says from behind me. "You will need to start procuring your own food. Preparing your own meals. You'll be given your own account at the Commodities Exchange, like we talked about. If you have any questions . . ."

I shake my head. I long to tell her that she doesn't need to worry, that I won't go hungry. Because my husband cooks. But I don't want to talk about meal planning, and neither does she. Not really.

When I turn from the sink, she is smile-frowning, which means she is about to say something I probably won't like, but I should accept it because she's my mother and she means well.

"It is always hardest the first time," she says. "Sometimes it takes a few tries. To get it right." Her lips barely move. It's almost like she hasn't spoken, except the words lie heavy and sharp between us, like a treacherous mountain I don't dare attempt to climb.

We didn't fool her at dinner.

She is my mother; she knows something isn't right between Aaron and me. But she assumes if we can get past our first embarrassing attempts at lovemaking, things will somehow get better. Of course, she expects we've at least made an attempt. If nothing else, Aaron should have forced my submission by now. Our awkwardness has somehow led her to believe the first time went badly and now we're reluctant to try again.

Or is it only me? I'm probably the reluctant one in her eyes, the one who must be chided and coerced. Talked into another attempt. It's my duty as a wife, after all.

I'm not sure how to respond, and the silence drags on. Should I tell her there has been no such attempt? That there never will be, if I have anything to say about it?

I hold my tongue as Aaron and my father pass by the window. The low tone of my husband's voice and the even deeper one of my father's waft past without settling. What are they discussing? How best to maneuver me into Aaron's bed? Are these the things men talk about when they're together? Maybe that's what tonight's dinner was really about. Divide and conquer. Probe and lecture.

"It is an expression of love. And God wants us to love. You may not believe me now, but someday you will see it as such."

"But I don't love him."

"Not yet. But you will," she promises. "That is the beauty of submission. Do as he asks, and love will follow."

I shiver at the echo of Phoebe's words in her mouth. "He hasn't asked anything of me."

When I finally meet her eyes, they are worried.

"I know this marriage is not what you expected."

"Not what I expected? Is that what you think? That I'm somehow confused by all this? Or shocked at the prospect of intimacy? That I can't handle living with a man?" I wave the dish towel at her as the words pour out like lava, hot and painful and unstoppable. Not that I want them to stop. They're all true.

"Maybe the sudden, complete . . . *upheaval* has unhinged me. Maybe I've gone completely mad with . . . with . . ." I stomp my foot when I can't find the right word, and as if by magic, it appears. "With regret."

"It is this way for everyone," my mother says.

And at that, I realize an awful truth. I've been so wrapped up in my own tragedy, I haven't given a moment's thought to my friends. Maybe Rachel is struggling as well. And what of Delilah? How does she feel, not being chosen? Being sent away?

"That was the point of resuming the Lessons," my mother continues. "So you could draw strength from one another."

"I don't need strength. I need someone to listen to me."

She frowns—a slight pucker of her lips and a wrinkle across the bridge of her nose. "This is the only way. You spoke to him, after all. What did you expect?"

"I expected you to understand, for one. You're my mother. I was only trying to help him. I didn't think it would . . ." I throw down the dishrag. "I don't want to be married to him. I don't want to be strong, because I don't want it to continue. I will be weak if it will undo this thing."

"Miriam. You couldn't be weak if you tried." She touches my wrist, but I yank it away.

"And anyway, it would not matter," she says, and perhaps only I would be able to read the hurt on her placid face. "When you spoke, you created a bond. And once a bond is consecrated by the Prophet, it cannot be broken. It is one of the tenets of our faith."

"It isn't a bond. It's a mistake." I clench my fists, forcing each word from my lips. "Surely you can see that. Surely everyone can see it."

She bows her head. "I have heard of some of the women who felt this way after the first Matrimony. But they soon realized God had a plan for them. Just as He has for you. What about your dreams? Have you been journaling?"

I haven't. Daniel still has my journal. I don't want to tell her this, though. It's unusual that he's kept it so long, and only a matter of time before he will want to talk to me about the lies in it. "I forget," I mumble.

She presses her hand to her heart. "You must have faith. Pray, and He will guide you. There are no mistakes. There is only God's will, which, sometimes, is hard for us to fathom."

"How can you know that? How can you be so . . . so calm? Aren't you listening to me? I can't do this."

"Of course you can. Miriam . . . what choice do you have?"

She knows the answer as well as I do. I'm a woman. I have no choice.

"How?" I manage to whisper. The words I normally struggle to hold back have vanished into a vapor that chills my hollow chest.

She grasps my hands, and this time I let her. "Submission. And dreams. This is our way. Open your body to your husband, your dreams to Daniel, and your heart to the Lord."

The Lord has sent me dreams of Caleb. But I can't tell her this, or anything else. Not anymore. Eventually she kisses my forehead, tells me "Keep faithful," and leaves me to finish drying the dishes alone.

It's only after she's gone that I replay our conversation in my head and realize she said "women." Some *women* have felt there was a mistake. Not men. Of course. In our community, the men don't own their mistakes. They do what they like and leave the women to pick up the pieces.

20

CALEB

"What are you doing with that?"

My heart stutters so hard I see nothing but stars. When they recede, Susanna stares back at me.

She grabs the letter with a finger and thumb and yanks it from my grip. "That isn't addressed to you."

She pulls out a set of keys and fumbles with them, trying to fit one into the lock on the other drawer. This is my brother's wife. Though God may not have chosen her for him. Yet another of the many riddles I can't answer. They're piling up.

I step around her, but she kicks the chair out to block me. So she takes her job seriously. That's something, at least. It might be part of what Marcus sees in her. If only I didn't blame her for his downfall and my misery.

I still have the envelope. Zzyzx, I know, is the old name for New Jerusalem. But I've never heard of Santa Cruz, and I have no idea what the string of numbers means. In the opposite corner, there's a bright picture of a blue butterfly, partially obscured by a black circle with some fuzzy writing in it. I look closer. It's a date. Last September. Which means whatever was supposed to happen in thirty days has long since transpired.

Susanna finally succeeds in opening the drawer. Without looking at me, she holds out her palm until I place the envelope in it.

"This is from Naomi. Rachel's mother."

"I know who Naomi is," she snaps.

"Has Daniel seen it?"

She hesitates just long enough that I can't tell if she's lying. "Of course. It's his letter."

"So why do you have it?"

"I'm his secretary. It's my job to take care of his correspondence."

Even correspondence that's more than six months old? But her glare dares me to contradict her, so instead I ask, "What did Daniel say about it?"

"I don't know. We didn't discuss it. He reads his letters, I file them."

"But you must have read it."

"*He* reads them. I file them."

I'm not sure if I'm disappointed or relieved by her answer. Naomi's words are shocking and blasphemous and not meant for our eyes. But at the same time, I need someone to help me figure it out. Naomi seems to be accusing Daniel of taking Rachel away from her, which is ridiculous. She was the one who sinned. And when she was ordered into the desert, to spend her seven years wandering like an animal, as is the law, she begged Daniel to keep Rachel so she could be raised to Shine with Righteousness.

She doesn't even mention Azariah. And the other things she's written? About the Outside? They must be lies. They have to be.

I watch as Susanna shoves the letter back into the envelope, slides the envelope into the drawer and locks it. I wait for her to leave, but she doesn't.

"What are you doing here?" I ask, suddenly suspicious. "Why aren't you at the Gathering?"

"It's a husband-and-wife Gathering." She fiddles with the key and bites her lip. "Somehow, I seem to have lost my husband."

"But how did you know he was here?" I ask.

"Marcus is here?" The whites of her eyes gleam as she looks about the darkened room.

She's acting odd. Nervous. Did she follow Father and Marcus here without them knowing? "I thought you said . . ."

"I read the letter," she blurts, her voice low and husky, like there's something caught in her throat. "And I know what Naomi did. The sin that was so terrible, no one can talk about it."

I knew I wasn't the only curious one.

She cocks her head and smiles up at me in a way that feels dangerous. "Do you want me to show you?" She raises her hands to her chest, and I look away, embarrassed. When I look back, she has slipped open the top button of her shirt and is working on the second.

Oh.

No.

Please, God. I've never seen a naked woman before. Yes, I've prayed for it, but that was wrong. I see that now. I've changed my mind. Make it stop. Make her stop.

But God isn't answering tonight.

"For God's sake, stop!"

Her laugh is low and mocking, but she drops her hands. She doesn't button back up. "Anyone who has dreamt of a woman lustfully has already committed adultery in his heart," she whispers.

I don't think that's the way the verse goes. But she has me so confused, with her wet lips and her gaping shirt. I've never dreamt about her, never even thought about her until tonight. And these are thoughts better left un . . . well, unthought.

She steps closer and I back up, jabbing the corner of the desk into my thigh. I'm suddenly aware of how alone we are. Somehow, whispering in the dark feels much more intimate than anything I've dreamt of doing with Miriam. My heart pounds so loudly, we both hear it. What is wrong with me? She's my brother's wife. What is wrong with *her*?

Before I can figure it out, she whirls away, moving noiselessly across the room and out the door.

When I can breathe again, I realize she never asked me where Marcus went.

21

MIRIAM

ONE WHO IS RIGHTEOUS IS A GUIDE TO
HIS NEIGHBOR, BUT THE WAY OF THE
WICKED LEADS THEM ASTRAY.
—*Proverbs 12:26*

It's only the second day of my wool-washing sentence and already I think I may lose my mind. When Lydia announces we are out of wool, I don't wait for her to give me another assignment. I simply grab a basket and run out the door, pretending I can't hear her calling me back. I'll deal with her accusations later.

"You said we were out of wool. I was only doing what you asked."

I imagine her shocked face, unable to form a logical retort, and I giggle. For a small moment, I remember what it feels like to be content. To be walking alone and free in the glorious outdoors. The wind nudges me gently along while the sunshine warms my face.

Then I see the Farmhouse and the barn, and my delight in these simple pleasures abandons me once again. Things will never be as they were. Rachel is someone's wife now, as am I. We both live in cramped apartments, on opposite sides of the old motel. And while Aaron and I learn to weave, she works beside Jacob on this farm, set back behind a wide expanse of scrub-brush lawn.

This used to be Caleb's home. And before that, Daniel's. My parents', too, back in the beginning. Back when New Jerusalem was just a dream, a scattering of dark caves and broken buildings in the middle of the desert. Long before Daniel built the Council House up on the hill. Before my mother and father became one of the first married couples to move into the tiny concrete-block houses down in the flatland. Even before my father stood on that dais in the firelight and chose my mother, in the first Matrimony so many years ago.

I pass the pasture on my left, and as the breeze shifts the goats bleat softly. They've already learned the scent of their caregiver, Rachel, now standing in wait at the mouth of the walkway, where the tight, pebbled path widens into a welcome smile.

Rachel's hair, like mine, has a tendency to frizz, and she usually wears it cinched tight and wound around her head. Now that she's married, it stays hidden under her brightly patterned head scarf. It makes her look older, and if not for the way she folds her arms over her work dress as she leans on the fence post, I might not even recognize her. Does she look happy? I can't tell from this distance.

I take a deep breath and open my arms so I can soak up all of the freedom of this open space. If only I could take a bit of it back with me to our dark, boxlike apartment.

"'I shall lie down in green pastures,'" I sing.

Rachel hurries forward and catches me into a hug. "Miriam," she chides me, a hint of laughter in her voice. "You haven't changed. No singing outside of Chapel. Don't make me report you."

"I'm praising God," I argue. "How can I resist, in a place like this? How can you? You should be singing with me. You're so lucky you get to work outdoors like this."

"I *am* lucky." Rachel beams, her slightly sallow complexion taking on a warm glow, which I doubt is due only to her Vocational assignment.

"You're happy with your marriage, then."

Her smile widens so much I fear her cheeks must ache. Then she blushes.

"Yes. I'm happy. I never dreamt I would be good enough for a man like Jacob."

Rachel's circumstances lie heavy on her shoulders. She has a lot to live up to, or perhaps the better word is *overcome*. She does it with a smile and a willing heart, always the first to quote scripture or raise her hand in class. Even those who insist on reminding her of the shame of her mother—Phoebe, for one—have to admit Rachel has proven herself to be above that.

We used to speculate about Naomi when we were young, sharing whispered little-girl fantasies between our twin beds after my mother tucked us in. About how she escaped the heat of the desert and went to cool herself in the ocean with the whales. Or sometimes, we imagined she was still wandering out there, a kind of Prophetess, sharing Daniel's Word. And one day she'd come home, bringing more followers with her, and Daniel would have no choice but to welcome her back into our fold, just like a lost sheep.

We stopped the game when we got older, mostly because Rachel refused to play. Was it because she knew her mother was dead? But she couldn't have; if she did, she would have told me. We've never kept secrets from each other. Until now.

Rachel is oblivious to my scrutiny as she loops her arm through mine and squeezes me close. "And you? I've missed you. We have so much to talk about."

I've missed her, too. Up until yesterday, we at least had the consistency of seeing one another every day at Lessons, even if we didn't have an opportunity to talk. But now that we've begun our Vocations, I have no idea how often our paths will cross. It unnerves me how much my life has changed in such a small amount of time. How much I've lost.

"Have you heard anything about Delilah?" I ask. "Will we be allowed to say goodbye?"

Rachel shakes her head, studying our sandaled feet. "I only know what Susanna's said in class. She's supposed to be taking this time to be alone with her family, before . . ." She stops, shudders. "Can you imagine?"

"No," I say, because none of this is like anything I ever imagined.

"Tell me about Aaron," Rachel says, changing the subject. "He is so handsome, yet so quiet. Mysterious." She bumps my hip with her own. "What's he like?"

I struggle to come up with a truthful answer, one that will satisfy her without bringing more questions about our relationship. I settle on "He's a good cook," and immediately regret it.

"He cooks?" She says this in the voice she might have used had I told her he falls asleep in Chapel.

Clearly, Rachel wants an explanation. Yet Aaron is my husband. Should I defend him? Pretend his cooking is normal? Isn't that what spouses do? I've watched my mother over the years, stressing my father's strengths, downplaying his weaknesses. But Aaron and I are not my parents.

"You mean he helped you prepare the Council meals?" she asks, rubbing at the bridge of her nose.

I hesitate. I've already given too much away. Aaron took care of all of the cooking even when the Council was sending meals; now that they have stopped, I've refused to shop for food, much less cook it. Or at least I intended to refuse. In reality, Aaron has never asked. He just does it himself. "He likes to do it."

"Jacob loves my cooking. He says it's nearly as good as the Council meals." She smiles. "I've promised him I'll work on it. Once we're through our Private Period, I'm going to ask your mother for advice. Then we'll have you and Aaron over for a Gathering." She's still smiling but her eyes are troubled, and I know she's concerned about me. "We can't really visit yet," she adds. "What brings you by?"

"Wool," I say, holding out my basket. This is at least true enough that it shouldn't get either of us in trouble.

She pulls me forward by our still-linked arms. "Come. There is wool in the barn."

"How about a cup of tea? I'm parched."

She presses her lips together, and I know she's weighing her duties as hostess against the rules for newly married women, which call for our socializing to be kept to a minimum. Once we've passed through our Private Period, we will be allowed more freedom, but early on we must confine our visits to Lessons and sanctioned Gatherings. Like the one I missed last night. Only I'm sick of feeling so confined.

"Oh, come on, Rachel. I doubt tea violates any rules. We're allowed to take sustenance."

She gives me a look I know well, one of weary exasperation. "We're allowed sustenance with our husbands, you know as well as I. How else will we learn they are our first priority?"

"I'm sure someone will find a way to remind us. Repeatedly," I say. My words might be filled with disdain, but I am enjoying this exchange—far more than I should. Not only does a visit to the Farm offer me open space, it gives me a chance to use my voice. Though

Rachel works hard to keep me faithful, she also loves me enough to tolerate my vocal complaints without too much chiding.

"Don't involve me in your anarchy," she says, as she pulls me into the barn. "I don't want to start my marriage with a Shaming."

It's an invitation to tell her what mine was all about; I can tell by the wary gleam in her eyes. But I don't want to talk about it. She'll be more disappointed in me than she already is.

"Where is Jacob?" I ask, changing the subject.

She smiles at the mention of her husband, and envy whispers faintly in my heart. "He's shearing. I'll join him shortly. Not because he needs help," she's quick to add. "He's . . . not as fond of the crops as he could be, but he's good with the animals. He must have learned a lot from your mother. Remember how he used to hang around the Medical Shed all the time?"

"I think he just did that as an excuse to see you, Rachel." I give her a knowing look, and she blushes.

"He helped her," she insists. "He's a natural healer."

We step into the office in the front corner, and Rachel stops short, nearly jerking my arm loose.

"Judith. I thought you were up at the house . . ." Rachel trails off, then gestures to me awkwardly. "Miriam has come. For the wool."

I hold up the basket once again, my cheeks burning as I await Judith's reproach.

But Caleb's mother merely smiles and says, "Of course. Welcome, Miriam." She puts her hands on both my shoulders, and I try not to flinch under her careful scrutiny. Once, I had hoped she would become like a second mother to me. Can she read the longing in my face?

Judith drops her hands and turns away. "I imagine before you get the wool, the two of you might like a visit."

"Oh no," Rachel protests. "We were just going to—"

"Sweetheart, please. I remember what it was like, those first few weeks of marriage. How lonely." She moves to a cozy corner of the barn, where a few wooden chairs form a half circle around a small table with a teapot on a hot plate, as well as a few cups and spoons. Judith wraps her hands briefly around the insulated pot. "I think this is still warm. You've been working so hard, Rachel, here from nearly dawn to dusk. And Miriam, too, I imagine. You and . . . Aaron, isn't it?" Her face darkens briefly, as if in disappointment. But that might just be wishful thinking. "Don't worry." She squeezes Rachel's arm gently. "Take your time. Catch up. I'll cover for you in the barn." She winks at us on her way out.

I settle into one of the creaky chairs as Rachel takes the pot from the burner. "What do you think of married life so far?" she asks, pouring for both of us.

My pulse beats wildly. Can I share my fears with Rachel? If not with her, then with whom?

"It's wonderful, isn't it?" she continues, handing me a cup. "Just like Daniel always promised."

The flutter in my chest slows as I sink down into the chair. Rachel won't understand. Still, she knows me almost as well as my own mother.

"You're unhappy." She sits in front of me and rests her cup on her knees. "Marriage isn't what you expected."

I bite my lip and blink the tears away. "He's not who I expected."

She cocks her head. "Ah. This is about Caleb."

The mere mention of his name sends a jolt through me, and I slosh tea onto the hem of my dress. "Aaron made a mistake," I say, after looking over my shoulder to be certain Judith has really left us.

Rachel frowns and sips her tea. "There are no mistakes."

"If one more person says that to me, I'll scream."

"Perhaps you're hearing it so often because it's true."

"Caleb would have chosen me. I'm sure of it."

"How can you know that? Miriam?" Her voice is sharp as she taps my knee with her fingers. "There is no interaction allowed before marriage. Even you wouldn't—"

"Of course not," I say, grateful she is willing to grant me that small concession of faith. Even if she's wrong. "Caleb and I only exchanged glances. I just know."

She laughs. "Always such a dreamer. There is no way of knowing what is in another's heart. Especially a man. Not until you lie with them."

Little does she know, I have lied with a man. Just not in the way she means; Caleb and I are both liars.

"Remember how it used to frustrate us, the Separation?" She says this as if it were years in the past, and not just last week when we were forbidden to exchange a single word with any of the boys. "Now that I'm married, I understand."

"I don't want to talk about your marital bed."

"Don't worry. I'm not Susanna."

"Thank heaven."

"I'm talking about . . . well, talking. Don't you and Aaron ever just talk?" Her eyes sparkle. "After, I mean?"

"We don't . . . anything."

"Miriam!" Her cup clatters against the saucer, tea sloshing over the side. "Have you resisted him?"

"He hasn't asked." My voice is ragged, the words tiny enough to slip into the empty chasm left in the silence of my admission.

Rachel stares at me, the spilled tea soaking into her apron as she tries to contemplate such an aberration.

"He shouldn't have to," she finally says, sounding even more certain than unmarried Rachel, who used to lecture me incessantly on the virtues of marriage. The virtues of anything, really. "You must speak to him at once."

"I can't talk to him. Not about this."

"You can and you must. That's what I'm trying to tell you. To speak to your husband, and only your husband, it's a special kind of intimacy. Sharing your hopes and dreams. That's why Daniel urged us to keep silent all those years. Think of the confusion if we had shared openly! Our hearts and minds would be clouded with all that unnecessary chatter. It's so much better this way. Now Jacob and I know only each other. The same way you and Aaron will know each other."

I yearn for her absolute conviction, and at the same time, I'm frightened. Is she right? Has the intimacy confused me somehow? I'd much rather feel a connection to Caleb. But Aaron and I have shared details about ourselves. He has dined with my parents. Cooked for me. Told me stories about the Outside. He knows my secrets. My weaknesses. What does that make us?

What does it make me?

I jump to my feet. "I must get back."

Rachel pulls me into one last hug. "Keep faithful," she tells me. But she's too late.

22

MIRIAM

BUT EACH PERSON IS TEMPTED
WHEN HE IS LURED AND ENTICED
BY HIS OWN DESIRE.
—*James 1:14*

I'm not ready to go back yet, to Aaron and Lydia and the never-ending piles of wool. So I take the wool from Rachel and head the long way around the pasture, which gives me plenty of time to count my multitude of sins. Loving another man—probably the biggest. And what about lying? I've lied to nearly everyone I love at some point this week. Rachel. My father and mother. Aaron. Not that I love him. But I have an obligation to honor him, and surely lying to your husband is worst of all. And then there's lying *about* your husband, which I do every time I speak of him. Or how about lying in bed too long in the morning, because I can't bear to face the emptiness of my life? The same word for so many terrible thoughts and actions. It's unfair I should have to count them all. It's really only one sin. *Thou shalt not covet.* Daniel's teachings echo in my head. *"Coveting is the sin that begets more sin; marriage is the only cure."* So why does my marriage, condoned and sanctioned by God, feel like a condemnation?

I round the bend near the copse of juniper trees, and there he stands, tall and beautiful, backlit by the waning sunlight. For a moment I think I've summoned him with my lustful thoughts. God created man perfect, in His image. I've never believed this more than when I look at Caleb.

My heart pounds as I check the path behind me. But it's deserted. No one comes this way unless they have to. I made it all the way to the Farm and back without passing another person, all of them busy elsewhere, finishing up their day of work.

We are completely alone.

"Caleb? What are you doing out here?" My whole body is vibrating, as if singing out in joy at his presence, but I manage to keep my voice calm.

He puffs out his cheeks and looks back at me, his eyes wide.

"I'm setting a trap," he finally says, his voice sounding strained. "For a coyote. Daniel thinks we have a problem."

"We do have a problem."

He goes pink but pretends not to understand. "I haven't found any tracks. But he's insistent. How would they get in?" He squats and runs his fingers through the dirt. Probably so he doesn't have to look at me.

I take a deep breath, willing myself not to fall apart, even as my heart splinters. This is how it will be now between us, always. Part of me has known it since the day Daniel and I kneeled together in the baking sand and tried to pray away the sin. My body still aches from those hopeless hours. But this reality is a pain all its own. We are neighbors now, and that is all. Anything else—everything else—has to remain a dream.

"Don't worry. I'm going to take care of it."

"It's too late." The words are out before I think about them, and definitely before I figure out he's still talking about the coyote.

"Miriam. Please . . ."

How can my name sound so much like a prayer on his lips?

"You left me messages," I say, my voice cracking. "You held me in your arms. You said . . ." I rub my knuckles with my thumb. My cheeks are fiery red, I'm sure, and not because of the midday heat. Sometime this past week, I began to doubt. Did any of it mean what I thought it did? Maybe I assigned too much import to what were just scratches in the dirt. Perhaps I exaggerated the heat of his voice, the urgency of his breath on my neck. How much was my imagination? It's so hard to keep my thoughts clear when I'm never allowed to speak them.

But somehow, I find the courage to ask, "Was it all a lie?"

"*You're* calling *me* a liar? After what you . . ." He steps toward me, but pivots and kicks the fence when I back away.

"After I what? What did I do that was so terrible?" I shouldn't push him. It's spiteful. I know what I did. I was punished for it, and for all I know, he was punished, too, for refusing to choose. But I need to hear him say that he doesn't want me anymore.

"Daniel told me." He threads his fingers through the wire and grips it so tight his fingers turn white. "About you and Aaron. That you and he . . . were together. Before the Matrimony."

Hot tears and words of protest claw their way up my throat, but it's so tight I can't even breathe, much less speak or cry. Caleb can't look me in the eye. He hates me now. I deserve this. It's like Daniel said— my sin has touched everyone.

"It's true, then," he whispers. He reaches out a shaky hand, and suddenly I know that even though he may hate me for what I've done, he still wants to touch me, as much as I want him to. I can read it in the twitching of his fingers, in the way his sad gaze caresses me. "How could you?"

"He'd been bitten by a rattler. What was I supposed to do, leave him there? He could have died." I dash away a tear. "You know the treatment as well as I."

His expression changes in a matter of seconds, but I don't know him well enough to read them all. Sadness to disbelief, maybe? Does he think I'm lying?

"What are you talking about?"

"The night of the Matrimony. When I . . . touched Aaron. That's what you're asking, isn't it? Why I would risk everything for him? I know it was wrong, but I still think—"

"Does Daniel know this?"

"Daniel knows everything."

"It was just that one time? And all you did was . . . ?"

When he trails off, I know he's thinking of the intimacy. Of my lips on Aaron's body. "It was his heel. And he was barely conscious. What else could we have done?"

"Daniel made it sound like . . ." His shoulders sag.

"Made it sound like what?"

"He called you an adulteress."

"Adulteress?" I bark a laugh, but my throat is tight with fury. "That's ridiculous. Me? I'm barely allowed to speak, much less make a choice to do *that*. But it always comes back to us, doesn't it? The *girl's* temptation, the girl's fault. Maybe men should take some responsibility for once. If you all feel tempted, maybe it's your own weakness and not ours." I whirl to leave, but Caleb grabs my arm and I drop my basket.

"Wait. I'm sorry. You're right. It wasn't your fault. It was Marcus and Aaron. They . . ." He breaks off and shakes his head.

"They what?"

"Never mind. Look, I tried to make this right. I spoke to Daniel."

Hope flares in my chest. "And? What did he say? Has he changed his mind? He told me it was a sin, that I would be Banished if I asked for . . ."

It isn't until he says, "Asked for what?" that I realize we don't know each other well enough to leave sentences unfinished. But I also can't bring myself to say the word *divorce*.

After a second, before I can reply, Caleb says, "Daniel says your marriage is God's will."

"God's will." I know this; everyone has told me. If anything, hearing Caleb say it out loud should finally make the reality easier for me to swallow, or at least make these feelings go away. Instead, my arm burns where he holds me, and the temptation to touch him, to feel his skin beneath mine, is so great I am light-headed.

"So that's it? We just . . . forget about each other?" I don't think I can. Is it easier for him?

"What else can we do?" He looks down, at his hand on me, and lets go. As if I'm on fire.

I understand why. Even being together, alone, feels like sinning. But I'm enjoying it far too much to stop now.

"I could help you," I say, gesturing toward the box. Though really, I can't. Not without inflicting punishment on both of us. But I'll try. "We're still neighbors, right?"

He looks away, then back at me, as if weighing the decision in his mind. "Sure," he finally says. "I could use some help."

The lure of even a few moments more with him is too strong to ignore. I pick up the box at his feet and shake it, the contents inside shifting with a metallic jangle. "So this is the coyote trap?" I'm tongue-tied suddenly. Why is it easier to talk of marriage and adultery than of ordinary things? Aaron and I talk about mundane things every day—food, wool, the weather. Is this awkwardness normal? Is this the difference between love and marriage?

Caleb nods, apparently as lost for words as I am. "Daniel thinks one might have gotten in somehow. Maybe it slipped in under the fence."

"I hear them at night. Howling. They sound sad."

"They howl to communicate. So maybe they're trying to find the lost one? But I don't think they have feelings."

"Lost is a feeling." It's how I've been feeling all week. But as the sun sinks and the long shadows stretch out into the desert, pulling Caleb and me into their comforting arms, somehow I don't feel quite as lost anymore. How sad that I feel less alone here than in the company of my own husband.

I hand Caleb the box. "Where are you going to put it?"

"I was thinking of the bathhouse," he says, nodding toward the burnt-out shell of the building at the bottom of the hill. "It'd be the perfect place for a den."

"But . . . has anyone actually seen this coyote? What did Daniel say, exactly? Are you sure he meant a real animal? Not a dream he had?" Daniel dreams about animals a lot. And monsters. And natural disasters. Honestly, it's a wonder the man gets any rest at all.

"Yes, I'm sure." He shifts his gaze from me to the space above my head. "I mean, he talked about coyotes. And danger. But he also called you . . . well, you know." His ears go pink.

Just then, a coyote howls in the distance, as if we've provoked it with our talk.

"That sounded closer than usual," I whisper, backing up against a tree trunk.

Caleb edges away from me and makes a show of scanning the area for predators. I can't see any in the encroaching darkness, but that doesn't mean they aren't there.

"You should go," he says, placing a hand on the branch above me. "It might not be safe out here."

But he leans toward me, even as his words deny me, and I can feel his breath on my face, sweeter than the wildflowers surrounding us. He steps closer, and the distance between us becomes a roaring fire consuming air and reason. His gaze is locked on mine, and my heart pounds with every blink of his lashes. My skin grows hot as I remember that night in the cave, the softness of his skin against mine. I should look away from those smoldering eyes, forget about those strong arms. Instead, I give in and move closer, tripping over the basket at my feet. My cheek brushes his chin, and it burns gloriously.

Then I tip my face to his.

His lips feel like the sun on my skin, like coming home, like touching the face of God. I am heady with the pleasure of his arms around me, the smell of verbena heavy in the air. How can anything so amazing be a sin?

We drink each other in until we're both spent and breathless, our thirst for each other incited rather than slaked. When we break apart, our breathing is the only sound other than the wind blowing mournfully through the tree branches, a sort of wailing that makes me cry.

Dear God, what have we done?

I press my hand against my mouth, but I'm not sure if it's to keep myself from speaking or from kissing him again.

"Miriam. I'm sorr—"

He's interrupted by a muffled cry. A human this time, not an animal, and it comes from somewhere behind us, down the hill.

Caleb pulls me down, so that we're crouching behind a tall creosote bush.

"Who is it?" My heart is pounding, both from the kiss and from fear. If we're caught here like this, I'll be branded an adulteress and Banished. No question.

The voice grows louder. It's unmistakably a woman, and she's upset. Angry. Has she already seen us?

"It's Susanna," Caleb says, shoving my basket into my hands, his whisper hardly more than hot breath in my ear. "Run."

23

CALEB

Susanna is on the bend beneath the hill, just outside the old bathhouse.
And she's not alone. Her companion is a man, judging by his pants,
but his face is hidden in the shadows of the wreck. Though I can't tell
who it is from this distance, his wild gesticulations tell me he's angry.

The bathhouse is a remnant from the inhabitants who settled
here before New Jerusalem was founded. It's a burnt-out structure,
home now to only a large number of rats and scorpions. Lightning
struck it back in the early days of the city. Daniel was inside, along
with Mishael, Azariah, and my father. Miraculously, God spared them
from the fire, so it's a holy reminder of His power. It's also dangerously unstable. What would anyone be doing in there? The same
thing Miriam and I were doing?

I can still taste her, bittersweet, like lemon and honey. The smell
of her hair, the feel of her in my arms. I love her, and it's a physical ache.
Not only in my heart, but everywhere else. This is what it's supposed
to be like, a love between a man and a woman. Passionate and real.
This is what I've given up.

No.

This is what's been taken from me.

Susanna swipes her arm dismissively toward whomever she
is with, then whirls up the path, right toward the spot where I'm

standing. I quickly kneel and dump out the contents of my box, sifting through the metal. I snap the trap open and closed, over and over, willing the pain and the longing to subside. But not the anger.

I stand as Susanna skirts the tree. She's caught up in her own thoughts, which she mutters under her breath, her mouth twisted. When she sees me, she stifles a scream and jumps backward, her hand on the bare part of her chest, where her buttons are half undone.

"Caleb. You scared me." Her eyes are wide with fear. Of me? Or whoever she was with?

"What are you doing out here, Susanna? I heard you cry out. Did someone . . . hurt you?"

Her expression cools into something almost predatory. "I could ask you the same thing," she says. "What are *you* doing out here? All alone."

Am I imagining it, or is she implying that she knows something? There's no way she saw Miriam. Right? I let my gaze slip casually over the ground, looking for anything Miriam might have left behind. But there's nothing. I hold up the chains. "Coyote trap."

"The only thing you're going to catch in there is some unsuspecting Brother or Sister."

I snap it closed in my hand and she startles. "Maybe they should be careful where they're wandering. Especially in the dark. Alone. Like you are. You are alone, right? Because it's strange. Earlier, I thought I saw"—I cock my head—"a man. Coming from the bathhouse."

She tosses her hair, and I notice a dark blotch on her cheek. Is it a bruise? It could just as easily be soot. "I'm a married woman, Caleb. It's inappropriate for you to ask me these kinds of questions."

This means far less to me than it would have even an hour ago.

Yes, she's a married woman. But so is Miriam. It seems adultery is easier than we've all been led to believe.

"No matter how well you think you know my husband," she adds, lightly touching the spot with her fingertips.

No matter how well I know her husband? What is she saying? That she was with *Marcus* in the bathhouse? That he raised a hand to her in anger? I think of the angry gestures. Wouldn't I have recognized them if it was Marcus? I shared a room with him my whole life. I should know my brother's body language like I know my own. But I can't be certain.

The anger of moments earlier vanishes, leaving me with only an aching sadness. For Marcus and for me. All I want is for Susanna to say something that will absolve us both. Tell me she isn't saying what I think she's saying: that her husband would never hurt her; that she doesn't know what Miriam and I have done.

Instead, she says, "Aren't you supposed to be with Delilah?"

Delilah is being sent Out today. Daniel asked me to escort her to the gate. "Hell." I leave the trap in the dust and take off in the same direction as Miriam, Susanna's mocking laughter ringing in my ears.

When I saw Miriam heading to visit Rachel, I thought I had plenty of time to check the fence line before I was due back. After all, the most logical place for a coyote to break in would be near the goats. But Miriam stayed longer at the Farm than I thought she would, and I wasted far too much time pretending to inspect the fence so I could accidentally bump into her.

I didn't plan to sin, I swear. So what did I think would happen between us? I didn't think it through any further than wanting to see her, maybe hear her voice. Because I'm an idiot. I'm also a coward. And a liar.

And now, an adulterer.

That's what Daniel called Miriam—adulteress. But she wasn't. Not until today. So why would he say that to me? Was he just mistaken? But Miriam said he knew everything about what happened between her and Aaron. Unless she meant "Daniel knows everything" as in "he's our Leader and he sees all." I want to ask him, but I can't. If I do, I'm afraid he'll know I spoke to Miriam. And if he knows we spoke, he'll ask what else we've done. I'm not sure I can lie to him.

But for the first time in my life, I'm not ready to tell him the truth either.

24

MIRIAM

HUSBANDS, LOVE YOUR WIVES.

—*Ephesians 5:25*

Aaron has dinner ready when I return to the apartment. Yet another reminder of all the ways I'm failing. As a wife, this is one of my duties. Work the Mill, cater to my husband, cook his meals. Kissing another man is nowhere on the list.

Will he be able to tell what I've done? What about Daniel? God already knows. I'm surprised I wasn't struck down on my way home. I'm sure it's only a matter of time. A wanton woman, after all, is the worst kind of sinner.

The spicy aroma makes my mouth water. I toss my basket on the couch and rip off my head scarf.

"Why are you cooking?" My voice is sharp, which isn't fair. It isn't him I'm irritated with. But at least if he's angry with me, he won't ask me what I've been doing. Or whom I've been doing it with. "Haven't you figured out by now that men don't do that here? You're making us look bad."

He's pulling a pan from the oven, so I can't tell if the motion in his shoulders is a shrug or a muscle twitch. He puts the chicken on top of the stove, pulls off his oven mitts, and flips a switch on top before he answers. "I don't really care what the rest of the men do. We've both been a little bit . . . overwhelmed. With all the changes. It wouldn't be fair to leave all the chores to you. And I told you, I like to cook." He turns, taking in my flushed face and the spilled wool. I wait for him to ask his questions. Where have I been? What was I doing? Who was I with?

Will I answer honestly? Will I confess? Or will I lie and sin again?

"So, are you hungry or not?"

I grip the back of my chair as he sets down a plate of food. A small piece of chicken flecked with herbs, some mixed greens, a fluffy pile of rice. All of his meals are like this—bright and simple. Even when the Council sent prepared meals, he would somehow take them apart and reassemble them into something lighter and tastier than anything I'd eaten before. He must be getting ingredients from the Commodities Exchange, or from Sarah, but I haven't bothered to ask. I haven't even looked in the refrigerator since we moved in, though my mother probably did at least ten times a day. I always thought my marriage would resemble my parents', but this is nothing like it.

"How is Rachel?" he asks, tucking a napkin beneath my fork.

How does he know I was with Rachel?

He points his chin toward the couch and my basket of wool, which I never did take back to Lydia. "I see you got more wool. Lydia will be ha . . . less unhappy?" he finishes uncertainly, and despite myself, I smile.

"How angry was she after I left?" I ask as I sink into my chair. "Or . . . what's the word you always use? Pissed?"

I think it's the first time I've heard him laugh. I'm not sure why it surprises me. He's made no secret of the fact that he's as unhappy as I am. Maybe it's that his laughter is contagious, easing my dark mood a little. But I don't want to share anything with him, not even this small moment of mirth.

He waits until I'm settled before he sits. "Pissed is right," he says. "God . . . I mean, gosh. You should have seen her face." He's still smiling as he shakes his head. "I reminded her that she's the one who asked for wool. Big mistake. She set me to work nailing down loose floorboards. I think I've got about a dozen splinters." He holds up his bandaged fingers. "Luckily, your mom helped me out."

"You saw my mother?" I force myself to pick up my silverware, ever so casually, gripping the cold metal tightly so as not to betray my trembling hands. "Without me?"

"Well, you weren't there, and some of those suckers were in pretty deep. I needed help. And antibiotic ointment." He spears a piece of chicken. "She says hello. And keep faithful. How about you?" he continues, before I can ask more questions about my mother. Like, did she wonder where I was? Does she know what I've done?

"How was your visit with Rachel?"

"It was fine," I say, spreading my napkin in my lap. "She invited us for dinner. Once Daniel allows it, of course."

"Sure. Right. And about how long do you think that'll be?"

I watch him scoop up a forkful of rice. He's the opposite of Caleb in every way: a thicket of dark hair instead of closely shorn blond; skin and bone instead of muscle.

His eyes meet mine, and I look down at my plate. "I don't know. This is the first Matrimony we've had in my lifetime. And there are so many newly married couples. It's hard to say how long it will take us all to adjust."

He nods as he chews. "How many families are there again?"

"There were twenty-two." I flatten stray grains of rice with the back of my fork. "Twenty-three once your family joined. And now there are thirty-tw—" I pause. Thirty-two is automatic, from our Lessons with Phoebe, when we talked about how the community would grow after the Matrimony, when we'd form new families. Only Delilah didn't get the chance to form her own. And Caleb refused. Does he count as a family on his own? Delilah is being sent away, for Education, or so Daniel says. I know what it really is— punishment. For being Unworthy. But what about Caleb? He is still here, doing Daniel's work. Is his not being a husband somehow less an affront to God than Delilah not being a wife? Or is it just because he's a man?

Aaron watches me, waiting for an answer. "I think there are thirty-one families now," I finally say.

"And the others can still socialize," he says. "The original families."

"Yes. It's just us who need to learn"—I swallow back the lump— "how to be married."

"And what if we socialized before Daniel says it's time? Say we invited Rachel and Jacob over. Just to chat. How does that fit in on the whole sin scale?"

"The sin scale?"

"Yeah. Like how bad would it be?"

I know what he's asking, but I don't think I like the question. Aaron may look fragile, but it would be a mistake to call him weak. His voice is steel when he says, "I'm just asking. Give it a number. One to ten. What if we ate with someone before we had Daniel's permission? What would happen?"

"I don't know." I look down at my plate. "I've never thought about it. Penance? Added chores? Anyway, it doesn't matter. Rachel would never do anything without Daniel's permission."

"But you would?" He grins, as if he can tell he's hit a nerve. "Just kidding. I get why following the rules would be important to Rachel, given her history."

I freeze with my fork halfway to my mouth. "What's that supposed to mean?"

"Never mind. It's not important."

"It's important to me. You're talking about her mother."

Aaron pinches his lips together. "Can we just forget I said anything? How do you like the chicken?"

"I don't understand. How do you know about Naomi?"

He flinches when I say her name. "Daniel told me," he says finally, wiping his mouth and pressing his napkin into his lap.

"Why? We aren't allowed to talk about her. And you never even knew her. So why would he mention her to you? He's always assured us that the sins of the mother don't—"

"What was her sin again?"

My cheeks flush. "I don't know. Something Contemptible."

"Contemptible, huh? What does that mean, exactly? I mean, I hear you guys use those words. *Shameful. Contemptible.* It's kind of vague, though, isn't it?"

"A sin earns you a public Shaming. That's when Daniel singles you out during Chapel and makes you recount your sins. After that, if you're found to be without remorse—Contemptible—you are Banished. Ordered to wander the desert with the wild animals. And your name is removed from the Book of Truth."

"And that means . . ."

"Didn't you pay attention in Lessons?"

"No, I know. When the end is upon us, the Book will be unsealed. And only those in the Book of Truth will be saved." He rolls his hand.

"But in here, specifically. Do you know what happened to Naomi and . . . what was her lover's name? Phoebe's husband. Azariah?"

I blink, shocked to hear his name spoken out loud. Azariah ran off, like a dog in the night. Naomi at least accepted her punishment honorably. Not that it did her any good. But something in Aaron's avid expression bothers me. He doesn't believe in any of this.

"We're not allowed to talk about Contemptible acts." Not that it's ever stopped me before. "Besides, I thought you said Daniel already told you."

Aaron has been nothing but honest with me since that night in the cave. I've been the one with all the secrets. But his face changes when I question him, and for the first time, I think he may be hiding something.

His smile looks forced as he says, "I'm sorry. I didn't mean to upset you. Of course we can have dinner with Rachel and Jacob. Once Daniel allows it. I know she's your best friend."

I don't like his tone, but I can't find fault with his apology. "Thank you."

"Is she happy with her marriage?" he asks.

"Why do you care?"

He winces.

"I'm sorry. That was rude. I didn't think that was the kind of thing any man would concern himself with. A woman's happiness? But yes. Rachel and Jacob are perfect together."

Aaron chokes on his food and takes a drink. "Perfection is overrated."

"Perfection is something we should all strive for."

"'Perfection is not for the pure of soul; there may be virtue in sin.'"

My throat tightens so my next words come out sounding breathless.

"Virtue in sin?" He knows about Caleb. He must. He's threatening me. I mouth the words silently back to myself. They don't sound like a threat. They sound more like . . . an invitation?

"It's a quote. Kahlil Gibran."

"Right. Your prophet."

The silence stretches out between us, until I think the scraping of our forks against our plates will drive me mad. "What do you know about coyotes?" I ask, searching in desperation for a topic that won't upset either of us. "Daniel thinks there might be one in New Jerusalem."

He studies me for a moment. "Doubtful," he says, after a beat. "Coyotes don't have any use for humans. They're pack animals. Did you know they mate for life?"

"Really? Just like u—" I gulp my water instead of finishing the word.

Aaron quirks an eyebrow. "It's ironic, when you think about it. Coyotes get a bad rap. In all the mythology, they're always the trickster. The thief. The weak traitor. When in reality, they're more loyal than humans."

More loyal than I am, for sure.

"This chicken is good," I say, too loudly. I hear the strain in my voice as I change topics, though for once I'm not lying. It's moist and juicy, with a burst of flavor I couldn't repeat if I tried. "Usually, chicken is so dried out."

He wrinkles his nose. "You mean the slop the Council passes off as chicken?"

"My mother cooks for the Council," I remind him, and feel slightly mollified when his face turns even pinker. I'm not the only one who says the wrong things.

"I like to cook," he says again, an edge to his words this time. "Besides, there's a saying on the Outside. Don't drink the Kool-Aid."

"What is cool aid? And why can't you drink it?"

His eyes glitter with a spark of something I can't identify. Humor? Fear? "It's a kind of drink. Like juice, only sweeter. And with less nutritional value. It means you shouldn't take whatever someone offers you at face value."

"Face value?" These two words have no meaning to me when squashed together.

Aaron's impatient, though I can't tell if it's with me or himself. "People have an agenda, Miriam. You shouldn't always buy into their empty promises. Just because someone tells you something, you don't have to believe it."

I can't help but think he's talking about someone in particular.

"And just because they give you drink, or food"—he gestures with his fork—"that doesn't mean it's good for you."

I look down at my own plate as his meaning sinks in. "You think there's something wrong with the Council's food?"

"Don't worry, your plate is fine. That's why . . . Never mind." He shoves another forkful into his mouth, as if to silence himself.

I nod, though I don't understand whatever thoughts twist his lips into two thin lines.

"What about our marriage vows?" I ask, laying my fork down. "Are those not just another set of empty promises?"

His jaw clenches in unison with his fist, and he mumbles something I can't understand. When I ask him to repeat it, he says, "Don't go there."

"Go where?"

"It means leave it alone. I'm doing the best I can."

"The best you can?" I cry out. "What does that even mean?"

"It means I'm trying," he says, his voice low. "I'm walking the walk. I'm playing the game. If anyone suspects we're not happily married, it isn't because of anything I've said or done." He raises his head on these last words, which are as sharp as his gaze.

"*You* picked *me*," I say, shoving a finger in his face and then my chest.

"I'm aware."

"So when are you going to make me . . . ?" I wave my hand toward the bedroom, but I can't finish the sentence.

He barks a laugh. "Is that what you're worried about? Sex? Relax. I'm not interested."

Tears well up, but I can't tell if they're from relief or humiliation.

"Hey. Don't cry. I'm not trying to hurt your feelings. I thought . . . Jesus." He tries to take my hand, but I fling it away.

"You didn't hurt my feelings. I never wanted *you*," I say, with more venom than I expect.

"So you have no interest in me, but you're offended I have no interest in you. Is that what you're saying?"

"That's unfair," I say, though he's partly right. "I just—people can tell something is wrong. Rachel already wonders. So what are we going to do?"

"Nothing."

"Nothing?" I don't know why I'm pushing him, other than because I'm angry and ashamed and afraid. "So this is it? The rest of our lives? We just live like this?"

"Damn it, Miriam. It's not the rest . . . I have a boyfriend." He spits the words, his hands clenched into fists beside his plate.

His abrupt change of subject confuses me. "What are you talking about?"

He dashes a tear with his fist. "I'm in love with someone else. On the Outside. A man."

The chair beneath me tilts, and I grab the table to hold on to as I shrink back from him. I have heard of these things, but only in a remote way, passages about long-ago sinners in the Bible, whose crimes were so terrible no one would repeat them today. "If a man lies with another man as he lies with a woman, he has committed an abomination."

"Stop!" He covers his ears. "I've heard it all before. It isn't going to change anything. Falling in love with him wasn't a choice." He hurls his glass at the wall above my head.

A shard bites my cheek as it shatters, and I cry out. Milk runs down the wall and pools at our feet. I touch my face, and my finger comes away wet with blood.

Aaron leans forward. "Oh my God. I'm sor—"

"Don't touch me!" I shove myself back from the table, out of his reach. Then with a sweep of my hand, I send the plates and silverware and food crashing to the floor. "It wasn't a choice? That's your defense?" I skirt the table, wading through soggy rice and vegetables as milk soaks the hem of my skirt; anything to get away from him and his dirty sins and his pathetic excuses.

From inside the bathroom doorway, I finally look at him—this stranger, my husband—and point a shaky finger in his direction. "You're a man. You don't have the right to complain about choices."

I slam the door before he can respond. As far as I'm concerned, the mess is his to clean up.

25

CALEB

I pass Delilah's parents on the steps of the Council House, Chloe's face buried in Gideon's shoulder. I nod at the guard, guilt burning a small hole in my stomach. If I had chosen Delilah at the Matrimony, they wouldn't have had to say goodbye to their daughter.

No. I can't think like this. I did the right thing.

"This makes no sense. You did nothing wrong. If anyone is Unworthy, it's—" Phoebe paces in front of the door, but stops mid-sentence as I enter the foyer.

Part of me wishes she'd continued. I know gossip is the devil's tongue in a woman's mouth, but I'd still give up all of the meager table scraps my mother has managed to smuggle me to know whom Phoebe was about to name.

Beside the door, Delilah sits on the bench. Her face is pale as ever, but her eyes are rimmed red and swollen, like she's been crying. She isn't crying now, though. She's staring out the window, arms tight across her chest. When she looks up, the ice in her gaze stops me cold.

I feel like I've walked in on the middle of something intimate, though I can't imagine what. They knew I was coming; it can't have been anything too private. But then again, they're women. My mother likes to grumble about my father keeping things from her, but it's the women who have all the secrets. Every man knows that.

"It doesn't matter now." Delilah balls her hands into fists. Her face turns the color of her hair, and so does her neck. As if she's bleeding.

This is the girl whose name was whispered to me at the Matrimony, when Miriam was no longer an option. If I had chosen her, my children would have had hair this color. Little tomato babies.

"It does matter," Phoebe says, each word clipped as short as her hair. "So what if no one chose you? There are other options."

She looks at me like I'm some kind of vermin that must be exterminated. She's wondering why Delilah is being sent Out, but not me. By Daniel's grace, I have been allowed to stay. I don't dare question his decision. Neither should Phoebe. I've had my own punishments to endure. Like this task, escorting them to the gate. Daniel said it was part of my job as Security Officer, but he wants me to see exactly what I did when I ignored the word of God. How my actions affect everyone.

"We've been waiting for some time," Phoebe says. "I trust whatever caused your delay was important? Not marital duties, obviously."

She sounds exactly like my mother. The perfect blend of politeness and guilt. Hard to believe she never had kids.

"I assumed you were with Daniel. I will need to speak with him before we go."

I'm not used to a woman addressing me like this. But as Daniel's close advisor, Phoebe has been allowed certain privileges. It just feels wrong. I glance toward Daniel's office. "I . . . uh, he's not with me?"

"Is that a question?"

"No." Was that a snicker? I glance at Delilah, but she's staring blankly out the window again. "I thought maybe you were asking me a question: Do I know where Daniel is? I don't. Have you checked his office?"

Crossing her arms over her chest, Phoebe says, "Yes, I've checked his office. He's not in. Nor is his secretary."

I know where Susanna is, but Phoebe scares me. She might be the last person I want to have that information right now, especially if what Susanna implied is true. I don't need her mouthing off to her teacher before I have a chance to talk to Marcus.

Phoebe stares at the door to Daniel's private quarters, then straightens her back. "Very well." She crosses the room and grasps Delilah's hands. "I know you're feeling confused right now. But Daniel says this is an honor. Sometimes we have to deal with the unexpected and trust that God knows what He's doing. Keep faithful," she says, and it almost sounds like she's talking to herself. "This will all work out."

Delilah doesn't say a word.

I understand why she's confused. Daniel founded New Jerusalem to keep us safe and protected. Why would he want anyone to leave? Phoebe isn't married, and she got to stay. Of course, those were different circumstances. She was married once. Is it because unmarried women are too susceptible to temptation without proper training?

"Let's go," Phoebe says to me. As if I've been the one dawdling, instead of patiently waiting for them to finish their conversation.

Delilah smiles, as if she can read my thoughts, and slowly unfolds herself from the bench. She hands me a suitcase, and Phoebe shoves her own canvas bag into my other hand.

"Let's go this way." I turn to the right without waiting for a reply. This is the long way around the city, but I'm the man here. They will have to defer to my suggestion. The last thing I want is to run into Susanna again.

We follow the dusty path that leads down the hill in uncomfortable silence. "Are you scared?" I blurt, mostly to fill the uneasiness in the air as we pass the girls' schoolroom and walk around the edge of the housing circle. Since Delilah is unmarried, she isn't supposed to speak unless spoken to, but her silence feels like a personal slight.

"Why? Are you planning to hurt me?" she asks.

I stumble over a rock. In a way, I already have. Does she know that she's unmarried because I refused to pick her? Or does she think I might physically cause her harm?

Delilah stops and hooks her pinkie finger through the chain link of the fence.

Phoebe glances back impatiently. "Hurry up. I need to speak to your father before we go."

When Delilah lifts a foot to pry a pebble from the bottom of her shoe, Phoebe throws up her hands and marches on without us.

"I meant, scared of going Out," I say, watching Phoebe get farther ahead, until she disappears into the shadows.

"Yes." Delilah switches to the other sandal. "But maybe it's still better than where I am now."

Her words remind me of Naomi's letter. But how could she know about that? Is there something about Naomi that all the women know and I don't?

"Where we are now is Sanctuary."

"I meant . . . being the only girl who's never been chosen." She waggles her finger back and forth between the two of us. "We're both unmarried, but it's different for you, isn't it? Because you're a man." She narrows her eyes. Or maybe she's just peering into the darkness. "I really thought you'd pick Miriam. She thought so, too."

Silence drags on, heavy and hot, and I think we're both imagining how different everything would be if I'd actually chosen Miriam. But that still wouldn't have changed Delilah's status.

"You can't understand how humiliating it is," she continues. "To be called Unworthy, not because of any choice I made, but because of someone else's."

"I didn't make a choice," I say, "because I couldn't. And I've been punished, too." Why did I think it was a good idea to talk to her? Talking never brings me anything but trouble.

"Not choosing is still more choice than we get."

I start walking again, mostly to stop the conversation, but also because I want to get this over with. Once Delilah is gone, she won't be a constant reminder of whatever mistakes I made. Or didn't make. As we get close enough that we can see the floodlights above the front gates, I finally say, "It's not like you're being Banished. Daniel is sending you to be Educated. He says you'll come back. Eventually."

"I wouldn't be too sure about that," Delilah says.

But before I can ask what she means, we've caught up to Phoebe. She's standing a few feet back from the gate, around the side of the guard shack. And she's arguing with my father.

". . . between you and Daniel?"

I don't hear the first part of Father's question, but Phoebe's body goes rigid, and even I can tell she's lying when she says, "Nothing."

She has her back to us and doesn't see us approach, but Father does. His cold gaze rakes over Delilah, then flicks to me and away. Dismissing us.

"This isn't right, Han," Phoebe says. "You know as well as I. After that debacle of a Matrimony, we should have at least had a Council meeting to discuss—"

Father slaps her.

I jump between them and grab Father's wrist. "You can't hit her! She's not your wife or your son."

Father curls his lip. "I'm still your father, regardless of how high you think you've climbed." His tone is frigid, but he takes a step backward. A small one, but I notice. Something has shifted between us, maybe because I'm bigger than him now. Or perhaps his anger is no longer a match for my own.

"Daniel will hear about this," Phoebe says, her hand pressed hard against her cheek.

"He will," Father agrees. "And he isn't going to appreciate you questioning his judgment."

I've never heard any man disrespect Phoebe so openly before. Yes, she's a woman. But she's also one of Daniel's closest advisors. She's always had his protection. What has happened that Father no longer cares about any of that?

And what did she mean by *debacle*?

Delilah suddenly makes a guttural sound, drops her suitcase, and collapses into the sand.

Father looks down at her, his face blank, then shifts his gaze behind me. I hadn't even heard Marcus walk up, but there he is, looking dazed, his face flushed and his hair damp with sweat. His clothes are rumpled. As if he's been fighting.

"Are you going to do something, or just stand there like an idiot?" Father barks.

The rebuke is so familiar I take an involuntary step forward before I realize he's talking to my brother.

Delilah moans and curls herself into a ball as the van—a battered, dusty contraption shaped like a moth larva and painted the dull brown of a tepary bean—pulls to a stop in front of our awkward semicircle, blocking our view of the rest of the city. It makes a belching sound, sending a cloud of noxious fumes into the hot desert night.

Father turns his back on her. "Get them in the car," he says to me.

Technically, not my job. But this isn't the time to argue Church law with him. Instead, I kneel beside Delilah to help her to her feet. "I need you to tell Miriam something," she says, looking suddenly more alert as she clutches at my shirt.

Despite the sweat sticking to me—from both the heat and the tension—I go cold. Why would she ask me to get a message to Miriam? What can she possibly know about us? I look to see if anyone else has heard, but Father has his head bent toward Marcus, who is climbing into the front seat on the other side of the van, and Phoebe is already climbing into the back. Only Abraham is within hearing distance, and he sits silently behind the wheel, his eyes hidden by a pair of dark glasses as he stares out the open window.

I disentangle Delilah's fingers from the fabric. "Tell her what?"

"Tell her not to worry. I'll be all right," she whispers in my ear, her voice as insistent as the whine of the engine. "In Abraham's care." She sways, as if dizzy, and I let her lean against me as we walk to the van. "Who's more faithful than Abraham?" She smiles and touches my hand. "Will you tell her that? Promise me."

I nod. "I will. I promise." I help her into the back seat, then walk toward the passenger side. I need to ask Marcus about Susanna and the bathhouse. I try to get his attention before he gets in the van, but he ignores me as he slams the door.

"Marcus," I call, but the van is pulling out, and I have to step back. He looks past me, back toward the city. Searching for something. Or someone.

Susanna? Would he really hurt his wife?

"Why is Marcus going?" I ask, after Thomas goes to close the gates behind them and Father and I are alone.

"It was Daniel's suggestion." Father yanks on the collar of his shirt with both hands, then smooths out his sleeves. "He didn't want to go at first, but I persuaded him. Your brother needs to get back in the Prophet's good graces. He hasn't been as fortunate as you."

Fortunate. Father *would* think it's all luck. No mention of how hard I've worked to earn Daniel's respect. Or how much I've sacrificed. Marcus is married to the woman he loves and I'm alone and yet I'm the fortunate one? I'll never understand my father.

"I'm assuming Daniel only agreed to let him go to scare him," Father continues. "Give him a taste of what real suffering is like."

Am I only imagining it, or is this message meant more for me? And if it's truly as dangerous Outside as we've all been taught, why send any of them Out at all?

26

MIRIAM

WIVES, SUBMIT TO YOUR HUSBANDS.

—*Ephesians 5:22*

I lock myself in the bathroom. It's the only place in this apartment—in my life—in which I'm allowed privacy. I stare into the mirror, at the cut on my face, and sing one of my mother's songs for comfort.

"Miriam? Please open the door."

Apparently, both time alone and privacy are privileges I don't deserve.

I'm tempted to ignore him, but he is my husband. Will this ever be my struggle: Honor him, because I have been told I must? Because it's God's will? And yet, what choice do I have? Daniel will not unbind us; he's already made that clear. Of course, that was back when I thought I was married to a boy, not a heathen. Perhaps now he'll reconsider.

"I have a confession to make," Aaron says, when I open the door.

"Another one?"

A ghost of a grin flits across his face. "This one isn't quite as shocking. I looked at the papers. From your bedroom? The song lyrics?"

"How did you know . . . ?" I whisper, then shake my head. "It's not allowed. My mother . . . used to sing to me. She stopped when she realized I might repeat the words where someone else would hear them. Some of her songs I've forgotten, so I had to make up my own. I wrote them down so I wouldn't lose those, too."

"Well, I'm glad you did. They shouldn't be lost. You have a beautiful voice." Aaron holds something out to me. It's a Joshua tree blossom. "So now I know your secret, and you know mine. Truce?"

I take the peace offering from him, the wilted petals soft in my palm.

"It fell out of your hair. That night. In the desert." He blushes and looks at his feet.

"And you've kept it all this time?"

"It's a reminder to me that not everyone here is a terrible person." He points at my cheek. "We need to clean that up," he adds.

I duck out of his reach and he pushes past me to the sink, where he wets a washcloth and then gently wipes the blood from my face.

He is standing so close I can count the hairs on his upper lip. I turn my head away, idly stroking the soft petals of the flower.

"Can we talk about this?" he asks.

"What more is there to say? I assume you're telling the truth." I grimace. "I don't need details."

"I shouldn't have lied." He rinses the cloth and wrings it out over the sink, then opens the medicine cabinet.

"Words are precious. Only a man would waste them by stating the obvious." I try to leave, but he puts out a hand to stop me, turning me toward the toilet. He gestures for me to sit.

I don't.

"Look, you have no idea . . ." He trails off and wipes his forehead with the back of his hand. "I didn't mean to screw things up this bad. You have to know that."

A terrible idea has begun to nibble at me, like a rat on rotting food. I've prayed for a way to end the marriage, and God has provided one. Daniel will be furious, but he won't make me stay married to an aberration like Aaron. I will be free.

"We must tell Daniel."

Aaron doesn't respond. I say it again, quieter, determined.

He finally meets my gaze in the mirror.

"He already knows."

I sit down hard on the toilet lid. "He knows, and he let you choose a wife? Why didn't he let us negate the marriage? What can he possibly expect from us?"

Aaron kneels in front of me, dotting ointment onto my cut. "You're only partly right," he says. "Daniel knows, but he didn't let me choose. He *made* me choose."

"But . . . why would he do a stupid thing like that?"

It's the first time I've ever questioned Daniel's authority out loud, and the words lie heavy between us, a boulder that has shifted precariously, threatening a landslide of doubts I'm afraid to voice. A tear slides down my cheek and over Aaron's thumb. "How does he expect us to . . . ?" Embarrassment chokes off the sentence.

"He expects my wife to change my mind."

"That's not going to happen."

He peels open a Band-Aid and presses it against my cheek. "Brutally honest. That's my Miriam." His face darkens. "I can't believe your mouth hasn't gotten you into more trouble."

"You'd be surprised."

He cocks his head to the side.

"There are many things you don't know about me. Maybe not as many as I don't know about you . . ." But I can't finish. It sounds like an invitation for intimacies I'm not ready to hear.

He stands and throws the wrapper into the trash can. "One secret at a time," he says.

After a few moments of silence, I find some courage. "Who is he?" I shouldn't care, but once again, my mouth is ahead of my mind.

"His name is Tucker."

"And if you are both . . . men, then who chooses whom?" It may be wrong to ask, but I can't help myself; I'm curious. These are the kinds of sins I've wondered about my whole life.

"It's not like that in the real . . . out there. You just, I don't know, you meet someone you like, you start up a conversation, and if you're both interested in each other, you go out."

"Out where? Aren't you already Out?"

"Out like on a date. To dinner. Or a movie, or something."

"When did you find time for all that?"

"Our days aren't as regimented. You have free time—days off. And you get to choose how you spend them. Sometimes we'd just pack up and spend the whole day at the beach."

Though I am dying to hear more about the beach my mother used to sing of, he looks like he might cry. I feel the same, so I change the subject. "And your parents? What do they think?"

He sits down across from me, on the edge of the bathtub, and in the confines of the small room our knees touch. I shift mine away.

"That's why we're here. To remove me from the 'negative influences' outside."

"Well, of course they want you to find love with a woman."

"Why 'of course'?"

"Because it's a sin."

"Is it? Preachers, prophets"—he wrinkles his nose—"they like to put a lot of emphasis on sex. Like that is the ultimate sin. Personally,

I don't think God is any more interested in what you do with your reproductive organs than he is in your elbow. I think he just wants us to be kind."

I am at a complete loss for words. That doesn't happen often.

"I've had girlfriends," Aaron says, maybe to fill my silence. "My first crush was a girl. Emma Cameron. She was kind of amazing." He smiles at some memory.

"And what happened to her? Why didn't you marry?"

His face goes blank. "It didn't work out," he says. "We were just kids. And I was thinking about what other people wanted for me, instead of what I wanted for myself."

"I'm sorry." I don't want to hurt him with painful memories, but something else he said has caught my curiosity. "She had two names?"

He shifts his feet and glances toward the living room, at the mounted speaker. "Do those things work both ways?"

"Both ways? They're for us to hear Daniel's word. Why would he need to listen to us?"

An embarrassed silence falls between us as I wait for an answer and he struggles to find one.

"Right," he finally says. "Everyone on the Outside has more than one name. Most of them have three, sometimes more. But everyone has at least two. Except maybe rock stars. But they don't really count. They usually change theirs."

"What are rock stars?"

"Musicians. Famous people."

"Musicians?" I lean toward him.

"Yeah. People sing and play music Outside. As much as they want. Some do it for a living."

The thought is an ache so deep, for a moment I can't breathe.

He glances at the ceiling once more. "I've got three names, in case you're curious. Aaron Okita Thompson."

"Was it always Aaron? Or did you change it?"

"No, I was always Aaron." He grimaces. "And to answer your next question, my parents weren't always Abraham and Sarah. But Daniel really encourages the biblical names. There was no way I was taking Isaac, so I guess I got lucky."

"Why not Isaac?" But I can guess the answer, even before he speaks.

"Are you kidding? Abraham sacrifices Isaac." He shudders. "I didn't want to give them any ideas. Fortunately, since there's an Aaron in the Bible, he didn't push too hard."

"And what about Okita? And Thompson? Why do you need so many names?"

He stretches out his legs, putting his feet on either side of mine. "It's mostly to keep track of who's who, I guess. I mean, there are a million Aarons. Thompson sets me apart. And it identifies my family. We all share the same last name," he says. "My mom and my dad and his parents and grandparents. And Okita was my mom's last name. Before she married my dad."

"She had to change it to match him? The Outside must be a scary place, if you have to share a name to stay connected. We're all family in New Jerusalem," I tell him. "And there is only one of each of us." The words echo off the white block tile like hollow excuses.

A strange look passes over his face, but all he says is "*You* are an individual. I'm not so sure about the others."

I think he means it as a compliment. But the bandage is enough. I don't want his praise, so I change the subject. "And what does Tucker think of you being here?" It's probably a sin to even think of such things, much less talk about them. But this is the first concrete picture

I've gotten of the sins that have been preached to me my whole life, and my curiosity outweighs my shame.

"He thinks this is a terrible idea." He chokes on the words. "Or he did. I assume he wants me to come home, but I don't know. We aren't allowed communication with Outsiders. And even if we were, I'm sure I wouldn't be allowed communication with him."

Even though I know Aaron is a sinner, my heart breaks a little for him. "Is he your coyote?"

"Maybe. We weren't together long enough before I came here for me to really know. We'll see if he's still . . ." He shakes his head, a lock of hair falling across his forehead. "Anyway. You know what it's like. To think you love someone you can't be with."

So he knows about Caleb. It's true Aaron and I do have this heartbreak in common, but something he says bothers me. "What do you mean, I *think* I love him?"

"I mean you barely know him. Sure, your life would be easier if you'd married Caleb," he continues quickly. "But sometimes, love means having to sacrifice your vision of perfection. If you're lucky, you end up with something better than you ever imagined. And if not"— he shrugs—"well, love's a gamble. There aren't any guarantees."

"But other people?" I ask. "If you hurt them, is love worth that sacrifice?"

"You're the only one who can say."

"We were talking about you, not me."

"Fine." His breath shoots out in a rush. "Do I wish I could make people understand? Yes. Do I want the people I care about to accept me for who I am? Absolutely. But if they can't, because of mistakes I've made, in the eyes of God or whatever"—he waves a hand—"will I change myself?" He slumps low. "I can't. And why should I? That's like saying who I am isn't enough. And that's just fu— messed up."

My own eyes well in sympathy, which makes me either a compassionate wife or a traitor to my faith. Possibly both. How can I sympathize with him, given what he is? But what is that, really? Daniel would call him a monster, but he doesn't look like one. He is only Aaron, who has cooked for me and shown me kindness. Turning my back on someone in a time of need—isn't that a worse sin? So instead of preaching, I tuck the flower behind my ear and reach for his hand.

And this is how I become complicit in my husband's sin. Curiously, it's the first thing I've done that makes me feel like a real wife.

27

CALEB

The raised voices wake me from a dream that slips away when I open my eyes. Daniel and someone else, maybe more than one someone else. And he is displeased.

Is this about Miriam and me? I'm tempted to hide in my room and pray whoever it is will go away, but Daniel hates cowards, possibly even more than adulterers. And I need to know who saw us. It can't be Susanna who's downstairs now. No woman, aside from Phoebe, would be welcome here after dark.

By the time I pull on my pants and reach the first floor, Daniel, Abraham, and my father have stopped arguing and are staring at each other in gloomy silence. The tension is so thick, my skin itches.

"If the gas station was in a populated area, she could be anywhere—" Father breaks off as he registers my presence. "What are you doing here?"

I'm so busy chewing over his words that I barely hear the insult. What is a gas station?

Daniel's eyes flick toward me, then away. "Caleb is in charge of Security," he says. "I welcome his perspective."

Father says, "I don't think that's such a—"

"Such a what?" When he doesn't answer, Daniel continues, "Fine. We'll finish this in my office."

He hasn't exactly invited me, but he hasn't told me to go back to bed either, so I follow. The last time I was here, it was so warm I thought I might pass out. Now, the fireplace is a dark void, and the harsh lighting and the chill between the other men makes me almost miss the heat.

Once we're all inside, Daniel standing behind his desk and the three of us in a semicircle in front, he points to Abraham. "Start again."

Abraham stares at a spot above Daniel's head for a second, maybe taking time to compose himself, though he doesn't look nearly as agitated as the others. More like angry. If possible, this is a man who carries more rage than I do. It makes sense. He is—was—an Outsider. It's evident just by looking. His dark hair and beard are clipped shorter than those of the Elders. And at least one of the lines around his eyes is a puckered scar. My mother says most of the people who live Outside have scars, but that not all of them are visible.

He spreads his feet, folds his hands in front of him, and says, "We stopped for gas just over the California-Nevada border. Right on schedule. Delilah asked to use the restroom."

"Delilah?"

Abraham silences me with a cold glare and continues, "She was gone for approximately ten minutes before Phoebe tried the door. When she got no response, she asked the attendant to unlock it. The room was empty. Delilah went out through the open window above the sink."

So this has nothing to do with Miriam and our adultery? Maybe Father was right. I don't have any business down here. I don't know anything about the Outside.

Daniel snaps his fingers in my face and I jump a little, which almost makes him smile. He points to a chair, and I sit. It gives me a chance to watch them all. Abraham is the only one fully dressed; he must have come to Daniel right from the gate. Daniel has one of his ceremonial robes thrown haphazardly over his shoulders. The front is still open, and he isn't wearing a shirt underneath. Father is, but his is buttoned wrong. He must have been in a rush to get here quickly. Did Abraham alert him to the problem?

"Why didn't Phoebe accompany Delilah to the restroom?" Daniel asks, folding his arms.

Abraham presses his lips into a thin line. "It was a single-person room. The window was high off the ground. We had no reason to suspect she'd run, let alone that she'd be able to do so."

An image of Delilah crumpled in the sand swims to the surface of my mind.

Daniel looks completely calm, even as he slams his fist to the desk. "Her chaperones had one job. One." He picks up his chair. "Job." And slams it down.

None of us are willing to respond, and the room goes silent, the sound of splintering wood echoing inside my head.

I don't know where I find the courage to speak up, but someone has to tell him. I lean forward. "Delilah didn't want to go . . . wherever you were sending her. She was afraid."

"Afraid? Everyone is afraid." He gestures toward the darkened window. "It's why we stay here together. So we can be safe from the anarchy Outside." He turns to me. "How well do you know her?"

Why am I the only one seated? I struggle to my feet. "Not well. But she is like most of the other girls. She'd never survive on her own Outside." Her earlier words echo in my head. *Maybe it's still better than where I am now.* It almost sounded like she *wanted* to leave. What changed in that short amount of time, from walking down the hill to arriving at the gate? Or was she lying?

Father doesn't like agreeing with me, but he says, "Caleb is right. Delilah's like the rest. No skills whatsoever."

I bristle at this criticism. That isn't what I said. They have skills. Miriam has her memory for scripture, and her beautiful voice. And she was more than willing to help me with the coyote trap. Before we got distracted by . . . other things.

"You said she was afraid," Daniel says, interrupting my sinful thoughts. "Could she have been afraid of someone in the van? Abraham, perhaps? Or Marcus?"

We all shift our gazes to Abraham, who looms over us like the shadow of a mountain. A solid, angry mountain.

Who's more faithful than Abraham? "She wasn't afraid of Abraham," I say, wishing I could take it back as soon as the words leave my mouth. Damnation. If it wasn't Abraham, does that mean she was afraid of Marcus? Marcus isn't violent. That mark on Susanna's cheek was probably soot. I don't even know if he was the man with her in the bathhouse. I need to talk to him. Why isn't he here, telling us his version of events?

"Marcus was there when she ran," Father says, echoing my thoughts. "Perhaps we can send him back out to look. Maybe he can find her before too much damage is done."

Does Father know something I don't? Even if Delilah is in danger, sending Marcus back Out seems unreasonably risky. And while Father craves admiration from our Leader above almost anything, surely even he wouldn't sacrifice his own son for a pat on the back. Then again, am I any better?

Daniel turns to Abraham. "What *was* Marcus doing during all this?"

"Marcus was in the van. Where I told him to stay. I went in to pay for the gas, and Marcus thought—"

"He thought wrong," Daniel says.

How does Abraham know what my brother thought? Daniel is already angry at Marcus. Abraham is just making it worse.

Father swallows hard, a sheen of sweat shimmering on his forehead. "Marcus has never been Out before. It's overwhelming the first time. He thought he was doing right by Abraham, protecting the vehicle."

"I sent him along to guard Delilah. But instead, it appears that your son is the one in need of guidance."

My father's eyes flick to me, then away, hitting me like a punch to the gut. I don't flinch. I just stare at a point on the wall above his head, my hands balled into fists. Why is that his first reaction? Daniel says his son screwed up, and he looks at me, even though I had nothing to do with this. I've been appointed to the Security team by our Leader himself. What more do I need to do to earn his respect?

"He meant Marcus." Abraham sounds amused, though his face is like rock.

"And what about *your* son?" Father fires back. "I'm told someone saw him with Delilah just yesterday morning. What was that all about?"

Why was Aaron with Delilah? Or is this just Father trying to shift the focus of Daniel's anger away from my brother? I've seen him do it countless times. It's not personal; he'd offer up anyone convenient. Usually, I'm the convenient choice.

"Are you suggesting my son is somehow to blame?" Abraham's tone makes clear what he thinks of Father's suggestion. "Aaron has nothing to do with this."

"Neither does Marcus."

But Daniel shakes his head. "I'm not so sure. He was there, Han." He flicks his hand at Abraham. "Put Marcus on watch. If he stumbles again . . ." He lifts one shoulder. "You know your duty."

"What about Delilah?" I ask, afraid to think about how he might finish that sentence. "Who will go out to look for her?" I pray he doesn't say me. But at the same time, she is our Sister. Someone needs to find her.

"Delilah is no longer our concern," Daniel says. "She chose to run; she is dead to me. The rest do not need to be put in danger because of her folly. In fact, I think we need to beef up security. What if she joins another community? Gives away our secrets? After all, which is worse? A distant enemy, or one who has stood inside your gate?"

Abraham and Father's faces are still, so I can't tell if they share my shock. Delilah isn't our enemy; she's just a girl. What secrets does she possibly know that could warrant what amounts to a death sentence?

Daniel continues, "Beginning tomorrow, the boys will start combat training."

Abraham straightens. "That seems . . . extreme."

"We're safe here," Father agrees. "We don't need to arm ourselves."

At the mention of arms, Abraham crosses his, his black T-shirt straining against the muscles beneath.

"We are at war with evil." For a second, Daniel looks haunted, his eyes going black with fear. He claws at his own chest, raking angry red gashes into his skin. "It's the holiest men the devil tries hardest to sink his teeth into."

"We're talking about one girl, Daniel." Father lowers his voice. "One scared girl. Her . . . mistake . . . shouldn't be an excuse for anything else. Don't make it one."

He's trying to soothe Daniel. I know, because it's the same tone he uses on Mother, usually after he's lost his temper. I'm just not sure why he needs to do so now. Because Delilah has run away, we are all in danger? It doesn't make sense, but I don't say so. Abraham also remains silent, and I don't know him well enough to guess if this is because he's smart, or because he's as baffled about what's happening as I am.

"Maybe Delilah didn't run away." I don't know where the words come from, but I have their full attention now. I can't look at Abraham, though I can feel his stare drill into my skull.

Daniel tilts his head to the side, and Father curls his lip and says, "Don't be ridiculous. What else could have happened?"

I don't know. But I have to say something to get their attention, convince Daniel he needs to find her. What else *could* have happened? It wasn't Phoebe; she's a woman. And Delilah wasn't afraid of Abraham, and even if she had been, I can't bring myself to accuse him while he's standing here, radiating anger like body odor. That leaves Marcus.

Please, God, don't let it have been Marcus. "Maybe she was just trying to get back home, where she felt safe. Like Daniel says, we have enemies. Out there," I say.

"Such as?" Daniel asks.

"Naomi." She's the only Outsider I know, and as Daniel said, she once took refuge inside our gates.

"Naomi?" scoffs Father. "Please. Surely even you aren't that stupid. She's long gone."

I turn on him, fists clenched.

"Temper, temper," Daniel chides.

"I thought Naomi was dead," Abraham says.

"Laugh all you want, but she's not dead. She's worried about

Rachel. And Rachel and Delilah are friends." I'm thinking out loud, but I'm immediately sorry. I wish I could bite off my own tongue.

Abraham gives me a look, but I can't read it.

"And how do you know that?" Daniel's voice is cold, like the darkest part of night when the animals hunt.

"I saw the letter she sent," I whisper.

I don't even flinch as Father strikes me. I deserve the blow for so many reasons, only the least of which is invading Daniel's privacy.

"Get out of my sight," our leader orders, and I don't hesitate. I need to find my brother. Before Daniel does.

28

MIRIAM

BETTER A SMALL SERVING OF
VEGETABLES WITH LOVE THAN
A FATTENED OX WITH HATRED.

—*Proverbs 15:17*

This morning, after the Call to Prayer, Daniel announces that instead of their Vocational Duties, the men will begin a new kind of train-ing. Which means that I must endure Lydia's harsh criticism and Mishael's leering gaze on my own. Daniel also declares that our Private Period is at an end, and reminds us it is our duty to social-ize with other newly married couples. It takes less than an hour for Rachel to hurry down the hill from the Farm to the Mill to extend Aaron and me an invitation to a Gathering in the Communal Dining Hall this evening.

As young girls, Rachel and I witnessed dozens of my parents' Gatherings. We even planned our own. Whom we'd invite, what we'd serve, which Bible passages we'd study. But now that the moment will soon be upon me, I feel sick to my stomach. Which is almost funny, since that is the excuse I plan to use to get out of attending.

But when Aaron returns from his mysterious new training, tight-lipped and sweaty, he insists we go. I have no idea what he's thinking.

We have far too many secrets. We'll never get through an intimate dinner without giving ourselves away.

Just before sundown, Rachel and Jacob greet us at the door of the Hall. "Welcome!" she says, while Jacob merely nods, his arm around her shoulder. I envy them their easy affection. It's the kind of thing Aaron and I will never have and won't be able to fake.

Aaron reaches for Jacob's hand, shaking hard. "Jacob. Thanks for the invite. So thoughtful. And so . . . spontaneous."

Jacob winces and rubs his hand when Aaron finally drops it. "Honestly, Rachel's been planning this for a while," he says. "We were just waiting for Daniel's announcement."

"Sure. You'd need to be ready at a moment's notice, wouldn't you? So whenever the opportunity presented itself, you could just"—Aaron snaps his fingers—"snap it up." His words are friendly, but his eyes are cold.

Jacob jumps at the sound but doesn't answer. Instead, he blinks and looks away. What is going on between them? They're allowed to say whatever thoughts pop into their heads, yet they hold so much back. I'll never understand men.

"Now, don't get upset. It was Susanna's idea." Rachel links her arm through mine and pulls me away, into the warm alcove tucked between the Dining Hall and the Communal Kitchen. The space is not intended for dining; it's more of a storage area. The shared wall with the kitchen has a pass-through window, and the opposite wall is the back of the brick fireplace in the Dining Hall. But it's cozy, much more suitable for the four of us than the cavernous hall. One long table has been pulled in from the dining area. Rachel has dressed it with one of her tablecloths and candles, the flames glinting off the glass doors of the cabinets. She must have been preparing all afternoon.

"Why would I be upset? This is love . . ." I trail off. The table is set for six, not four. And then I notice Susanna leaning against the kitchen doorway on the other side of the room.

Suddenly, I regret not faking that stomachache. But it's too late now. For one brief moment, I consider fleeing, the way I did yesterday. I can't do this. I can't act like a proper wife with an audience. I certainly can't do it in front of Susanna and her husband, the brother of the man I've committed adultery with. I stagger backward, bumping into Aaron. He's maneuvered himself somehow so he is holding me in place, his arm wrapped firmly around my waist, his foot in front of mine. He's supporting me, literally, and I'd be irritated if I weren't so grateful.

"Hello!" Susanna calls, waggling her fingers at us. "Isn't this darling? Only a few days of marriage, and already Rachel is the perfect hostess." Her white dress is cotton, the same as mine and Rachel's, but she's unbuttoned the top three buttons and cinched a red woven scarf tight around her waist. I doubt Daniel would approve. Even I don't.

We stand awkwardly in our newly formed couplings as Susanna slinks slowly around us like a cat looking for a place to sharpen its claws. Marcus trails behind, already having figured out that his wife is used to being the center of attention and seemingly happy to oblige her. When she stops in front of Aaron, my mind chases through a dozen awful things she might say to ruin us.

"The last time I saw you, you were flat on your back" is what she decides on, tracing a single finger down his cheek and resting it on his shoulder, "with Miriam on top of you."

He flinches and jerks away, and there is a moment of shocked silence, though I can't tell if it's from the implication behind her words or the intimate way she's touched my husband. Or maybe I just can't hear anything beyond the buzzing in my own head. Aaron and I may as well be naked and copulating on the table in front of them, the way everyone looks at us.

Aaron's face is redder than mine, his embarrassed gaze lingering on Rachel. Even he recognizes my best friend as the paragon of virtue in this group.

Rachel breaks the tension with a wheezing laugh and wipes her fingers against her apron. "Susanna! What an odd thing to say!"

"For God's sake, Susanna. Don't—" But my words are no match for her poison.

"I'm talking about the night of the Matrimony," Susanna says. "Miriam, you remember. You and Delilah were running across the desert. Trying to escape your fate, perhaps?"

For once, I'm speechless. Some part of me knew Susanna would find a way to use that night against me. Still, Daniel already knows about my transgression. I've been Shamed for it; I've paid my penance. Why does she still care?

Aaron snorts and mutters something under his breath, but I catch only the words "too late," and I hurry to cover his voice with my own.

"We were running because we were late." I hate her even more for making me explain myself. I don't tell them that if I'd known what the future held I would have run in the opposite direction.

Susanna continues, "Aaron was on the ground. Miriam must have tripped right over him. I'm not sure what he was doing down there."

"I'd been bitten by a snake." Aaron tenses, his fingers digging into the flesh at my waist.

"A snake!" Rachel reaches through the pass-through to grab an onion, which she clutches to her chest. Her response is overly dramatic, but it serves to cut some of the tension. "And on our wedding night! How awful."

"Was it?" Susanna is more amused than concerned. "I hadn't realized. I suppose that's why she put her lips on him then. Poor Miriam. Never can control her mouth."

I suppress the urge to scream, but barely.

Rachel rescues me once again. "Who's hungry? Jacob, can you check on the roast? I just need to finish dicing some vegetables." She throws visual daggers at me before turning her back to search the drawers for a knife, and it's all I can do not to weep. Instead, I exchange a guilty look with Aaron before glancing hastily in the other direction. If murder weren't a cardinal sin, I'd snatch the knife from Rachel's hand and turn it on Susanna. I still may have to, if only to keep my best friend from using it on me.

Jacob hasn't moved. I'm sure he doesn't know how to check a roast. Under different circumstances, I'd offer Aaron's assistance. "Shall I check the meat?" I ask, louder than I intend.

"Forget it. I'm sure it's ready." Rachel points the knife at me. "Sit, and I'll bring it in."

Jacob takes his chair at the head of the table, offering me the spot on his right. I slide onto the bench and Aaron follows, while Susanna and Marcus settle themselves across from us. I give Marcus a tentative smile, ignoring his wife. "So, Marcus, heard any good riddles lately?"

He stiffens his back, eyes wide. "No. Why? What have you heard?"

"Oh. Okay." His reaction is so unlike the cocksure boy I used to know, fearful, almost, that it catches me off guard. I take a drink of my water to fill the awkward silence. "Okay," I say again. "I've got one. Where was Solomon's temple?"

"Oh, please. Everyone knows that. It was"—Susanna hesitates for the briefest second and glances at her husband—"his head. On his head." She crosses her arms with a smirk.

Marcus switches from tapping his temple to scratching his eyebrow and angles a tiny smile in her direction.

So, the arrogant boy I knew has finally learned to humble himself. Too bad it wasn't for someone worthy.

Rachel carries in a platter piled high with lamb and turnips. Though we're fully capable of serving ourselves, she ladles the food onto our plates as we thank her. Rachel has always ministered to others, even back when she was the least fortunate of all of us. Now her luck has changed, but still she thinks of us first. She deserves every blessing she's received.

As if she's read my mind, Rachel beams down the table at us, at Jacob, blissful in her role as wife. I'm supposed to be sharing that bliss. Marcus certainly is. He watches Susanna, a faraway look on his face that clears only when she smiles. Meanwhile, Aaron pushes the food around on his plate, pretending to take small bites when he thinks someone is looking. I could probably read his thoughts if I tried. It's a trick my parents have perfected. But we are not them.

Daniel intends these Gatherings as a time for fellowship, a time to bring us closer. But right now, I feel further from these people than I ever have. I once thought this life was what I wanted. Dinners with friends. Gathering wool. Together, we weave a tapestry, sharing our stories and our lives. It's what I was taught to work toward my whole childhood. Could it still make me happy? All I have to do is give up my foolish fantasies about Caleb, and the hope of ever experiencing true passion. Like my memory of that kiss. If I want to end this . . . whatever it is I've been doing, all I need to do is take my husband's hand. Make a silent declaration that I choose him. It's that easy.

Aaron shifts and tucks his hands under the table before I can make up my mind. "You're working at the Farm now, right?" he asks Rachel. "I heard it used to be Daniel's home."

"Yes. When Daniel first received his dreams of—" Rachel stops herself mid-lecture. "Actually, Jacob probably knows the story better than I. Jacob, why don't you tell him?"

Susanna drops her fork with a clatter. "Why should Jacob tell the story? Marcus lived there, up until our marriage. Why doesn't he tell it?"

"He's our host, Susanna," Marcus mutters, staring at his plate.

"What has gotten into you?" she asks. "You've been acting strange. Ever since that stupid thing with Delilah."

Marcus makes a noise somewhere between a cough and a swear. She furrows her brow. "What? No one said I couldn't talk about it."

"Talk about what?" I don't mean for it to come out so loud, or so sharp. I lower my voice. "What 'thing' with Delilah?"

Susanna twists a blond curl. "I suppose you wouldn't have heard yet."

"No one's heard yet." Marcus sounds like he's chewing a mouthful of glass.

"What's happened to Delilah?" I ask, and this time I'm begging.

But before anyone can answer me, the door slams against the wall, and Caleb fills the doorway, his chest heaving with exertion. In one breathless moment, I am beneath the tree again. Caleb's body pressed against me. His lips on mine. My heart stops beating, and in the silence I hear a sound like screaming. I hope it isn't me.

He looks confused. And then determined. Like a hawk that has spotted its prey. He rounds the table, and for a second, I think he's here for me—to declare his love, or take me away. Instead, he grabs Marcus by the arm. "We need to talk."

Marcus stands so quickly he nearly knocks over the bench, and Susanna has to jump to her feet to avoid being thrown to the ground. "Not here. Outside," he says.

They leave so abruptly, I can't find my voice in time and when my questions finally do come—"What's happening? Where is Delilah?"—they are left to linger in the silent room, unanswered.

29

CALEB

Marcus paces beneath the spindly pinyon trees that protect the Picnic Pavilion, the moonlight casting a snakelike shadow behind him. He's agitated, angry, but so am I. And my temper has had a full day to build. In addition to assigning the men to combat training, Daniel also called for increased security. So instead of looking for my brother first thing this morning, I spent most of the day patrolling the fence line. When Thomas finally arrived to relieve me of duty, I headed straight for Marcus's apartment, only to be told by Eve, through the window next door, that he was at a Gathering.

I've had a lot of time to interrogate my brother in my head, to deliberate on his imaginary answers and find them lacking. It feels like we've already been arguing for most of the day, and I'm out of patience. "What the hell happened out there?"

"You have no idea what it's like." Marcus twists his mouth in distaste. "Do you know how many cars there are on the road, all at one time? It's so loud. And filthy."

"I'm not interested in cars! What about Delilah? Where is she? And where were *you* last night? Why did you allow Abraham to come to the Council House and speak for you?"

"Abraham said it would be better if he talked to Daniel." He must read the disbelief in my face, because he adds hastily, "We knew Daniel was going to be mad. Abraham said he could handle it."

Marcus is supposed to be the smart one. Why is he being so dumb now? Doesn't he know how weak it makes him look, to need another man's protection? "Of course he did. But what if he's involved? Did you ever think of that? Where was he, anyway? While you were with the van. Could he have taken Delilah?"

"Taken her where?" Marcus frowns and flicks his wrist. "He was inside. Paying for the gas. There is no Exchange. They use *money* for goods." He curls his lip.

For love of money is the root of all evil. That's a verse even I remember. Though I can't tell you who said it, other than Daniel. "Marcus!" His name comes out like the cry of a wild animal, sobering us both. "This is important," I say. I speak slowly, trying to hold back my temper. "What. Happened. To. Delilah?"

"I don't know! She must have crawled out the window, though how she managed I have no idea. It was seven feet off the ground and tiny. I'm surprised she didn't get stuck trying to wiggle through. She probably wasn't gone more than a minute or two when we noticed." He slams a fist against the tree. "We could have caught up to her. But no. Phoebe had to call Daniel first, and he ordered us to return without her." He rubs his hand, his breathing as hard as mine. "If anyone is to blame, it's Phoebe. Why don't you talk to her, instead of yelling at me?"

Temper is a family trait, and I'm reminded of the bruise on Susanna's cheek.

"Did you . . . do something to her? To Delilah?" I lower my voice. "I'm your brother. You can tell me."

"How can you even ask me that?" He narrows his eyes. "Is that what Daniel thinks? And Father? They both blame me. For everything." He kicks one of the picnic tables, the wood shrieking against the concrete floor. "Daniel is just looking for some excuse to punish me."

I hesitate. If I agree with him, does that make me disloyal to Daniel? But the fact is, Daniel does blame him. Both for Delilah and for whatever happened at the Matrimony.

"Daniel says we're in danger. Because of Delilah. So if you know something—"

Marcus turns, and though he's shorter than me, I take a step back. "Daniel says. Daniel says. Do you hear yourself?" He shoves at my chest. "What about me? About my feelings?"

"Daniel says"—rage simmers in his eyes, and I hurry—"anger is a worthless emotion."

He mumbles a word that sounds like *hypocrite*, and I know what he's thinking. Daniel does say this—a lot—but Daniel also gets angry. Though his behavior is excusable; the only times he's truly angered is when one of us strays from our Path. It's Daniel's job to keep us faithful. When we fail, he fails. And this is a huge failure.

"You should have talked to him. Right away. Explained yourself. Why didn't you?"

"I went home," he says, so quiet I can barely make out the words. "I needed to see Susanna." He looks toward the Dining Hall. "I was . . . worried. About what might happen to her. While I was gone."

"Worried? She was safer than you were."

"You're not married. You wouldn't understand."

He knows me well enough that he can deliver a blow without even using his fists. But so can I. "It wasn't because you'd hit her? Earlier?"

"Hit her?" His stare pierces me. "Please. I'm not Father. Or you."

He's practically daring me to punch him, but I don't. I may not be as clever as him, but I'm no fool. I need to keep my head if I'm to get any answers out of him. "I saw her. In the abandoned bathhouse. Just before you took Delilah Out." I swallow. "She had a bruise on her cheek." I lift my hand to my face. "She was scared, Marcus. Of you."

He grabs the collar of my shirt with both hands, twisting it tight against my throat.

I've never considered my brother a threat. He may best me in an intellectual test, but usually, there is no physical contest at all. Tonight, love—or more likely guilt—has made him strong.

He shoves his face close to mine, his breath hot. "Neither of us were in the bathhouse. So I don't know what you think you saw"—he twists the fabric—"but I suggest you forget it."

The fury growing inside me is as familiar as my brother's voice, though his words are foreign. Is he *threatening* me? I gather all of the heat of my anger into my fists, tightening them. But I don't hit him.

"You promised." I struggle to form the words, to speak instead of exploding. "We *both* promised. We'd never be like him."

"We were kids then," he says. He loosens his grip, and I take a gasping breath. "What did we know? With our stupid ideas about love. And loyalty."

"What are you saying? Love and loyalty are—"

"You want to talk about loyalty?" he interrupts. "That's rich. Fine. Answer me this. Who killed a quarter of humanity?"

As usual, I don't know the answer. I also have no idea why he's picked now, of all times, to ask me a riddle.

"Give up?" He shoves me as he lets me go. "It was Cain. When he betrayed his brother, he took out one of the four people on Earth."

"I'm not trying to betray you." I yank on my shirt to straighten it.

"They are making me out to be a devil. And you're helping them."

I don't know what to say. I've been so focused on finding answers, I haven't stopped to consider what my questions might mean. Do I really believe my brother is a monster? That he would hurt his own wife? Do worse to Delilah?

I want the answer to be no. But I hear the echo of our father in his show of temper, and it does nothing to calm my fears.

30

MIRIAM

WINE IS A MOCKER, STRONG DRINK
A BRAWLER, AND WHOEVER IS LED
ASTRAY BY IT IS NOT WISE.
—*Proverbs 20:1*

"Delilah's gone," Susanna finally says, as she peers out the window into the darkness after Marcus and Caleb. Is she . . . smiling?

"Is that what Caleb is so angry about?" Aaron asks.

Normally, any discussion about Caleb would command my full attention. But I need to know what's happened to Delilah. "Forget Caleb. Gone where?" I slap my hands on the table.

Susanna turns and smiles, enjoying my discomfort. If I could reach her, I'd slap her. Ironically, if Delilah were here, she'd know exactly what I was thinking, and she'd try to stop me. But only so she could hit her first.

The silence drags on, until Susanna finally says, "Out somewhere. Only the Lord knows at this point," just as I am about to scream and launch myself over the table.

Aaron lays his hand on my arm. "She wasn't chosen. At the Matrimony, right? So she's been sent Out. But she will return?" He means to reassure me, but his questioning tone does not.

Susanna shrugs. "She did go Out. Marcus and Abraham went along. To chaperone." She leans forward, eyes flashing with excitement. "But when they stopped, she jumped out and ran. Just took off." She snaps her fingers.

I don't dare look at Rachel, because if I do I'll burst into tears. "So she's missing?" The thought makes me weak with fear. The room swims, and I close my eyes. A mistake, because now all I see is the grinning, gap-toothed Delilah of my childhood, the little girl with even more curiosity than she had freckles.

"Jesus," Aaron says softly, gripping my hand.

I open my eyes and gulp back a sob.

"Who wants lemonade?" Rachel tosses down her napkin and jumps to her feet.

"After all this drama, I'd rather have wine." Susanna brandishes a green glass bottle from the countertop behind the table. "Who's with me?"

Everyone stares at her. Susanna likes to stir up discontent. Over the years, we've all learned the quickest way to stop her is to ignore her or change the subject. But for once, I want her to keep talking, since she seems to be the only one who knows anything about Delilah. Jesus turned water to wine. Perhaps it's not such a bad idea after all.

"I'll take some," I say.

Rachel carefully tucks her fork next to her plate. "Wherever did you get wine?"

"Commodities Exchange," Susanna says, as if this is the most normal thing in the world. Only I've never tasted wine, and I don't think anyone else here has either. Except maybe Aaron. Do they drink wine on the Outside?

"I don't know where we'd find wineglasses," Jacob says.

Susanna puckers her lips and scans the room. "Aha!" She points to the china cabinet. "What about those?"

"Those are Daniel's goblets," Rachel says. "I think they belonged to his mother or something. No one ever uses them."

"Then tonight seems like the perfect time to start," Susanna says. "Daniel told us to Gather, after all. Didn't your parents ever serve cactus wine at a Gathering?" She throws open the doors to the cabinet. The intricate cut glass catches the candlelight and scatters tiny rainbows across Rachel's tablecloth as Susanna pulls the goblets out.

"I don't think . . ." Jacob begins, but Susanna ignores him and passes the goblets around the table. Then she holds the bottle over Aaron's glass. He covers it, and Susanna leans in between us, as if maybe her nearness will entice him. But he ignores her with a determination I can't help but admire. There are many things I could like about him, if I only had the heart to try.

Susanna shrugs and dangles the bottle neck between her fingers. "Anyone else?" She fills Rachel's glass along with mine, then sits down and takes up her own, clearly more interested in wine than in her husband's fight with Caleb, or Delilah's fate. But I'm not letting the subject go that easily.

"Delilah is one of our Sisters," I say. "Someone must be looking for her. Abraham?" I turn to Aaron, but he shrugs and shakes his head. If Abraham was sent out to find her, he didn't tell Aaron.

"Fine," I say, taking a deep breath. "If no one else will go after her, I will."

Susanna laughs, long and loud. "Please, Miriam. No one likes a martyr." She swirls the pink liquid around her glass. "I'm tired of Delilah. Let's talk about something else." As if she weren't the one who brought up the subject in the first place, knowing the distress it would cause the rest of us. And now that it has, she's bored and ready to move on to another topic. "Jacob, weren't you going to tell us how you and *Rachel* ended up tending the Farm?"

Her strange inflection on Rachel's name makes Aaron wince, while Jacob coughs and shoves his glasses up the bridge of his nose.

"Jacob was going to share the *history* of the Farm. For Aaron." Rachel's withering glare silences us all.

"The history. Right." Jacob folds his hands. "Well, the Farmhouse is where Daniel and the founders lived when they first arrived. Out of all the buildings, it was the only inhabitable one."

We've heard this all before, in our history Lessons, though I can never picture New Jerusalem looking any other way than it does now.

"Makes you wonder what happened, doesn't it?" Aaron's question sounds like a challenge, and for some reason, he seems to be issuing it to Rachel. "To the people before you, I mean. Who abandons a place like that? And why?"

Jacob manages a thin smile. "I imagine there was a time when people found New Jerusalem too isolated. It was once preferable to be closer to the rest of the world. Before it all went bad."

"And you guys were just lucky enough to find this place when you did."

"Daniel saw it. In a dream." Rachel echoes the words in my head— the way we've heard him tell it so many times—exactly as if I've said them. Exactly the way we're all thinking them. All of us but Aaron.

"A dream. Right. So the fact that it used to be a prison doesn't bother anyone?" He glances up and down the table, looking genuinely curious, as Rachel makes a choking sound.

"It wasn't a prison," Jacob snaps. "It was a health facility. People came to partake of the waters and be healed."

It's Aaron's turn to choke. He covers his mouth with his napkin. His eyes water and he grabs at his empty wineglass, then shoves it aside to get at his water. After gulping down a swallow, he asks hoarsely, "*Health* facility? Do you mean Zzyzx?"

The hair rises up on my arms. "How did you know that?" I ask.

"'Zzyzx. The last word in health and vitality,'" says Susanna, raising her glass. Rachel shudders as the pink liquid sloshes dangerously close to the top.

"What infomercial did that come from?" Aaron snaps. "Zzyzx wasn't a health facility. It was a scam."

Susanna gulps her wine, slopping a few drops onto the tablecloth. Rachel stares at the stain, her jaw tight, then flushes and looks away when she sees me watching.

"What's a scham?" Susanna asks, slurring the word slightly.

"The owner was a fraud. He took their money—those poor, sick people—and gave them nothing but bottled water." Aaron reaches over and slides Susanna's glass out of her reach. "That's what *scam* means. He cheated them."

"He healed them." Susanna leaps to her feet. It might be the quickest I've ever seen her move, though she knocks over the bench. "For my reason returned to me! And my faith and my splendor were restored!"

I don't believe it. She's quoting Daniel, or at least she's trying to.

"Majesty," Rachel mutters under her breath. "'And my *majesty* and my splendor.'"

"What can a heathen like you possibly know about our city?" Susanna leans over Aaron, her shirt gaping open.

Aaron politely turns his head to address Rachel. "Quite a bit, actually. It's pretty common knowledge Outside. Zzyzx is kind of a joke. I mean, the guy, Howe, he made a bunch of money by building an 'oasis' in the middle of the desert." He hooks his fingers as he says *oasis*. "The lake, the hot springs. None of it was real. You've got to give him credit, though. He must've been a hell of a salesman. To get people to come all the way out here. Voluntarily." He shakes his head. "Especially considering that before he owned it, it was a prison camp. Zero escapes, even though there were rumors of secret tunnels. Like the Marriage Tunnel."

He looks from one of us to the other, then shrugs. "I guess the cons figured, why bother? They were stuck out here in the middle of the desert. Even if they escaped, where would they go? Kind of ironic . . ." He trails off abruptly and coughs into his napkin.

Susanna imitates his hooked gesture, then stares at her fingers as if she's never seen them before.

I'm not sure what to think. Why is Aaron telling us all this?

For a minute no one speaks, then Jacob breaks the silence. "I don't know where you've gotten your information, but you're wrong. The man was a *doctor*. And the Lake of Fire is real. Where else would we get our water from? Or fish?"

"If by *real* you mean it's a body of water, then yeah. It's real. But it's manmade. I'm surprised no one's told you all this. The history of your town shouldn't be a secret. Should it?"

But Susanna dismisses him with a wave of her hand. "This wasn't a prison. This was sacred ground. Know and understand this! When the Anointed One comes, New Jerusalem will be rebuilt, with streets and with a trench." She whirls on Aaron, poking a finger, but he's not looking at her. "And why do we need a trench? For the *water*."

Instead, Aaron is watching me as I raise my own glass. He purses his lips and gives one small, violent shake of his head.

Don't drink the cool aid.

Is he still worried about poison? Susanna's already downed her entire glass, and she seems fine. Sure, she's a little red-faced and excitable. But if anything, she's making better points than usual, using scripture instead of her normal insults to make her arguments.

I raise my glass and lift it to my nose, to sniff it, and Aaron slaps it out of my hands. The glass shatters, wine splashing in an arc across the table and floor.

"What the—?"

"Sorry. My hand slipped," Aaron says, as the sticky liquid spreads across my white skirt like a bloodstain.

I stand as the dampness seeps into my undergarments.

"I'll help you clean up." Rachel pulls me from my seat. She shoots a glare in Aaron's direction, but he has knelt to pick up the broken pieces of glass.

As soon as the kitchen door swings shut behind us, I ask, "Did you know about Delilah?"

Rachel pauses for a split second on her way to the cupboard and shakes her head.

"What are we going to do?"

"What can we do? Pray is all. You know I love Delilah, but she was always too headstrong. You heard Susanna. She made up her own mind to run."

"What do you think she was running from?" The words come as a whisper, and Rachel shakes her head again.

"There's no use trying to figure it out. It's a problem better left to the Lord." She hands me a bar of soap and wets a cloth under the faucet. "I don't want to think about it anymore."

And she won't. Rachel's always been better than me at putting unpleasant thoughts from her head.

"What about the wine?" I ask, changing the subject as I rub the bar of soap against the stain, which is rapidly spreading across my stomach.

"I know he's your husband, Miriam, but really? He broke one of Daniel's mother's goblets! How will I ever explain this to the others? And he ruined my best tablecloth." She wrings out the cloth and kneels before me.

"I meant Susanna." I stop scrubbing. "And why did you let her use the glasses, anyway?"

"Oh, Miriam." Rachel snatches the soap from my hands. "You know how she is."

This from my best friend, who's never once failed to correct me when I've strayed from the Path of Righteousness. Why is she suddenly so accepting of Susanna's transgressions?

I stare down at the top of her head. "Marriage has changed you, Rachel."

She scrubs harder, and I have to lean back against the counter. "Nonsense. I'm just saying, Susanna is like a force of nature. You won't change her. Why bother?"

"You've never given up on me," I say.

"Because I know you can be better." She grasps my hands, but I slip them free.

"Why did you invite them here, Rachel? Tonight? You know being with Marcus only reminds me of . . ."

She takes the rag to the sink. "He is Jacob's friend. And this is how it will be. You have to accept it. This Insubordination, this Blasphemy— it was fun when we were little. But we're adults now. You're married. You need to embrace that."

"I have embraced it." I turn to the sink and rinse my skirt as best I can, the stain going from bright to pastel pink. It's strange, but lying to my best friend feels like more of a sin than anything I've done with Caleb—in reality, or in my dreams. Maybe because she's always thought better of me than I do myself.

"Don't you ever wonder if this is all there is?" I ask, watching the soapy water circle the drain. Is this the kind of thought that made Delilah run?

"What are you talking about? It's exactly like Daniel always told us. This is the way to Righteousness. We've been waiting to be wives our whole lives, Miriam. Remember how we dreamt of this? Gatherings with our husbands? And now here we are." She turns from me. "Soon we'll have babies. A real family. Of my very own."

She doesn't mean it as an insult. We took her into our home, but I know how much she longed for her own mother, her own siblings. A house filled with love and laughter. So did I.

"I remember," I say, to her reflection in the window above the sink. She's behind me, arranging berries on a platter. "It's just . . . different than I imagined, somehow."

But I know exactly how. Rachel and I are drifting apart, and it's my secrets separating us. If I were to let go of my foolish dreams and accept my marriage and my responsibilities, I could make things right between us.

Aaron's voice drifts in from the other room. How easy it would be to follow them all down this path. How natural. How safe.

How empty.

I lean toward the window, until my reflection disappears and I can see into the yard. Caleb is out there, sitting on a picnic table with his head in his hands. And he is alone.

I turn to Rachel, who is intent on making her dessert platter the prettiest it can be.

"I need some air," I tell my best friend. "Excuse me for a moment."

Then I slip out through the back door, and follow my heart into the darkness.

31

MIRIAM

THOU SHALT NOT COVET.

—*Exodus 20:17*

A sliver of moonlight slices through the darkness as Caleb catches my hand, pulling me into the shadows of the tin-roofed Pavilion. I trip, and he helps me find my balance. We're standing so close together. Too close. The last time we were this close, we were kissing.

I lean back against a wooden post and he follows and I forget about Rachel and Delilah then, forget about everything but him. We kiss, until hours have passed, or maybe days. I can no longer tell, and I don't care. My world has shrunk to only this space, only this moment.

A coyote howls. We startle and move apart, and I can see my own guilt reflected in his eyes. This is a sin. I need to end it. Right now. I need to tell him that we can't do this. Then I need to go to Daniel and confess. This path is as clear to me as any of the endless passages of scripture I've memorized.

"I'm sorry," I blurt. Sometimes my thoughts trip over themselves and I don't know which will make it to my lips first. I'm grateful it wasn't "my God, you're beautiful," or "kiss me again."

His forehead puckers into tiny lines. When he puts his hands on my shoulders, I melt. "For what?"

"We can't do this." The words lack the conviction to convince myself, much less anyone else, but I'm thankful that my runaway tongue still knows the difference between right and wrong. At least when it's not otherwise engaged.

"You know scripture better than me," he says. "Isn't there anything in the Bible about a duty to love?"

"What are you saying? That we should"—I fumble for the words—"be unfaithful?"

The thought is equal in horror and in thrill. Adultery is a sin. It isn't something I can condone, even for a moment. And yet. To never touch him again? To only have the memory of my lips against his? I think I'd rather die. Sin or death. Are these my only choices?

"We already have."

I close my eyes and breathe him in. He's right. We've already sinned. What's one more meeting? One more kiss? One more touch? A little more time together, a few more memories to hold on to. After that, I'll be strong enough to do the right thing.

Oh, the lies I tell myself.

"Are there degrees of sin? Or infidelity?" He hooks his pinky finger around mine, his touch burning me with a glorious heat.

"Degrees? No. Maybe." I open my eyes and exhale. "I don't know. We're taking too many risks. Someone will find out, and then what?"

"I don't care," he says, his words as reckless as the way he presses his body against mine. "I'm not ashamed of how I feel."

"I'm not ashamed either. I'm afraid," I say, pushing weakly against his chest. His heartbeat thumps beneath my hand, an invitation I'm not sure I'm strong enough to turn down. "We've crossed a line. There's no way back from this. The only way to avoid Banishment now would be to leave before we get caught."

And leaving isn't really an option. It would mean saying good-bye to our friends and our families. Turning our backs on Daniel. And yet, something about the idea lights a match, deep inside. "Delilah is already Out there somewhere. If we went Out, we could find her . . ."

He pulls away, and the wind blows cold between us. "We can't leave. This is our home."

"What about Delilah? Is it true, what Susanna said?"

He glances toward the Dining Hall. "I don't know what she said, but Delilah . . ." He hesitates so long, at first I think he's going to tell me something terrible. "Ran away," he finally finishes.

So Susanna wasn't lying. At least not about this. "And she's still Outside? Is no one trying to bring her back?"

"Shhh. We can't talk about Delilah anymore." He presses a finger softly to my lips.

I shake it off. "Delilah is my friend. Our Sister. We can't just . . . leave her. She could die out there." My words are angry, bitter on my tongue. Because I *am* angry. Is this why I have such an overwhelming need to speak all the time? Because the only way I can know my own heart is to name the feelings inside it?

Caleb takes my clenched hands in his own. "I saw Delilah. Before she left. She asked me to give you a message. She said not to worry, that she would be all right. And she wanted me to tell you, 'Who's more faithful than Abraham?'"

"'Who's more faithful than Abraham?'" I echo. "Is that some kind of riddle? Because she wasn't all right, was she?" Unless she was planning to run all along, and she didn't want me to worry.

"Maybe she was scared of someone," he says. "And that's why she ran."

"Who would she be scared of?" But I think maybe I know. Maybe it's not a riddle at all. Maybe it's just the name that's important.

"Abraham?" I ask, at the same time that Caleb says, "Aaron?"

He's asking as much as he's suggesting, but his guess is even more ridiculous than mine. "She barely knows Aaron." Yet, she did ask Caleb to give *me* the message. Not her mother. Or Rachel. Because she thought I would understand it? Or because she thinks I'm in danger, and might need Abraham's help? "That's ridiculous. Aaron isn't dangerous."

Caleb presses his thumbs against mine, over and over. "How can you be sure? He's not a believer, you know."

A chill crawls across my shoulder blades. "Why would you say that?"

"You don't have to defend him just because he's your husband. How much do you even know about Aaron? He's an Outsider. If he was involved in Delilah's disappearance, Daniel should be told. With him gone, you'd be a free woman."

I pull my hands from Caleb and wrap my arms around myself to get warm. "He didn't do anything to Delilah," I say. "The whole idea of it is absurd. I saw him; he was as shocked as I was when Susanna told us she'd gone missing. If he were lying, I'd know it." I study Caleb's face. "Is that what this is really about? You want to get rid of Aaron so we can be together?"

"Don't you?" he asks.

"I . . . no. How could you think that? I don't want to hurt him. And anyway, Banishing Aaron won't make me a free woman. It's too late. Everyone would assume . . ." I can't say it out loud, but he must know. We've been married for more than a week; they all think I've shared his bed. "I'd be humiliated. Shunned. Like Phoebe." I shudder

244 · *Shannon Schuren*

at the thought. "You claim to love the sound of my voice, but I don't think you're hearing what I'm saying."

"That's the first time anyone's accused me of not listening," he says. "Daniel says I listen too much, when I should be taking action. And that's what I'm trying to do. Just deal with one obstacle at a time."

"That's how you think of Aaron? As an obstacle?" My voice climbs, and I force myself to lower it. For all I know, our argument is carrying right through the kitchen window.

"How do *you* think of him?" Caleb asks me.

I'm not sure I can answer. What is Aaron to me? Not husband or lover, but not an obstacle either. Friend, maybe? Even though he's a man?

Caleb senses my hesitation and leans closer. "There is something, isn't there? Something that makes him . . . unsuitable. Something he might have done. You must tell Daniel."

He's hinting at something. Does he know Aaron is not attracted to women? Maybe there are no secrets in New Jerusalem.

"You seem to know better than I. Why don't you just say it?"

He ducks his head and rubs a hand roughly across the back of his neck. "My father saw him," he finally says. "With Delilah. The day before she left."

"So?"

"And then there's . . ." He presses his lips together. "I think he's in love with . . . someone else. I promised Marcus I wouldn't tell, but . . ."

My heart thumps hard in my chest, this time from fear rather than desire. "Promised you wouldn't tell what?" I ask.

"Marcus told me. They planned it all. Before the Matrimony. It's Blasphemy, I know," he says quickly, before I can respond, "but Marcus was acting out of love. I don't know what Aaron's excuse was."

How can you plan to fall in love, with man or woman? Blasphemy, Caleb calls it. Daniel would have stronger words. But then I think of Aaron, bandaging my cut while he laid his own wounds bare for me to judge. I slowly shake my head.

"We can't tell anyone about this. I made a promise, too. And I'm not prepared to sacrifice him for my own happiness. Daniel knows anyway, so what does it matter?"

"What about *my* happiness? Does that matter?" Caleb slams a fist into the post above me. "If Aaron had just picked Susanna, like he was supposed to—"

My scalp tightens. "How do you know who Aaron was supposed to pick?"

Some emotion I can't read darkens his eyes. "Never mind . . . I can't tell you. It's only for the men to know."

"Only for the men." I mimic him, my voice dripping sarcasm. "You men with your secrets. What are women, then? Property? I'm trapped in my marriage, and all because of some secret you won't share. You know what would solve a lot of problems? If women got a say in who we married."

"That's not the kind of decision women are equipped to make. God doesn't speak to you."

"But he speaks to you? What does he say, exactly? 'Pick Miriam, but tell her to keep her opinions to herself'? Or maybe, 'I'm willing to look the other way on the breaking-of-the-commandments thing, as long as you've got a solid plan to get rid of her husband.'"

Caleb backs up against a picnic table as he tries to escape the trap of his own words. "I'm not proud of what we've done," he says, contradicting his earlier declaration. "I know it's wrong. I'm just trying to find a way to make it right. There isn't another option."

"That's what I used to think, too. But you know what? There is a choice. I could keep being good Miriam, the girl who does what she's told. The one who goes along with what everybody else wants. The one who keeps her mouth shut." I step back, farther into the shadows. But if I keep being this Miriam, I may as well disappear altogether.

"Or what?" he asks, leaning forward. "What else can you do?"

"I can start thinking for myself."

32

MIRIAM

AND THERE AROSE A DISAGREEMENT

BETWEEN THEM, SO SHARP

THEY PARTED WAYS.

—*Acts 15:39*

Caleb moves toward me. "What does that mean?"

I turn my head. Something deep inside me feels shattered. I don't want to deny him like this. But hasn't he already done the same to me?

"You aren't thinking clearly," he says. "We need to talk about this."

I'm tired of men telling me what I need to do. In the distance, a door slams and someone calls my name.

"Meet me tomorrow night. At the Mill," Caleb says, ducking around the back side of the pinyon tree and into the shadows.

I don't have a chance to answer, scarcely even a moment to breathe, before Aaron is at my side.

"What are you doing out here? Are you alone?" he asks, scanning the Pavilion like he's trying to memorize it.

"I needed some air," I say, avoiding the second question. "Did they miss me inside?"

"It isn't me they want to talk to."

"I should say goodbye," I say, though I can't bear the scrutiny I'll receive from Rachel.

"I took care of it. I told them you weren't feeling well."

I should be grateful. Instead, I'm suspicious. "Why would you do that?"

He turns to the tree, and my insides turn liquid with fear. "I assumed you had your reasons for leaving. I didn't think you wanted to explain them to anyone."

"How thoughtful."

"No problem. This is what we do now, right? Lie to cover each other's asses?" He walks away and leaves me staring after him, open-mouthed.

After a moment of stunned silence, I hurry to catch up.

"I'm sorry I put you in that position," I say, as we cross over the main road, "but I never asked you to lie for me."

"Whatever. Where the hell did this all go so wrong?"

He sounds like he's talking to himself more than me, but I agree with his sentiment. At least the parts I understand. "It's like a puzzle that's been jumbled. Like someone tried to jam some pieces in where they don't belong."

"It's my own damn fault. If I hadn't been late, I'd be married to Rachel and you'd be happily married to Caleb."

"What?" This is the last thing I expect him to say. "Rachel? You said that Jacob wanted Rachel. That they were perfect together."

He swivels so suddenly I have to jump back. Then he grabs my arm and pulls me through the line of the palm trees that rim the courtyard, so that we are hidden from view of the road. Alone. "No, *you* said that," he whispers. His eyes dart away from me. "The truth is, I thought about choosing Rachel."

I'm stunned. And suspicious. Does he like Rachel? I think back to dinner. Did he show any interest in her? Any sort of affection? No. And what about his boyfriend? There's something else going on here. What did Caleb say? Aaron was supposed to pick *Susanna*. So who's telling the truth? And how is it they all seem to know these secrets about each other and the Matrimony, secrets that allow them to discount what I've always been taught is sacred? I need to know more.

"So what about Marcus and Susanna? Were they supposed to be married?"

I expect a shrug, or an "I don't know." Instead, Aaron says, "No. I was supposed to pick Susanna. Marcus was supposed to choose Rachel."

He may as well have struck me. "You just said you were going to pick Rachel."

The cobblestone is cracked, buckled by the heat, and he toes at the gravel collected inside before stooping to pick up a rock. "You really want to know how it works, Miriam?" he asks, tossing the stone from hand to hand. "Because it sure as hell isn't some divine selection. We're supposed to pray. Real hard. And then we go to sleep and wait for God to send us a vision of our wives. And if we've prayed hard enough and long enough, we dream of her. Which all sounds great. A message from God? Who wouldn't want that? Except who we marry isn't decided by God. It's assigned by Daniel. It doesn't matter who we dream of; Daniel interprets the dreams however he wants."

I don't believe him. I can't. "You're lying," I say. It's the only thing that makes any sense. "Only God can choose. He's the one who calls for the wedding in the first place. Why would Daniel care who chooses whom?"

"That's the question, isn't it? I told Daniel I dreamt of Rachel. Many, many times. So why would he say that God wanted me with Susanna? And that Marcus was meant to marry Rachel?"

"Maybe He—God"—I emphasize the word—"thought Susanna's beauty would . . . change your mind. About . . . you know."

"Maybe." He turns from me, toward the Lake of Fire, and chucks the rock. It bounces smoothly across the surface with a soft *thup thup thup* before clanging against the base of the fountain.

I have so many questions. Some I'm afraid to ask. But I have to know. Because whomever Aaron dreamt of, it clearly wasn't me.

"So why me? If you dreamt of Rachel. And Daniel . . . told you to pick Susanna."

"Marcus and I came up with a different plan. We were going to switch. Quietly. Why would it matter to anyone if we just both picked the girls we dreamt about? We thought no one else would get hurt. Clearly, that didn't work."

He and Marcus. A plan. Is this what Caleb meant by Blasphemy? I was thinking of a far worse sin.

"Jacob must have caught wind of what we were doing. Somehow. And I was late. He went before I got the chance." Aaron runs a hand across his hair, which shines blue in the moonlight. "I was backed into a corner, and you were nice to me. When I finally made it to the cave, it was your name that came out." He puffs his cheeks and blows out. "Ironic, right? That I actually listened to my heart in there, instead of to Daniel? And look where it's gotten us."

His heart? I shake my head. I don't want to hear about how I was in his heart. There are too many other problems with his words. "Hold on. You said it was Daniel who picked the wives. But that can't be true. Because then Daniel would know you switched."

"Daniel does know we switched. Why do you think he's so pissed off?"

I shake off the memory of Daniel, the day of my Shaming. Of his rage. "No. He could have just stopped the Matrimony."

"Not without admitting he was the one who arranged it in the first place. And not without telling everyone that our dreams—and God—have nothing to do with it. Otherwise, Marcus and I should have been free to do what we'd planned and choose the wife God named for us. Right?"

I can't quite wrap my head around his logic. Everyone keeps telling me my marriage to Aaron is part of God's plan. Deep down, I've never believed them. So what he's saying makes a twisted kind of sense. But then where does God's influence end and Daniel's begin? Did Aaron's parents bring him here to be married off to a woman because God told them to? What about the snakebite? Was that God? And who told Aaron's heart to offer my name instead of Susanna's? And why Susanna in the first place? If Aaron is to be believed, that wasn't God either.

It was Daniel.

Daniel, who built his own house high on the hill so he could watch over us and protect us. Who gathered us here, near the tunnels, so we could be safe. Because God told him to.

Unless that's not true either.

"All that stuff you said tonight . . . about Zzyzx? Was it true?"

"Yeah, it's true."

"And the tunnels? The handwriting on the walls? You called it something." I squint into the light of the flame atop the fountain, trying to remember. "Pet—"

"Petroglyphs."

"What is that?"

"Rock carvings. Left by indigenous peoples." He shrugs. "I don't know much about the history of the area, but in general, there were a lot of nomadic tribes, and they used the carvings to communicate with each other. You know, where to find food. Water. That kind of thing."

I only know part of the words he's saying, and none of it makes sense. "But that's the handwriting of God."

He starts to smile, then sobers when he sees my expression. "Look, I believe the cave might have had some spiritual meaning for those people. Just like it does for you. But those carvings were made by human hands."

"How can you be so sure?"

"We studied them. Back in high school. They're well documented throughout the world."

Throughout the world. So, not special at all. Which means maybe New Jerusalem isn't special either. In fact, if I can believe Aaron, it used to be a prison. I look back toward the city, to the Council House looming over us like a beacon. Or maybe like a guard.

"But why would God send Daniel dreams of a prison?"

"Don't you get it yet? God didn't have anything to do with any of this. Daniel's father was the guy who ran the old resort scam. He owned all this land, long before you guys came here."

"His father?" I've never pictured Daniel with a family, other than us. Though of course he must have a mother and a father. For some reason, the idea makes me uncomfortable. "How do you know all this?"

A fleeting expression of pain ripples across his face. "I did my research. Before we . . . joined. I—I mean, my family—had a bad experience with a community like this once before."

"What do you mean, 'a community like this'?"

"Look, Daniel wants you all to believe it's you against the world, that you're the chosen people. But it's not that simple, okay? There are a lot of religions, a lot of belief systems. Some are more . . . mainstream than others. Some just prey on the weak. And when I was a kid, that's the kind we ended up in."

My head feels stuffed, like too much information has been packed in much too tightly. "Pray on you? How?" I picture a pile of adults kneeling on top of a young Aaron.

"They brainwashed me," he says, not looking at me. "Beat me. Drugged my food. I was lucky to get out. That's why—" He breaks off, as if the thought is too painful to finish.

"That's why you dumped my wine."

He rubs his hands over his face, as if to scrub out the memory. "I may have overreacted back there. It's just, sometimes this place reminds me so much . . ." He shakes his head.

"But New Jerusalem isn't like that place. You're safe here. You've found Salvation."

As I say the words, though, I can't ignore that somehow, they don't hold the comfort they used to. Did Delilah have doubts like this? Is that why she ran?

Goose bumps tickle my arms and I say, too loud, "Caleb gave me a message from Delilah. About your father. I need to talk to him."

"What kind of message?" he asks sharply.

"She said, 'Who's more faithful than Abraham?'"

I watch him closely, to see if these words mean any more to him than they do to me. But he just jams his fists into his pockets and tilts his head back. I mimic him, but I don't find any answers, just the same vast expanse of stars and sky stretching far beyond the limits of the city.

"I guess we could go see my parents," Aaron finally says. "They'd like to spend more time with us, anyway. Get to know you."

"I guess they probably find it odd. You being with a woman."

"Miriam!"

"What? We are alone." I gesture to the empty courtyard.

"Are we?" This isn't the first time he's implied that he thinks someone is listening.

"Yes," I snap, impatient with his fear. "And why does it matter, anyway?" It's like I told Caleb. I'm tired of following someone else's rules all the time, especially when a lot of them seem like they're designed to control me rather than to help me. "Why shouldn't we talk freely? We're married, after all. We aren't supposed to have secrets."

He raises one eyebrow, and shame washes over me, so sharp I shrink back another step. But he has no right to be angry. "You know what doesn't make sense to me?" I ask. "Why you'd dream of Rachel."

"What are you talking about?"

I look him directly in the eye. "Because she's a woman." The last word comes out bitter. I'm angry, too. Not at his betrayal, but because he lied. Either about loving a man or about his reasons for wanting to switch wives with Marcus.

"Don't do this," he says, his voice quiet. "Not here. Let's go back to the apartment. We can talk about it there."

I try to remember my exact conversation with Caleb, but it's jumbled with our kisses and our argument. "Caleb said you were in love with someone else. I thought he meant Marcus, but he was talking about Rachel, wasn't he?"

Aaron presses his lips into a thin line and looks away.

"I don't care what you do, or who you do it with," I continue, though it isn't exactly the truth. Mostly I try not to think about it, because when I do I have too many questions about how it all works. "But you could have at least been honest with me."

"I have been as honest with you as I can." He grabs my wrist. "It's your boyfriend who's lying. I knew I didn't trust that guy."

Like a reflex, I pull away. But Aaron doesn't let go.

"Look at me," he commands. When I don't, he flings my hand, as if tossing trash. "For fuck's sake."

I wince at his vulgarity. I've heard men swear before, my father in particular, but Aaron is usually more civil.

"It didn't matter to me who I ended up with. For obvious reasons. But Marcus is in love with Susanna. I know, because he whined about it Every. Fucking. Day before the Matrimony. So I figured I'd help him out. Tell him I dreamt of Rachel, offer to switch."

I massage my wrist as he stomps back to the road, toward our apartment building.

"I don't know what to believe," I call out. Marcus does love Susanna, that seems apparent. And Aaron has been brutally honest with me about everything else. Why would he lie about this? But he also said he'd dreamt of Rachel. So which is true? My mind turns it over like a ball of yarn unraveling.

Aaron turns and walks back to where I stand. "I don't know why Caleb told you any of this in the first place. If he had just kept his mouth shut . . . You were better off not knowing." He pounds his fist against his forehead and mutters, "What the hell was I thinking?"

"You may not trust Caleb," I say, "but you sound just like him. All of you men think you know better than us what we women need."

Aaron tilts his head, as if he's listening to the echo of my words. "You're exactly right. And do you know why?" He enunciates each word carefully. "Because we're parroting Daniel. Just like we've been taught." He's standing too close, and his lips graze my ear. The intimacy of the gesture unnerves me, and I back away.

"Parroting him?" I'm tired of Aaron's tirade. I start for home, skirting the places the palm tree roots have buckled the road. "We aren't birds. We're . . ." I'm about to say *followers* but suddenly that sounds weak. I decide on "apostles" instead.

"Apostles." Aaron snorts. "Because he's what, God?"

"He's not God," I say automatically. "He's the Living Prophet. He guides us."

"Guides you to what?" Aaron asks, following behind me.

"To Righteousness."

"If you keep following him, you're headed somewhere. But it sure as hell ain't righteousness. Trust me."

"Why would God choose him, then, if he isn't righteous?"

"How do you know God chose him? Because he told you?"

My heart is pounding uncomfortably fast. None of what Aaron is saying is true. It can't be. He's just trying to shock me with his nasty words and insinuations. "You make it sound like he's a terrible person. But he's saved us. He protects us from the dangers Outside." Doesn't he? The doubt itches like dirty wool, and I try to push it from my head as Aaron shoves past me.

"I envy you your trust, Miriam."

And because I'm watching him instead of where I'm going, I stumble and trip over one of the cracks. The foundation my life is built upon is more precarious than I have been led to believe. It's all crumbling beneath me, and I have no idea where I stand anymore.

33

MIRIAM

I CONTINUED WATCHING BECAUSE
OF THE AUDACIOUS WORDS THAT
THE HORN WAS SPEAKING.

—*Daniel 7:11*

There are seasons, even in the desert, and spring is the season of marriage. It's also the season of planting, and every day Daniel finds new ways to tie the two together. Chapel, which used to be a source of comfort for me, is now a chore. Where I once thought I could pray away all my doubts and sins, I'm now suffocated by them. Packed into this room, with the hundred other members of the community, I feel both smothered and exposed.

"We reap and we sow," Daniel cries. As he dances about the pulpit as if the fire of the Holy Spirit burns beneath his feet, I sit beside Aaron on the hard wooden pew, careful not to let our bodies touch.

What are we sowing, any of us? If I am to believe Aaron, none of these marriages were sanctioned by God. Does my mother think this way, too? Is that why she never talks about her own marriage? I seek out her bowed head, across the room. No. My mother has always been one of Daniel's most faithful followers. If she believed for one second that God didn't approve of her marriage . . . But what would she have done? What *could* she have done? All the times she told me, "This is what God wants"—did she really mean what Daniel wants?

"God cannot be deceived. He who sows for pleasures of the flesh will only reap destruction; we all know this."

He may as well be talking about Caleb and me. But we've sown something else, too: falsehood and infidelity. I shudder to think what kind of harvest that will bring.

Caleb. Just thinking his name makes my heart ache, but where it used to hurt from love, now the pain comes from disappointment. Women can't speak to God; we aren't capable of making our own decisions. How could he say those things to me? How could he think them? But I know how. Daniel has sown this, too, this imbalance between the men and the women; unlike the meager vegetables we harvest from the sandy desert soil, the roots of this belief go deep.

Up on the stage, Daniel lifts his arms high and cries, "I have had a dream!" He throws his head back, eyes rolling like sun-bleached stones. A low rumble rises from the room, a frisson of excitement that surges through the crowd like an electric current. Only today, the charge misses me. Instead of the usual tingle of anticipation, I feel only a hard brick of doubt settling in my stomach, weighing me down.

What is wrong with me?

I shift in my seat, peeling my cotton skirt away from the backs of my legs as I try to mimic the exultation on my neighbors' faces.

"And in this dream. Four. Terrible. Beasts!"

But this isn't revelatory. So why do they all act as if it is? The Dream of the Four Beasts is straight out of the Book of Daniel. We've studied the teachings of Daniel since before we could read.

Why did we bother? If we're here because we need Daniel to interpret for us, both our dreams and his own, then why study the

Bible at all? Isn't God's word, sent directly to our Prophet's ears and then passed down to us, enough?

I shake my head, hard. Where are all these questions coming from? *Dear God, please make them stop.*

"Lion, bear, leopard." Daniel ticks them off on his fingers as the rest of my Brothers and Sisters wait with bated breath to hear what these all mean. Even though he's interpreted this particular passage for us dozens of times. "England, Russia, Germany. We've watched these once great nations crumble under corrupt leaders. And the great monster, with its iron teeth and its ten horns—America, feeding on itself. The horns, as we know, phallic, a symbol of the sexual degradation that plagues our country."

"What the . . . ?" Aaron's harsh whisper draws a few glares from the seats around us. Interesting, that he of all people would question sexual degradation.

Daniel slows in front of us, his robes rustling as they sweep the floor of the darkened room. Sometimes, the windows in the cupola above are opened to let in the sunlight; sometimes, like today, Daniel relies upon flickering light from the dozens of candles that rim the stage and the enormous chandelier above the pulpit. "I know what you are thinking," he says.

My heart sinks. Because for the first time in my life, I don't think he does.

"You're thinking this all sounds a bit too familiar." A few nervous titters echo in the room. "But here's the thing. I finally know what God was trying to tell me all those years ago. And this isn't easy for me to say, but I . . . I made a mistake."

The collective intake of breath is so sharp I feel the cut. A mistake? How does the Living Prophet make a mistake? Unless . . .

"I thought—we thought—that the birth of New Jerusalem was the starting point. We thought we had seventy years here. But the timing was wrong."

This makes no sense. Seventy years is straight from the Bible. It's knowledge we've been raised on; it's why we're here. My mother keeps a calendar in her kitchen that counts down the days. If not seventy years, then how many? No one breathes as we wait for his revelation.

"In my dreams, God has revealed the truth. This isn't the beginning. It's the end. Brothers and Sisters, we are at the *End* of Days!"

There is a moment of silence, and then the crowd erupts. Women crying, men struggling to their feet. Only Aaron remains seated beside me, perhaps as unable as I am to process this news. Daniel was *wrong?* Does this mean Aaron is right? Our Prophet is not infallible?

"There will be a war, great and terrible. Many of those who sleep in the dust of the earth shall awake, the Faithful to everlasting life, the rest to shame and contempt. It has been written in the Book of Truth, and there is no going back. The Tribulation has already begun."

Keep faithful. That is our greeting and our goodbye, the mantra by which we live. But I have not kept my faith. Is it my doubt that has brought this upon us?

The light in Daniel's eyes darkens to take on a sharper focus. And as he holds the Book aloft, everyone quiets. The sight of the cracked leather and wax-sealed pages paralyzes me, too. The Book of Truth and the promise of Salvation are the prophecies taught to us from childhood. Everything I've done in the pursuit of righteousness has been recorded in this text. So despite all my questions and doubts, part of me still desperately wants to know if my name is written in those pages.

"The Prophecy has long been sealed, but we know what it says.

The Lord has promised safety to the Faithful. To the people of New Jerusalem. As long as your name is in here"—he waves the bound leather volume in the air—"you need not worry."

Then he slams the Book down on the pulpit, and the chandelier above him sways, candles licking wildly at the darkened ceiling. "As for the rest—the liars, the godless, the lustful—" He pauses and we all lean in, even though we know what's coming. "Once we break the seal, your sins will be revealed. There is no hiding from the eye of the Lord."

He holds out his cupped hands. "This is your final chance at Salvation. If you've sinned, now is the time to confess and beg for mercy. Because now, more than ever, we must distance ourselves from the unrepentant. Cut ourselves off completely from the evil Outside. Cling to me, and I will cling to you. Keep you here, in the palm of my hand. When the end comes—as it will, soon—I alone will offer you up to God."

Somehow, this seems to calm the others. Daniel lifts his cupped hands, and they rise up, smiling and clapping and mopping at their tearstained faces. I must be the only sinner here, the only one with doubts. Because instead of feeling calm, I am terrified.

Does no one else realize his palm is much too small to hold us all?

34

MIRIAM

Do not be deceived: Bad company
corrupts good morals.
—1 Corinthians 15:33

When Daniel finally finishes his dire warnings of destruction and releases us from Chapel, the sun is high overhead, blinding and dizzying. Instead of lingering to talk to my friends and family, as on a normal Sabbath, I run. I make it as far as the courtyard before my knees buckle and I have to sit on the low wall. Aaron follows me and kneels before me as I try to catch my breath. I've never felt like this before. The faith that's filled me my entire life is shrinking, leaving behind a gnawing emptiness that threatens to swallow me whole. I guess doubt takes up less space.

"Are you okay?"

This is his fault. He planted these questions with all his talk of the Matrimony, and Daniel's involvement. "It can't be true," I manage, before my voice breaks. Either Daniel is the One True Prophet or he's just a man, human like us, who made a mistake. Both can't be true. Can they? It doesn't really matter. Either way, I don't know if I trust him to save us anymore.

Aaron shakes his head. "End of Days, my ass."

His statement is so absurd, for a moment I forget my fears. "What does your ass have to do with anything?"

He almost smiles. "Sorry. It's an expression. A stupid one. It means he's lying."

The pit in my stomach grows larger. There's that word again. How casually Aaron dismisses the man I've always revered. "What makes you so sure? Tell me," I add, desperate.

"What did he say, exactly? He twisted that dream from the Book of Daniel for his own means. Most scholars agree those teachings were meant to reflect what was happening in that specific time period. They weren't meant to be deciphered like some prophetic puzzle and applied to the future."

"What are scholars?"

"That's a job. Outside. People, smart people, who study the Bible. And not even they can agree on what it all means. It's not cut and dried, you know? What you believe, where you place your faith . . . that's more about what's inside of you than anything else."

I don't know what's inside me or what I believe anymore. I take a breath and it comes out like a sob. "It's the same thing. Belief and faith."

"I disagree. A belief is in your mind. Something you choose to agree with. Or to disagree with." He pauses and gives a reluctant smile. "Like Daniel's whole argument. I don't *believe* the world is ending. There are supposed to be signs, right? Fire and brimstone. Floods. Locusts." He shakes his head. "I don't remember all of Revelation. But even separate from all the biblical stuff, if things were really going wrong out there, you can bet there would be crowds, hundreds of people at the gate of New Jerusalem, trying to get in."

"That many? Why?" But I already know the answer. They'd be looking for Salvation. Maybe a better question is why haven't they all come already.

"Because desperate people will believe anything," says Aaron. "That's what I'm trying to tell you. A belief is a choice. But faith?" He whistles softly. "That's trickier. Faith is a feeling in your gut. It's the belief without the proof. It's the foundation your belief sits on." He makes a fist and lays a hand flat on top. Then he shakes his head. "I'm not explaining this very well."

"No, I understand what you're saying. But that's *why* we all believe. Because we have faith. In Daniel and in his dreams."

His expression darkens. "*Blind* faith is different. The faith I'm talking about is more like trust. In yourself, in the people you care about. But only people who have earned it. Not some random guy who gets his kicks out of convincing you his dreams are messages from God."

"What do you mean, 'convincing us'?"

His expression is closer to pity than unkindness when he says, "Miriam. You of all people must know this dream stuff is a crock. God may communicate with us in a lot of ways, but it's not by sending anyone dreams of the future. I mean, come on. Haven't you ever had one of those dreams where you're standing in front of the class with no clothes on? Or how about the one where some animal is chasing you, but you can't run? What is God trying to tell you in those dreams? To always wear clean underwear, and never piss off a bear?"

His words are a cold wind that reaches deep inside me to steal my breath. How dare he ask what I dream about? That is between me and God. It has to be. What am I, if I'm not a Dreamer?

The courtyard is starting to fill as the other couples head home to the apartments. "Come on." Aaron grabs my hand and pulls me to my feet. I'm still reeling from his assertion; can everything I've ever known really be no more than a lie? I let him pull me across the cracked cobblestones and past the welcome shade of the palms, toward the housing circle. To everyone else, we must look like a married couple out for a stroll. How shocked they would be if they could guess my doubts, if they had heard the things Aaron said. He must be wrong. But he sounded so matter-of-fact about it. So confident. Just like Daniel. What *would* Daniel say to all of this?

" 'Hear my words! If there is a prophet among you, I the Lord make myself known to him in a vision; I speak to him in a dream.' "

"Jesus Christ!" Aaron tosses my hand aside, then checks behind us and lowers his voice. "Quit parroting all the shit he's told you and start thinking for yourself, would you? I know you're smart enough."

We're close to his parents' house now, and as we step up the walkway, Sarah flings open the door and throws out her arms in greeting. It's obvious she's missed him, and I have a strange pang of longing. For what, I'm not sure.

"Aaron. Miriam. What a surprise! Welcome!" She grabs my hands and pulls me inside, away from Aaron and into the kitchen. Before I can say anything, he has walked off, and I'm left with a woman I hardly know.

From the outside, this house is identical to the one I grew up in. Inside, Sarah has given it her own personal touch, and though I love the pots of herbs growing on the kitchen windowsill and the tiny figures decorating her mantel, I can't help but wonder what Daniel must think of the graphic display of personal belongings.

"They're called netsuke. I collect them."

The detailed carvings—most no bigger than my pinky—are as

delicate and beautiful as their owner. I reach out a hand, then quickly pull it back.

Sarah laughs. "You can touch them. They're not that fragile." She picks one up and drops it into my palm, and I see that what first looked like a ball decorated with abstract hatchings and designs is actually a pile of turtles. "This one is my favorite. He has a secret." She leans forward and presses the carving with her fingernail. To my amazement, one of the shells springs open, revealing a tiny compartment inside.

"Has Daniel seen these?" I ask.

Her face goes blank, and I immediately regret my words. It sounds as if I'm shaming her. "I mean, you probably shouldn't have them on display," I say. "If he hasn't seen them. He doesn't like"—I fumble for the right words—"this kind of stuff," I finish lamely.

She is quiet for a moment. "That's good advice, Miriam. Thank you." She gives me a brittle smile as she takes the carving and puts it back, and I know I've offended her. I'm not even sure why I said it. I'm the last person she should trust to give her advice on Daniel's laws.

We make our way to the living room, where Abraham and Aaron are seated together on the couch, underneath the framed portrait of Daniel. Abraham is big and bulky, and though he and Sarah have the rhythms of a married couple, I can't imagine them embracing. He'd crush her as if she were one of those tiny figurines. I wonder how long they've been married. My parents have grown to resemble each other, or perhaps they have just become washed-out paintings of the people they used to be. Were they ever as different as Aaron and I, or as Sarah and Abraham?

"I'm glad Aaron has finally brought you to us." She takes my hands.

"I told you, Mom. We would have come sooner, but I wasn't sure about the rules for Gathering. I didn't want to get in trouble." Aaron stares pointedly at her until she nods.

This isn't entirely true. I explained the rules of Gathering to him, that they only apply to visiting other members of the Second Generation, not the first. So why *have* we waited so long to visit them?

"Of course," Sarah says. "We have just been so anxious to spend time with the woman you . . . selected as your wife."

Why is it none of our parents can speak of our marriage without choking? Do all marriages begin as a chalky, dry word that won't go down naturally? Perhaps only the passage of time makes the idea palatable enough to swallow.

Sarah links her arm with mine. "Come. I made dinner earlier. There's plenty to share."

The table is decorated with a bouquet of fresh herbs, and Sarah motions for us to sit while she gets two additional place settings from the kitchen, the napkins folded into swans. Aaron grabs the tail and gives it a gentle shake, and I do the same.

"I see where Aaron gets his cooking skills," I say, when she serves a bowl of cold rice studded with bright red, green, and yellow vegetables. It smells of lime and something else I can't identify. The lemonade she pours contains whole slices of lemon and tiny purple buds.

"Lavender," she explains, when she sees me frowning at the glass. "It's calming."

"Aaron tells us you're talented," Abraham says as he shakes out his own napkin.

"Talented?" I tilt my head. He can't possibly be talking about my weaving ability, or lack thereof. A couple of days of Lydia's tutelage have done nothing to improve my skills in that area.

"He says you have quite the singing voice."

My fork clatters to my plate.

"Did I say something wrong?" Abraham lays his palms on the table, waiting for my answer.

I clear my throat. "I don't sing."

They look in question, first at each other, then at Aaron.

"Women don't sing," I try again, and am relieved to see they understand. But there's a flicker of something else, too. Do Aaron's parents share his doubts about this place? Do they question their choice to leave the Outside?

They need someone to guide them, to help them along. A few weeks ago, I could have been that girl. Now, I sip my lemonade and try to swallow both the doubts and the secrets Aaron and I are keeping.

But there is one secret we don't need to keep, not from them. The realization feels like waking from a dream. These are the only other people in the world who know the truth about our marriage. If I wanted, I could talk about it. Because they know. They know about Aaron, and presumably, they know what that means about our relationship.

"Not ever?" Sarah asks, her voice a whisper.

"Not—?" I stop myself. She's still talking about the singing. "No. I mean, yes." I take a gulp.

"But it's scripture." She pauses and looks to her husband for confirmation. "We should lift our voices in song."

She's right. It is scripture. This is the same argument I used to make to my mother when I was younger. And because I don't have a better answer, I give Sarah my mother's reply. "We can sing together. Not alone. We are all children of God. None of us is better than another. The singing of praise we may do together. Singing alone is reserved for Daniel."

"But Aaron has heard you." It's not a question, and though the statement scares me—clearly they've discussed my sins—she is calm and nonjudgmental.

My cheeks heat. I don't know how to answer. I don't want to lie to my husband's mother. He shouldn't have put me in this position. I finally manage, "This is our way." But it's starting to sound less like a mantra and more like an excuse.

"Mom, drop it."

"Forgive me, Miriam. I'm afraid there is so much I've yet to learn about the rules of the community. Perhaps you can help me?" Without waiting for a response, she continues, "For instance, I'm told I talk too much. Daniel says he'll indulge me for a short period of time so I can get it out of my system. Apparently, he thinks I'll run out of steam and have nothing left to say."

"'For if we could control our tongues, we would be perfect and could control ourselves in every other way.'" The verse slips out, and they gawk at me.

"You know a lot of scripture," Sarah says, her voice tight.

"I do. Sorry." I wince. "Sometimes the words just pop out. That one, Daniel and my mother have been repeating since the day I learned to talk."

To my surprise, she throws back her head and laughs. "Please. Don't feel the need to quiet yourself in this house. We don't."

Maybe not yet, but she will. Not because she'll run out of ideas. More like her ideas will soon become muzzled. Abraham will learn to do it, if she can't do it herself. According to my father, this is a husband's job.

I move the rice around my plate as these strange thoughts continue to pour in. Does married life always lead to morose notions?

Perhaps the activities we're supposed to be engaging in are meant to quiet the voice in my head. Instead, the doubts are gaining strength. Because instead of encouraging them, Aaron is supposed to silence them. Which is only one of the reasons God made a serious error with this pairing.

Only God didn't make this pairing. And He doesn't make mistakes. I used to think Daniel didn't either.

"Aaron tells me you have questions about Delilah." Abraham wipes his mouth with his napkin and lays it beside his plate.

Her name floods me with fear and guilt. Delilah needs help, and what have I done about it? Nothing. "Yes." I wrap my fingers tightly around my glass, slippery with condensation. I can't bring myself to ask the most terrifying question, so I say instead, "I heard you were there. When Delilah . . . when she ran away."

Abraham chases an errant pea across his plate. "I drove her," he says, casually, as if mentioning a stroll through the courtyard and not a trip to God knows where.

I pour more lemonade from the pitcher on the table, to gather my courage and give myself time to think. I can't decide if it makes sense that Abraham would take her or not. After all, he used to live there. Or presumably near there. Wherever "there" is. But shouldn't newly joined members have even harsher restrictions than the rest of us? At least until they've lost the temptation to return to their old lives of sin.

"Why did she run?" I ask.

"My guess would be to avoid ending up wherever Daniel wanted us to take her."

"And where was that?" I ask.

Abraham takes a sip from his glass. "I can't say," he says, lifting one shoulder. "The address was in Vegas."

"And you think that's what she was afraid of. Not someone here."

"That's another possibility." Abraham studies me for a moment, flexing his fingers open and shut, then gives me a tight smile. "She had nothing to fear from me, if that's what you're asking. I wouldn't hurt your friend."

"Of course you wouldn't. Who's more faithful than Abraham?" I say, watching his face to see if he reacts to Delilah's words.

But Aaron interrupts, stealing Abraham's attention. "She's better off wherever she is, if you ask me."

"Aaron." Abraham barks his son's name.

"What is that supposed to mean?" I turn in my seat, so I'm facing him.

"My guess is that eventually, Daniel would have decided Delilah had been punished enough. You know, for her sin of being 'Unworthy.' And he would have brought her back, to live with him and 'play house.'" He keeps making his weird finger gesture. "Just like Phoebe."

My face flames with embarrassment. "Daniel isn't like that! He takes in women who have nowhere else to go. After Azariah left her, Phoebe needed a home, and he needed the support of an educated woman." But the familiar words suddenly feel awkward on my tongue.

Aaron curls his lip. "Use your head, Miriam. Educated women speak their minds, and we all know how Daniel feels about that."

"That's enough, son." Sarah smiles, but I see the steel behind it.

He mutters something and shoves a piece of bread in his mouth.

I know Aaron is trying to tell me something. But I'm ashamed to say that I don't understand. After all this time, how is it I know so little about Daniel, and New Jerusalem? Is *anything* I was taught true?

"But . . . Delilah was going to be Educated. Daniel told me. She would have liked that, much more than being someone's wife." Tears prick my eyes as the realization hits me: She's never coming back. And I never even got to say goodbye. "She's not . . . dead, is she?" I choke out the words.

Abraham swallows a forkful of food. "No one's found her body."

"Dad! Jesus!" Aaron slaps the table.

I can feel the blood leave my face.

"Well, I'm not going to lie to her," Abraham says. Then he looks at me, and something in his expression softens. "What I'm saying is, I don't think you need to worry. Delilah's a smart girl. She'll be all right."

"What about your other friends?" Sarah asks, in a transparent move to change the subject. "Aaron tells us you're good friends with Rachel. She's Naomi's daughter, right?"

I nod, unable to speak around the lump in my throat. Who told them about Naomi? Daniel? Or Aaron?

"And she just got married?" Sarah continues. "Like you and Aaron?"

Images of Delilah and Rachel flash through my head, pictures of all of us together. It wasn't supposed to be like this. We had our futures all planned out. So happy. And hopeful.

"Yes. Everyone gets married. When the Lord says it's right." We would all be married. We were certain of it. Though now that I think about it, Delilah wasn't all that certain. She was worried, that night in the desert. Did she have some sort of premonition about what was to come? Was she already planning to seek refuge somewhere else?

"Is she happy?"

"Who, Rachel?" I slump against the back of my chair, suddenly exhausted. "Yes. Rachel prayed for Jacob. And he chose her."

"Like in the Bible."

"Well, yes. But that's not why . . ." I stop. Aaron said Jacob wasn't supposed to pick Rachel. That he lied at the Matrimony. That if he hadn't, she'd be married to Aaron. Or Marcus. I never asked him about Delilah, but I should have. Who was supposed to say her name? Because that's why she was at the Matrimony. She was supposed to be chosen. Which means she wasn't sent away for her own sin, but for someone else's.

My head feels light, like it's floating away from my body. Like one more breath, one more word, one more dark thought will loosen it entirely. I press my hands against my ears, as much to hold it into place as to block out their words.

"Miriam? Are you all right?"

"I don't feel very well," I say, hearing the words from far away.

"It's the lavender," Sarah says. "It can be potent if you've never had it before. Let's get you somewhere quiet. Abraham, help me."

I let them carry me to a twin bed in a room much like my old one. It smells of cinnamon and musk. The sheets are cool, and though I don't mean to, I drift into sleep before I can come up with a logical explanation for the doubts that are gaining volume in my mind.

35

CALEB

Daniel's speech today, about the beasts and sinners and the End of Days, terrified me. I'm still shaking. The world is ending, and there is nothing we can do. In fact, it's our sins that led us here. Delilah's escape. My adultery. Marcus and his secrets. It's no wonder Daniel says we must confess and repent. What choice do we have?

Miriam may think that finding Delilah will help, but how can it? We can't leave. Not now, when everything is falling apart. Outside is the last place we should be. I wish I had made that clear to her last night. I wish I had said a lot of things. Why do I always think of the right thing to say when it's too late? I should have told her the truth about the Matrimony. How Marcus and Aaron screwed everything up. Then she'd understand that her precious husband isn't what he appears to be. But as always, Daniel's voice is in my head. And he would never approve of me sharing that information with a woman. Especially not one he called an adulteress.

Except she wasn't, not then. I have made her one.

Guilt hits like a sucker punch.

I must look like a crazy person, muttering to myself as I take the path behind the pasture to check the coyote trap. It's empty, which may be a good thing. I'm not sure what I'd do with an animal if I caught it. I'm so hungry, I might be tempted to eat it. I haven't had a full meal in days. It's my own fault, and Daniel has made it clear that he isn't interested in relieving my suffering in this area. I'm not used to this constant feeling of hunger. It gnaws at me, like wild animals. Like guilt. I'm far more used to anger, feeling powerful and in control. These other feelings leave me weak, at the mercy of Daniel and his Beasts.

Last night, I waited until the others left and then snuck into the Communal Kitchen and ate their leftovers cold, right out of the refrigerator. Handfuls of cold potatoes swallowed whole, hunks of meat, fat already congealing, torn with my teeth. The food stuck in my throat, and I held my mouth under the faucet to drink and to wash the grease from my face. I felt shame, but also a strange connection to Miriam. It was food we should have eaten together, as man and wife. Instead of sharing meals, we've been reduced to secret meetings where we end up either kissing or fighting.

The kissing. Even now, I can't stop thinking about kissing her. I am strong; why does even the thought of her make me weak? I have to tell Daniel. But first I have to see her. One more time. I asked her to meet me at the Mill tonight. After Daniel's pronouncement, she's probably reached the same conclusion I have. But if not, I'll convince her that we both have to do the right thing and confess.

While I wait alone in my room for dark to fall, I decide to sneak down to the kitchen to see if there's any food left over from whatever Phoebe served Daniel for dinner. I've done it before. Once, I found a bag of tiny colored discs with an *M* symbol stamped on them. They made me think of Miriam. As I held them in my hands, the color started to bleed onto my skin, and I quickly put them back where I found them. If I can't find anything else tonight, I will risk Daniel's wrath and eat them. What's one more sin? I may as well have a full belly when I accept my fate.

As I slip silently through the side door into the darkened hallway of the Council House, I notice a light in the kitchen. Who would still be up at this hour, long after dinner? I wait in the shadows, listening for voices, but I hear only the soft click of utensils against a plate. The hungry beast in my gut howls loud enough to give me away.

"Daniel? Is that you?" Phoebe smiles expectantly as I step into the room. "Caleb." To her credit, she sounds only slightly disappointed. "What are you doing here so late?"

My stomach begins a seemingly endless series of growls as I stare at her plate.

She slides off her stool. "Are you hungry? Here, sit." She pushes the plate in front of me. "Eat. I'll make more."

She goes to the counter at the back of the room to make another sandwich, as I tear into the one she's already bitten. I don't even chew it before I shovel in a forkful of potato salad as well.

"I told Daniel it was an evil sort of punishment, making you go hungry like this. It would have been an easy thing to ask one of the Council Women to cook for you."

I shrug and try to chew slower. It's the first food anyone has given me in a long time. Why is Phoebe being so nice to me? When we escorted Delilah to the gate two days ago, she made it clear she blamed me for the girl's fate, and she's right. I was supposed to pick her as my wife. All of this is on me.

"It's my own fault," I say, around a mouthful of bread and cheese.

But Phoebe places her hand over mine. "You were trying to do the right thing. We . . . Daniel . . . believed that God would choose Miriam for you."

I take the glass of milk she pours. "Miriam believes God should let the women choose," I say, once I've washed down the sandwich. I shouldn't tell her this—I'm all but admitting we've spoken. But somehow it seems to matter less now. Soon everyone will know anyway.

Phoebe wipes off the counter. "That sounds like Miriam." She pauses, the sponge still in her hand. "Would it be such a bad thing, do you think? Perhaps women have more insight into the human heart. Happy wife, happy life."

"Is that scripture?"

"No. Azariah used to say that to me." She turns her head, and I'm struck by how beautiful she is, considering she's probably my mother's age. She has neither long hair nor scarf to hide behind, but if anything, that makes her more attractive. Her close-cropped cut hugs the angles of her skull. She reminds me of the herons that land near the lake sometimes, lean and elegant.

"But . . . that's not how it works. God doesn't speak to women." Thank goodness. If he did, I fear there'd be even more men married to the wrong wives.

Phoebe's back stiffens as she stares out the darkened window. I can't tell if she's sad or angry when she says, very quietly, "What would you know of our communication with God?"

"I just . . . I would know. Daniel would have told us."

"Because you're a man?" She shakes her head. "This must be hard for you. You hold all the power. I can understand that even the idea of giving any of that up is frightening."

"We don't hold all the power. I used to think that, but . . . you women have a certain power, too. Over us. I sometimes feel like you know more than we do." I duck my head. I sound stupid. I shouldn't have admitted that to Phoebe. But how is it that Miriam can consume my every thought, even when Daniel has told me it isn't right? And the night that Susanna tried to undress in front of me. She stirred something in me, even though she belongs to my brother. On top of that, she's a terrible person. Maybe an adulteress. And still, I was drawn to her.

"It's not in men's best interest to notice things."

I bristle at the insult. "I notice things."

"Do you? So you know, then, that women have something to offer? Aside from their service to you?" She brings her plate to the counter and sits beside me. "Because if that's true, you're much more observant than your brethren."

The last bite of sandwich lodges in my throat. I am different. Didn't I choose to remain single, rather than take a wife merely to meet my own needs and appease God and Daniel? I look down at my plate. Then again, I did just sit here and eat Phoebe's food while she made herself more. "Thanks. For the meal," I say, feeling more shame than I can admit to her.

"I owed you a debt," she says, running the tines of her fork through the mayonnaise on her plate. "For defending me. Against your father."

Ah. So that's why she's fed me. I shrug and ball my napkin in my fist. "Not a big deal."

"It's bigger than you think. Not many people stand up to Han. You're either brave or foolish." She raises an eyebrow as she nibbles at her sandwich.

"Probably both."

"I wish I were," Phoebe says, dropping the bread to her plate and dusting off her hands. "Braver, I mean."

Is she talking about the End of Days? Surely Phoebe has no sins to account for, other than her husband's. And she's already paid for those. But Marcus did say if anyone else were involved in Delilah's escape, it would be Phoebe. I watch her closely. "Are you scared?"

She wrinkles her nose, just the tiniest bit. "I wish I could say no." The muscles in her neck tighten as she swallows.

"What about Delilah? Is she . . . damned? Without Daniel's protection?"

Phoebe drops her gaze to the timeworn table. "I hope not. I hate to think of her Out there . . ." Her voice trails off, and then she straightens her back. "But where she was headed wasn't any better."

"Is it all connected?" I ask. "Her escape and Daniel's dream? Because they've happened so close together. Is Da— I mean God, angry?" I don't need to ask about Daniel. I already know the answer to that.

"I don't know. I used to think I understood him. But lately . . . all of this . . ." She sweeps her hands upward, as if trying to encompass the whole community. "It scares me."

Phoebe is an Elder, as well as Daniel's confidant. Maybe she can answer my questions. I have no one else to ask.

"I found something," I tell her. "A letter from Naomi." She flinches, but I can't tell if it's the name itself that upsets her, or something more. "Did you know that she was alive?"

She stands abruptly and goes to the window. "She's of no concern to any of us anymore."

"But. If she's still Out there . . ." I'm having trouble putting it all together in a way she'll understand. "Do you think . . . I mean, could she have had something to do with Delilah going missing?" When she doesn't answer, I keep going. "What about Azariah? Do you know where he is? Could he have taken Delilah?"

Her gasp is painful. "Do not say his name. Ever."

I'm flailing blindly for answers without thinking about the injuries I might inflict, but I don't have time to worry about them now.

"Please," I say. "I need to know. Daniel blames Marcus for her disappearance. But I know my brother. He couldn't . . . he can't be involved. And I need to prove it. Before it's too late."

She closes her eyes briefly. "Daniel doesn't blame Marcus. Not for that."

"For what, then? The Matrimony? Because if it weren't for Susanna, tempting him—"

Phoebe holds up a hand to stop me. "I know what you must think about her. And yes, sometimes Susanna uses her looks to gain some measure of control. It's because she thinks that's all she has. And that's my fault. I should have taught her better. I should have let them all know that their thoughts and feelings matter. Instead, I spent too much time trying to avoid my own shame. It's funny, right? That my shame is really someone else's? But that's the burden we women must carry."

Then she jerks, as if remembering where we are. Who I am. "But that doesn't mean . . ." She pauses. "You can't talk about a woman like this. In public." Her gaze darts to the doorway and back to my face. "Even a hint of gossip will damn her. She isn't allowed the chance—"

"Her shame is her own," I say, interrupting. "She tried to seduce me. After the communal Gathering. In this very building."

Phoebe's face goes white. "Susanna was *here*? At night?" She drops the fork with a clang and stumbles off her stool, tripping over her own skirt. "That's impossible. Daniel would never allow such a breach . . . No." She's talking more to herself than to me. "No. Not Susanna." She pushes past me and out of the room, whispering something under her breath that sounds like ". . . too young."

But we're never too young to commit sin. Daniel's been teaching us that since we were kids. And I'm proof of it. Even after learning how close we are to the End of Days, I'm still going to meet Miriam at the Mill.

Phoebe didn't finish her sandwich, so I grab it. But rather than eat it, I wrap it in a napkin and stuff it in my pocket. My hunger for Miriam is even stronger than my appetite. Or my guilt.

36

MIRIAM

I HAD A DREAM AND IT MADE ME FEARFUL.

—*Daniel 4:5*

The tunnel is familiar, yet not. Similar to the one I walked on my wedding night, though this one has no light to guide me. And I'm alone. A frigid wind blows through the corridor, icy hands pushing at my back. The only way out seems to be forward, so I clutch my wool wrap for warmth and step carefully, avoiding the rodent-like shadows skittering just beyond my sight. I trail my fingers along the rock wall, which is somehow gritty and slimy at the same time. There are symbols here as well, just like in the other tunnel. Most are foreign, but some I recognize, like the pair of spectacles, our notation for *seek*. And the tower, which stands for *refuge*. And beside that, dozens of question marks, which we sometimes scribble in the margins of our notes when we find a passage confusing.

Then I see Delilah, standing at the end of the tunnel, awash in moonlight. She looks just as she did the last time I saw her, that night in the desert. Her white linen dress glows like a beacon. Unlike me, she seems unbothered by the biting wind that flattens the fabric to her body.

"Delilah! What are you doing here?"

She frowns and tilts her head. "Where else would I be?"

"Home," I say. "When are you coming home? Are you lost?"

She tilts her head, her eyes filled with such sadness, I begin to weep. "Oh, Miriam. You're the one who's lost. Not me."

"No—" I start to say. But she's already gone, disappearing into the shadows like smoke. On the wall behind where she was standing, Daniel's name is scrawled in big letters. But when I look closer, I see it isn't D-A-N-I-E-L. It's D-E-N-I-A-L.

I jerk to wakefulness. The darkness pulses as I blink away the residual effects of a headache. I'm in Aaron's old bedroom and the door is shut, but though the outside walls of these houses are concrete, the interiors are paper thin.

"Intentional community, my ass. Call it what it is—it's a cult." That's Aaron, and based on the way his voice carries, he's down the hall in the dining alcove. "These people are sheep. He tells them how dangerous it is out there, so they shut themselves off completely. And now he's got them convinced the world is ending? It's fucking crazy!"

"Aaron! Lower your voice!" Sarah says. Her next words to him are muted, and I have to get out of the bed and move to the door to hear better. Even then, it's difficult to make out what she says. ". . . not their fault. You . . . better than anyone." Sarah sounds genuinely upset. Unlike me, who doesn't know the meaning of the word Aaron's just used. Based on context, *cult* must be some kind of expletive. He knows a lot of those.

I slowly turn the doorknob, holding my breath as I crack the door. "And we have more pressing concerns right now." Sarah is still talking. A pause, then she says, "We need to think about an exit strategy."

"What? No way. I may have screwed up, but I'm committed."

That's Aaron. He hasn't lowered his voice, despite his mother's admonition, and it carries clearly.

"He's right. We still have work to do." The deeper voice must be Abraham. "Our goal hasn't changed."

Goal? I mouth the word.

"There's nothing else Aaron can do here." Sarah. "Without being married to Rachel."

Nothing else he can "do" here? What is she talking about? And what does Rachel have to do with it? Maybe I'm still dreaming.

"We're a team. We stick together." Of the three of them, Abraham is the only one who doesn't sound agitated. "It's unfortunate that Miriam's involved, yeah, but we play the hand we're dealt. His leaving is only going to draw suspicion. And we won't get another shot at this."

"It doesn't matter. I'm not leaving."

Sarah says, "You heard Daniel. 'If anyone has sins to confess, come forward now.' He's trying to force someone's hand. We have to face the possibility that he might be starting to suspect something."

"Or maybe he's just looking for a scapegoat for the Armageddon he's trying to manufacture," Aaron says. "We can't just leave Miriam here. Or any of them, for that matter. He'd sell them all into prostitution if it served him somehow."

Prostitution? Like in the Bible? I know the rest is about Daniel's miscalculation, but it doesn't make sense to me, and I can't tell if the muffled sensation is because I'm still woozy or because they're talking nonsense. Leave us here? This is our home. Where else does he think we'd go?

"You're overreacting," says Abraham. "Delilah was an isolated case. And partly our fault."

Partly their fault. So Abraham *was* involved. As Aaron would say, *shit*. I liked them.

"Trust me, I'm not overreacting. He spent the morning teaching us how to use assault rifles," Aaron says.

"This community has no history of violence. The research is solid."

"No history, huh? That's exactly what they said about Jonestown. And Waco. You know why? Because anyone who could say different was dead."

"Have you said any of this to Miriam?" For the first time, Abraham sounds concerned. Not about Aaron's words, but about the idea he might have shared them with me. Strange. "You're influencing her in ways that probably aren't—"

"I'm just trying to get her to think for herself," Aaron says. "But don't worry. I doubt it'll take. She's had a whole lifetime of indoctrination. And Daniel's never given them any lessons on the dangers of cult membership."

I repeat the strange words to myself and make a mental note to ask about them. Who, I'm not sure. My mother, maybe. Or Rachel.

"You know that could easily backfire on us. Knock it off. She's not our concern," Abraham says.

"They should all be our concern! Or have you been drinking the Kool-Aid, too? After all the lectures you've given me? Jesus Christ."

I press my back against the wall as Aaron stomps down the hall toward me. But he keeps going, and I see his back through the crack as he goes into the bathroom and slams the door.

I wait for my heart to start beating again before getting back in bed. But Abraham and Sarah aren't finished.

"We shouldn't have let him come. He's not ready. After—"

She doesn't say after what, but I can fill in the blank. After the awful place Aaron spent his childhood.

"If he doesn't want to leave, we can't force him. It would only arouse suspicion."

They're quiet for so long, I think they must have moved, though I didn't hear their footsteps. I have my hand on the doorknob when Sarah speaks again.

"Did you know? About the guns."

"No."

A pause. Then she says, "So what does it mean?"

"It means Daniel's becoming paranoid. And he doesn't trust me, not completely. If he did, he'd have given me a weapon. To shoot Delilah in the back, if nothing else."

"A.J.!"

"Sorry. Don't worry, love. She's safe. He won't find her."

She's safe. He won't find her. Abraham is talking about Delilah. Delilah is safe. From . . . Daniel?

"And Miriam?"

"I'm not sure what to do about Miriam," Abraham—or A.J.?— says. "Clearly, Aaron is becoming attached. She's going to be a problem."

My stomach clenches and my breaths come faster, in the same rhythm as my pounding head. My father-in-law—the same man who has "removed" Delilah, supposedly for her own safety—thinks I am a problem.

I sink to my knees and fumble for the trash can, emptying the contents of my stomach into the bin. If only it were that easy to get rid of all these doubts.

37

CALEB

I wait outside the Mill all night, until the sun rises to beat the moon from the sky, bruising the edges a soft purple. Miriam doesn't come. I've conditioned my body to withstand a great deal, but losing her is a pain I don't know how to bear.

38

MIRIAM

IF WE SAY WE HAVE FELLOWSHIP WITH
HIM WHILE WE LIVE IN DARKNESS,
WE LIE AND DO NOT PRACTICE THE TRUTH.
—*1 John 1:6*

When I open my eyes again, Aaron's head is on the pillow next to mine. For a moment, I don't remember where I am. Why are we in bed together?

Aaron presses his finger to my lips as I try to speak, and I resist the urge to bite it. Barely.

He must see something in my expression, because he snatches his hand back and tucks it under his cheek. "Daniel's on his way over," he says. "He wants to talk to us."

From the way he wrinkles his forehead, I know he's debating if he should say more. Does he know I heard him talking to his parents? I don't remember anything after throwing up. Did I get back in bed? Or did he put me there? Or maybe he's wondering if I'll keep my mouth shut about everything he's told me. I don't give him a chance to ask. Instead, I sit up and scoot away from him, but the bed is small. He rolls to grab my arm just before I fall.

"Calm down. We have to act normal."

Normal! Who is he to talk about normal? He's the one who's planted all these doubts in my mind. He and his family, who are clearly up to something . . . something not good. Did they really take Delilah? Does Daniel know? Is that why he's coming here? Or is it because he knows about me and Caleb, and our sins? Or my ebbing faith?

"I can't act normal! I don't know what that is!" I yank my arm away and tumble off the side of the bed. Luckily, the sheet I'm tangled in pads my fall, but the floor is just a thin layer of carpet over concrete, and the pain in my hip is going to translate to a big bruise later today.

"Are you all right?"

"I'm fine." I untwist the sheet from around my ankles and throw it across the room.

"For the record, being so afraid to touch your husband you'd rather injure yourself falls into the 'not normal' category," he says, swinging himself into a sitting position. His tone is light, but I can tell I've hurt his feelings.

"I'm not afraid to touch you." To prove it, I take the hand he offers and pull myself up. "I'm still getting used to your—you know. Your inclination."

"The word you're looking for is *gay*." He grabs his shirt from the hook on the back of the door and shrugs into it, doing up the buttons while still watching me. "But don't ever use it. Daniel will wonder where you learned it. And I told you. It isn't an *inclination*. It's just part of who I am." He sniffs, then wrinkles his nose. "Did you get sick last night?"

I shrug and use my foot to slide the garbage bin behind me. "And Daniel knows you're gay?" He's already confirmed it, but this is the part I can't reconcile. Daniel has taught us there is no virtue to be found in a sinner. I find it unfathomable he hasn't cast Aaron out, that instead he has bound him to me. Doesn't he worry Aaron's sin will damn us both? Doesn't he care about the fate of my soul?

"He does." Aaron's face is a cold mask of anger, and I recognize this as the expression he dons when our Leader's name is mentioned. "Look, he may ask questions. But you don't have to tell him everything you know."

"You want me to lie?" In my mind, I still hear their whispered words. *Cult. Armageddon. Prostitution. A.J. Miriam's going to be a problem.* But he doesn't know I heard those things. What then does Aaron want me to keep quiet about?

"Not lie, no. Just answer only what he asks. Don't give him any more—"

"I had a dream," I say, partly to make him stop talking, and partly because I need to talk about it. "It was about Delilah. She was here, in the tunnels. I thought she'd come back because she was scared, but she wasn't. She was worried about me. She said I was the one who was lost. What do you think it means?"

Aaron's expression flickers between interest, surprise, and then anger. Clearly, he doesn't believe me. I don't know why I told him. *Cult. Armageddon. Problem.*

"Never mind. Daniel's the one I need to ask."

Aaron groans and rubs a hand over his face. "That's exactly what I'm talking about. I told you, your dreams are not a prediction of the future. It's your subconscious. You're worried about Delilah, so you dreamt of her. It's totally normal, but it doesn't mean anything. And for the love of God, do not bring up Delilah to Daniel."

I'm pissed—to use a favorite word of his—that he dismisses my dream so quickly. "Why can't I ask Daniel?"

"He's already suspicious. We weren't exactly sociable after Chapel yesterday. And somehow he knows we spent the night here." He chews on the corner of his lip. "I'm just . . . worried about what he's going to think."

"Well, *I'm* worried about Delilah." I twist my skirt around and smooth the front of my shirt. "And Daniel interprets our dreams, so—"

"Don't you get it? The 'dream interpretation'? It's just another way to manipulate you. He makes you keep those stupid dream journals so he can read them and use the information. Either to make you think he's some kind of oracle or to keep you in line."

"Stop that! Why must you question everything he says? Everything we do?"

He throws up his hands. "Why don't you?"

I can't answer. I've just remembered—Daniel has my dream journal. It seems a lifetime ago that he took it from me, though it was only a few days. That must be why he's coming here. He knows I lied in it, and worse, he knows how I feel about Caleb.

The door opens.

"He's here," Abraham says.

I let Aaron take my hand and lead me into the living room behind his father. This is how I'm expected to act—docile and compliant—and while the warmth of his hand in mine is a small comfort, it occurs to me that many of my duties as a wife are designed to make me feel small.

Abraham moves toward Sarah, who stands near the window with her arms crossed over her chest. While tiny in stature, she has a presence even her husband can't overshadow. Maybe that's because he doesn't try.

Daniel leans on the fireplace mantel, which has been cleared of all the netsuke. Did Sarah take my advice? Behind him, I see part of a book and a shoe, which are odd decorations, even for Sarah.

Our Leader turns as we enter the room. He is unreadable, his face so devoid of emotion it may as well be chiseled out of rock.

"Good morning." He holds out his hands to us.

I take a hesitant step forward, but he drops his arms before I reach him.

Aaron laces his fingers through mine and squeezes. A show of support? Or a reminder to hold my tongue?

"I'm told you slept here last night," Daniel says, his gaze flicking back and forth between us. "A slumber party of sorts."

Aaron's hand crushes mine before I can speak. His reflexes are even quicker than my mouth. It's probably for the best. I have no idea what a slumber party is. How can you have a party while you're sleeping?

"And I noticed you left quickly after Chapel yesterday," he continues, linking his hands behind his back, "without staying for Fellowship. I'm not sure that children who flee from God's embrace deserve Salvation."

I'm not a child anymore. I'm a woman. But like everything else, that title holds meaning only when it's convenient.

From the corner of my eye, I see Sarah take a step forward. "It isn't Miriam's fault—she began feeling ill while at Chapel. We invited them for dinner, and when her headache didn't improve, we let her lie down—"

Daniel doesn't turn toward her. In fact, his posture does not change at all as he says, "For if we could control our tongues, Sarah, we would be perfect and could control ourselves in every other way."

I threw that same quote at her last night. Tears of shame blur my vision, so I can't be sure if Abraham means to hold her back or embrace her as he wraps his arms around her shoulders.

The protective mother. What was it she said once? Mothers worry? But she isn't my mother. I want to trust her, and she did just lie for me, but I don't know if I can. Does she also think I'm a problem, like her husband does?

"Well?" Daniel stares us down. He's waiting for some kind of reply, but I have no idea what he wants to hear. He didn't ask us a question, which means there is probably no right answer. Clearly, he found Sarah's explanation lacking. Part of me still itches to confess my sins. To tell him of my doubts. To ask him what all of this means—Armageddon, Delilah, cult. And not just because I want to see his reaction. Because he's always been my spiritual guide, and I could really use some guidance now. If I can't put my faith in him, then where?

But I have too many questions running through my head, and for once the words won't come.

"Cat got your tongue?" He tilts his head back and laughs, as if he finds my newfound obedience hilarious. "It's a bit late, don't you think?"

A question with no right answer. The intensity of his stare is mesmerizing. It's as if he can see inside me, deep down into the depths of my soul. He knows about Caleb and me. He knows about the sins we committed, and those I've only dreamt about. How does he do that, if he isn't a messenger of God?

He circles me, the heels of his sandals slapping the floor in punctuation. "You speak to a man, you mark him as your husband. You take to his bed, you become his wife. You turn your back on the Fellowship of God and family"—here he pauses and takes my chin in his fingers—"you invite sin into your heart."

The shame that has been slowly kindling in my chest sputters. He's still talking about leaving Chapel yesterday. He's not talking about Caleb. Why isn't he talking about Caleb?

"Are you a sinner, Miriam?"

"Yes," I whisper. And it's true. I'm suddenly just not sure to what degree Daniel knows it.

Beside me, Aaron makes a noise that could be a cough or a curse.

"And what are we going to do about that? Time is running out."

This time I know the answer, but I still have to force the word out. "Pray."

He grips my shoulders and pulls me close. "Prayer only works for so long," he whispers in my ear. "Then it's time for Confession. And Repentance." He releases me so suddenly I stumble, and Aaron steadies me.

Daniel turns back to the fireplace and grabs the book on the mantel. But it isn't just any book. "I've had a chance to read through your journal," he says. "I don't encourage self-analysis. But you have an interesting perspective." He taps the cover. "The dream you had on your wedding night. About the fountain. You seemed to recognize then that your need to run your mouth is your biggest weakness. I'm impressed."

My heart thumps so wildly I feel faint. Impressed? My dream about the fountain was a complete lie; my interpretation almost word for word his own. How does he not recognize this?

He hands me the journal and I take it with a shaking hand, waiting for the reprimand, or at least the questions: Why is it so sparse? What have I left out? What about my dreams of my lover? But he doesn't ask.

"Since I've had this," he says, "you obviously didn't have a chance to record the last few nights' dreams. Were they odd, I wonder? Because sometimes, wine has lasting effects. It clouds our judgment. Blurs our insight. Perhaps it was the cause of your headache."

That was two nights ago. How does he know about the wine? Aaron and I exchange a look, and his contains an additional warning. *Don't mention Delilah.*

"Do you remember . . ." For one brief second, I think Daniel is going to bring my friend up himself, but he finishes with "the story of Asa? With his diseased foot? You may recall that he refused to turn to the Lord to save him, instead relying on others." The smile Daniel gives us doesn't reach his eyes. "He died, of course."

Is Daniel threatening me? Or merely saying my headache is a product of my own wavering faith?

"The headache wasn't wine or disease," I say. "It was worry. About Delilah. I dreamt of her last night." Aaron told me not to bring her up, but I don't care. This may be my only chance to learn what Daniel knows.

After a glance toward Abraham, Daniel looks at me curiously. "What do you know about Delilah?" he asks, fiddling with the other item on the mantel.

It's a shoe. A sandal, like I wear. Like all the women wear. Tightly woven of yucca, the straps of frayed rope. When he flips it over, my stomach turns with it. Because I recognize the doodle on the bottom.

I steel myself to look him in the eye. Abraham said she was safe. So why does Daniel have one of her sandals? "Where did you get it?"

Daniel's gaze holds mine as he picks up the sandal. "I have heard rumors," he says. "That you wish to mount a search for our lost sheep. I'm here to tell you that will be . . . unnecessary. And unwise."

Aaron curses softly, and I wonder if he's thinking the same thing

I am—how does Daniel know so much about what happened at the Gathering? The wine, my resolve to go after Delilah. It's as if he was there.

"Delilah was—is—a good person. She's done nothing to deserve punishment or shame. Even if she had, she's still our Sister. Someone should be looking for her."

A flicker of emotion crosses Daniel's face, and then it's gone. Disgust, maybe? Or pride? "As I've told you many times, there is no protection outside these gates. Especially not for sinners." He tosses the shoe, and it lands at Aaron's feet. "Delilah is dead."

I feel woozy, and I hear a high-pitched noise, like the mewl of an injured cat.

It's coming from me.

Aaron wraps his arms tightly around me and bends my head to his chest. I stare down at the shoe, listening to the heavy thud of his heart as my own splinters. The doodle on the bottom is our symbol for refuge. Is this the last I'll ever see of her drawings?

"We told Miriam as much. Last night," Abraham says. He clears his throat. "She was upset. We all are. Understandably."

I squeeze my eyes shut. He most certainly did not tell me that. But he sounds convincing now. So what is true? Was he lying last night, when he told me not to worry? But he also said the same thing later to his wife when he thought no one else was listening. *She's safe.*

Safe. Refuge. I blink my eyes open. The tower on the bottom of the shoe seems to wave at me through my teary gaze. What if Delilah left the shoe behind on purpose? What if it's a message? Like the message she sent through Caleb. *Who's more faithful than Abraham?*

I desperately want to believe this. I *need* her to be safe. But if Abraham is telling the truth, that makes Daniel the liar.

So whom do I believe? My Leader? Or an Outsider?

Daniel is the Living Prophet. It has to be him. Except. He didn't recognize my made-up dreams from among my real ones. He hasn't called out my sins. And he can't seem to tell that all of us are lying.

Abraham's motives remain unclear. All I know for sure is that he was the last person to see Delilah.

I can't let them see my doubts, so I raise my head from Aaron's chest and say, "She was my friend. I didn't want to believe it. I'm afraid I carried on so much, I made myself sick."

Daniel studies me, blinking only once in what feels like an eternity. He's looking for signs of deceit, but I channel my mother and adopt her mask of serenity.

"Next time, you'll do well to confine your sickness to your own house." He nods, first to me, then to Aaron, Abraham, and Sarah. "And Miriam? Keep faithful."

I'm starting to feel like that's no longer an option, but he's gone before I can say another word.

Aaron and his family surround me then, and though no one has asked the question, I can feel the weight of it between us. Aaron opens his mouth first, and I raise my hand. "Please. My head still hurts. Can we go home?"

As he ushers me to the door, Sarah pulls me close. "You did good," she whispers. I want to believe her, but nothing about this feels even remotely good. When she hugs me, her bosom makes a curious clacking noise.

She's hidden the netsuke in her bra.

39

CALEB

Miriam does not want me. The realization pounds in my head, keeping time with my heavy steps along the path behind the pasture as well as the throbbing behind my eyes. I have not slept. I waited all night, but she never came. The message is clear; she has chosen her husband over me. Which means my sins were for nothing. I gave up my right to be in the Book just so that she could turn her back on me. On our love.

I want to break something. Hurt someone. Hurt myself. Physical pain is much easier to bear. I try to focus on my headache, inviting it to take hold and push out everything else. But it remains stubbornly weak and ineffective. Just like me.

Why is this happening? I can't lose her. Not now. Not after I know what her voice sounds like as she whispers in my ear, what her hair smells like, what her body feels like. There has to be a way to win her back. I just need a plan. Food, then sleep. And then a plan.

Susanna is already at her desk when I stumble through the front door of the Council House, and I have to hold back the curses that hover on my lips. What is she doing here this early? Even if I were capable of holding a normal conversation without screaming, it wouldn't be with her.

"Caleb." Susanna raises her eyebrow. "You've been out and about early. Or late. What have you been up to? Ducking your obligations already?"

Her question unnerves me. What does she know about me and my obligations? "What are you talking about? I'm following all my obligations. Are you?"

"Poor Caleb. All that love in you, and yet you're alone. No one to share it with." She stands and moves around to my side of the desk. When she gets close enough that I could touch her, or she could touch me, I stumble backward and out of her reach. She makes me nervous in a way I can't explain, except I know it has to do with all the preaching I've heard my whole life about carnal urges. I don't love her—I don't even like her—but I'm always aware that she's a woman. I'm drawn to her, somehow, and I'm afraid that when we're alone together some primitive power will take over and I'll end up touching her in a way Daniel might understand but I know Marcus won't.

"I don't . . . what is it you want?"

"I need your help," she says, her blue eyes shiny with unshed tears.

It feels like a trap. Why would she need my help? She's married to my brother; he's the one she should ask for help. Unless this is about him. My head hurts from lack of sleep and trying to figure out her agenda. So I swallow and say, "What kind of help?"

She flips her hair over her shoulder and turns her head, as if the purpling bruise on her neck is some kind of offering. "I think you know."

I'm overcome by an all-too familiar sensation, the same blend of anger and disappointment that colored my childhood. *Oh, Marcus. What have you done?*

Susanna wraps her hands around her neck as if to hide her

shame, then presses herself against my chest. The flowery scent of her hair tickles my nose. She is temptation in the flesh, if I'm not careful.

"Please," I say, aware of how weak begging makes me sound. "Not Marcus."

Instead, she tilts her head to look into my eyes. "Haven't you figured it out yet? He's the coyote."

"What? No. How can the coyote be a person?" What had Daniel said? *The devil takes many shapes. A coyote, a wolf in sheep's clothing.* But she's right. He didn't ask me to hunt for wolves.

"Don't be an idiot." She pushes away from me and crosses her arms over her full chest, any trace of amusement gone. "Did you really think Daniel was asking you to catch an actual coyote? He's looking for a traitor. Your brother is the traitor."

My sympathy for her deflates so quickly it leaves me weak, and I sag against the desk. "No," I whisper, even as Daniel's words echo in my head. *Sometimes even a brother.*

"Yes," she argues. "He's responsible for all of this—" She waves her hand between us. "Your lack of a wife, my suffering, Delilah's disappearance."

Marcus can't have done all those things. Yes, he has a temper. But he's not a monster.

Susanna leans forward and traces her finger slowly down my cheek. "I know how much you both struggle not to be like him—your father," she whispers. "But only one of you is succeeding."

Her words are eerily close to my darkest thoughts, the ones I've tried so hard to bury. I slap her hand away. "You don't know anything about me."

Her smile hovers somewhere between wise and wicked. "I know you're in love with Miriam."

"How could you possibly . . . ?" I'm not sure how I form the words. My lips are numb. My whole face is numb.

Susanna blinks widened eyes at me. "I'm a woman."

She's toying with me. I see it now. Damn Marcus and his weakness for her. What else has he told her? Before I can ask, she continues, "What you *should* be concerned about is whether Daniel already knows. He's with Miriam, right now. What do you suppose they're talking about?"

The words are a threat, a dagger perfectly aimed. I clench my fists tight at my side, the urge to lash out so strong I'm afraid, for her and for me. I can't speak, for fear of what the words might set in motion.

"He's going to open the Book, Caleb. Soon. And your name isn't going to be in it."

I force myself to take a breath. And another. Each exhalation where I don't hurt her is a victory for me. And a reprieve for her, though she's too stupid to realize it. *Breathe.* Finally, I'm calm enough to say, "Neither are you. You're as much an adulterer as me. Only I am Daniel's trusted advisor. His beloved apostle. You're nothing but a secretary. A mere *woman*."

That seems to amuse her. "An adulterer and a woman. Is that all?" She cocks her head. "The time will come when you'll realize you've underestimated me. And you aren't going to want to be on my bad side when that happens." Her voice singsongs up and down on the words.

She's trying to fan the fire of my anger—I can feel it happening—and I'm powerless to stop it. Only the sound of approaching footsteps stops me from doing something I'm not sure I'd regret.

Susanna straightens and dons an expression of piety probably only I can see through. "It's you or him, Caleb. So do us both a favor and give Daniel what he's asking for," she says, bending forward just enough to whisper in my ear, "Give him the coyote."

Her hot breath sends a shiver of revulsion through me. As if it's that easy. He is still my brother. I must honor him. But is there a way to do that while still remaining in Daniel's favor? Or while regaining Daniel's favor? Because if Susanna has told him about me and Miriam, I may have already lost it. I don't want to believe her, but she's right about one thing. Daniel is going to open the Book. And I don't know if my name will be inside. And what about Miriam's? If she is barred from the Kingdom of Heaven, will she ever forgive me?

It all feels so hopeless. What can I do?

My gaze falls on Susanna's desk, on her blotter. And her keys. She said it herself: Daniel doesn't want a coyote. He wants a person. A nonbeliever. A traitor to our faith.

That, I can give him.

And just like that, the weight upon me is lifted. Keeping all these secrets while accomplishing nothing has felt unnatural; this decision to act is like removing a barbell from across my neck.

40

MIRIAM

I lean over the spinning wheel, my head still churning with everything that's happened: Abraham's cryptic reassurances about Delilah, the strange conversation I overheard between Aaron and his parents. Daniel's lies.

Is he a liar? I can't believe I'm even entertaining such blasphemous thoughts. But nothing makes sense anymore. Daniel says Delilah is dead; Abraham says she is safe. That reassurance holds small comfort for me, since I don't know if I can trust him. I once thought we were all safe here, but that doesn't seem to be true either. How did this happen? I'm losing everything I believe in.

Even Caleb. All of those comments about women and God. He talked as if we were inferior. Does he really believe that? And what about whatever went wrong at the Matrimony? How much does he know? He wanted me to meet him here last night. What must he have thought, when I didn't come? Did he wait? I look around the room but see only wool. There is nothing out of place, nothing he's left for me. No evidence he was even here. Maybe, like me, he found it difficult to throw off his obligations for even one evening.

I feel the impossible weight of Aaron's stare as he asks, "Are you ready to talk about it yet?"

While Aaron possesses the admirable quality of sensing when I need silence, it appears even he has his limits.

"What is there to talk about?" I take a rolag of wool from the basket Lydia's left and twist one end around the spindle. Today I'll finally spin our wool into yarn, which we can either trade for other commodities or use in our own weavings. As girls, we were all taught to use the spinning wheel as part of our education, but I was never good at it. I suspect one of the reasons Lydia has gone to help with the shearing today is so she can rejoice tomorrow when my yarn comes out snarled and fuzzed.

And just like that, I've already snagged the wool on the bobbin. "Damnation."

"Let me help, Sleeping Beauty." Aaron gently pries the wool from my hands and begins to untangle my mess.

"I'm not sleepy," I say, leaning away.

"I meant . . . because of the spinning wheel. You know, the fairy tale?"

He sees something in my blank expression, because he closes his eyes and sighs. "Never mind. Not even a goddamned fairy tale?" he mutters, yanking harder on the thread. "Doesn't he let you read anything in here?"

We're face to face now. I can smell his breath, minty with a hint of sweetness.

"We read the Bible."

"And nothing else?"

"Daniel tells us stories. How many other books can there be?"

He snaps my bobbin back into place. "The more you talk, the more I worry."

I don't blame him; I'm worried, too. I want to ask Aaron about the conversation I overheard, but I'm afraid he'll confirm all my suspicions. For now, as long as I can keep the doubts to myself, I haven't become Faithless.

"You could have told Daniel the truth this morning, but you didn't." He twists a piece of yarn between his fingers. "Why?"

Holding back all my questions and my fears is like trying to hold back a flood. Once they're out, I won't be able to take them back. Worse, what if Aaron confirms them? "Your mother lied to protect me," I say. "I felt I . . . owed her."

"She wasn't just protecting you. She doesn't want anything bad to happen. To our family."

Is that what they meant by "Miriam's going to be a problem"? "No one's trying to hurt your family."

He reddens. "I told you about the place I grew up. They weren't big on family there, and sometimes . . . it's hard to forget. That's all I meant."

He sounds matter-of-fact, but I can see the hurt little boy beneath the surface, and I'm not sure whether to laugh or cry. For an awkward moment, I think I might do both. Aaron looks away to give us each time to compose ourselves.

"What's a cult?" I ask, partly to change the subject. But mostly because my curiosity is stronger than the dam holding it back.

"Where did you—" He jerks his fingers through his hair as he scans the room. "Shit, Miriam, you can't—"

"Just tell me. I want to know."

"Fine." He gets up and paces once around the wheel. Twice. "Okay. Okay." He puffs up his cheeks, then blows the air out. "A cult is . . . it's a kind of religious group. It's usually run by a single leader. One leader who sort of twists things"—he twists his hands together—"for his own benefit. A leader who manipulates people into believing everything he says. Who makes rules you have to follow, no matter what you want. Like here . . . in the Children of Daniel."

"No." I shake my head violently. "No. That's not true." But my head starts buzzing, and I have to grip the bobbin to stop shaking. Daniel *does* make all the rules. Rules that sometimes feel impossible to follow. And when we fail, he's right there to dole out the punishment.

"It's true," he insists. "You believe every crackpot thing he tells you. Look at yesterday. The beast with horns? Phallic?" He shakes his head. "Come on."

"Are you saying Daniel's . . . his interpretation is wrong?"

"I'm saying I don't think the guy who wrote Daniel all those years ago was worried about sexual tendencies, yours or anyone else's. It's classic projection." Seeing my blank expression, he adds, "Projection is when someone is focused on a particular failing in other people because they're committing it themselves. Like your Prophet, who seems awfully preoccupied with sex."

"Daniel isn't a sexual being. He's married to the Word." Isn't he?

"Right. That's why he lives in that big house up on the hill along with a bunch of single women."

"It isn't a bunch. Just Phoebe. 'And then the Lord said, it is not good for man to be alone.'" Of course my first instinct is to quote scripture. It's what we've been taught to do in times of crisis. Proclaim our faith, loudly and repetitively. But why is that? Whom are we preaching to? Everyone in here already knows it.

"See, that's exactly the kind of manipulation and fallacy a cult leader uses. That quote, that's from Genesis, and it's referring to Adam and Eve—one man and one woman. But Daniel uses it to justify getting it on with whoever he wants."

This time, I choose my own words. "*Phallic* and *fallacy* sound an awful lot alike."

Aaron's mouth twitches. "That's the kind of thinking I know you're capable of. It's also the opposite of what Daniel wants. He doesn't want you to know the truth. He prefers you ignorant and scared."

"Fine. Since you claim to know so much, tell me: Is Delilah really safe? Because your dad says she is. But she's Out there somewhere, alone. So how can she be safe?"

He hesitates. "Daniel wants you scared. He has you brainwashed into believing that everything Outside is terrible, that there's no way anyone could survive out there. But there's so much goodness in the world, Miriam."

"Like what?" He's evading my question about Delilah, but I have to know. What is it really like out there?

"So many things. Coffee shops. Books. All the music you can possibly imagine. Green grass. Kittens and puppies. Freedom. Choice."

"It sounds terrible." I'm lying. I suddenly want to know what "all the music you can possibly imagine" sounds like, more than anything.

"Really? *That* sounds terrible? As opposed to being married to me and lusting after another guy. Listening to a false prophet who controls who you marry, where you live, what you eat. And you can't fool me. I know how much you hate weaving. But you're supposed to do it the rest of your life? No complaints. No choice. Well, guess what? Outside, you can be whoever you want. If you want to sing, you sing. And if you never want to look at a goddamn loom again, you don't have to."

He's baiting me, but I refuse to bite. Surely it can't be as great as he says. There's a reason my mother fled all of that. Her fear is real, real enough to keep us here my whole life. "Hurricanes. Floods. Fire?" I counter. "Death. Pestilence. Are you going to tell me those are just lies, too?"

"People die in here, too!" He takes a slow, deep breath, as if to calm himself.

What is he talking about? Who has died in New Jerusalem?

"Look," Aaron continues. "There are problems everywhere. But they're not as widespread as Daniel would have you believe. God isn't raining down fire and brimstone the minute you walk out the gates. And a lot of people—the *majority* of people—think that freedom is worth a few problems. I mean, let's face it. Here in New Jerusalem, you've done the opposite. You've traded freedom for safety."

"For Salvation," I correct him, the word feeling hollow. Because I've just realized: It doesn't matter how wonderful the Outside is, or how terrible. Either way, it's too late for me. If Daniel is right, this is the beginning of the End. And my name isn't going to be in any Book.

If he's right.

"How far away is it?" I ask, my voice loud. As if that might drown out the doubts.

He cocks his head. "How far away is what?"

"Outside. Do you have to travel far, once you leave the gates?"

"It depends on where you're going."

"Outside," I say again, my frustration mounting.

"Miriam, *everything* is outside. Once you leave New Jerusalem, you're outside."

"So I've already been Outside, then. At the Matrimony." The news is deflating. It's just an empty expanse of sand and sky.

"There are cities, too," he says, perhaps sensing my disappointment.

"Cities? More than one?"

He nods. "More than ten thousand."

I shake my head. "That's not possible. There is New Jerusalem, and there is Outside. Aren't they equal?"

He stares at me for a long moment; his expression holds a hint of sadness, along with a touch of wonder. And maybe fear. "How is it you can be so well educated about some things and so clueless about others?"

I don't know how to answer. *Clueless* is another word I don't know.

"Here. It's easier if I show you." He walks to the drawers against the wall, extracts a piece of paper and a pencil. "This is California." He looks at me as he draws. "Do you know about California? California is the state we live in. Fifty states make up the whole United States."

I'm already shaking my head. "I've heard of the states. But New Jerusalem doesn't belong. We've seceded," I say, repeating what I've been taught, though it occurs to me I don't know the meaning of that word either.

"No, you haven't. Daniel can say you've seceded, but that doesn't make it true."

Another lie from Daniel? They're lodging in my throat. Any more and I don't think I'll be able to breathe. Could this really be a cult, like Aaron said? "What's that?" I point to a line on the side of the page, which separates all he's been showing me from nothingness.

"That's the ocean."

"The ocean."

"Yes. You know, under the sea," he sings.

Clearly he's heard me singing more than I thought he had, since he's already memorized the words. "I've dreamt of the sea," I tell him, touching the paper with my fingertips as if I can feel the water. "It doesn't seem so far when you draw it. You've been there?"

"Many times."

"But how did you get through the desert?"

"Draw me what your world looks like." He hands me the pencil.

I draw our city in the middle of the page, the wall that surrounds us and protects us. Then, on the far edge of the paper, I draw a small body of water. "I'm not sure of the direction," I say, feeling the need to apologize. "I only know it's very far."

Aaron studies my drawing.

"What?" I ask. "Have I drawn it all wrong?"

He's quiet for so long, I fear he won't answer. When he does, his words don't make sense. "Everyone has their own definition of Hell. I know mine. I'm trying to figure out if you know yours."

My cheeks burn. "New Jerusalem is your version of Hell? What about your last . . . cult?"

He chews his lip and braces himself on the wheel. "Same difference."

"That doesn't make any sense. And anyway, you're wrong," I tell him, pushing his hands away as I sit and feel for the treadle with my foot. "Hell isn't a place. It's a feeling. Of loss. Of losing your most important thing."

"Then I guess we're both right. Because we're both here, and we've both lost."

He's right. Caleb. Delilah. My faith. Maybe I am in Hell. I

slam my foot against the pedal, and the fiber tears in my hands. "If you hate it here so much, why are you still here? It shouldn't be hard for you to leave. You've done it before." *Go, and take my doubts with you.*

A Call to Prayer blares out from the speaker on the wall, and Aaron and I both glance up, then at each other. This isn't the normal time. They're coming more frequently now, a reminder that we all must prepare to repent.

I stumble from the spinning wheel, my muscles too stiff with fear to kneel, even if I wanted to.

Aaron reaches out a hand to steady me. "It's okay to have doubts," he says.

I pull my arm away, and the muscle in my shoulder seizes up. How does he know of my doubt?

Aaron winces in sympathy and motions me to turn around. When I do, he lays his hands on my shoulders. "I'm just going to try and work out the knot. Is that all right?"

I relax my shoulders and nod. "How did you know?" I whisper. "About my doubts?"

"It's pretty common. You've been taught your whole life to be faithful. So, being unfaithful . . . even having unfaithful thoughts, it causes anxiety. And nobody likes feeling anxious. We want to get rid of the feeling, as soon as possible. So we tend to revert to our old habits. We do the thing we've been trained to do in a time of crisis. For everyone here, that means turning to Daniel."

For some reason, the soothing touch of Aaron's hands coupled with his soft voice makes me start to cry.

"Hey, don't feel bad about it. That's the thing with cults. They mess with your head." He stops rubbing for a moment and taps his finger gently against my skull. "Daniel's been up in there your whole life. It's not that easy to get him out."

The muscles in my neck have loosened, but now my chest tightens. "And if I can't?"

Aaron squeezes my shoulder. "Look. Maybe you should just forget everything I said. Like my mother keeps reminding me, you were happy before. Maybe I shouldn't have told you any of this. Confused you."

Was I happy? That seems so long ago, and any happy memories I have—skipping and laughing with Rachel and Delilah—seem like they happened to another girl. One who never listened to stories of the Outside, who never ate the food her husband cooked for her. Who didn't know what it was like to feel the sunshine on her face while she kissed the boy she loved. Who still believed the word of her Prophet.

I don't think I could be happy here again—not knowing what I know. And certainly not without knowing what's happened to Delilah.

I shake my head. "No. I'm glad you told me. I just have a lot to think about."

He stares at me for a long time, but I'm not sure he's really seeing me. Finally, he takes the single skein of yarn I've managed to finish and inspects it. "Not bad," he says. "Maybe we should trade it."

"What? No one is going to give us anything for that but grief."

"My mother will. And besides, there's something I think you should hear. From her."

41

CALEB

Your brother is the traitor.

Give Daniel the coyote.

I leave Susanna without a goodbye or a "keep faithful," entering the door to Daniel's inner chambers and locking it behind me. Then I stand in the darkened hallway, heart pounding, trying to figure out what all of this means.

She has to be mistaken. Or lying. My brother has never done anything to betray anyone. Unless you count taking Susanna for a wife instead of Rachel. But that wasn't really a *betrayal.* A lie, maybe. A misstep. But it should have been between him and God. Daniel wouldn't call him a traitor for that. Would he?

So this all must have to do with Delilah. Daniel blames Marcus for her running away. I need to prove that isn't true.

I have to find Delilah and bring her home.

It makes perfect sense. I don't know why I didn't think of it sooner. Once I bring her back, she can tell Daniel herself that Marcus had nothing to do with her disappearance. Daniel will be so pleased. And almost better than that, Miriam will be happy. She was so worried about her friend. This will ease her mind; this will bring her back to me. This must be what love is—the willingness to risk anything to make her smile. I have kept faithful to Daniel all my life. But

I've never wanted anything like I want Miriam, and I don't know how to stop. I can only hope God will forgive me this one sin.

Daniel's forgiveness is another matter, though if I can find Delilah, I suspect he'll give me anything I ask for.

I pace the hallway outside Daniel's office, the eyes of the Prophet's painting following me. He is still asleep, and ideally, I need to leave before he wakes. But I'm going to need help, both to leave New Jerusalem and to find Delilah. Marcus is the obvious choice. He's been Out once already. But I don't want to get him in any more trouble than he already is. That leaves Abraham. He's been Out, too. Hell, he knows how to drive; he used to live Outside. The problem is, I don't know if I can trust him. I try to think back to the night Delilah went missing. Did he seem overly concerned about her well-being? I can't remember. If anything, he seemed more worried about Marcus. Which could work in my favor. And what was it Delilah said to me? *Who's more faithful than Abraham?* I can think of about a dozen people, off the top of my head. But none of them have access to the gate and the van. And none of them were there when Delilah ran.

There's also Naomi. When I suggested to Daniel that she might be involved, I was mostly trying to take the blame off my brother. I don't know if she has anything to do with Delilah's running away. But I do know she's still alive. And I know where to find her. If she can't tell me where to find Delilah, she will at least be able to help me navigate Outside.

I need to get her letter.

I crack the door open, hoping Susanna has left her post. She hasn't; worse, Phoebe is with her.

Their voices are so low at first, I can't make out what they're saying. Phoebe stands in front of the desk, her muscular arm wrapped through the handle of a woven basket. Her face is puckered with concern, while Susanna just looks smug. But then, Susanna always looks smug.

". . . heading down a bad path," Phoebe says, her voice rising at the end of her sentence.

"It's my choice. You're just jealous." Susanna pushes back her chair and reaches for the basket, ripping it from Phoebe's hands so violently it makes me wince.

"It may feel like a choice, but it's a mistake. Trust me, I know." Phoebe rubs at the scratch marks left behind on her arms. "God always recognizes sin. Even when Daniel condones it."

My jaw drops at her outspoken Blasphemy. Susanna merely rolls her eyes. "Out of my way," she says, pushing past her teacher. "I've got shopping to do. Daniel will be hungry."

"And what about your husband?" Phoebe asks, straightening her shoulders.

Susanna's gaze flicks in my direction, and I jump away from the door crack. "Marcus has bigger problems than breakfast," she says, slamming the door on her way out.

Cold sweat trickles down my forehead as I wait in the darkness for Phoebe to leave. If Daniel wants a coyote, I will give him one. But I have to hurry, before Susanna gives him my brother.

When the room is empty, I slip through the doorway and go straight for Susanna's desk. But the drawer is locked. I'll have to break it. With any luck, by the time she realizes it and thinks to accuse me, I will be gone. Or maybe even back already, our lost sheep in tow.

What exactly was it that Daniel said to me, when he asked me to bring him the coyote? Something about someone among us who was weak. He wasn't talking about Delilah at the time, but she fits that description. Her fear has made her weak, and her foolishness has put us all in danger. I must be the strong one now.

The keyhole is just that—a hole. If I can find something small enough to jam in there, I can turn the lock. I seize Susanna's letter opener and work it into the opening. I'm both surprised and vindicated when it works. Who says I'm not the smart one? How's that for a riddle, Marcus? Who killed a quarter of humanity? How about: Who saved his brother's soul?

The letter is still in the drawer and I grab it, stuffing it into the waistband of my pants. I'm about to close the drawer, still savoring my victory, when I see something lying in the bottom. Another set of keys, this one with a tag that bears the same logo as the van.

Maybe I won't need Abraham's help after all.

42

MIRIAM

ALL HER PEOPLE GROAN AS THEY
SEARCH FOR BREAD; THEY BARTER
THEIR TREASURES FOR FOOD TO
KEEP THEMSELVES ALIVE.

—*Lamentations 1:11*

We cross through the city and head toward the Commodities Exchange, greeting our neighbors as we pass. The day is heavy with the smoky scent of creosote, and everyone is out, taking advantage of the clear weather while we still have it. In the distance, the sky has darkened to match the asphalt, the occasional zigzag of lightning the only way to separate the cloud line from the road. As I nod and smile at the younger girls who used to be my classmates, or their parents and siblings, the word *cult* loops through my head like wool on a spindle, so loudly I fear I may scream it out to anyone who tries to engage me in conversation. My expression must be unnatural, but at least it keeps everyone at a polite distance.

These are my friends, my family. If I voice my doubts, I will be Banished and I'll never see any of them again. Is that really what I want? Why can't I just shut my mouth and accept things the way they are? The rest of my neighbors have, and they're happy. Aren't

318 · *Shannon Schuren*

they? We pass Leah, and in the morning light, she looks pale and tired. She's probably a bad example. I think about Rachel, who got to marry her love and work the Farm. Certainly she and Jacob are happy. I think of my mother, who loves it here so much she panics at even the thought of leaving. Who knows what would have become of her if she'd stayed Outside? What would have become of me? All I know for sure is I wouldn't be here, married to Aaron, marking my time with knotted bits of yarn.

Aaron turns back as my steps slow. "Are you all right?"

I nod, then shake my head as the tears slip down my cheeks.

He puts an arm around me. "Everything is going to be okay. I promise. Let's talk to my mom."

Sarah works in the Commodities Exchange, a rectangular building of metal and cinder block. Since Aaron has taken on the cooking and the shopping, I haven't been inside since I ran errands for my mother before the Matrimony. It's as depressing as I remember—one long room, separated only by the metal shelves that hold the basics of our survival, available for barter or begging. Dim lights hug the ceiling high above, trapped in wire cages along with the dust that coats the bulbs.

Sarah is behind the counter near the door, sweeping the cement floor. A line of ants gives her a wide berth as they march toward a mound of sand in the corner of the room. She straightens and gives us a smile when we enter, along with a warning glance down one of the aisles.

I'm not interested in whatever concerns her, not until I turn a corner and run smack into Caleb.

Even with all that's happened between us, my body jolts and fizzes when I see him, like a kind of electrical shock. He must not have a similar reaction, because his eyes are ice as they glide over

Aaron and me, taking in my tears and his hand on my shoulder. He turns and goes back to studying the shelves with a tiny frown, as if he hasn't noticed us.

I know the importance of appearances, but I also know how hurt he must be.

"Please. Can we talk?" I ask.

Caleb turns and I take a quick step back, suddenly aware of how cool it is in this room because of the heat in my face.

He pastes a casual smile across his face as he glances from me to Aaron and back. "Maybe you can help me. I need some food I can carry. For a long distance. I'm not very good at this kind of thing. I don't have a wife to shop for me."

Aaron clears his throat and jerks a thumb over his shoulder. "I'm gonna go talk to my mom."

Once he has walked away, I can speak to Caleb freely. "I know you asked me to meet you last night," I whisper.

"You don't have to explain." He won't look at me; instead he studies the shelf intently. But I can read the pain on his face like the words to a song. He thinks I didn't come last night because of some choice I made. Doesn't he know I don't have that right?

"I was at Abraham and Sarah's house," I say. "For dinner. I couldn't just leave. Not without drawing suspicion."

"Sure. Right. What about tuna? But I'd need a can opener."

I don't owe him an explanation. He knows as well as I what my obligations are. But his indifference makes me angry. He needs to know the things I do. He doesn't understand, not yet, but he will. "I planned to leave early. But then, we talked of Delilah." I falter. "And I grew ill. They put me to bed, and when I woke it was morning and Daniel came to speak to us."

Now I have his attention. "Why did Daniel think to find you there?"

"I'm not sure." I didn't question it at the time, but now that Caleb has, I wonder, too. I doubt Sarah and Abraham called him, not when they seem eager to protect others from Daniel. So who told him we were there?

From the front of the store, Aaron clears his throat. Loudly. When I look up, he tilts his head, past Caleb.

"Miriam. And Caleb." Susanna sidles up next to Caleb, grabs his arm, and presses herself against him. "That's a strange combination, isn't it?"

Caleb yanks himself free of her grasp. "Are you following me?"

"Don't be stupid." She turns to me. "And how about you, Miriam? I'm not used to seeing you in here. Your husband, yes, but you . . ."

"Miriam's been busy. Weaving." Aaron joins us, holding up the skein of yarn like it's a source of pride rather than embarrassment.

Susanna runs her thumb over it. "I suppose God will grant you peace, if nothing else."

Aaron balls the yarn in his fist and shoves it in his pocket. "He'll also grant us fish."

"Fish? This time of year?" Caleb asks. "Doubtful."

Aaron nods at the long white package tied with string in Susanna's basket. "Not for Susanna, apparently."

Fish is a prized commodity, reserved for women who have a talent they can trade for it or who are married to husbands with high-ranking positions. As far as I know, Susanna has neither.

Her smile cools. "Everything is available, for a price. Even fish."

"You must've had something pretty special to trade," Aaron says. "Don't you work for Daniel now? Opening mail and scheduling his appointments? What commodities come of that?"

"There are other commodities besides yarn." Her sniff reminds me of her mother.

"Sure, sure. Love, for instance," Aaron says.

I don't understand the glare Susanna gives him, but Aaron seems vaguely pleased with her response, while Caleb looks like he's going to punch one of them. Or both.

"Love isn't a commodity," I say, horrified. "It should be given freely, not bartered away."

"Tell that to Susanna," Caleb mutters.

"Everything's a commodity," says Aaron. "Isn't that right, Susanna?"

"You're wrong." I answer for her, but it comes out so weak even I don't believe myself. Because isn't my marriage—all our marriages—proof he's right? Each of us traded to the first man to say our name. Aaron spoke and I was handed over, just like a piece of fish. Susanna is beautiful, but she also has a sharp mind and an even sharper tongue. Still, to most of the men here, she's nothing more than an object. Even Marcus, who loves her, probably doesn't see past that perfect face. The sad truth is we are all commodities. Aaron was right, that night he told his parents that Daniel would sell us all into prostitution. In a way, he already has.

"You know what's a commodity?" Susanna asks us, though she's only looking at Caleb. "A coyote. That's a real commodity."

Caleb's face goes white and then red, in such quick succession that it could be the weak lighting.

"Did you catch the coyote? In our . . . your trap?" The words are out before I can think about what they might reveal to Susanna about my relationship with Caleb. Based on the wicked smile that slowly crawls across her face, she doesn't miss their significance.

"Just because you're willing to barter with my brother's life, that doesn't mean I am," Caleb says to Susanna.

"We'll see." She blows Caleb a kiss as she rounds the end of the aisle.

Aaron and I watch her go, but when I turn back to Caleb he is staring at me with a strange intensity. "I know I've said some things to make you unhappy," he says.

My cheeks go hot. Aaron is still looking after Susanna, a puzzled frown on his face.

"I'm going to make it up to you," Caleb continues. "I have to do something, and when I get back—"

"Back?" Aaron interrupts.

Caleb glares at him, then turns so he is between us, his back to Aaron. "When I get back, everything will be better. I promised you I would fix things, and I finally figured out how." He lifts a hand, as if to touch me, then perhaps remembers where we are. "I'll see you soon," he whispers. As he walks past Aaron, he bumps him with his shoulder, throwing my husband off balance. It looks like he may have done it on purpose, but I can't know for sure.

Aaron and I both watch as Caleb hefts several jugs of water onto the counter and signs his name to the register.

"Go back to the Mill and wait for me there," Aaron says, not taking his eyes off Caleb. "It's important that you act normal, stick to our routine. Don't make anyone suspicious."

"Suspicious? What are you—"

"I'm going to stop your boyfriend from doing something completely fucking stupid."

43

CALEB

I drag the last of the jugs of water into the garage and pull the door shut behind me. It's dark, no windows, and I give myself a minute for my eyes to adjust and for my pulse to stop racing. A minute to see if anyone has followed me. I cut around the back of the Kitchen and the Pavilion, avoiding the main road. But I wasn't exactly inconspicuous, lugging all this water. If anyone asked, I was going to tell them that Daniel wanted it stockpiled in the tunnel.

The air is thick with the smell of gasoline, and under it, a faint but unmistakable hint of rain. Thunder rumbles in the distance, an unnecessary confirmation. When you live in the desert, you learn to smell rain before you learn to walk. I've got to hurry. I've only ever driven a tractor, and though I'm guessing the van operates on the same general principles—engine, steering wheel, pedals, gearshift—I'm sure there's going to be a learning curve. And I'd rather not do it in a washout.

I've committed to—and then discarded—a dozen different plans. Right now, I think the best course of action is to load the van, then figure out if I can drive it myself. But turning on the lights is going to attract attention. I'm going to need a flashlight. In the corner, I can make out the shadowy outline of a cabinet. I squeeze past the van and yank open the metal door, wincing at the rusty shriek. The shelves are crammed with a jumble of tools and junk—screws, rope, cans of paint, a chipped mug, a ball of rubber bands, a pile of dirty rags, a box of rat poison. I pick through it, tossing aside the rags to reveal a flashlight. *Praise the Lord.*

I pull it out, sending a pile of screws raining down onto the concrete floor in a chorus of metal. "Damn it." I curse quietly and flip the switch on the flashlight.

Aaron's face appears out of the dark like a devil.

"Jesus Christ Almighty!" I leap backward, banging into the cabinet door.

"What the hell are you doing?" he asks. He keeps his voice low, but it carries a warning that makes the hair go up on the back of my neck.

"How is that any of your business?" I whisper. I try to look behind him, to see if he's alone, but all I can see is what's in the small circle of light between us. I switch it off.

"It's my business because you're about to make a huge mistake that's going to fuck everything up." He holds out his hand. "Give me the van keys."

I clench my fist around them.

He tilts his head. "Come on. I know you have them. Probably stole them, right? From Daniel? No? The guard shack, maybe? Do you even know how to drive?"

I'm not going to take orders from this guy. He isn't my Leader. He isn't even faithful. "Of course I know how to drive. Now leave, before you get us both caught."

His lip twitches, like I've said something funny. "That's noble of you. But Miriam would never forgive me if I let you do something this stupid. You're going after Delilah, I'm guessing?"

I blink. "How did you . . . "

"That was my more charitable guess. The other was that you

decided to cut and run, leaving Miriam to deal with the fallout of your little—"

My temper revs into overdrive. "I would never—!"

There's a sudden pounding on the roof above us, and we both instinctively crouch and look up. "The rain's started," I say. "I need to get out of here."

Aaron shoves me. The blow isn't hard, but it catches me off guard and I go down, my elbow scraping the concrete. The keys clatter to the floor, and he snatches them up.

"This is a bad idea," he says. "Delilah isn't someone you need to worry about right now. You've got way more important problems to deal with, right here." He unlocks the driver's side and pulls open the door, reaching around to pull the lock on the back.

I stand and brush myself off. There's an oil stain on my pants, and my fingertips are black. "You don't know anything about my problems. Marcus is in trouble," I add, though I'm not sure why I'm telling him, other than he's part of the reason. "Daniel's had it out for him ever since you two arranged your stupid switch."

Aaron wrenches open the back door, then stops as if to consider my words. "Why Marcus?" he asks.

"I don't know! You tell me. Maybe because Delilah—"

"Marcus didn't have anything to do with Delilah. Okay? She's safe where she is. Safer than here," he mutters, hoisting himself into the back seat.

What does that mean? How does he know Delilah is safe? And what the hell is he doing in the back seat? "You're not coming with me," I say.

"Neither of you is going anywhere."

A crash of thunder shakes the garage, while a blinding streak of lighting illuminates the open doorway—and Daniel.

44

MIRIAM

I slam through the Mill door and am brought up short by Lydia's presence.

"What are you doing here?" I ask, pressing a hand against the twinge in my side and trying to catch my breath.

"Today you dye," she says, lips pinched with disapproval.

"What?" I stumble backward, raking my fingers against the rough wood wall behind me.

"The wool." She cocks her head, and her glee at my discomfort is so palpable it nearly chokes me. Belatedly, I see she's lined the counter and stove with stainless steel pans and piled the table with more wool.

The last thing I want to do is spend the afternoon with Lydia. Not when I'm still trying to figure out what Aaron meant when he said he had to stop Caleb from doing something "completely fucking stupid." And not when I still have all these doubts piling up in my head, much like these unending piles of wool. But Aaron told me I had to act normal.

"Fine," I say, pressing my hands across my apron and forcing myself to sound calm. "But I don't know what I'm doing."

"Put these on." She throws a pair of rubber gloves at me. "You'll need to protect your skin."

"From what?" I peer down into the vat of water. It's not boiling.

Her tone is impatient. "The mordant—it helps the dye take. It can damage your skin." She unrolls a fleece of wet wool from a towel and slowly sinks it into a vat the color of mustard, so slowly I have to bite my lip to keep from screaming.

"The wool has to be wet when it goes into the dye," she tells me, yet another of the dozens of rules she's thrown at me in recent days. She can't possibly think I'll remember them all. The only explanation is that she's hoping I'll fail. On a normal day, I'd rise to her challenge; I'm stubborn enough to want to prove her wrong. But right now, all I want is for her to shut up and leave.

"Otherwise we'll get uneven color," Lydia continues to lecture, mistakenly believing I care. "Now we wait for it to soak up the dye."

Such a terrible word, *dye*. Dyeing. Dying. How fitting today, when I don't know what my future holds. What if I have lost my faith? What if it is the End, and my name isn't in the Book? Worse, what if everything Daniel's ever told us has been a lie? What if none of us are in the Book? I fight the urge to burst into tears and instead force myself to take a breath. Act normal. Make her leave. And pray she doesn't ask where Aaron is.

Before she can say anything else, I ask, "Does it hurt the wool? The dyeing?"

She rolls her eyes heavenward. "Wool can't feel anything."

"I meant damage," I say, though I didn't. Not completely.

"We aren't damaging it. We're making it better. Why would we

328 · *Shannon Schuren*

want this dirty pile when we can have something pretty?" She unrolls another piece. "Put this one in the red."

I shove the wool into the churning liquid, grimacing as the crimson stain eats into it. It reminds me of blood, and torture. Death.

"Stop that!" Lydia snaps, and I snatch my hands back, splattering red dye across my apron.

"What? What did I do?"

"The humming," she says, her blue eyes flashing. "I won't have it."

With shaking hands, I pull the wool from the bath and wrap it carefully in a towel. I didn't realize I was humming, though now that she's caught me, I recognize the song. It's one my mother used to sing. She lost her voice as I grew older, but I'd memorized them long ago.

The one about not weeping for your memories. As a child growing up in New Jerusalem, I found the thought of crying about someone's absence ridiculous. Why would I worry about forgetting someone? Our community was so tightly knit, no one ever left. But here I am, dashing my own tears with the back of my wrist. If I lose everything, all I'll have are memories.

"Your color is uneven. That's the problem."

I swallow a sob, as well as the urge to rip pieces from the vat and hurl them across the Mill. "How do I fix it?" I ask, praying she doesn't tell me to start over.

"You'll have to pull it out and start over." She shakes her head and turns, but not before I see the smile tickling the corners of her mouth. My failure brings her pleasure like nothing else. If I were a better person, I'd be happy she's found this small source of joy. Instead, I imagine her suffering some terrible accident at work. Getting her hand caught in the loom. Falling into a vat of dye. Who knows? If she doesn't leave soon, I may push her.

Instead, Susanna comes to my rescue. Or maybe Lydia's.

"Have you heard the news?" she asks as she sweeps into the room, shaking rain droplets from her golden hair. She doesn't even bother with a greeting. But then, why should she? Her mother will always welcome her; any greeting I extend will be false. Now that Aaron has pulled back the veil to reveal the rot inside the core of our community, I can't unsee it. How much of our daily life is a lie? Words, prayers, deeds, all performed by rote and without soul or heart. Has Susanna known this all along? Certainly, she's refused to conform to many of the rules the rest of us have blindly agreed to follow: covering her hair, talking about the men. Keeping her mouth shut. Is this the reason I hate her?

"Daniel caught Caleb and Aaron trying to leave the city. Chloe was on her way to take Gideon his lunch, and she saw the whole thing. Word is, they've been arrested!"

The blood leaves my head all at once, as if my brain has decided it has no need for it any longer. I stagger toward the table, and then somehow, my face is resting on the wool.

Aaron. Caleb. Leave the city. Arrested.

"Arrested!" I can see the shine in Lydia's eyes, even from here, and *this* is the real reason I hate them both. Not because I'm jealous, or because of some failing on my part. Because they are horrible human beings.

"Get out," I say. But the words are muffled in the wet wool beneath my cheek.

"Your husband may be Faithless. But you still have work to do," Lydia reminds me.

I push myself up and turn to pull a hunk of wool from the vat. "I refuse to allow you to disrespect my husband," I say, slapping it down on the table. Dye splatters across the wood planks, narrowly missing Susanna.

"The wool won't dye itself," Lydia says, raising her voice to match my own. She may be blind to my rage, but Susanna isn't.

"Let's go, Mother." She steers her to the door, pulling it shut just in time to avoid being hit by the hunk of wet wool I hurl at their backs. It hits the wall with a splat, trailing dye as it slides to the floor.

When I wipe my tears with the back of my hand, it comes away red. As if I'm crying tears of blood, like Jesus in the garden of Gethsemane. Just before he was crucified.

45

CALEB

"Running away?" Daniel asks. "Only the wicked flee when no one pursues."

Light floods the room, and I blink in the sudden glare. It's not just Daniel. He's brought guards with him. Thomas and Gideon. Damn. We're in bigger trouble than I thought.

"I'm not running away," I say. How could he even think that? "I was only trying—"

Daniel steps forward and backhands me across the face.

The blow catches me off guard. I touch my lip, half expecting to see blood. But our Leader isn't all that strong, at least not physically. That's why he has me.

Aaron is still in the back seat of the van. He hasn't spoken or moved, and for a crazy moment, I think he may be planning something terrible, like running over Daniel and crashing through the garage door. Should I try to stop him? Or join him?

But then he crawls backward out of the vehicle, his hands raised in the air as he slowly turns to face Daniel. Is he praying? He looks like an idiot.

"Put your hands down," I mutter.

Daniel raises an eyebrow. "Not the partner I expected to find you with."

"This is all a mistake," Aaron says. "Whatever you think is happening, it isn't . . ."

"Shut up," Daniel says, almost conversationally. "Your lies and denials are nothing but the pitiful cries of the damned. But you, Caleb." He shakes his head back and forth. "I expected more of you. What have I told you? If you lack wisdom, your only other option is righteousness. And now you're left with neither."

"I am right—" I begin. Okay, maybe I'm not righteous. I've committed adultery, after all. And I was about to leave the city without permission. But only for a worthy cause. Only to redeem my brother. And myself. It was a good plan. Right up until I got caught.

"I'm wise," I say softly. But that might not be true either.

Daniel certainly doesn't think so. He jerks his head at the door, and the guards shove us both out into the rain, which has become a downpour. In a few short hours, it will wash out roads and flood the low-lying buildings. It happens every few years. We get so little, the ground can't absorb it all when it comes. Today, the skies are weeping. Thunder and lightning crack in the distance, voicing the anger I can't, as Daniel leads and Gideon and Thomas push Aaron and me through wet sand and ankle-deep water.

"Where are we going?" I ask through chattering teeth. But the wind steals my voice and the rain threatens to drown me, so I shut my mouth and continue on. Are we being thrown out? Aaron, I could see. But me, Daniel's faithful servant? For this one infraction? He hasn't even let me explain myself.

But he stops before the tunnel door, and then I understand. He's going to lock us in the tunnels. I've heard rumors of this punishment from the other men, but I thought it was only for the worst sinners.

"Wait. This is all a misunderstanding. I wasn't running away. I was going to get you your coyote."

Aaron stares at me like I've sprouted horns. Daniel just ignores me as Thomas rolls back the door and we step into darkness. Water runs through the tunnel like a fast-moving river, splashing over my sandals and numbing my feet. My wet clothes cling to me, offering no relief from the cold air. I long for a fire or the desert sun or even the comfort of my warm bed in my lonely room.

"Wait here," Daniel orders Gideon. "Don't let anyone else in. Or out." He takes the flashlight from the guard, then shoves me forward while Thomas and Aaron follow close behind. I duck my head low and press my hands against the wall, feeling my way through the darkened space. When we come to the handwriting, I run my fingers over the carvings. Daniel's told us many times at our Lessons what it says, but I can never remember it word for word. It has something to do with why we're here, and the sins of the Outside we're trying to avoid. As I peer closer, I'm surprised to see images instead of words. One looks like a man holding a spear. And there's an animal—maybe a deer or a coyote. People standing near a river. Is it possible Daniel got the message wrong?

Before I can say a word, Daniel strikes me between the shoulder blades, muttering bits of scripture under his breath. "You have turned your back on me" I recognize. I think that one comes early in the Bible. And "lake of fire and sulphur" is Revelation, one of Daniel's favorites. But I don't recognize "lie down with dogs."

"What book is that?"

He hits me again, and I slip in the ankle-deep water and bang my head against the wall.

"The Book of Daniel." Spittle hits me in the face. "You want to drive?" he asks. "So be it." He pushes me farther down the tunnel. "You will be driven far from your people. You will wander the desert like animals."

The quote is vaguely familiar to me, but in my panic and my shame, I can't place it.

"I wasn't trying to leave," I say again.

When he stops to throw open the door, I realize we are in the Marriage Cave. It feels like another life, another Caleb who stood on that stage just a few weeks ago. I started that night with such hope, and by the end I was furious and heartsick.

I guess not much has changed.

Thomas shoves Aaron forward, and he falls to his knees.

"This will be your new home," Daniel says, his voice magnified by the rock walls and his rage. "I've removed the ladder, so there will be no crawling out of the pit. Let's see how resourceful you truly are. If you really want to escape, you can probably find a way. But you should give serious thought to whether you wish to brave the desert at night. Also"—he waves at the entrance to the tunnel, where water is flowing in at an alarming rate—"this is going to flood soon. I strongly suggest you keep this door shut if you don't want to drown."

With that, he pulls the door shut, plunging us into darkness. Maybe it's the cold, or the shock, but it takes me a few seconds to process what has happened. The quote *is* from Daniel. From when Nebuchadnezzar dreamt of exile as punishment for his sins.

We aren't just being punished.

We've been Banished.

46

MIRIAM

> AND YOU WILL KNOW THE TRUTH,
> AND THE TRUTH WILL SET YOU FREE.
> —*John 8:32*

As soon as Susanna and Lydia are gone, I leave the Mill, heading out into the rain without an umbrella or a plan. I just know that I can't sit by myself and worry. I need to do something. I need answers.

The trouble is, I don't know where to get them. Daniel? I don't know if I trust him anymore. My mother? What will she know about Caleb and Aaron? I stop and lean against a pinyon tree to catch my breath, though the rain is doing its best to drown me. Where can I go? Daniel's eyes are everywhere inside these gates, as is his law. What I need is an ally, though I feel like those are being stripped from me, one by one. Is this deliberate, or am I starting to see demons where they don't exist?

Like Caleb. I used to think I'd do anything to make things "right," so that we could be together. But what has he done? When Aaron left me, he said he was going to stop Caleb from doing something stupid. Now they've both been arrested. Trying to leave the city? What were they thinking? When I told Caleb I'd thought about going, he laughed at me. Did he change his mind? He'd never leave New Jerusalem, not for good, but maybe my concern about Delilah finally got through to him. But then why didn't he tell me? Maybe he was trying to, earlier, at the Commodities Exchange, and somehow Aaron got caught in the middle. My thoughts swirl together so quickly I can scarcely pull them apart, and my head swims. How did our need to be together become so great it overshadowed the hurt we'd inflict on everyone else? Because now Aaron is in trouble, too. He told me he didn't trust Caleb, and he was right.

So why did I? Because I loved him? Or at least, I thought I did. Though he said nice things, and held me in his arms, I don't really know him. And he certainly doesn't know me. My thoughts. My dreams.

Though Aaron says my dreams aren't real. That I only dream about the things I'm worried about. What did he call it? My subconscious? What does that even mean? Under-conscious? Beneath my conscious. Or beneath my conscience? Because I've certainly dreamt about things my conscience doesn't approve of. Or at least Daniel wouldn't approve of. But if dreams are messages from God, why would that be? The thought makes my gut twist tighter. It's not true. Aaron must be wrong.

I shake my head, water spilling from my curls. I can't think about this now. I need to do something. Aaron and Caleb. How can I help them? Aaron told me he wanted me to talk to his mother. That there was something she had to tell me. Of course, that was before we ran into Caleb, and Aaron went after him and sent me back to the Mill. But maybe Sarah can help me now. At the very least, she should be able to answer my questions. She and Abraham both know what happened to Delilah. Maybe they also know what's happened to Aaron and Caleb.

I run all the way to the housing circle and knock at their door, not at all sure of my welcome. After all that's happened, how can I have faith in anything? But I must have answers.

Abraham stands silently in the doorway as rain drips off the eaves of the porch and down my neck.

"Can I come in?" I ask, and he steps back to let me pass, then sticks his head outside once more before shutting the door.

"Miriam!" Sarah comes into the room, stopping when she sees my disheveled appearance and rain-slicked face. "What's wrong? Where is Aaron?" Her concern is for me as well as her son, and it's my undoing. One second, I am standing in their living room, the next I am sobbing in her arms.

She leads me to the sofa and rocks me, smoothing my hair. "It's all right. Shh. Abraham, get us some towels."

She dries my tears and helps me out of my clothes as best she can without leaving me naked, then wraps me in a blanket. As she gathers the rest of my wet things, the speaker on the wall crackles to life. "All citizens report to Chapel in one hour. All citizens, report to Chapel in one hour."

I lift the towel from my damp hair. "Why is he calling us to Chapel? It isn't the Sabbath."

"You tell us," Abraham says.

"A.J." Sarah's voice is sharp, and my apprehension gives way to full-blown terror at her use of this different name. They promised to give up all the remnants of their former lives when they came into this community. The fact that she calls him something other than the name Daniel gave him, right in front of me, fills me with a terrible foreboding. "Can't you see she is upset?"

And then to me, "Be careful," she whispers and points to the speaker mounted on the wall. So Aaron has shared his suspicions with them. Or they shared theirs with him. I appreciate their concern, but in this case, it's unfounded. If he were using the speakers to listen to us, my mother would have been Banished for her singing long ago. Besides, how would he ever keep all the voices straight? We all have at least one speaker, and most homes have more.

I shake my head. "He can't hear us like that. He has other ways of keeping track of us."

"Well, just to be safe," Abraham says, and then yanks out the cords. "That will cost us, but we don't have time to worry about it now. Why are you here, Miriam? Where's Aaron?"

"I don't know." I fight the urge to cry again and pull the blanket tight around my shoulders. I need to be strong. They deserve the truth, and I need their help. Even if it means confessing my sins and my complicity in Aaron's arrest. I take a deep breath. "I don't know where Daniel's taken him, but I think I know why. Caleb"—my voice catches on his name—"Caleb and I were . . . unfaithful."

Confessing this to these good people feels like ripping my heart out and handing it to them. "I'm so sorry. We—I—never meant to hurt anyone. Least of all Aaron. He just . . . got stuck in the middle somehow." I twist my fingers together and stare at the tangle.

Sarah grips my hands with warm fingers. "We understand more than you know."

Abraham narrows his eyes, as if he has less faith than his wife, but he keeps his mouth shut.

I give Sarah a grateful smile, then swallow it. "I don't know what happened. Aaron went after Caleb, earlier today. He said he had to stop him from doing something stupid. And now Susanna says they've both been arrested."

Sarah's grip turns painful. "Damn it."

"How convenient," Abraham mutters. He closes his eyes and pounds a fist against the fireplace mantel.

"She said they were trying to leave the city." I tear up again. "That can't be true. Why would they do that? They must have known how much it would anger Daniel."

They exchange a look I can't decipher. "Do you think he might be . . . violent?" Sarah asks.

With all I know, I can't defend him any longer. "Yes. I think he could be violent." I take a deep breath. I need to know everything. "I heard you. Last night. I know about the cult. And Delilah." I look at Abraham. "I also heard Aaron say something about prostitution. What did he mean?"

Abraham clears his throat. "My orders were to drop Delilah at a brothel in Vegas. Daniel didn't know what else to do with her, so he got in touch with a madam who agreed to take her."

My vision darkens to a few tiny stars of light, and I sway as the blackness closes in. Someone holds my shoulders to steady me. I blink, trying to clear the dizziness and confusion. If this is true—if any of it is true—that would mean Daniel is worse than a liar. He's a monster.

But I can't think about that. I need to concentrate on Delilah. "You said you got Delilah somewhere safe. Is that true? Were Caleb and Aaron helping you? Is that why they left?"

Abraham says, "It's true that Delilah's safe. But I didn't know anything about Caleb and Aaron. He wouldn't have been that stupid. Would he?" He glances at his wife, who shrugs. "If he's really been arrested, then we're all in trouble. You've been honest with us, so I'm going to lay our cards on the table."

I glance at the empty coffee table, and Sarah stifles a sad smile. "He means we're going to tell you the truth."

340 · *Shannon Schuren*

"We'll help you, even take you to Delilah if you want. But we need something in return. We need you to help us get a message to Rachel."

"Rachel?" I couldn't have been more surprised if he had named Daniel himself. "Why Rachel?"

"Naomi wants her daughter back," says Sarah.

"How do you . . . ? Naomi's dead."

Sarah is shaking her head before I finish. "She isn't dead. She's living right here in California. Healthy. But sick with worry about Rachel."

I can't comprehend what she's saying. Daniel told me Naomi— But of course. Yet another lie. Still. "That doesn't make sense. When Rachel was a baby, Naomi committed a sin so Contemptible, Daniel had no choice but to Banish her. But he offered to keep Rachel and raise her in New Jerusalem, so Rachel had a chance at being Saved, despite the stain from her mother's sin."

They stare as if I'm speaking in tongues.

"That's the story Daniel told you," Sarah says.

"To cover his own ass," Abraham adds.

I look from one to the other, bracing myself on the couch against another wave of dizziness. "Prove it."

They exchange a look. Finally, Abraham ducks his chin, and Sarah stands to retrieve one of her netsuke, a tall woman holding a vase. She turns it over and uses her pinky to retrieve a tightly wrapped piece of paper from the bottom.

When she hands the roll to me, I smooth it out across the table. It's actually two pieces of paper. A note addressed to Rachel and signed "Mom," and a photograph. I study the photo. But I've never seen Naomi, and I don't know what she looks like. "This could be any woman," I say, my throat so tight it burns.

Any woman with Rachel's dark eyebrows and the same dent in the bridge of her nose.

So it's true. Rachel's mother is alive? That means Daniel lied to me. And then I realize. Everything I've been told—everything Daniel has ever said—it's all lies. My vision blurs, and I'm not sure if I'm going to faint or throw up.

"What about Azariah?" I whisper his name from habit. "Is he alive too? He and Naomi sinned. And then Azariah ran away. He was too cowardly to face his punishment. He left his wife behind, as well as Naomi and Rachel." Even as I repeat the story, I recognize this must also be a lie.

Abraham frowns. "We don't know what happened to Azariah. Naomi's looked for him, but she hasn't been able to find him. The thing is, Azariah had no reason to run."

This is the first thing he's said that I don't believe. "Sometimes men are weak."

Sarah makes a choking sound. "Oh, Miriam. I see why Aaron likes you. You're feisty."

I don't know what that means, but I think it might be a compliment.

"Everyone is weak, sometimes. But in this case, there was nothing to run from. Azariah didn't sin. He isn't Rachel's father," Abraham says. "Daniel is."

My head shakes of its own accord, and scripture jumps unbidden to my tongue. This time, instead of reciting it, I choke on it.

Sarah jumps up to get me a bowl, then holds it while I gag and spit. She rubs my back, whispering soothing sounds. I thought I'd looked all the way down into the darkness, that I'd discovered the depths of Daniel's deceit. But I was wrong.

Rachel's father. He had relations with Naomi and then threw her Out. Worse, he let Rachel bear the burden of his own sin. All that "sins of the mother" crap that followed Rachel her whole life. What about the sins of her father?

Finally, I settle weakly back on the couch.

"I know it's a lot to take in," she says.

Abraham hands me a glass of water and sits on the edge of the table. "We don't have much time," he says. "We don't know what happened to Azariah. What we do know is that when Naomi gave birth to his child, Daniel kicked her out and forced her to sign custody of Rachel over to him."

Sarah adds, "She entrusted Rachel to your mother, thinking it would only be a small amount of time before she could get her baby back. But she had some problems. And Daniel made things complicated for her. Legally speaking. She's been trying for years to get custody of Rachel. But she left here with nothing. She doesn't even have a birth certificate, so she can't prove she's Rachel's mother. That's why she hired us."

"Hired you?"

"We're private detectives," Abraham says. "We specialize in helping families who've lost loved ones to cults."

I thought I was done being sick. But now, my head spins and my stomach drops. "Wait. So . . ."

"We didn't come here to be saved. We came to save Rachel."

47

CALEB

I hear a splash, and in the second it takes me to react, Aaron is on me, punching and kicking. He may be small, but he's stronger than he looks, and he manages to land a few blows before I throw him off.

"You have no idea what you've done," Aaron says, struggling to his feet.

Daniel wasn't kidding about the flooding. As my eyes adjust to the dim light, I see water is flowing in under the door like someone turned on a faucet. The water is up to our calves now.

"What I've done?" I say. "You're the one who came after me! You probably led him right to us. If you had just minded your own business—"

"If I'd minded my own business, you'd either be here by yourself or dead behind the wheel of the van, you self-righteous bastard," he hisses. "Now you've put not only us but my whole family in danger. Including my wife."

"Don't call her that!" I lunge at him, fully intending to throttle him until he dies or at least passes out, but he moves out of reach and this time I end up in the water.

"How long was Daniel standing there?" Aaron asks as he stares down at me. "Think. This is important. Did he hear me tell you that Delilah was safe?"

"I . . . I don't know. I don't think so? How can you be so sure about her, anyway?" The icy water gives me sudden clarity and I remember what Father said, that night in Daniel's office. "You *were* with her. Before she disappeared. Was I right? You were who she was afraid of? Were you . . . lovers?"

"Oh, Jesus Christ, Caleb! Get a grip. I'm gay," Aaron says, crouching beside me. "And since you're probably not up on the lingo, I'll break it down for you. I like dudes. Present company excluded."

A wave of water hits me in the face, and I roll to my side, coughing and retching. Gay? That can't be . . . Is this the secret Miriam was willing to keep? *I won't sacrifice him, not even for my own happiness.*

"Miriam knows," I say. It isn't a question—more like a desperate plea for him to deny it.

"Miriam's a good person. She was protecting me."

"You aren't worthy to say her name." But I'm too weak to put any force behind the words. It takes all my strength just to stand up.

"Neither are you. But I know she cares about you. So there must be something decent I can't see."

I'm forever grateful for whatever she sees in me. But she also sees something in Aaron.

"And what about you?" I ask. "How does she feel about you?"

"You'd have to ask her."

Our gazes lock, then skitter away.

"Look, we don't choose who we love. But we do get to pick our friends. Miriam and I are friends," Aaron says.

"Friends," I repeat. "And you only like guys. Not girls. Not even Miriam? So why'd you choose her, then? Did Daniel tell you to pick her?"

"I picked her because I thought she was a good person. And

because I didn't have a lot of options at that point." He rubs his chin. "How long have you known? That it's Daniel and not God doing the choosing?"

I shake my head, fast, so that my vision blurs. "What? No. That's not what I . . . I don't know why I said that. I just meant, did Daniel tell you your dreams were about her?" But that isn't what I meant. I was thinking of the voice, at my own supposed Matrimony. The voice that whispered "Delilah." It was the voice of God. Wasn't it?

Aaron is silhouetted beneath the faint light filtering down from the opening of the pit. He stops digging his knuckle in his ear and tilts his head toward me. "Lame, right?" He deepens his voice. "Yes, Marcus. I understand you've dreamt of only Susanna. But I'm telling you it means God wants you to choose Rachel. Why? It's a mystery only God and I understand." He shakes his head, then tips his ear to the floor and says in a normal voice, "I can't believe he thought that shit would work."

"But . . ." I have so many questions. "It did. It does. I mean, it works if we all listen. I dreamt of Miriam. That wasn't a lie. We were supposed to be together. And you were supposed to . . ."

"Haven't you figured it out yet? There was no way everyone was going to be happy. Daniel got a little too power-hungry, and he fucked the pooch, as we say on the Outside. He overplayed his hand," he says, when it's apparent I have no idea what he's talking about. "He tried to maneuver all of you into the marriages he wanted you in. But let's face it. There was no way that was ever going to work. Someone was going to walk away from that Matrimony unhappy. Daniel was just gambling on it being someone who wouldn't complain too loudly. Or someone he could call out as a sinner so he could shut them up if they did."

My mind is reeling. This can't be true. Only . . . hadn't I said almost the same thing to Phoebe? Only I'd said that having the girls choose would have left someone unhappy. But maybe Aaron is right. Maybe someone was always going to be married to the wrong woman. Or not married, in my case. Because if Aaron and Marcus hadn't switched, Marcus would be as unhappy as I am now.

Doubt floods me like the rainwater in this cave, which is steadily rising. "Oh my God. Is that why he's so angry? Not because you switched, but because . . ."

"Because we showed everyone he wasn't the 'Living Prophet'?" He shrugs. "Maybe. But we've got other problems now. Like getting out of here. And I'm worried about my parents. And Miriam. You know Daniel better than me. Will he go after them? Punish them for whatever he thinks we've done?"

I rub my face with numb fingers. "I don't know." It's so cold. Temperatures drop suddenly in the desert, but we're hardly ever out of doors when it happens, and never far from shelter.

"Does he know about you and Miriam?"

"I don't know," I repeat. "How did you . . . Never mind. I don't think he does. Except, when he saw you in the van, he seemed surprised. Like maybe he was expecting someone else."

"Shit. She isn't safe. Daniel is escalating. It's only a matter of time—"

"Escalating?"

"I don't have time to slow-walk you through this, so try and keep up," Aaron says. "Short version—you're living in a cult. Daniel has you all brainwashed into believing the world outside is some kind of lawless wasteland. It's not. Miriam was starting to understand, and to have doubts of her own, so that makes her a threat to Daniel. He's going to use us, our attempt at escape"—he makes a weird clawlike gesture with his hands—"to try and reassert his dominance. Regain control. At our expense. Trust me. I've seen it before. This isn't gonna end well for us."

I resist the urge to cover my ears with my hands. "I don't know what you're talking about, but if this is what you've been filling Miriam's head with, it's no wonder—"

"Screw it. Don't believe me. I don't really give a fuck. I'm getting the hell out of this cave, then I'm going to find Miriam, and we're leaving. You can do whatever you want."

I want out of this cave, too. The rest—but I can't do this now. I'll think about the rest later.

"We need to stop the water, or at least slow it down," I say. "It's coming in from both directions. We can't do anything about the opening to the pit, but maybe we can stop the water from the tunnel if we stuff something underneath the door."

Aaron pulls at his wet shirt. "Clothing?"

I'm not comfortable with the idea of being naked alongside another man, especially one who doesn't seem to care that his choices are going to get his name excluded from the Book. But the bigger problem is I don't think the clothes will stop the water. I shake my head. "The fabric is too thin. We're going to have to use sand."

We drop to our knees, side by side, and scoop handfuls of wet sand and gravel from beneath the water. Push it against the crack under the door, over and over, until it's covered.

I crawl up onto the stage, exhausted. Aaron sits on the edge, then flops onto his back and breaks the silence. "Daniel's unstable. But would he really leave us here for the rest of our lives? Too many people would question what happened to us."

I can't answer him. We've been taught to live our lives in service to God, and at the end he rewards us with Salvation. As promised, it sounds glorious. The problem is, if I believe any of what Aaron has told me, we might've been promised a lie. In which case, there won't be Salvation for anyone, sinner or not. There may not even be a tomorrow.

48

MIRIAM

"I don't know what you mean, 'private detective,'" I say. *"But Rachel* isn't the only one who needs saving." I struggle free from the blanket cocoon Sarah's wrapped me in. I thought I could trust these people. Does no one tell the truth anymore? "What about the rest of us? What about your son?"

"Aaron isn't our son. He's working with us. Undercover. As a teenager," Abraham says.

I fall back onto the couch. "What? Not your . . ? Then who am I married to?"

"No one," Abraham says. "Daniel doesn't want the government involved in his dealings here, so he doesn't file certificates with the state. None of these marriages are legal."

Though I don't understand half of what he said, I latch onto his final words. None of the marriages are legal. Days earlier, hours, even, this would have been joyous news. Now, it's too much for me to comprehend.

"Is anything Aaron said true? About you living in a cult once before? His boyfriend? How old is he?"

"He told you about Tucker?" Sarah asks, at the same time Abraham says, "Twenty-four."

They exchange a look I can't decipher, then Abraham continues,

"Aaron lived in a cult as a kid. With his parents. I'm not sure what he told you, but it messed him up pretty good."

"We had reservations about bringing him along for this," says Sarah. "Given his past."

"But his past is what makes him good at what he does." It sounds like an argument Abraham's made before, and he waits for my reaction, arms crossed, occasionally looking out the window.

I try to put the pieces together.

"So . . . you said 'detective.' What does that mean?" I ask. "Do you detect danger?"

"Sometimes. Mostly, it's work for hire. A client pays us to find information. Or people," says Abraham.

"Did someone hire you to save Delilah, too? Is that why you helped her escape?"

"That wasn't a planned operation. But after Daniel told me where he was sending her, we were obviously concerned about her safety. So I followed my gut and had Aaron tell her the truth about Daniel. After that, she wanted to leave, and we helped her. You can join her. If *you* help *us*."

"Miriam," Sarah interrupts, "let me explain. Naomi is very concerned about Rachel's well-being. She knew Rachel would be forced into marriage once she was old enough. We tried to swing the Matrimony so she'd end up with Aaron. When that didn't work, we needed a plan B."

"Plan B?" I sift through her words for something to grab onto, but none of it makes sense.

"You're plan B," Abraham says. "You're her best friend. She trusts you. If—when—you tell her the danger you're in, she'll listen."

"I still don't understand. If Naomi has been trying to reach Rachel since she left, why is this all just happening now?"

"We're not the first people she's hired. But Daniel is pretty adept at covering his ass. Combine that with his pathological suspicion of outsiders, and it's all but impossible to get information about this place," Abraham says. "We've been working on this operation for over a year."

We hear raised voices outside the window, though I can't make out the words. Abraham presses himself against the wall and peers through one of the window-blind slits. "Council Members. On their way to Chapel." He takes a step forward and pulls me to my feet. "You need to talk to Rachel," he says. "Convince her you both need to get out of here."

The knock at the door renders us all mute and immobile. Before I can react, Abraham shoves Naomi's letter into my hands and pushes me down the hall. I slip inside Aaron's old bedroom and behind the open door.

"Hello." I recognize Susanna's voice. "Daniel has called us to Chapel."

Abraham is the first to recover, impressing me once again with his ability for deceit. In New Jerusalem, we welcome any intrusion, however annoying. "Welcome, Sister. How nice to see you," he says, stepping into the living room and blocking her view of the hallway. "We were just discussing this unusual summons."

"It's time to open the Book," Susanna is saying. "For the truth to be known, for the names to be revealed. Is anyone else here with you?" she asks, and I imagine her trying to crane her neck around Abraham, though I can't see from my position, pressed into the corner.

"Who else would be here besides my wife?" Abraham asks.

"Aaron?" Susanna asks, and I have to bite my lips shut to avoid

352 · *Shannon Schuren*

crying out. Why is she lying to them? She knows Aaron has been arrested. She's the one who told me.

I picture Abraham weighing his words. "Aaron isn't here. I assume he's at his own apartment. With his wife." Perhaps it's only because of all they've told me, but I hear a challenge in his words. "Or maybe he's already heading to Chapel. Were you interested in speaking with him?"

Susanna laughs, as if she has no worries about lying to her neighbor's face. "Not at all," she says. "I just thought as newer citizens, you might have some concerns. So I've come to escort you."

"How thoughtful of you," Sarah says. "You must be very close to Daniel," she continues, "for him to send you personally."

"Daniel didn't send me," Susanna says sharply. "I came on my own. Idle gossip is the tongue of the devil," she adds.

I have an urge to rip her own tongue right out of her mouth.

"Thank you, Sister." The door creaks open, and Abraham's voice grows momentarily louder. "We're grateful for your support. Let me just grab an umbrella." He sticks his head into the room, glancing back and forth. When I peek my head around the door, he presses his finger to his lips, then drops it and mouths one word: *Rachel.*

"Let's go," he says, turning back to the hallway. "Sarah, darling, are you ready? Such a momentous occasion. Tell me, Sister, what will become of those whose names Daniel doesn't read?"

Susanna's reply is lost in the slamming of the front door, but it doesn't matter.

It's become evident to me what Aaron has known all along, what I should have seen long ago. The Book isn't real, because none of this is real.

Daniel is no more prophet than I am.

49

CALEB

Rain is still pouring through the opening above the pit; if it weren't, I might try to scale the rocks. But they're slippery, and I'm too weak at this point. Instead, I pace, just out of reach of the rain, and try to think of a plan.

Aaron sits on the dais, his back against the wall, looking tired and defeated.

"Abraham and Sarah will help us," he says. "Unless they've already been arrested. Or worse. Shit. What if he heard me? What if I put them all in danger? Just to help save your ass?"

He keeps blaming me. Repeatedly. And I'm sick of listening to him.

"You *did* put us all in danger! I didn't need your help!" I raise my voice on the final word, as if someone might hear and come to our rescue.

"Shut up!" says a third voice, from somewhere above us.

I freeze, my skin clammy and not just because of the water. "Is that Daniel?"

"Well, it's not God, is it?" Aaron snaps.

How long has he been up there? Is he guarding the pit in case we try to crawl out? In the rain? I can hear him yelling, quoting scripture, but I can't make out the words over the noise of the storm. His voice fades in and out, as if he's pacing toward and then away from the opening. Something about curses and dust.

A shower of rocks plunks into the water near my feet as his head appears above me.

"'And the serpent was more crafty than the other beasts, and he said to the woman—' Don't you see? It's always the woman!" Daniel says, fast and breathless. "For the serpent convinces the woman, and then she urges the man to sin. I am the one who must stop it; I am the one who must open your eyes to the temptation. For I am the One True Prophet, called by God to lead His Chosen People. Don't you see?"

I don't know how to answer. As sermons go, this is the most disjointed I've ever heard. And his frantic tone is making my skin crawl.

A metallic clang, then, "May your God whom you serve deliver you!"

Something splashes into the water beside me.

"Daniel?"

He doesn't answer, but whatever he's dropped is moving. Alive. I can't make out the shape in the dark, but the rattle is unmistakable.

Fear shocks me like a lightning strike. I don't move. I don't breathe.

"Are those fucking snakes?" Aaron asks, his voice so high-pitched it's almost a squeal.

Something grazes my groin as it slithers past in the water, and instead of answering him, I suck in air and retch, vomit splashing the water beside me.

"They can swim," I try to say, but no words come out. It feels like there are dozens of them, wriggling and gliding around me. I need to get away, but I'm frozen. Movement might interest them. Or worse, anger them. I cast a frantic look toward Aaron and the rock dais, which seems miles away. Lucky bastard. Not really, though. The snakes probably want dry ground as much as I do.

I back toward him anyway, lulled by the illusion of safety.

"Dude, what are you doing? We need to split up, not give them a single target."

"Fine. Then you get in the water and let me climb up there!"

One of the snakes swims past, twitching its body through the water as easily as if it had fins. Then it switches direction and slides up on the raised rock in one easy motion.

Aaron leaps off the other end and into the water.

"I don't think we've given enough consideration to scaling the wall," Aaron says, dragging himself through the water to stand beside me. Wasn't he the one who said we needed to stay apart?

"Climbing is too risky," I say. "One slip or scrape and we'll be adding the scent of fresh blood to the situation. Can snakes smell blood?" They can smell fear. Or is that coyotes? Fear has rendered me as stupid as Marcus used to claim I was.

"So, the tunnel then." Aaron holds his arms high and scans the water around us. "We'll swim for it."

"Drown, or get attacked by a den of snakes," I say. "God really doesn't like sinners."

"Maybe it's not as bad as we think."

"Being poisoned by rattlers?" Has Aaron completely lost his reason?

"The tunnel," he says. "What if Daniel just told us the tunnel floods to keep us in here? That would be just like him, actually. Keeping us prisoner with our own thoughts."

Is Aaron right? Is Daniel really that manipulative? There's only one way to know.

As if sensing we're attempting an escape, more of the snakes slide onto the dais, one after another, like sentries lining up for battle.

Slowly, I turn my back, motioning for Aaron to follow. The soft sound of rain grows louder, echoing off the cave walls. But it isn't rain. It's the rattlers.

I shudder, take a deep breath, and pull open the tunnel door.

A wave of water gushes over our heads, dragging us under.

50

MIRIAM

After they leave, I wait, alone, as the rain beats relentlessly on the roof. I don't believe Susanna had any altruistic motives for coming here. Why Abraham and Sarah? Does Daniel know something about their secret? Is that why Aaron was arrested? Maybe Caleb was just in the wrong place at the wrong time.

But speculating will get me nowhere. I must do what Abraham asked, and talk to Rachel.

I take the back way to the Farm, keeping to the shadows. I don't want to run into any of my friends, asking why I'm not heading toward Chapel. I'm hoping Rachel is still at work. While she will obey Daniel's Call without question, she will need to tend to the goats first.

When Rachel answers my frantic knocking on the barn door, I fall into her arms.

"Good heavens, Miriam. What's wrong?"

I pat self-consciously at my hair, aware of how I must look. "I'll tell you everything, but it'll take some time. Where's Jacob?" Despite Sarah's assurances that they only want to help Rachel, I'm putting us all in danger by coming here. Rachel will understand once I explain about Naomi, but I don't want that decision in her husband's hands.

"He's out in the pasture, trying to round up the goats before Chapel." Worry puckers her forehead. "Why are you here?"

I don't know where to start. "I had to see you first. It's about your mother," I blurt.

She jerks her head back. "Come in and get warm. I think we have time for a quick cup of tea."

She gives me dry clothing to change into. When I come out of one of the barn stalls, she hands me a mug and I wrap my hands around it, grateful for the warmth.

"It's a long story," I say. "But I have reason to believe . . . that is, someone has recently told me that Naomi—your mother—is alive. She's alive, Rachel! And she wants to see you!" I pull out the letter I took from Sarah's house, but she bats it away.

"My mother may not be dead, but she's dead to me."

"You don't mean that. Remember the stories we used to make up about her when we were kids? What if they were true? What if everything else we've been told about her is a lie?" I bend over to retrieve the paper, smoothing it on my knee.

"Who would lie?" she asks, her voice high. "Everyone in the community? If you love me, Miriam, if you value our friendship at all, you will never speak of that woman again."

That woman. Despite the heat from the wood-burning stove in the corner, my skin goes cold. What if Abraham and Sarah are wrong? What if I can't convince Rachel to come with me? I can't just leave her here, knowing what I know.

"Now." Rachel straightens her skirt. "Are you going to tell me why you're running around in the rain? I have a feeling it has something to do with your marriage." She closes her eyes and pinches her lips together. I have anticipated her disapproval, along with her disappointment. Rachel always does the right thing, and she expects those she loves to do it, too. I may as well get my confession out of the way. Perhaps my honesty will earn her trust in the rest.

"Aaron and Caleb have been arrested. Susanna says they were trying to leave, but I don't believe it. I think they were trying to find Delilah."

"My God, Miriam, what were they thinking?"

"They were thinking she needed help. They would've come back. Caleb would never leave New Jerusalem without me." Though everything else I've believed has been proven false, I still trust in his devotion to me. My feelings for him are more complicated, however.

"What are you saying?" Rachel asks. "That you coveted another man?"

"I'm aware of my sins," I say, grateful she doesn't know what else I've done. "But have you ever really thought about that one? *Thou shall not covet.* How? How do you stop wanting something? It's like trying not to breathe."

"You pray."

It would be that easy for her. "I tried that. But love doesn't just go away. And if God wanted me to turn to Aaron, why would he continue to send me dreams of Caleb?"

She goes to the stove in the corner of the barn and opens it, sending a flurry of sparks into the air. "I'll tell you what you shouldn't do. You shouldn't go around arranging secret meetings with your lover." She shoves a log onto the fire.

"I didn't arrange— Wait. How do you know about that?"

She goes still.

"Rachel?" I set my tea down on the table. She doesn't look at me. My mind flips through memories of the last few days, slowly, as if digging under a rock, afraid to unearth a scorpion's nest. Our first kiss, on the path just down the hill from this house. Our heated exchange under the Pavilion. "How long have you known?"

She makes a sound halfway between a laugh and a sob. "Please. You didn't even try to hide it. Have you no shame at all?"

"I believed I loved him."

"What do you know of love?"

"What do you?" I snap back. "Married to a man only because he picked you? And what if I told you it wasn't even supposed to happen? That's right," I say, as her eyes widen in surprise. "Daniel wanted Jacob to pick Delilah. You were intended to be Marcus's wife. And you would have just gone along, wouldn't you? Given yourself to him, at his will, and told everyone it was fine, all because Daniel sanctioned it. How is that better than me and Caleb? He and I making the decision to be together because it was what we both wanted?"

"None of that is true. My marriage is real, and it is God's will."

"God's will." I snort. "God had nothing to do with it."

Rachel shakes her head. "You're wrong."

"I'm not. Have you never noticed that God's will only functions to keep Daniel happy? What about the rest of us? What about your mother? What if she didn't want to leave you here?"

Rachel shrinks back as if my heretical thoughts are contagious. "You're much further gone than I thought," she says. "Susanna was right. We should have stopped this sooner."

"What did you say?"

She clutches her chest and takes a step back.

"What does Susanna have to do with this?"

She stumbles against the wall and turns her head from me.

"Is this your doing? Did you say something to Daniel?"

Silence.

I think back to this morning, to Daniel's cryptic remarks about the Gathering. And the wine. My desire to go out to look for Delilah.

"Answer me, Rachel. Did you tell him about the Gathering?"

Slowly she turns her head back and meets my eyes. "It was Susanna," she whispers.

"But you didn't try to stop her. Or warn me." The heat in my chest burns so fierce, I want to scream but fear if I do, it will be fire instead of sound.

"I did try to warn you. I went to your apartment last night. But you weren't home." Her words hold an accusation. "So I went to the Mill. You weren't there either. But Caleb was."

I flinch. It seems a lifetime ago that he asked me to meet him. "I was ill, so we spent the night at Abraham and Sarah's house. But I suspect you already know that."

Her face turns a blotchy purple. "Someone had to do something. Before you sinned so badly, even Daniel couldn't forgive you."

"I thought you were my friend," I say.

"And I thought you were mine." Rachel's fury matches my own. "You of all people know the burden I carry because of my mother. First she is Banished because of her Contemptible ways, and now you?" She shakes her head, fast. "I couldn't let that happen again. We had no choice. You were past reason."

Does she believe that her confession will convince me to see it her way? But I know the truth about Daniel, and my eyes are open wider than hers will ever be.

"You didn't go to Caleb, and Daniel knows that. He will understand," she continues. "You must confess and repent now, though. For coveting. Before he opens the Book."

362 · *Shannon Schuren*

She reaches for me, but I just stare at her hand. "Because that's all it would take? I confess a sin I am not sorry for, and take my punishment? Because you can accept me being a sheep, but not a woman with desires."

"Listen to yourself." Her voice turns cold. "You sound like a harlot. Clearly all you care about are your carnal desires. I'm telling you, as your best friend, you need to go to Daniel right now, get down on your knees, and beg him for forgiveness. If you're lucky, he'll let you stay."

"Stay, and be Shamed. Only you would think a lifetime of suffering a fair penance."

"That's because I know from experience."

"And that experience is based on a lie. We all accepted Daniel's story about your mother, about her sinning with Azariah. Him running away and her abandoning you. But what did we really know? Nothing but what he told us. It was all a lie. Daniel is your father, Rachel. Not Azariah. And your mother is still out there. Alive. Trying to get to you."

"No. No no no." She presses her hand to her throat, perhaps to hold back a scream. It's a gesture I've made myself, a thousand times. But even as she denies it, I can read the doubt on her face. The quivering of her lips, the tears shining in her eyes. They belie the shaking of her head. She knows I'm right. And she's weakening.

"Just read what she's written," I plead. "Then if you still don't believe me, I'll do whatever you ask."

Her hand trembles as she reaches out and slowly takes the paper from me. But instead of reading it, she turns and tosses it into the open stove.

"Rachel, no!" I jump to my feet, but it's hopeless. The flames have already consumed it.

"Please, Miriam," she whispers. "You mean more to me than some woman I can't remember. Just repent. For me."

"It's that easy, is it?" I ask, watching the fire as tears run freely down my cheeks. "Repent, and everything will be all right?"

Relief floods her face. This is a question she's been taught how to answer. "Of course! It's Daniel. Don't you think—"

"No, Rachel." I turn away, from the fire, and from the girl I love like my own sister. "That's the problem. None of us think. *Your father* won't allow it."

51

CALEB

I thrash about in the water, coughing and choking, as I try to regain my footing.

"I don't suppose you get much chance to practice swimming here," Aaron says as he pulls me to my feet. The water is almost waist deep now.

"I can't swim," I manage, once I spit out the rest of the dirty water. A gritty residue still coats my mouth.

"Daniel knows that, I'm assuming?" Aaron slaps me on the back. "Of course he does. Between the water and the snakes, we have got to get out of here. Pronto."

Above the dais, a gush of water splashes onto a pile of snakes and they scatter, their rattling a violent hiss that raises the hair on my arms.

"Where'd that water come from?" Aaron asks, scanning the wall. We spot it at the same time. A thin opening, maybe shoulder height. Tucked into the darkened corner. "Is that another tunnel?"

"I . . . I don't know. But I just realized. We call them tunnels."

He blinks at me, the whites of his eyes bright in the gloomy cave. "What's your point?"

"Don't you get it? Not tunnel. Tunnels. The tunnels are sacred," I say, echoing part of the story.

"As in, more than one," Aaron says. "Well, shit!" He grabs my shoulder and shakes it.

"But we don't know where it goes." I'm sure he's as aware of this as I am, but I point it out anyway. "Could be a dead end."

"True. But there are no snakes in there, right?"

"Not that we know of."

"Excellent. So we're in agreement, then." He pulls through the water, moving slowly to the left, around the front of the ledge, to the side with the now snake-free puddle. "No sudden movements," he says from the corner of his mouth. "They're distracted. Let's keep it that way."

Aaron climbs up and then kneels on the rocky floor, planting a foot and lacing his hands together. "Here. Step into my hands." He mimes lifting me up into the tunnel.

"Why should I go first?" I ask.

"Because you're bigger and stronger, and you have to be able to pull me up once you're in. Come on. We don't have time to argue."

He's right. I put my foot into his hands and grasp the ledge above me, heaving myself up as Aaron lifts. Once my chest is over the ledge, I wiggle into the tunnel and lie on the floor to catch my breath.

"Hurry up!" Aaron urges, his head bobbing in and out of view.

Below, one of the snakes rears back, then lunges for Aaron's ankle, jaws wide. I grab his hand and pull. His feet scrape against the wall as he scrambles up, kicking the serpent in the head. Another rattler strikes, but too late, and Aaron rolls into the tunnel beside me. He scoots into a sitting position and slouches against the wall, holding up a hand, in victory, maybe. When I weakly mimic his gesture, he slaps my open palm. "High five," he says, then shakes his head at my confusion. "We did it."

We did . . . something. I'm not sure what. Survived, maybe? I'm going to wait to celebrate.

He holds out an arm toward the darkness in front of us. "You wanna lead, or should I?"

I shrug and begin crawling forward. The ground slopes up slightly and water flows past us, but not nearly as deep as in the bigger tunnel, covering only our hands and knees. After a few minutes, the tunnel opens into a cavern-like room, not as big as the Marriage Cave but big enough to stand up in. There's no pit, just a rounded ceiling with a couple of slits that cast moonlight near our feet like scattered stones.

The tunnel branches, and we look at each other silently, weighing our options. Aaron takes a step toward the right. I hesitate, then head for the left. We need to explore both paths.

"Hey!" he calls, when he realizes I'm not following him. "We've gotta go this way. It's the running water. It means there's a way out."

A way out. I hesitate and start to turn, but my foot slips on something smooth—a large rock, maybe?—and I go down hard on my knee.

"Caleb? Did you hear me?" When I don't answer, Aaron sticks his head around the corner. "What the hell, man? Let's g—" he starts.

Then he sees the bones.

52

MIRIAM

I shouldn't be surprised, or even angry because Rachel refuses to hear the truth. My best friend has always been the most faithful person I know. Next to my mother. Which makes me wonder: What does my mother know? She took Rachel in when Naomi left. Did she know she was raising the daughter of her Prophet?

My mother is still home, though my father, a Council Member, has already left for Chapel. She takes one look at me standing on her doorstep and pulls me inside. "My baby. Your father says Aaron has been arrested. What on earth is going on?"

As she pulls me close, I feel a flood of shame at all the lying I've done. I'm not used to keeping secrets from my mother, and I fear if I open my mouth, it will all come pouring out.

"I don't know, Mother." Secrets and now lies. I don't even recognize the woman I've become. For a second, I long to be the old, naïve Miriam. I long to curl up in my mother's arms and let her stroke my hair and tell me everything will be all right.

But I can't. And not just because she won't sit still long enough to let me. Even as she waits for my explanation, as we're minutes away from either Salvation or Damnation, she's still tidying her house. I follow her into the kitchen, where she grabs a rag and starts to wipe down the refrigerator.

"Mother, stop. Does any of this matter right now?"

She pauses her vigorous scrubbing long enough to say, "I won't go into the Tribulation with a messy house."

I choke back a laugh that ends on a sob. "Some of us have worse things on our conscience than a messy house."

She clutches the rag to her chest. "Miriam."

All that disappointment balled up in one little word. How does she do it?

"Please don't. I'm a woman now, remember? My sins are my own to make." I slump into a chair at the kitchen table.

"As is your repentance." Clearly, my mother has been talking to Rachel.

"What if I'm not sorry?"

A lesser woman would be shocked at my outspokenness, but she merely shakes her head and slides into the chair across from me and reaches for my hands. "This is the wrong time to be headstrong. Your future is at stake."

I don't tell her I can no longer imagine a future here. Instead I ask, "Do you never question the hypocrisy of it all?"

"What are you talking about?"

"I know about Naomi, Mother. Daniel told me she was dead, but she's not." I pick at a woven placemat, gauging her reaction from the corner of my eye. "Why would he lie? And why would we believe him?"

"He is Chosen. And we are here because he has Chosen *us*. To hear the True Message."

"What if there is no True Message?" I ask. "What if he's just a really good storyteller?"

She blinks, wide-eyed. "How can you say that? You've witnessed his gift firsthand."

She's talking about the prophecies he's made about the Outside, the wars and the murders he predicted. Sometimes he'd share a dream, and the next day he'd share reports that confirmed his predictions. Only now I know that none of it was true.

"You didn't grow up here," I say. "You followed him, voluntarily. What made you leave everything else behind? Please, Mother. It's important that I know." Part of me is curious, but another part needs to know how she did it. How to gather the courage to leave everyone— including my own mother—behind.

"I was your age," she says. "We heard about this man who was traveling the country. He drove around in a van and did dream interpretation out of a tent. He was set up outside Bakersfield, and a group of us drove out to see him."

"You drove?"

Her expression is pained, as if it hurts her to talk of these things. And maybe it does, dredging up those memories after all this time. "I didn't drive that night. Though I did know how." She fiddles with the rag, then stops and folds her slender fingers in her lap.

"Who went with you? Father?"

"I didn't know your father at the time. It was just some people I used to know. Friends."

I can't picture this at all, my mother on the Outside, riding in a car with a group of people I don't know that she calls friends.

"My older sister was with us, too."

Older sister? I have a thousand questions, but as in every conversation with my mother, I hold them back. This time, not because I think she won't answer but because I fear my interruption will stop the flow of words. And though the information she is giving me is new and terrifying, it's also exhilarating. She has—had—a sister. On the Outside. Whom she left behind.

She is quiet for a long time, staring up at the cracks in the plaster ceiling. "I didn't believe," she says finally. "Not really. I didn't think Daniel would actually be able to see my dreams." She looks right at me. "But he did. The things he saw." She stops and clutches at the crucifix around her neck. "I never told anyone about the nightmares. Or about my father—"

"Your father?" I can't help myself. The words spill off my tongue, dangerous, like jagged ice. I know the term for my mother's father—*grandfather*—because I learned it in Lessons. But it has never been spoken in my house, or any other in New Jerusalem I know of. Daniel teaches that we are all the family we need. Those the First Generation left behind are inconsequential.

"He was not a nice man. He did . . . things . . . that a father shouldn't do to his daughter."

My mind reels, and my heart aches for the girl she used to be. "Mother." My voice cracks.

She shakes her head. "It was a long time ago. And Daniel saved me. He took me away, brought me here. Showed me what it means to love. Gave me a home, and a future. He made me a wife. And a mother." She smiles then and reaches to grip my hands tight. "Miriam. You are the best thing that's ever happened to me. I can't bear to lose you." My mother, who has always been serene in the face of any crisis, is crying tears as heavy as the rainfall outside. "You are my life. Believe me when I tell you that New Jerusalem is a refuge in a sea of sin and debauchery." She pushes a lock of hair from my cheek. "I didn't want you to ever witness any of that. That's why I came here. To be safe."

"But New Jerusalem isn't what you envisioned. There's sin here, too."

She just looks at me, sadly. And though she doesn't acknowledge the truth in my statement, she doesn't deny it either.

"Tell me about Naomi," I say. "Did you know she was alive? That she was trying to get Rachel back?"

"Naomi made her choice, long ago."

"What does that mean?"

I can see the emotions warring on her face. She's keeping something from me. "Tell me."

"You have to understand, we were different back then. Just a handful of us who understood the truth about Daniel and his abilities. We had all been hurt; we'd all been told that we weren't worthy. And then we met Daniel. And he believed in us as much as we believed in him. At first, we all lived out of a bus. We'd stop somewhere, set up the tents. Daniel would do a reading, and if he managed to touch a soul, they would come with us. About the time I thought we couldn't fit another person in that vehicle, Daniel dreamt of the tunnels."

Though she smiles at the memory, I feel sick to my stomach as I recall something Aaron told me. *Daniel's father owned this land.* Which means Daniel's dream of the tunnels didn't come from God. It was just a memory.

"And so we came to New Jerusalem," my mother continues, oblivious to my distress. "But it was still a small community. All of us living together, crammed into the Farmhouse. We were . . . close." She slides her crucifix back and forth on its chain. "When the Joshua trees blossomed the first time, it was a message from God. Because of the temptation to sexual immorality, we were all to partake in the Matrimony."

She's quoting 1 Corinthians. Loosely.

"Those of us who had been here since the beginning were joined. Mishael and Lydia. Hananiah and Judith. Azariah and Phoebe. Gideon and Chloe. Your father and I." She waves her hand in the air. "All the Elders. And it worked out perfectly," she continues, "one woman for each man, the way God intended. And then Naomi came to us." She jerks her head back and forth, as if to shake off the memories. "Daniel was still going Out regularly, trying to find Outsiders who might be saved. One day, he came back with Naomi. We had all been wed. But she didn't have a husband. Maybe that should have been a warning to us. But she was so lost, so alone. We let her join, and we paid the price. Phoebe most of all." She smiles sadly. "You know the rest. Azariah ran off, before he could be punished. Naomi gave birth to Rachel, and then she gave her up . . ."

"But Rachel isn't Azariah's daughter." I want so much to believe her, but I don't. Sarah's version of this story makes much more sense. Why else would Naomi need to hire detectives to get Rachel back? Because she can't take her from her father. There's probably a rule about that.

"Who told you that?"

"It doesn't matter. I can tell by the look on your face that it's true. All these years, you all just kept on lying. And what about Rachel? How do you think she felt, believing her father to be an adulterer? Although I guess being a false prophet isn't any better."

Her face goes white, then pink. "Daniel couldn't claim Rachel. His responsibility is the community as a whole. He is husband and father to us all."

I shiver with revulsion. "All except Naomi."

"Naomi asked to leave. Begged, actually. And he let her go. Don't you see? It was her own choice. Just like it was Aza's to run."

But Abraham's questions have awakened an instinct for truth I didn't know I had, and I point out the flaw in her story. "But Azariah wasn't Rachel's father. He wasn't the guilty one. So why would he run off? Why not stay and protest his innocence? Tell people the truth about Daniel?"

My mother apparently doesn't possess the ability to question. She blinks. "Everyone is guilty of something."

"And what about Phoebe? Why didn't anyone ever tell her that her husband wasn't an adulterer?"

"It wasn't my place." Wearily, she pushes back from the table and stands, moving to the small mirror on the wall to adjust her head scarf.

I can't even look at her.

"Daniel is not a bad man, Miriam," she says to the mirror. "Flawed, yes, but aren't we all? He is the Living Prophet. He will save us. And he is loyal to those he cherishes. That's why I stayed. He deserves my loyalty—all our loyalty."

"So you're telling me that Naomi's sin, the one so Contemptible we must never speak of it, was having sex with Daniel and then choosing to leave when he tossed her aside?"

"You're being deliberately obtuse."

"I'm obtuse?" I jump from my chair. "You knew, and you all stuck around and kept swallowing his lies!"

She turns to face me. "Not everyone knew. I only knew because Naomi told me. We were friends, you see. Our daughters were sisters."

Sisters? Suddenly I can't breathe. No. She can't mean . . . I take a step backward, stumbling on the chair leg. Is she saying what I think she's saying? Not just Naomi and Daniel, but her and Daniel?

"You aren't the first person to sin in the name of love, Miriam, and you won't be the last."

Daniel and my mother. Daniel, who sent Naomi away and told us she was dead. Daniel, who doles out punishment to the wicked.

Daniel is my father?

"But . . . if he was the one . . . why did he let you stay?"

"Boaz chose me. My pregnancy could be explained. But Naomi was unwed . . ." She doesn't finish the sentence, but she doesn't need to. She means that Naomi's baby was evidence of sin. And in order to deflect from his own guilt, Daniel pointed to Azariah. But why didn't Phoebe's husband defend himself? Was he so enamored of his Prophet, he took on that sacrifice? Or so afraid, he'd rather face the cruelty of the desert?

My mother adds, "Naomi could have stayed. All she had to do was admit to her sins and ask for forgiveness."

But that isn't all, and we both know it. She would have had to accept the Shame as her due, while she watched the rest of them revere the real father of her child. She would have had to live a lie. Like my mother did, with my father—or the man I was raised to believe was my father—Boaz. This is my bloodline, my inheritance. "That's why you took Rachel in."

My mother nods. "You're sisters." She smiles through her tears. "You needed to be together." Mother pulls me close, and though I can't stand to touch her, her revelation has left me too weak to struggle. "I know of your dreams. You are more like him than you know."

My dreams. But she's wrong about those, too. I didn't dream of Caleb because God wanted us to be together. I dreamt of him because I wanted him. Daniel built this community on falsehoods and fantasy. Because Aaron was right: That's all dreams are.

"And now you must beg for forgiveness and banish your sinful thoughts."

Banish them. I don't know how to do that. For the first time in my life, I'm thinking clearly. Like the thoughts in my head are my own, and not something I've memorized and repeated so many times they've lost all meaning. Now, I'm looking for the meaning. Instead of biting my tongue, or spewing out scripture, I want to say the words in my heart. Instead of ignoring those feelings, or pushing them down, I want to let them out. I want to feel them.

I don't say any of this to her. I wish I could. She isn't supposed to share these things about her past, and I know she wasn't supposed to tell me about Naomi, or my . . . Daniel. She only did it so I would choose the path she thinks is best. But as strong as her love is for me, her devotion to Daniel is stronger.

"You will repent?"

"I'll think about it," I say. And then, because I don't want the last thing we say to each other to be a lie, "I love you, Mother. Always. I hope . . . I hope you remember that. No matter what happens."

"Of course. Keep faithful," she whispers, kissing my cheek.

"I can't. But I gave it a fighting chance. Just like in that song you used to sing." I try to smile, to soften the pain for both of us, because the sorrow etched deep into her face is enough to gut me.

We both know the truth. I don't belong here anymore.

53

CALEB

We stare at the skeleton. Though it's obviously been picked by scavengers, the rotting pants and shirt hold the bones in the loose form of a man.

"Fu-u-u-ck," Aaron says, drawing out the word as he crouches beside them. He tugs at a piece of the fabric with a finger and thumb, and it crumbles. "Do you know who this is?" he asks, looking up at me.

"Of course not. Why would I?" But my outrage is hollow. The clothes, or what's left of them, clearly resemble the simple, handmade garments we're both wearing. There's also a chain coiled around one of the bones. With a cross. Just like the Elders wear.

"Azariah," he says softly, cradling the crucifix in his hand. "It has to be."

I want to deny it, but I can't. Most of us had always assumed he wouldn't survive Outside. "He must have tried to escape through the tunnels," I say. "And gotten stuck somehow."

The look Aaron gives me is familiar. It's the same expression Father wears, right before he calls me an idiot. "Why would he try to escape through the tunnels?" he asks. "Why not just walk out the front gate?" He brushes his hands against his pant leg.

"Maybe the guards wouldn't let him leave?"

"There were no guards back then. Not until after he and Naomi left." Aaron stands and turns around, studying the ceiling. "No," he says, "Daniel put him here."

"How do you know—"

"Just like he put us down here. Think about it. Is he up there, right now, telling everybody how he put us in the pit to drown? And threw in a bunch of poisonous snakes for good measure? Or is he explaining to your neighbors that he caught us red-handed, trying to leave? And that we've been thrown out?"

I look from the bones to Aaron and back again. "You're saying that Daniel . . . killed . . . Azariah? For committing adultery?" Sweat breaks out on my forehead, even though the cave is freezing.

"I'm saying he killed him. I don't know why. But we need to get the hell out of here, before we're next." He grabs me by the collar and pulls me toward the other tunnel. "Come on."

"Shouldn't we do something . . ." I wave at Azariah's remains. "We can't just leave him here."

"There's nothing we can do for him now."

He's right. If we stay here, we'll end up like him. I turn away from the bones to follow Aaron, but I take with me the knowledge of what Daniel will do when cornered. If Aaron's right, Miriam could be in danger, too. But I don't want Aaron to be right.

We take the tunnel, sloshing against the flow of the water for what feels like hours, until we finally come to the end. It's partially blocked by a pile of rocks, but Aaron doesn't even hesitate before he scales them. I'm bigger, but there's just enough room to wiggle my way out through the opening behind him.

The rain has stopped, and the bright moonlight after the darkness of the cave fries my eyeballs. I fall to my knees in the sand, hacking phlegm and bile onto the ground. Dizzy and weakened, I sag onto the boulder behind me as Aaron rolls onto his back.

"Shit," Aaron says, finally raising his head to look at the familiar surroundings, the Chapel in front of us and the Council House looming over our shoulders. "I guess we don't need to worry about how to get back in." Then he drags himself to his feet.

I pull myself up, using the rocks that form the base of the ridge beneath the Farmhouse. "Has this tunnel always been here? How could we not know?"

Aaron kicks at some of the stones. "My guess is the opening used to be covered—by sand and these rocks—and the rain washed it away. Whoever hid it did a damn good job. I'd heard there was another way out, and I've been looking for it since I got here. Still, I never noticed this."

Another way out. Why did he even come here? Just to fill Miriam's head with lies? To make us question our faith?

"Something's wrong," Aaron says. "Where is everyone?"

He's right. The city is eerily empty. Yes, it's night. But it's not a normal night. Shouldn't people be worried about our whereabouts? Or did they not even know we were gone?

"They're at Chapel. Daniel's going to open the Book."

The voice is Miriam's, and my whole body pulses with emotion: fear, anticipation. Desire. Her hair is wild, and she's dressed in clothing that clearly wasn't made for her, the top too big and the skirt too short. But she still looks like an angel, bathed in moonlight.

"Thank goodness you're all right! I thought . . ." She breaks off, swallowing hard. "Susanna said . . ."

"We're all right," I say. I want to pull her close, to hold her and never let go. But I can't, not here, in public. In front of her husband. Instead, I wrap my arms around myself.

"All right?" Aaron snorts under his breath. Louder, he asks, "Have you heard anything about my parents?"

Miriam nods. "I was at their house when Susanna came for them."

Susanna? With Aaron's parents? What is she up to?

"They told me," Miriam adds, staring at Aaron with an expression I can't decipher.

"Told you what?" I ask.

Miriam turns to me, a strange smile on her face. Is she crying? She places her hand on my cheek. Part of me is shocked, but I'm powerless to stop her.

"You're so beautiful," she whispers. "Everything I thought I wanted."

Without thinking, I press my lips to hers, and it's somehow both sweeter and darker than my memories. I kiss her with a fervor I've never possessed before, the emotions from the last few hours fusing inside me. The doubt, the fear, the anger.

Aaron coughs, and Miriam pushes me back. Gently. "We can't do this," she reminds me.

I start to agree, but then she says, "Not just because it's a sin." Her eyes fill with tears again, and I sneak a glance at Aaron, but he's turned his back to us.

"I need time to think," Miriam continues. "To sort things out. And I can't do that here."

Here. In New Jerusalem? What is she saying? "Damn it," I say, the words exploding from my lips. I move toward Aaron, but Miriam steps in front of me.

"Stop. This has nothing to do with him."

"He's a traitor. He doesn't deserve your loyalty."

"A traitor? Because he told me the truth? Daniel's the traitor.

He's the one who's been manipulating us. Lying to us. It isn't as bad Outside as he's told us. There isn't a war. Delilah isn't dead!"

The rest is nonsense. But how does she know about Delilah? I glare at Aaron. "What has he done to you?" I ask Miriam. "If he hadn't stopped me, I could have found Delilah. And if he hadn't put these ideas in your head in the first place, you could have asked for a divorce and we could have been married."

She stares at me, as if I'm a stranger she no longer recognizes, then shakes her head. "No, we couldn't. Daniel was never going to let us be together. Even if any of this"—she waves a hand toward the Council House behind her—"had been real."

Not real? How can she say that? This is our home, our life. "Our love is real. I love you. Do you love me?"

She hesitates, doubt shuttering her face, and my heart cracks inside my chest.

"So that's it then. You're choosing him. Over me."

"Oh, so *now* you think I should get to choose?" She doesn't look guilty anymore, nostrils flared and eyes blazing. "Don't you see? I don't have any say in my own life—not as long as I stay here. My name isn't going to be in that Book, but you know what? I don't care. I'm leaving."

I can't speak. She mentioned leaving to me once before, but that was nonsense. Just worry over her friend. She can't talk like this. This is Blasphemy. I don't know a way to save her now. Worse, it's clear she doesn't want me to.

Aaron says, "I'm sorry to interrupt your . . . moment, here, but we should get to Chapel." He waves toward the building. People are starting to file through the doors. "I need to see my . . . Abraham and Sarah." He turns to me. "And you need to find Marcus. Daniel's angry at him, just like you said. We need to be there when he opens the Book. Just in case."

In case what? But I can't break through the pain that fogs my mind to ask the question. I follow behind them down the path, as if in a dream. Only this is my worst nightmare.

When we get closer, Miriam stops. "There's Phoebe," she says. "I need to talk to her."

"Wait."

She pauses, and for a brief second, I'm grateful to Aaron. Even if he is my rival. Maybe he can convince her to stay when I can't. He digs in his pocket. "I think this belongs to her." And he drops the necklace into her open hand. "It was Azariah's."

"Where did you get this?" she whispers.

Aaron jerks his head toward the pile of rocks. "The tunnels."

"I don't understand. When were you in the tunnels?"

"Long story. But Azariah's dead. We found his . . . remains."

She closes her eyes, as if in silent prayer. When she opens them, she's looking at me.

"I didn't know," I say. "I swear." But it feels as if I'm apologizing for something else.

"Go on without me," she says, turning away.

Aaron urges me forward, but I can't move. *Go on without me.* Doesn't she know that isn't possible?

Without her, what do I have left?

54

MIRIAM

It isn't a decision I ever thought I'd make: my freedom over my faith. Saying it to Caleb, bearing his disappointment, felt like dragging a sick animal up a mountain and then pushing it off a cliff. But there is no other way. He still believes in Daniel, still feels the obligation to serve, an obligation I am ready to throw off like a tattered dress that no longer fits. For the first time in my life, I'm making a choice all on my own, and I know it's the right one. My mother wasn't lying: It's always hardest the first time.

"Phoebe!" I hurry forward to catch my teacher before she slips inside the Chapel. Before I do anything else, she deserves to know the truth.

"Miriam." She nods at me and tries to turn away, but not before I see her eyes are red and puffy.

"Are you all right?" When she doesn't answer, I grab her hand and pull her through the foyer and into a curtained alcove outside the sanctuary, usually reserved for mothers with fussy babies. "Are you worried about the Book?" I ask. "Because there's something you should know. It's about Azariah."

She starts to shake her head, then looks up sharply. "What about Azariah?"

I press the necklace into her hands. "Aaron and Caleb found that.

In the tunnels. He . . ." I stumble, trying to put it together in my head. Why were any of them in the tunnels? Susanna said Aaron and Caleb had been arrested. And Azariah was supposed to have run away.

Phoebe turns the crucifix over in her hands, then makes a fist around it. "This was Azariah's?" When she raises her head, she isn't looking at me, but past, to someplace I can't see. "How do you know?"

"Aaron said—" This is harder than I thought it would be. But telling her is the right thing. I'm so tired of all the lies. I can't be the only one. "Aaron said they found him. His remains." I use the same word he did, wondering what it even means. What remained?

A shudder runs through her entire body as she takes this in.

"Caleb and Aaron." She worries her dead husband's cross between her fingers. "I thought they were . . . Never mind. The tunnels?"

I need to tell her the rest. About Rachel and Naomi. But I can't find the words to hurt her further. "Why is Daniel opening the Book now?" I ask instead. "Does it have something to do with me and Caleb? Or Caleb and Aaron?" Everything is happening so fast, I haven't had time to think about all I've learned, or how it all fits together.

"Oh, Miriam. In some ways, you're as self-absorbed as the men. None of this is about you. It never has been."

My cheeks flame as if she's slapped them, but I accept the blow because I've just dealt her a worse one. Her honesty stings, but it also absolves me of the last of my guilt. It isn't my sin that's set all of this in motion.

"Azariah isn't Rachel's father," I blurt. "It was Daniel. My mother told me. She knows because she . . . and he . . . because Rachel and I are the same. Sisters." All my life, we lived like sisters, but now that I know we're blood, the word rings hollow, and I swallow back a sob.

All of the color leaches from her face, like wood left out in the sun, as she studies my face for signs of deception. Or maybe she's looking for clues to my parentage. Her lips move silently, either trying to absorb the information or more likely in prayer. Then she covers her face with a shaky hand. "Now I understand. Dear God, how could I have been so stupid?"

"I'm sorry, but I don't understand any of it. I mean, he didn't want anyone to know what he'd done to Naomi, so he sent her away. And he kept Rachel here because she was his daughter. But why would he let you think Azariah had betrayed you?"

Her whole body sags, as if her belief in Daniel was all that was holding her upright. "Do you remember our lessons about Vashti?" she asks, instead of answering me.

"What does Vashti have to do with anything?"

"What was her crime?" Phoebe asks, gripping my shoulders. "Think."

Her insistent fingers dig into my skin as I try to focus. "Vashti refused to dance for her husband and his audience. So, disobedience?"

"And why did she disobey?"

"Why does any of this matter right now?" I'm totally confused. Am I dreaming? But even Daniel couldn't interpret this one. The thought of him trying makes me want to laugh hysterically. I'm hysterical. No. I'm panicking.

"It's important that you understand," Phoebe says. "That I taught you something. Tell me what Vashti did."

"Okay. Okay." I nod. She's scaring me with her intensity, but if this is what she wants from me, this last thing, I can give it to her. "Vashti didn't want to dance for her husband. Naked. So she refused."

Phoebe is nodding, tears streaming down her face. "She didn't want to be stared at by strangers. Objectified. And yet, she was the one who was punished. Made to feel shame. But the shame wasn't hers at all, was it? And she knew that. Because *she* was strong." Her voice breaks. "I'm sorry, Miriam. I should have been stronger. For myself, and for the rest of you. It's too late for me, but you can still save yourself."

"How?" I ask, fear weaving a knot in my belly. No matter what's about to happen, I know my name will not be in that Book. But that's not what I'm afraid of. There's a freedom in not believing, but it comes with a price. Because not only do I not trust Daniel to save us anymore, I also don't trust him not to hurt us.

"He's conditioned us all to turn our minds from sin. To accept everything he does, because it's for the greater good. And if we question it, we're the perverted." Her smile is bitter. "He's going to keep doing it," Phoebe continues, shaking her head. "Before me, there was Naomi, and before her, your mother. It's his pattern, and his weakness. You see it, don't you?"

"I don't," I whisper. "Why are you telling me this? What can I do?"

"You're his blood. When your name isn't called, he won't Banish you outright. He'll call you forward. Give you one last chance to Repent. You have a chance to end this."

"End this?" My head is spinning so hard I feel like all the words she's saying are completely new and without meaning.

"I tried to be good, Miriam. Noble, even. Live up to his example. But I did it at the expense of common sense. Don't be like me. Stop ignoring that little voice inside you, the one that chides your faithfulness, and tell them what you know."

"I don't know anything!"

But then I think of all I've learned these past few days, the truths I was once afraid to face. I know Daniel is a liar. And so are the beliefs he fed us. For instance, that women are the weaker sex. If scripture says we have the power to bring a righteous man to his knees, aren't we the strong ones? Shouldn't we be listened to and feared, rather than shamed and ignored? And what was so disobedient about Vashti refusing to show her naked body to strangers, anyway?

But it wasn't that, was it? She embarrassed the king. She defied him. She spoke up. "Vashti used her voice," I say, and a glimmer of light comes back into Phoebe's eyes.

Now it's time to use mine.

55

CALEB

It was all for nothing. My sins, my guilt. My sacrifice. My prayers. None of it matters. I tried so hard to be a good disciple. To do the right thing. Yes, I sinned. I coveted. I dreamt about a married woman. I kissed her. I urged her to adultery. But I also tried my hardest to be righteous. I refused to take a wife I didn't love. I resisted Susanna's temptations. I protected my brother. I tried to save Delilah. I begged God and Daniel both for guidance, and when I got no answer, I still remained strong. Faithful. And it was all for nothing.

"Nothing!"

"Jesus Christ, Caleb!" Aaron shoves me back against the side of Chapel, just as a group of neighbors turn in our direction.

I lean my head back against the building and close my eyes. I'm tired. I'm cold. I'm hungry. None of that matters either. Because I'm also defeated. Miriam doesn't love me. I thought the night she left me alone at the Mill was the worst pain I'd ever endured. But back then, I could only guess at her change of heart. Knowing is much worse.

"Listen closely." Aaron's voice is urgent, but I can't even muster the energy to open my eyes. "Daniel thinks we're already dead. That's the only advantage we've got, understand? That means you've got to pull yourself together. We've got to get inside without anyone seeing us."

When I don't respond, he grabs my shirt and shakes me. "Miriam's in danger, man. Don't you care? Look, I know it hurts. Trust me, I've been there. But if you still care about her at all, you've gotta help me help her."

I open my eyes. He's standing much too close, and his breath is terrible. "She doesn't want my help."

"Doesn't matter. She needs us. They all do. What do you think is going to happen once Daniel opens that stupid book?"

"It's not stu—"

"It doesn't matter! Think about it! He's got the entire city crammed in there, and he's about to tell a bunch of them they're going to Hell. People are gonna freak out. It'll be anarchy, and that's best-case scenario."

My mouth is dry, and I have to swallow twice before I can ask, "What's the worst case?"

Aaron shrugs. "He kills them."

"You're crazy," I whisper. "He isn't—he wouldn't—"

"He is. He would. What the fuck do you think he was trying to do to us?"

No. He's wrong. I've lost too much already. Miriam, Daniel's favor. I can't believe this. I won't. "Maybe he wasn't trying to kill us at all. Maybe it was a test. The lion's den." I push myself off from the wall. "That makes more sense than your stupid idea."

He rubs his hands over his face, as if trying to scrub something away. His own doubts? "Fine," he finally says. "You don't have to believe me. I just need you to help me get inside. And then keep your mouth shut, at least until we know what's going on. Maybe you're right," he offers, though he's clearly lying. "In that case, cool. I'll back off. But for right now, let's just watch and listen. For Miriam's sake," he adds.

He's manipulating me. But the truth is, I'm not as certain of Daniel's motives as I pretended. Or of my reception. Daniel may not have tried to kill us firsthand, but he did leave us down there while he called everyone else to Chapel. "Okay," I say. "We can probably get in the back way without anyone seeing us." I lead him around to the other door. "Daniel uses this sometimes when he wants to slip in or out quickly."

The door leads to a dark alcove that wraps around the back corner of the sanctuary. There's a small washroom off to one side; on the other, a velvet curtain separates us from the stage where Daniel preaches. When I turn around, Aaron has a gun.

"Where did you get that?"

"It was hidden under the back seat of the van. I grabbed it just before Daniel arrested us."

"So you've had it the whole time? Why didn't you use it on the snakes?"

"Don't be ridiculous. You can't shoot a gun in a cave."

He raises the gun in the air as he pulls the door quietly shut, then checks the washroom.

"Who are you?" I ask, my suspicions growing.

"Who knows about this area?" he asks, ignoring my question.

"I'm not sure. The Security team. Maybe some of the Council Members? They aren't supposed to use it, though. It's strictly for Daniel."

"Good." He almost smiles, then waves me off to the side before moving the curtain with one finger.

The Council Members are seated in the front row, facing the stage. Behind them, some community members sit in pews while others mill about, trying to find seats. Marcus is in the second row, behind Mother and Father, and Aaron's parents are right behind him. I step closer to the curtain to peek through at the faces, the fathers and mothers and Brothers and Sisters, all my friends and neighbors. They look nervous. Some are openly crying. I suppose no matter how righteous any of us believe we've behaved, we've all done something we're ashamed of. Right now, everyone is united in one prayer: *Please, Lord, let me be worthy.*

I study my father, who looks more confident than my mother. He shouldn't. I've been waiting for his Judgment Day for a long time.

Daniel sweeps onto the stage, dressed in his purple sacramental robes. I drop the curtain and step back. Did he see me?

But his attention is on his audience. "It has been a terrible week of sin in New Jerusalem. I'm sure there is no need to remind you I foretold this." He sounds as if he blames them all for our downfall. "Some have already been Judged, but there is worse still to come, and we must guard against it."

Already been Judged. Does he mean me and Aaron? Or Delilah, maybe? Either way, none of us were Judged. We didn't receive a trial or have a chance to repent and be saved.

"These sinners are a cancer that will spread throughout the community if we let them," he continues. "We must cut them from our midst."

I peer through the crack again, in time to see them all nod, some more vehemently than others. I shiver in spite of the stuffy room, my damp clothes clinging to me like mold. Cut us. Is that what he was doing, leaving us in the pit? And Azariah? Did he really run, like we've always been told? Into the tunnels? Or was he cut, too?

"The time has come, my followers. Today, the Book of Truth will be opened; the righteous will be revealed." Daniel grabs the Book from the podium in the center of the stage and holds it aloft. Some people gasp, others look grim. "As you know, this Book was delivered to me, sealed by God, until the Time of the End. It is as He told me: 'At that time your people—everyone whose name is found written in the Book—will be delivered. And many who sleep in the dust of the earth will awake, some to everlasting life, but others to shame and everlasting contempt. The wise will shine like the brightness of the heavens, and those who lead many to righteousness, like the stars forever and ever.'"

"Hallelujah!" they exclaim, as one. The Elders kiss their crucifixes.

"Blessed is the one who reads the words of this prophecy, and blessed are those who hear and obey what is written in it. Because the time has come!" Daniel proclaims.

He opens the Book, wax crumbling to the floor as he cracks the seal. As one, the congregation falls to their knees and bows their heads.

Sweat drips down my forehead, and I glance at Aaron. His face looks gray, his lips pressed so tightly together they've gone white.

Daniel settles the Book on the podium. The room is silent as he rustles the pages.

"Hananiah," Daniel reads, holding out his outstretched palm toward my father, who merely nods once. As if this is his due. I lunge forward, but Aaron stops me, his arm across my chest. "Not yet," he whispers.

"My father is not righteous," I say, my voice quivering with rage. "He is a monster."

Aaron nods, as if no other explanation is necessary. My whole life, my word has meant nothing next to my father's. That Aaron, this nonbeliever, should accept it outright takes the breath from my anger.

"Judith," Daniel calls out, and my mother rises up, her hands held heavenward.

"Isaiah." Daniel reads the name of my younger brother, the one after Marcus.

My heart is pounding. So is my head. I thought maybe the Elders' names were being read first, but he must be going according to family. Which means he skipped both Marcus and me.

My mother starts to wail, until my father silences her with a look. Matthew, my youngest sibling, gazes up at Marcus, his lip quivering. Marcus merely folds his hands and bows his head.

I didn't think my name would be included. But I expected something more than damnation by default—some expression of regret at our loss, or a last chance for repentance. So what now? Despite Aaron's insistence, Daniel doesn't try to hurt Marcus, or eject him from Chapel. He doesn't even look at him.

Daniel makes his way through the rest of my family, concluding with Matthew. Then he moves on to Mishael, whose name is included, along with his wife. I don't know them very well, but well enough to be surprised. Though maybe the Elders have had more time to repent. Or maybe some sins are just worse than others.

"Susanna."

"What?" The word explodes from me, and this time Aaron is too late to hold me back.

"Shit." He fades into the background as I burst onto the stage.

Daniel startles at the sight of me, his eyes widening and his arm trembling as he lifts it to point. "Caleb." He thunders out my name, holding one hand toward me and lifting the other toward the chandelier, which sways above him.

Is he still reading from the Book? There is a long pause, as Daniel holds my fate in his hands.

"Her name cannot be in the Book," I say, taking advantage of the silence. It's bad enough that my father is in there. And Mishael. I have seen the way he looks at the young girls. But Susanna? "She is the whole reason Marcus was led astray. The women tempt. That's what you've always taught us! And she, she is the worst. She gossips. And she lies. I think she may have been unfaithful to her husband. She tried to seduce me!"

Susanna has risen to her feet, and she narrows her eyes at me now. The rest of the congregation starts to whisper among themselves.

Even Daniel looks flustered. "Our lost sheep," he says, trying to deflect from my accusations and draw the crowd's attention back. "You wandered from the herd and got tangled within the brambles of sin. God ordered you to the lion's den. And yet you have survived."

He moves to the front of the stage, talking more to the crowd than to me. He sounds angry, but he should be proud—both at my escape and the fact that I figured out the lion's den analogy. I'm finally starting to understand how his mind works.

Then I see the congregation, watching avidly as Daniel paces at the front of the stage, and a dizzying sense of dread strikes like a blow. Is *this* the lion's den?

"Come here, Brother." He holds out his hand, inviting me forward, so that we are standing left of center, directly in front of my parents. "Tell us of your ordeal. If God has saved you, He must intend for you to have a chance at repentance."

My limbs feel strangely heavy as I lift my feet to walk toward him. Chapel is much cooler tonight, especially after the rain, but my breath is shallow, and sweat runs in rivers down my back.

"What about Susanna?" I repeat. "Why is her name in the Book?"

"'Let he who is without sin cast the first stone,'" Daniel says, gripping my shoulder. "You alone have the chance to redeem yourself, Caleb. So I will ask again. Are you ready to repent?"

Me alone? Why is he trying to offer me a way out? I search the audience for Marcus. Was his sin really so much worse than mine? Or does Daniel have some other reason for offering me Salvation while he damns my brother?

"Caleb's right."

Everyone swivels toward the doorway, to Miriam, who stands at the end of the center aisle. "Susanna's name shouldn't be in that book," she says. "And neither should Daniel's."

56

MIRIAM

As I approach the stage, Phoebe hands me a microphone. I've never used one before, but I've seen Daniel, when his voice gives out after hours of preaching. I press the button on the side, and a shriek echoes through the room.

I'm not going to wait for him to expose me. I'm ready to speak now. I'm just not sure what I'm going to say.

As I climb the stairs to the stage, Daniel watches me, his flowing robes bathed in white light. In that moment, he looks more like the prophet he never was than I've ever seen him. On another day, in another life, I'd be drawn to him. Now, I see the illusion for what it is, and I'm repelled.

He falters when he sees my face, but it doesn't take him long to recover. His eyes roll back in his head, and I know what is about to happen. My heartbeat quickens. After so many years of relying on Daniel's visions, it's an automatic response. My first thought, however, is that his visions come at very convenient times.

My second is that Phoebe is right. I know what she was trying to tell me, and I know how to end this. It was never my dreams I should have been listening to. It was my heart.

"I have had a vision!" I yell, before Daniel can speak the words, and my voice booms out, filling the room.

Suddenly, I'm bathed in a circle of blue light. I've never stood up here, before the crowd as the center of attention. The feeling is electric. I can say anything in this moment. And they will listen.

"A vision of a boy. Who dreamt of wonderful things, or so he said. An oasis in the desert. A cave with the handwriting of God. A Path that leads to the stars of Heaven. He also dreamt of terrible things. War and suffering, death and destruction." I pace, like I've seen Daniel do a thousand times, though I keep to the opposite side of the stage from Daniel and Caleb. Everyone else remains rooted in place, fixated on my story.

"The trouble is, some of the dreams were lies. But the people— his *children*—they were so used to believing the dreams, believing the Prophet, they couldn't tell the difference anymore." I see Daniel out of the corner of my eye. He's trying to interrupt, but my voice drowns him out. No one seems to mind. They're riveted.

"He told them he would always protect them, as long as they obeyed. As long as they submitted to God's will. But it wasn't God's will at all. It was his."

Daniel motions for his guards, but they aren't paying him any attention. For the moment, he's powerless.

I know the feeling.

The book is still lying open on the podium. Daniel reads something in my expression and moves toward it. But I'm quicker.

People gasp as I snatch it from his reach.

"Don't worry," I say, putting the podium between me and Daniel. "I understand. You're afraid. I was, too. I was afraid to be judged for the things I've done. But look inside." I hold it up, open. Some of them turn away in fear, but many crane their necks for a better view, and I move forward to give it to them.

"This isn't God's handwriting. It's Daniel's. These people haven't achieved Salvation. They've just traded their lives to a false prophet, in exchange for a bunch of empty dreams."

Daniel's face is red. He snaps his fingers in Phoebe's direction, but her seat is empty.

"Daniel got so used to getting what he wanted," I continue, "he thought he was owed it. But he didn't open this book to reward us for our faith. No, this is a punishment. For his own failures. He didn't call us all here today because of some prophecy."

"So why are we here?" Caleb's voice isn't as loud as mine, but it carries from the side of the stage, where he's been standing, frozen, since I came in.

"It's about the Matrimony," I tell him.

I don't know why it took me this long to figure it out.

"Daniel was angry," I say. "We all knew that. But I also knew someone was feeding him information. How else could he know about Aaron's snakebite?" I look for Aaron in the crowd, but he's not there. Neither is Abraham. I see only Sarah, sitting alone, her expression grim. "Or the wine? Or that I threatened to look for Delilah, the night we Gathered at the Dining Hall?" Caleb winces at this.

"But what I didn't understand was why he cared. Was it because he wanted control? He does like to control us; look at our lives, our Lessons. Our marriages. All planned out in advance. Except for this year. This year, someone made a mistake.

"Have none of you asked yourselves what happened at the Matrimony?" I turn toward where my parents usually sit, but the light blinds me, and I can't tell if my mother is there. "I know you all questioned it. But God forbid we speak up."

Daniel finally runs over to the speakers and pulls the cords. The room goes quiet.

But I'm not done.

"Well, you should have," I yell. It's the loudest I've ever been in my life, and the sound of my own voice echoing off the walls gives me chills. "Because it had nothing to do with God. And everything to do with her." I point to Susanna, sitting in the front row. She shifts and crosses her legs, arching one eyebrow.

"He's told us he has no interest in our marriages, other than as God's interpreter. But like so much else he's said, that was a lie. It isn't the voice of God who decides who the men choose. It's Daniel. And for some reason this year, he wanted Aaron to choose Susanna. At first, I couldn't figure it out. Why those two? But then I realized—this is his pattern."

I look for Phoebe, but can't find her either. Hopefully, this is what she meant when she told me to end this.

"You see, he never planned for Susanna to stay married. He simply needed to give her to a man who he could later identify as a sinner. That way, he could Banish Aaron, and then move Susanna into the Council House with him."

Susanna's smile is frozen, but her eyes have narrowed to slits. If she could maim me right now, I've no doubt she would. But her sharp tongue is her best weapon, and it's useless against the truth.

Beside her, Mishael's face is bright red, while Marcus has lost all color. "That's why he's so angry with you," I tell him. "You took something Daniel wanted for himself. See, it worked so well for him the first time. With Phoebe, after Azariah ran off. Except it wasn't Phoebe's husband who made Naomi with child. It was Daniel. He stole her baby and tossed her out, like a piece of trash. He destroyed her. And then he took Phoebe in. The kind, benevolent Leader. No one else would touch her, because of the Shame. No one except Daniel."

My voice is the only sound in the room. I don't know if anyone else is even breathing.

"You doubt me, but Daniel is a sinner. And I have proof."

As much as they believe in him, they are now equally enraptured by me, at least temporarily. As much as they want to believe I'm lying, they also want to see my evidence. So I hold my arms wide.

"I am the proof. I am his daughter. Blood of his blood. Flesh of his flesh. How many of you knew? Some of you must have guessed.

"It's funny, he once told us those were the kinds of sins that happened on the Outside. Remember when he told us about the terrible men who like to lie down with girls? Yet he lies with Susanna now. Just as he lay with my mother and Naomi. Just as he lay with Phoebe. He isn't righteous or a prophet or our leader. He's just a filthy sinner."

There is one more second of quiet, then chaos. Gasps and shouting. People struggling to their feet, others collapsing. I search for my mother in the audience but can't find her. Does Daniel's relationship with Susanna remind her of what her father did to her? Maybe she'll go with me, after all.

In the confusion, someone grabs me.

Daniel's fingers are an iron band around my wrist.

"That's quite a story, Miriam," he says. "But as I've told you before, not all dreams are prophetic. And not all dreamers are prophets."

"You certainly aren't."

He studies me closely, and though I'm tempted to look away, I don't. "God wants your obedience."

"No, *you* want my obedience." I spit at his feet.

He slaps me, hard, and a salty, copper taste fills my mouth. His loss of control should shock me, but it doesn't. He slaps me again, my head bobbing back and then forward.

"Slow to anger," I say, watching droplets of my blood splatter the floor like raindrops.

He must become aware of the audience, because he straightens and turns toward them, still gripping my wrist. "It appears we have not only a prodigal son, but a prodigal daughter as well." He raises his voice, and some of the turmoil quiets. They are still his Children, and though I have just exposed him as a fraud, their instinct is to turn to him for comfort. I can't blame them. I used to think he possessed a unique gift for comfort as well. Now I know it's all manipulation. What was the word Aaron used? A scam. Daniel just puts us in the most uncomfortable situations, so we must turn to him for relief.

When he has their full attention, he says, "Your dear Sister thinks lying about me will save her from her fate. It will not." He snatches the book from my hand and holds it up. "And now we must add it to the list of other sins you've committed. Fornication. Covetousness. Adultery. They are all poison from the same tree. Really, Miriam, have I taught you nothing about self-respect?"

"No," I say, yanking my wrist free and spitting out more blood. "You've taught me how to bend my will to someone else's. You've taught me to shut my mouth when I wish to speak. You've taught me to smile and acquiesce when every fiber of my being is screaming out to resist. You've taught me to be obedient, to submit. But you've never taught me anything about self-respect."

"Why do you think we spend so much time preaching to you? Trying to keep you on the Path of Righteousness?" Daniel runs his fingers lightly across the book's leather cover. "But I'm a kind man. I'm going to give you a choice."

"A choice? For me? I'm a woman. I'm not allowed to make decisions," I remind him.

"That's not true. You've always had a choice. Be faithful. Or face the consequences."

I've never noticed it before, but *choice* sounds a lot like *voice*. I'm usually allowed neither. Perhaps now that I've used one, I should exercise the other.

"I don't believe in you or your empty threats," I say. "Nothing you say holds any power over me. I am leaving. By my own choice. Not yours."

I don't know where the words come from, exactly, but once they are free, so am I. There's no going back now.

But Caleb must disagree, because he steps forward from the shadows, holding a gun. And it's pointed at Daniel and me.

57

CALEB

I cock the gun, pulling the hammer back with a loud click. Daniel flinches, while Miriam looks stunned, her eyes wide and her mouth open. The rest of the congregation has gone still. I can't tell if they have been struck dumb by Miriam's revelations, or are just scared of the gun.

Only Thomas tries to move forward.

"If you take another step, I will shoot Daniel," I say. I won't, not yet, but they don't know that.

"You know I know how to use this," I say, eyes trained on my Prophet. "You taught me how."

Daniel licks his lips. "Do as he says. Drop your weapons." He sounds less like my spiritual leader and more like a scared old man.

Both Thomas and Gideon toss their guns to the floor.

Aaron steps out from behind the curtain, hands raised, and I pivot the gun slightly toward him. "Don't do this, man," he says.

"Shut up!" I yell. "Most of this is your fault anyway! Stop moving." Aaron freezes mid-step. "Sit down. On the floor."

"Me?" Aaron asks. "Or—" He gestures to Daniel.

"Yes. All of you." I back up, so they are all in my line of vision, and point the gun back at Daniel. "You too."

They lower themselves to the floor, Aaron's gaze on Gideon's gun, as if he's calculating the distance to reach it.

"Don't even think about it."

"Well, you stole my gun," Aaron says. "That's a little unfair, don't you think? Leaving me unarmed. Helpless. Knowing what you do now about this fraud."

"Shut up," I say again. Dear Lord. Not even a gun pointed at him will keep his mouth shut. I can't think while he's talking. "I just need a minute." All of the things Miriam said. They can't be true. Daniel and Phoebe? And now Daniel and Susanna? Rachel and Miriam are his daughters? He may not be infallible, but he's not evil.

But what about Azariah? We found his body.

I blink and rub my hand against my forehead. My head feels like it's on fire. I need someone to help me figure this all out. I look out at the congregation, at my family. Marcus? But his loyalty is to Susanna. It always has been. And my mother? Will always defer to Father, who will defend Daniel to the death. There is no one I can trust to be completely on my side. So I keep the gun trained on Daniel, while I step over to the guards' guns and use my foot to slide them out of the way, behind the podium.

Aaron presses his lips together and turns to look at the crowd. Trying to get help?

"Turn around," I order him, and wait until he scoots around so he faces me, his back to the room.

"Caleb, please," Miriam says. She presses her hands together, as if in prayer. "This isn't going to solve anything."

"And what will? You leaving?" I'm ashamed at the way my voice cracks. I'm stronger than this. "You can't go. This is all wrong. This is just a . . . a mistake." I search desperately for the words that will convince her. "We were supposed to be married," I say. "You know that's true. Daniel knows it's true." I shake the gun in his direction.

"But *he.*" I turn to Aaron. "He screwed it all up. If he hadn't, none of this would be happening. We'd be happy. Can't you see that?"

She shakes her head, her curls—those soft curls—brushing her shoulders. "It doesn't matter," she says.

"It does matter!"

"We can't go back. We can't change anything. And . . . I don't want to. I'm sorry, Caleb," she adds hastily, stretching out her hand, "I don't want to hurt you. But my eyes are open now. I can see the truth, and I'm glad."

"The truth? The only truth I know is that I love you. Isn't that enough?"

"That isn't truth," she says. "That's just a feeling. A feeling Daniel encouraged, because it served his purpose. But that doesn't make it real."

Daniel looks like he's going to argue, but Miriam goes on. "You say you love me. Then you should understand why I need to go. You can even come with me, if you want. Everyone can." She glances around the room, raises her voice. "There's nothing left for you here."

There is murmuring from the crowd, but I ignore it. "So what? You're just going to walk away?"

"Let her go, son," Daniel says.

"Don't call me son." I tighten my grip on the pistol, the butt of the gun slick in my hand.

"The devil is strong in her," Daniel says softly. "But you can still be saved. Because you know the truth."

But I don't, not anymore. Miriam is right. I can't separate truth from emotion. Maybe this has been my problem all along.

"You didn't even give me a chance to explain myself," I say, shaking the gun at Daniel. "I have done everything you asked! I tried to be righteous! And still, you blame me. At the Matrimony, I didn't pick a wife, because I knew it would be wrong. To take a woman God had not chosen for me. But where did that get me? Alone and punished, while the others got to go on frolicking and fornicating." All the anger and the sadness pours out of me, as if I've opened a floodgate deep inside. "You were angry about the Matrimony. But you didn't do anything about it! You didn't stop them! How can you call yourself a Leader?"

Daniel closes his eyes. His lips move, but no sound comes out.

"Are you praying right now? It's a little late, isn't it? On second thought, why don't you go ahead and call God. I have a couple of questions for him, too. Like—"

From the corner of my eye, I see Aaron trying to mouth something to Miriam. I turn the gun on him. "Don't talk to her. I will shoot you. It would be much easier than killing him."

Aaron snaps his mouth shut and nods once.

"I was trying to fix things," I say, turning back to Daniel. "I was going to get Delilah. Bring back your lost sheep. Or your coyote." His metaphors are getting jumbled in my head. I am the lost sheep. Delilah was the coyote. Or was that Marcus?

My vision blurs for a minute. The air feels thick, heavy. Susanna was the one who called Marcus a coyote. But if she's really been this close to Daniel all along—as close as Miriam said—was everything Susanna told me about Marcus a lie? Because if Miriam was right, then it wasn't Marcus I saw Susanna with, that night she was out after dark.

"Susanna was with a man. At the bathhouse," I say. "Was it you?" I focus on Daniel. I need to see his face. I need to know if any of it is true. But he keeps his eyes closed and his face blank. "Is that why you sent Marcus Out with Delilah? So you could have Susanna all to yourself? Is that why her name is in the Book? Because she's your lover?"

I lean down and snatch it from his lap.

406 · *Shannon Schuren*

I keep the gun aimed, using my extended arm to brace the book. As I flip through, the chasm in my heart grows wider and deeper. It is Daniel's handwriting. Worse, it's not just a list of names. It's notes. About all of us.

It's a journal.

"'Suitable matches for Matrimony,'" I read aloud, my voice hollow. "'Caleb and Miriam.'" I look at her, and she looks away. "'Marcus and Rachel? Aaron and Susanna.'" My heart is so heavy, it pushes the breath from my chest. "You did plan it. These aren't God's words. They're yours."

I shouldn't read on, but I can't help myself. I page back, spot Father's name. "'Hananiah has asked for his son to be placed on the Church Council,'" I read aloud. I look at Father, his face like stone. "'He is willing to pay handsomely for this honor. However.'" My voice cracks, and I have to clear my throat before I can go on. "'However, Caleb is not intellectually equipped for such a position. Perhaps Marcus would be more suitable.'"

I am gutted. I have nothing left. No heart, no soul.

No faith.

I drop the book. My vision is fuzzy around the edges, narrowed to a tunnel that contains only Daniel and me. "It was you? Not my father who said I wasn't worthy, but you?"

"Caleb," Daniel commands. "Look at me."

I can't help myself. I do it.

"I am your Leader. It is my job to assess your strengths, as well as your weaknesses. To help you be a better man. So that you may shine like the stars. That's all I was doing. You are a Child of Daniel; you deserve my best efforts. That's why you are here—for Salvation. New Jerusalem is an oasis from sin. But only if I keep it that way."

His words are tempting, like food to a starving man. But I can no longer be tempted.

"No. That's what it's supposed to be. But you've ruined it!" Tears and sweat burn my eyes, and I swipe them away with the back of my hand. "You've twisted it for your own means. You never cared about any of us. Or our salvation. You only care about being revered."

"I love all my children," Daniel argues. "Just as I tried to love you. But sadly, you aren't worthy. The stars of righteousness will never be yours. You're neither wise nor a leader." His tone is mocking, and the gun trembles in my hand. "Do you know why we're here right now?" he continues. "It's because of your temper, your total lack of self-control. How many times have I told you it would be your downfall?"

Too many to count.

"Put the gun down, Caleb." Daniel's voice is sharp, strong. The voice of a Leader. But he still hasn't answered my questions.

"What about Azariah? We found his body. In the tunnel. Did you kill him?"

For a crazy moment, I think he might tell me the truth. But I've forgotten. Daniel doesn't share knowledge. He wields it. Like a weapon.

"Caleb. Who are you going to believe? Your Prophet? Or an adulterous whore? Now either put the gun down or put it to good use." Daniel waves a hand in Miriam and Aaron's direction, then gets to his knees.

A part of me still wants to believe him, believe *in* him. Do what he says. Put everything back to normal. He is my Leader, and I am but a follower.

He is also the only one who can make Miriam stay.

Miriam. So beautiful. And so defiant. The way she stood up to Daniel and spoke her truth out loud. So brave.

And all at once I realize—this is what I've loved about her from the beginning. That she pushes back. That she knows her own mind. That she has a voice.

So I can't force her—to stay, to believe in something she doesn't. To live a lie. And I can't force her to love me.

That would make me no better than my father. Or Daniel.

"I'm sorry," I say to Miriam. And I am. For all the ways I failed her. And for what I'm about to do. "But you're wrong about one thing. I've always loved you."

Then I point the gun. And I pull the trigger.

58

MIRIAM

I wake with a scream in my throat. The dark room is quiet, and I wait, my heartbeat eventually slowing, as I try once more to separate reality and dream. It's been this way for the past seven nights, ever since we left New Jerusalem. The shooting, the screams, the blood, the fire. As hard as I try not to think about it during the day, as soon as I fall asleep, I'm right back in that moment. Aaron says it is my mind, trying to make sense of the incomprehensible. He says this is the way of dreams. Sometimes they are wishes, sometimes they are fears.

Sometimes they mean nothing at all.

"Are you okay?" Delilah whispers from the twin bed across the room.

I turn onto my side, just able to make out the shape of my friend's face in the predawn light.

"Just another nightmare," I say.

"They will pass. Eventually." She sounds confident, and she should know. "Was this one about Caleb?"

I roll onto my back, trying to trap the tears before they escape. They're all about Caleb, in some way or another.

"Do you think the rest will ever come Out?" I ask, mostly to change the subject.

"You have to stop saying 'come Out.' It means something different here," Delilah says.

"Everything means something else. It's not a closed community, it's a cult. Daniel's not a prophet, he's just a con man. How am I supposed to keep track?" I know Delilah is just trying to be helpful, but I'm still on edge from the dream.

"Daniel is an asshole," Delilah says.

She learned to curse from Naomi, and it seems to come naturally to her. She's adjusting better than the rest of us, but she's had more time. She also didn't witness what we did.

I've only had a few days, and everything is foreign to me. Crowds wherever we go. So loud and intrusive. They stick their microphones in my face and shout questions I can't answer, so they can show them on something called television, which is some sort of one-way viewing screen. Still, it's better than the police station we went to first. Abraham said we had to file something called charges, which meant I had to sit in a cold room and answer questions, a lot of them about Daniel, but some about Caleb and the shooting. Aaron says I haven't done anything wrong, so I shouldn't worry, but that some of what went on in New Jerusalem was illegal.

None of it makes any sense to me. Until recently, I didn't know we had to follow any laws but Daniel's.

The sheets are sticky with my own sweat, and I kick them to the end of the bed. I can hear the ocean beyond the apartment walls, whispering.

"I need some air," I tell Delilah.

Outside the bedroom door, I nearly trip over Naomi. She sleeps on the floor in the hallway every night, outside Rachel's bedroom. Of the three of us, Rachel is having the most trouble adjusting, and I can't blame her. I had time to live with the thought of Daniel as something other than our prophet, days where I watched him and listened to him and tried to untangle what I'd been taught from what I really believed, until finally I was able to wrap my head around all of his lies and manipulation.

Rachel had an hour.

I have to give her credit. I threw a lot at her—her mother was still alive, her marriage wasn't sanctioned by God, Daniel was her father— and though she didn't want to hear it, in the end she'd trusted me and jumped in the van with the four of us. She left New Jerusalem. I used to think she was just like my mother. But it turns out she's stronger.

Still, even the strongest people need support. That's why every day, Naomi invites someone called a deprogrammer to visit us, along with Sarah and sometimes Abraham. Those aren't actually their names, but we call them that. It's easier for all of us, especially Rachel, who sometimes has second thoughts about leaving our old home. And Jacob. I can't tell if knowing he defied Daniel to choose her as his wife makes leaving him behind easier, or harder. It's possible she doesn't know either.

As I tiptoe around her on my way to the stairs, Naomi stirs but doesn't wake. In sleep, her face is peaceful and unmarred by the perpetual worry lines she acquires upon waking. Daniel liked to surround himself with beautiful women, just like Phoebe said. My mother, my teacher, Naomi, Susanna. But they were also strong women. I wonder if he realized that? My mother, a survivor of abuse, who taught me to sing and to use my voice, even though she couldn't find hers in the same way. Naomi, who found a second chance at life and happiness after New Jerusalem. Phoebe, who was brave enough to teach us to be strong, even if she thought she wasn't. Susanna, I have a harder time being generous with. But she always spoke her mind. Who knows what she would have become, away from Daniel's manipulation? Did he recognize their strength? Was that part of the attraction? Or maybe he saw their light and couldn't help but try to snuff it out.

I glance out the front window as I pass through the living room. The news van is still parked outside, the crew ready to spring out at the first sign of life from inside. They all want to know more about the person they call Prophet Howe. That's his other name. And mine, or so they say. I suppose it's fitting. As in, how did we ever believe anything he said? How did he fool so many of us for so long? How could we ever have thought he was a living prophet?

I slip out through the patio doors, to the back deck above the beach. I love this time of day, when sunrise colors our view from inky grays to light pastels. The reporters aren't allowed to come back here, and so this is where I retreat when I need to be alone. If I could still pray, this is where I'd do it. After sixteen years, it's a hard habit to break. But I can't seem to separate God from Daniel in my head. Maybe it's because only one of them was there to begin with. Because that was how Daniel wanted it.

Still, every day I walk down the wooden stairs and onto the sand, out to where the spray salts my face and the water rinses my feet clean. I stay until the roar drives all the bad dreams from my head, and the wind has dried my tears. And each day I get a little bit closer to finding faith again, in things like love and kindness and friendship.

But not God. And not just because he let Caleb die.

Caleb shot Daniel in the shoulder. In the ensuing chaos, someone knocked over a candelabra, setting the Chapel on fire. For a long time, this was all I knew. Abraham and Aaron grabbed Rachel and me, hustled us into the van along with Sarah, and drove us out of the city.

Later, Aaron told me the rest. By the time the FBI raided the city, Daniel and Susanna had fled. Marcus saw them running down Zzyzx Road, on the wrong side of the fence. He said he called out to his wife, but she never looked back. The firefighters thought they'd managed to put out the fire without any casualties, until they found Caleb's body in the charred wreckage. At first, it was believed he'd been overcome by smoke, but there was evidence of a gunshot. Most likely self-inflicted.

Naomi says there are degrees of love. It's not all or nothing. It doesn't have to be all-consuming, like the adoration Daniel demanded. What might Caleb and I have been to each other, if left to our own decisions? Certainly, there were feelings between us. An attraction that felt like heat lightning. Out here, it's okay to spend time with someone, even if you're not sure you love them. Kiss them, even. Try to get to know them, learn what's in their heart. Show them what's in yours. Out here, no one gets married just because someone says your name.

But we never got that chance, and I mourn that loss almost as much as I mourn him.

When I turn, Aaron is watching me from the bottom of the staircase. He comes most days, too, but usually not so early.

I wipe my tears with my sleeve, then study his face as he approaches. I can read him well; our fake marriage has supplied me this benefit. "Something's happened," I say, when he gets closer.

He grimaces and shoves his hands into the pockets of his jeans, and something jingles there—coins or keys. "I've spoken to your mother," he says.

I wrap my arms around myself, to guard against the chill, and turn my face toward the sea. "And?"

"She's still adamant that this is all a misunderstanding. She thinks Daniel will come back, and when he does, he'll explain every-thing. Until then, she's not leaving New Jerusalem."

"Why am I not surprised?" Aaron has been trying to convince her to come Out—to come here. To be with me. But as always, I come second to Daniel. Even when he's gone.

"Don't be too hard on her," Aaron says. "She's not the only one. I'd say about half the Elders have refused to leave, and so far, most of their families have stayed, too. He had so much control over them, for so many years, they find it difficult to make decisions without him. New Jerusalem—and Daniel's law—is all they know. It's not uncom-mon in these kinds of situations."

I wish I could say my heart holds forgiveness for my mother, but I haven't been able to wholly accept what she did to me. Her life before New Jerusalem was even worse than anything I'd imagined. Her father—my grandfather—was a monster. But she ran from him straight into the arms of another monster. And stayed. Had his child. Swallowed his lies. Even if she thought she was doing right, how did she justify keeping so many secrets? Turning a blind eye to so many of his faults? Trapping me there? All in the name of her so-called belief.

Aaron says that's called playing God.

My mother would say keeping faithful.

I don't have a word for it. I just know it hurts.

"It's a hard transition. But it will get easier," he says. "Have a little faith."

I give a small snort of laughter. Aaron rarely has anything posi-tive to say about religion. It's one of the reasons I'm so grateful for his company these days. He understands what we've gone through like few people can.

He sighs. "Eventually, she'll have to leave. They all will. Daniel used the land in commission of his crimes, so the government will seize it."

"Seize it? What does that mean?"

"It's a process. There's paperwork that has to be filed. Lots of governmental red tape." He squints into the sun, and I wonder if he can see the gates as clearly as I can, wrapped in red and tied up in a bow. "It's better if it happens slowly," he continues, "if they have time to convince everyone to leave on their own. If they have to throw them off the property, things can get ugly."

"And then what? The government just gets to keep it? The land?" While I don't care if I never see New Jerusalem again, I also don't like the idea of a bunch of strangers taking over and living there.

"Not exactly. What they really want is for Daniel to stand trial. So they'll give notice they're going to take the compound. Which means Daniel then has thirty days to come out of hiding and file an appeal if he wants to keep the property." He pauses, and looks at the water with me for a moment. "Him . . . or his heirs. As his offspring, you have the right to file a claim, too."

"How many of us are his . . . offspring?" This question has plagued me since we left. How many of my so-called Brothers and Sisters are actually my blood?

"We don't know. It's possible that was part of why he was trying so hard to manipulate the marriages—he didn't want any of you married to your siblings."

This thought brings the sour taste of bile up my throat.

"We'll do DNA tests to be sure," Aaron continues. "Phoebe says she's been his only lover for many years. If that's true, it could be he was trying to avoid having the same . . . complications he did, early on."

The same mistakes, he means. "But then how come Phoebe never had any children?"

Aaron kicks at the sand. "Maybe she couldn't. Or maybe . . . she didn't want them. You'll see, out here, how much is possible. Not everyone wants to get married or have children." There is so much I have yet to learn, sometimes it makes me dizzy. But for now, I drop the subject.

"So if we did what you said—filed a claim," I ask instead. "Then New Jerusalem would belong to us? Me and Rachel?"

He shrugs. "The rest of his family is dead. His parents divorced when he was young. His mom had custody; his dad moved to Zzyzx and started that scam of a health resort. When he died, Daniel inherited the land. That's when he moved the cult out there. You know the rest."

It's a lot to take in. Especially if I think about the fact that this isn't just Daniel's family he's talking about, but mine. I shake my head. "I can't go back there."

"You don't have to. This will all be tied up in court for years. Assuming they catch him. Which they will," Aaron reassures me quickly. "You don't have to make any decisions now." It's something the other adults tell me every day. "But when you're ready—"

I finish the sentence for him. "The choices are all mine."

He takes my hand, his warmth staving off the chill of the morning, steadying me, the way his friendship does. Together we watch the ocean. It's more beautiful, more dangerous, more *everything*, than I ever pictured. Vast like the desert, but where the desert was stagnant, placid, submissive, the sea is demanding. The waves pound the rocks on shore, constantly pushing, constantly challenging their right to exist. The two extremes are a part of me—who I was and who I have become.

This world outside is nothing like I imagined, and more than I ever dreamt.

ACKNOWLEDGMENTS

This book is about the power of voice and the strength of women. And the truth is, this book would not exist without the support and counsel of three amazing women:

- My critique partner, Linda Davis, who read this manuscript approximately fifty-seven times without complaint, pushed me to keep going when I threatened to quit, and very calmly steered me to the right ending when I lost my way. I am forever grateful.

- My agent, Barbara Poelle, who from our very first phone call has been a fierce supporter, advocate, champion, coach, therapist, and fighter. How do you thank someone for handing you your dreams? Without her, none of this is possible.

- And my editor, Liza Kaplan, who is a genius, and whose attention to detail and ability to see inside my brain are both uncanny and unparalleled. She has a gift—she *is* a gift—and I am so honored that she chose this story, and so grateful for how she's strengthened it.

I am eternally grateful to the whole Philomel phamily, including Ken Wright, Jill Santopolo, Talia Benamy, Ellice Lee, and Jenny Chung. Thank you to Dana Li, Kristin Boyle, Lizzie Goodell, Kim Ryan, and the entire team at Penguin Young Readers.

I have been surrounded by strong women all my life. For better or for worse, they have all taught me to be brave and speak my mind, and for that I am thankful, especially to my mom and my stepmom, and before them, both my grandmothers. I only wish the latter two were still here to tell their stories.

Thanks to my dad, who first introduced me to Kahlil Gibran. And politics. I like to imagine he'd be proud of what I've done with that. I miss him every day.

I am graced with many friends who are always willing to offer encouragement—and wine! And who never stop believing in me. (Even after reading early drafts of this book!) Special thanks to Eric Gorshe, Katie Styra, Traci Hiebing, Tiffani Trumm, Stacey Rice, Alyssa Ziegler, and Tina Beining. It's no coincidence that most of you fit into the strong women category, too!

To my Hot Mamas—Cory, Melissa, Nannette, Jenny, Mindy, and Stacy—thanks for all the fun and laughter and bad Spice Girls renditions. No one has a bigger voice than we do!

I am indebted to authors Kathi Appelt and Todd Strasser, who offered early critiques of the opening pages—through the Adventures in YA Publishing blog and SCBWI, respectively—and gave me much-needed advice and encouragement.

A big thank-you to my kids, Emma, Arianna, and Cameron, who are and will always be my greatest inspiration. You make me want to be all and do all. Instead, I wrote this book.

And finally, Josh—I am grateful for so many things, but mostly thank you for being the strong and steady guiding force in my life. When I told you I was thinking about writing a book, you didn't even blink. You just bought me a laptop. If that's not love, I don't know what is.